"Berry" Delicious Praise . . .

Blackberry Crumble

"**Blackberry Crumble offers up a thrilling murder mystery!** Most people are not who they appear to be. I can't give away the really shadowy characters or the killer, but there is a killer—and this killer means business!"

—Gabi Kupitz

"**Josi Kilpack is an absolute master** at leading you to believe you have everything figured out, only to have the rug pulled out from under you with the turn of a page. *Blackberry Crumble* is a delightful mystery with wonderful characters and a white-knuckle ending that'll leave you begging for more."

—Gregg Luke, author of *Blink of an Eye*

Key Lime Pie

"I had a great time following the ever-delightful Sadie as she ate and sleuthed her way through **nerve-wracking twists and turns and nail-biting suspense.**"

—Melanie Jacobsen, author of *The List*,
http://www.readandwritestuff.blogspot.com/

"Sadie Hoffmiller is the perfect heroine. She's funny, sassy, and always my first choice for crime solving. And where better to solve a mystery than the Florida Keys? *Key Lime Pie* **satisfied with every bite!**"

—Julie Wright, author of *Cross my Heart*, www.juliewright.com

"The title of *Key Lime Pie* will make you hungry, but the story will keep you too busy to bake. Even when oh-so-busy amateur sleuth Sadie Hoffmiller vows to stay out of police business, life comes up with a different plan. **A missing girl, a very interesting man with bright blue eyes, and plenty of delicious recipes all create a combination even Sadie can't resist.**"

—H.B. Moore, www.hbmoore.com

Devil's Food Cake

"There's no mistaking that Kilpack is one of the best in this field. *Lemon Tart* was good, *English Trifle* was better, but with *Devil's Food Cake* she delivers **a polished novel that can hold its own anywhere.**"

—Jennie Hansen, *Meridian Magazine*

"Josi Kilpack whips up **another tasty mystery where startling twists and delightful humor mix** in a confection as delicious as Sadie Hoffmiller's devil's food cake."

—Stephanie Black, three-time winner of the Whitney Award for Mystery/Suspense

English Trifle

"*English Trifle* is an excellent read** and will be enjoyed by teens and adults of either gender. The characters are interesting, the plot is carefully crafted, and the setting has an authentic feel."

—Jennie Hansen, *Meridian Magazine*

Lemon Tart

"**The novel has a bit of everything. It's a mystery, a cookbook, a low-key romance and a dead-on depiction of life.** . . . That may sound like a hodgepodge. It's not. It works. Kilpack blends it all together and cooks it up until it has the taste of, well . . . of a tangy lemon tart."

—Jerry Johnston, *Deseret News*

PUMPKIN
ROLL

OTHER BOOKS IN THIS SERIES

Lemon Tart
English Trifle
Devil's Food Cake
Key Lime Pie
Blackberry Crumble
Banana Split (coming Spring 2012)

Pumpkin Roll recipes

Pumpkin Roll	10
Laree's Ginger Cookies	31
Baxter's Clam Chowder	46
Whole Wheat Pancakes	55
Broccoli in Brown Butter	94
Whitty Baked Beans	132
Cinnamon Twists	151
Whoopie Pies	236
Pot Roast and Yorkshire Pudding with Gravy	360

Download a free PDF of all the recipes in this book at
josiskilpack.com or shadowmountain.com

PUMPKIN ROLL

A CULINARY MYSTERY

JOSI S. KILPACK

SHADOW
MOUNTAIN

To my Kylee-Bear, the very best thing about October.
Love you, sweetie.

Visit us at ShadowMountain.com

Library of Congress Cataloging-in-Publication Data
Kilpack, Josi S. author.
  Pumpkin roll / Josi S. Kilpack.
     p. cm.
  Summary: Sadie Hoffmiller is in Boston, Massachusetts, with her boyfriend, Pete Cunningham, babysitting his three young grandsons. The boys insist that Mrs. Wapple, the woman who lives across the street, is a witch, and Sadie and Pete are anxious to distract the boys from such Halloween-induced ideas. Then Mrs. Wapple is attacked in her home, and Sadie finds herself embroiled in a series of unexplained occurrences with life-or-death consequences.
  "A Culinary Mystery." — t.p.
  ISBN 978-1-60908-745-6 (paperbound : alk. paper)
  1. Hoffmiller, Sadie (Fictitious character) 2. Halloween—Fiction. 3. Witches—Fiction. 4. Babysitting—Fiction. 5. Boston (Mass.)—Fiction. I. Title.
  PS3561.I412P86 2011
  813'.54—dc22   2011017598

Printed in the United States of America
Publishers Printing

10 9 8 7 6 5 4 3

CHAPTER 1

"So, what's the difference between a sociopath and a psychopath?" Sadie asked as she put the last plate in the dishwasher.

Pete Cunningham, Sadie's boyfriend—though that was such a juvenile term—looked up from where he was replacing a hinge on a flat-fronted kitchen cabinet. "One starts with an S and the other starts with a P," he said before going back to the task at hand—one of the two dozen items from his self-imposed honey-do list. They were in Jamaica Plain, a suburb of Boston, watching Pete's grandsons while Pete's son and daughter-in-law spent six days in Texas where Jared had just accepted a residency following his completion of medical school at Boston University.

"Funny," Sadie said with exaggerated dryness. "I meant in a psychological way—how are the disorders different from one another?" She sat down on one of the cheap kitchen chairs that went with the cheap kitchen table. Jared and Heather had been poor college kids for ten years, during which time they'd had three children; cheap was all they could afford. The din of little boys playing in the other room was at a moderate level, giving Sadie and Pete a rare chance at adult conversation.

Pete turned the final screw and stepped back to shut the cabinet, which now hung perfectly. "This question wasn't inspired by my grandchildren, was it?"

As if waiting for an invitation, three redheaded boys, graduating in height from tallest to shortest, ran into the kitchen. Kalan, the oldest, darted behind Pete, while Chance and Fig—a nickname somehow derived from Finnegan—held plastic swords above their heads, trumpeting a war cry in pursuit of their brother. All three boys had taken off their shirts to further emphasize their warrior physiques as only a six-, four-, and three-year-old could.

"Get 'em, Grandpa! Get 'em good," Kalan yelled.

Sadie smiled as she watched the show; it was her favorite— Grandpa Pete.

After using a series of karate chop actions to fend off the blows, Pete grabbed the plastic blade of one sword and then the other.

"I cut your hand off!" Chance yelled, tugging at his sword.

"Hand!" Fig repeated, pulling on his sword as hard as he could.

Pete lifted both swords until the boys had no choice but to let go. They stared at him with angry pouts.

"Gib it back!" Fig demanded.

Pete smiled. "I can't."

"Yeth you can." Fig held out his hand. "Gib it back!"

"It's almost time for bed." Pete put the swords on the counter behind him.

All three boys immediately began whining in protest.

"If you get ready by yourselves, we'll have dessert before story time."

Sadie lifted her eyebrows, and Kalan yelled, "Dessert!"

"Ice cweam!" Fig yelled.

"Not ice cream," Pete said, opening the refrigerator door. "Aunt Sadie made a pumpkin roll."

"Bread?" Chance asked, crinkling his nose and sticking out his tongue. "Bread's not dessert."

"Not bread—cake." Pete pulled out the platter of rolled cake with cream cheese filling.

"Cake!" all three boys said at once.

"But you've got to get ready for bed first," Pete said, lifting the platter out of their reach and looking to Sadie for help out of the mess he'd made.

She turned to Kalan. "Will you help your brothers put on their pajamas?"

Kalan was only six, but he understood what it meant to be the big brother, so he grabbed an arm of both younger boys and began pulling them out of the room.

"Are you sure cake before bed is a good idea?" Sadie asked once they were gone. It was after eight o'clock and the pumpkin roll was supposed to chill for a few hours so that the filling would set up—it had barely been two. She'd planned to have it tomorrow evening.

"What's the fun of having Grandpa stay over if you can't have cake right before bed?"

It was hard to argue with such logic.

"I should have asked you first, though, since it's your cake," Pete said, holding the platter with both hands as though trying to determine what to do with it now. "Sorry."

It was easy to forgive. "I wasn't planning to eat it all myself." Sadie took the platter and went up on her tiptoes to kiss Pete's cheek as she passed him on her way to the counter. "You're a fabulous grandfather," she said, putting the platter down and heading for the newly repaired cabinet to retrieve some plates.

"I don't know about that," Pete said, watching her busy about the kitchen. "This may turn out to be the longest week of my life."

Sadie laughed and grabbed a knife to slice the roll. "Haven't you ever played Grandpa full-time?"

"No," Pete said, moving to the sink to wash his hands. "Pat went a few times when the kids went on vacations or had babies or what-not, and we had Brooke's kids for a weekend here and there, but I haven't been called upon since Pat died."

Sadie looked up at the casual mention of his late wife, liking that he was becoming more comfortable merging his old life with the new possibilities of their relationship. "Well, then, I'm glad I could be a part of this new experience," she said. "And rest assured, you're doing wonderfully—cake before bed notwithstanding." She grinned at him as she carefully sliced the cake.

"I appreciate the validation," Pete said with a nod, leaning against the counter as he dried his hands with a dish towel. "Even if I don't really deserve it."

Sadie carefully lifted each slice of cake spiraled with cream cheese filling before putting it on a plate. It was so pretty. A moment later, Pete's arms snaked around her middle and his lips pressed against her neck, sending a tingle down and then back up her spine. She turned in his arms, holding the knife out to the side so as not to appear threatening.

"I couldn't have done this without you," he said in a tender voice. "Aunt Sadie is amazing with these kids."

"I'm glad it worked out," Sadie said. She'd been very uncomfortable with the idea when Pete had first invited her. Staying in the same house with him didn't seem right, given that her reputation had suffered some painful blows in recent months, but the more she considered the possibility, the more she wondered why she cared so much what people thought of her. She *was* a woman of high standards, and the people who truly cared about her knew that.

A phone call with Heather, Pete's daughter-in-law, assured her that the boys could share one bedroom, which would give Pete and Sadie their own separate rooms. Heather was warm and easygoing and loved the idea of having double coverage for her boys. Pete and Sadie had sat down and set specific rules—not venturing into one another's bedrooms, kissing kept to a minimum and only in vertical positions. Since attaining a new level in their relationship, they had both realized that age didn't factor into chemistry as much as they would have suspected.

It had been so nice to have uninterrupted time with Pete, and she'd always loved New England in the fall, which made the trip a good choice so far. She and Pete had arrived three days early—Pete stayed with the family, but Sadie had stayed at the Courtyard Marriott a few miles away in Brookline—so the boys could get used to them before their parents left for Texas. Sadie and Heather had hit it off as well in person as they had on the phone.

"It's been fun getting to know Jared and his family from the inside-out," she added, looking up at Pete and trying not to get lost in his hazel eyes.

"And they love you," Pete said. He leaned in for a quick kiss before eyeing the knife still in her hand. "Maybe I should let you get back to work before one of us gets hurt."

Sadie laughed and turned back to serving.

Pete pulled out a chair. "So, why the interest in psychopaths and sociopaths?"

Sadie shrugged. "I caught part of a *Law & Order* episode the other day. They seemed to be using the two terms interchangeably in the show. Are they two names for the same thing?"

"Well," Pete said, folding his arms over his chest, "they're both antisocial personality disorders, which means they function 100 percent on what they want."

"That means they have no moral code?"

Pete shook his head. "Not necessarily. Many of them still live by a moral code, but only because it gets them what they want. The terms are often used interchangeably, but to those who care to differentiate, sociopaths are generally classified as such because they don't fit very well in society. Psychopaths, on the other hand, have an uncanny ability to mimic the way normal people act. They can appear to play the part of average citizens whereas sociopaths tend to stand out more. Neither of them has a conscience—but one group can pretend that they do. The definition seems to change every few years though, so don't quote me."

"Are they all violent?" Sadie asked.

Pete shook his head again. "Many of them live relatively normal lives and are contributing members of society. They become dangerous once their disorder escalates to the point where they are aggressively acting on their most base instincts. They don't think rules—including laws—apply to them. That's usually where I end up coming in with my police badge."

"That's scary," Sadie said. "To think there are people with no conscience living their lives among the rest of us."

Pete nodded in agreement. "But, like I said, they aren't all criminals. For example, Pat was involved in the PTA for years, and I'm pretty sure there were a few psychopaths involved in that organization."

Sadie smiled to herself and moved to the table, putting a fork by each plate as she considered the vastness of Pete's knowledge. Then she paused. "Shouldn't the boys have been back by now?"

Pete cocked an ear toward the doorway. "I hate to interrupt them if they aren't screaming. . . . Wait."

Sadie heard it too. Whispers. She and Pete shared a quick look and then bolted toward the hallway that joined the kitchen and the living room. Sadie reached it first and came up short when she saw the three boys kneeling on the couch and peeking over the back in order to look out the big picture window. They were in their pajamas, she noted, but were obviously intent on something happening outside. She looked over her shoulder at Pete standing directly behind her, and he shrugged.

Slowly they moved into the room, Sadie veering to the left side of the couch and Pete toward the right. They leaned forward to look out the window, and Sadie scanned the street to figure out what the boys were looking at. After a few moments, she spotted a woman across the street, digging in a flower bed outside the house . . . in late October . . . at night. And she wasn't using a trowel to worry out some dead flowers; she was using a spade and making a pile of dirt on the sidewalk that led to the front door.

"Who's that?" Sadie asked Kalan, who was closest to her.

"Mrs. Wapple," Kalan said quietly.

"What's she doing?"

"Being weird."

"Does she do weird things a lot?"

Kalan nodded and folded his arms over the back of the couch, resting his chin on his hands. "We like to watch her when Mom turns off the TV."

"She's a witch!" Chance said.

"Witch!" Fig repeated.

Sadie's eyes flickered to the large cardboard cartoon witch on

the wall—one of a dozen decorations Heather had put up in prepa-
ration for Halloween next week.

"I think she's just . . . digging," Pete said. But Sadie knew he
found it strange as well.

"Mr. Forsberk's dog pooped on her grass, and she cast a spell on
it and it got hit by a car," Kalan said.

Sadie directed a look at Pete, inviting him with her eyes to help
her out. He didn't get the cue. "I feel bad for Mr. Forsberk's dog,"
she said, "but unless Mrs. Wapple was driving the car, then it was
probably just a very sad accident."

"It wasn't," Kalan said, still wide-eyed and sincere. "It was a
spell. Mama even said."

"Your mom said it was a spell?" Pete asked for clarification.

"Well, no," Kalan said. "But she did say Mrs. Wapple is a witch."

"A witch!" Fig said, loudly this time, and began jumping on
the couch. Apparently his interest had waned. "A witch, a witch, a
witch."

Pete tried to shush him, and Sadie once again launched into
her defense of the poor old woman digging across the street. Then
Chance pointed out the window, his mouth open. Sadie followed
his gaze and was startled to see Mrs. Wapple facing them, standing
on the sidewalk that ran parallel to the street rather than on the
walkway leading to her house. The streetlight down the block illu-
minated the gray hat made of some type of coarse fabric on her head
and her long dark hair that fell in frizzy waves past her shoulders.
As they watched, Mrs. Wapple lifted her hand and began drawing
pictures in the air with her index finger.

"Okay, boys," Sadie said, ushering them off the couch. "She's
just a silly old lady. And there's cake in the kitchen, so let's eat." She

chose to believe Mrs. Wapple hadn't caught them spying, but was simply . . . being weird, like Kalan said.

"Cake!" Fig shouted as he bounded off the couch. Chance and Kalan followed, though Kalan kept glancing over his shoulder. Pete finished herding them into the kitchen, and soon they were arguing about which piece of cake was the biggest.

Alone in the living room, Sadie hurried to the right side of the window near the floor lamp where the pull cord for the heavy blue drapes was tacked behind the curtains. Before she pulled the blinds closed, she turned off the lamp, hoping it would make her less visible. Then she looked at Mrs. Wapple one last time. The woman was still on the sidewalk. Still staring with her finger pointing toward the house. No, not the house—pointing at Sadie.

Sadie swallowed and pulled herself a little further behind the heavy curtains. But she didn't take her eyes off the strange woman outside.

Mrs. Wapple lifted her hand so that it was pointing at the sky, and then she closed her fingers into a fist. Still staring in Sadie's direction, she punched her hand upward at the precise moment that the lightbulb in the lamp next to Sadie exploded with a pop. Sadie jumped out of the way as a thousand tiny shards of paper-thin glass tinkled to the floor.

"What was that?" Pete asked, stepping into the doorway.

Sadie looked at him. "The lightbulb exploded," she said, refusing to consider the coincidence that it had happened at the same time Mrs. Wapple had punched her fist over her head. Didn't lightbulbs have to be turned on to shatter like that? She looked out the window again, but Mrs. Wapple was gone.

She wasn't on the sidewalk; she wasn't digging in the garden. She was gone.

Sadie felt a strange tingling sensation wash over her skin like a cold breeze as Kalan's words came back to her: "*Mama says she's a witch.*"

Good thing Sadie didn't believe in that kind of thing.

Pumpkin Roll

3 eggs
1 cup sugar
1 cup canned pumpkin
1 teaspoon baking powder
1 cup flour
½ teaspoon salt
½ teaspoon nutmeg
1 teaspoon ginger
2 teaspoons cinnamon

Filling
1 (8-ounce) package cream cheese (softened)
¼ cup butter, softened
1 cup powdered sugar
½ teaspoon vanilla

Preheat oven to 350 degrees. Grease a 11x15 jelly roll pan and line the bottom with parchment, wax paper, or a silicone mat. (The cake will stick to the pan otherwise since it's such a thin layer.) In a medium-sized mixing bowl, beat eggs. Add sugar; mix well. Add pumpkin; mix well. Add the rest of the ingredients; mix well. Pour batter into prepared jelly roll pan (mixture will be thick). Smooth out as evenly as possible. Bake for 20 minutes.

While cake is baking, spread out a large dish towel or flour-sack towel on the counter. Sprinkle with ¼ cup powdered sugar. After removing cake from oven, immediately turn cake out onto the sugar-coated towel. Remove parchment, wax paper, or silicone mat from bottom of cake. Roll the cake and towel up together the long way. (The towel keeps the cake from sticking to itself; the powdered sugar keeps the cake from sticking to the towel.) Put the towel-rolled cake on a cooling rack and let cool at least 30 minutes.

While cake is cooling, make filling by beating cream cheese until smooth. Add butter and beat until smooth. Add powdered sugar and vanilla. Mix well.

When cake has cooled at least 30 minutes, carefully unroll it from the towel. (It might crack; there's nothing you can do about that.) Spread with room-temperature cream cheese filling. Re-roll cake without the towel. Put cake on platter and cover. Refrigerate until serving—at least 1 hour, though 3 hours is best. (I usually cut the roll in half before I put it in the fridge or the freezer so it's easier to work with.)

Cake freezes well for up to 2 months when wrapped tightly in aluminum foil. Serve chilled or frozen.

Serves approximately 14.

CHAPTER 2

"That's it?" Shawn asked on the other end of the phone the next morning, the Monday of what should prove to be a busy week.

"Isn't that enough?" Sadie asked, annoyed that he was so hard to please. Kalan had wanted to walk the three-quarters of a mile to school so she'd obliged him and was speed-walking her way back in order to work off at least some of last night's pumpkin roll—and the additional slice she'd had that morning. Calling Shawn, her twenty-one-year-old baby boy, and catching up while she exercised was simply good multitasking. Her breath fogged in the air as she spoke; a cold spell had settled across the East Coast overnight, but she was staying pretty warm due to the exertion. "Exploding lights and drawing pictures in the air is pretty out there, if you ask me."

"Well, I mean, it's weird. But you're in *Boston*, Mom, and it's almost Halloween. You'd think you could drum up something a bit more exciting."

Sadie huffed extra hard to make a point. "I'm not in *Boston* Boston," she corrected him. "I'm in Jamaica Plain, a quiet little suburb, and I think the excitement of the last year has completely destroyed any sense of normalcy you ever had," she said with only slightly exaggerated disappointment. She really did worry that her involvement with five murder cases in the last twelve months had done some kind of damage to her son; he was a little too excited about helping her out with her newly formed PI business—Hoffmiller Investigations. Before he could defend himself, she changed the subject. "How's that skip trace going?"

"You don't have to call it a skip trace anymore, Mom. Use the lingo: skip."

"Fine," Sadie said, appreciating a turn-of-the-century Victorian home that stood on the corner. It had been beautifully restored—as had many of the historic homes in this area—and she wondered if it was on one of the walking tours the city offered. Sadie would love to see the famous hand-carved woodwork and stained-glass windows of the old colonial homes up close. And yet, while there were $700,000 homes on this street, Jared lived a few blocks away on a tired-looking street full of bland little rental houses.

The front lawn of the next house sported latex zombie hands sticking up from the grass and a giant spiderweb that stretched from the eaves of the framed porch to the bottom of the steps. A very large, though realistic-looking, spider hovered just above the front doors. Sadie preferred the zombies.

A gust of wind blew a swirl of fallen leaves around her ankles, and she picked up her pace, imagining the cream cheese filling melting off her backside with every step. She tuned back into the conversation with her son. "How's the *skip* going?"

"His mom's neighbor saw his car leave early in the morning. I'm pretty sure he's at least sleeping there. I've got a process server set up to go at eleven o'clock tonight."

"Excellent," Sadie said. "And you're keeping good notes, right?"

"Perfect notes," Shawn said.

Sadie could tell he was proud of himself and it helped her feel better about giving him some of her investigation work while she was out of town. She'd been an official private investigator—though Colorado didn't require an actual license other than the basic business license—for almost five weeks. On the one hand, most people would find what she'd done so far pretty boring work: locating parents who had skipped out on child support or heirs who needed to be found to fulfill the requirements of a will. She'd had one case of a cheating husband. On the other hand, however, Sadie loved the work! Most of her information hunting could be done over the phone or via the Internet, which made it infinitely flexible. And there was just something invigorating about unraveling a mystery— even a boring one.

During the first few weeks of being open for business, Shawn had helped her research a detail here and there, but when three full cases came in the day before Sadie was supposed to catch a plane to Boston, Shawn had said he would handle them himself. She had planned to supervise him, but he had hit the ground running and had done an impressive job so far without her.

"The other two cases are coming along as well," Shawn continued. "I have a lead on the deadbeat case that looks pretty good—I should know this afternoon. Do you have more for me to do?"

"I don't think so," Sadie said.

"But something new came in, didn't it?"

Sadie considered her options for a moment but couldn't deny that she had her hands full with three little boys and an inexperienced grandfather. Even if she wanted to do some of the work herself, the time simply wasn't there. Not this week. And she hated putting people off if she didn't have to, especially when she was still establishing her business. "I did have something else come in last night. It's a woman looking for an ex-boyfriend from fifteen years ago."

"Why does she want to find him now?" Shawn asked.

"She has a fourteen-year-old daughter," Sadie replied, with no need to elaborate. "I've already scanned the social networking sites. I found nothing, which leaves us with only her last known information about him."

"I see. Fifteen years is a lot of time to dig through."

"I know." Sadie began taking deeper breaths as her exertion caught up with her. "I have to tell myself not to wonder whether or not it's the right thing to find him. If he's a mess, I . . ." She paused for a breath. "I might tell her we didn't find anything. We might not be able to find anything anyway."

"Maybe you should give it to Jane," Shawn suggested. "She's good at the outdated stuff."

Sadie frowned. While it was true that she'd used Jane Seeley, a reporter she'd met several months ago, to find bits of information she hadn't been able to locate on her own, she had yet to feel completely comfortable with the younger woman. Shawn had made peace with his poor opinion of Jane from the past—her investigative skills had him in awe—but Sadie couldn't quite get to that point. Her own reluctance made her question her misgivings. Was she simply holding a grudge?

Yes, she and Jane had gotten off to a rocky start, and Jane had followed it up with an article that Sadie was still recovering from, but Jane had also been invaluable in Portland and nothing but helpful and encouraging since then.

"She's never taken an entire case," she said out loud, pretending that was her only concern.

"Well, give me the case, then, and if I need her, I'll ask."

Sadie bit her lip and slowed her pace, taking in a bit more of the holiday decorations. Not all homes were in the holiday spirit, of course, but most of them displayed some type of tribute to ghosts and ghouls. Of course, just being located in New England meant that every home was decorated for the season with vibrant colored leaves. Even living in small-town Colorado, with its rich foliage that made autumn a treat, didn't compare to the sheer number of trees here in Massachusetts and the celebration of colors that exploded this time of year.

Jared's house was on the next street and she was ready to cool down. "I've already given you three cases," she said. Part of her hesitation was concern that Shawn was overcommitting himself, but part of her also felt the itch of wanting to take this case herself. No, she didn't have time, and, yes, she'd committed to not make this a working vacation, but . . .

"I'm caught up in all my classes," Shawn said, driving to the heart of her objections. "I promised you I wouldn't take your stuff on if I couldn't do it, and I won't, but fall soccer is over and basketball registration isn't until next week so I don't have much to do this week." Shawn worked at a local youth recreation center in Michigan. "I can do this, and I could use the money. I've got to get my hands on the new Xbox—it's awesome."

"Okay," Sadie said with a laugh. Such a big man, and yet such a little boy at the same time. She needed to trust him to manage his own time. "I'll e-mail you what I've got, but use Jane only if you have to, okay?"

"Deal," Shawn said, his tone both relieved and lighter. Sadie wondered when he was going to tell her that he'd changed his major from sports medicine to criminal justice. She'd figured it out about three weeks ago, thanks to her new skills at uncovering information, but Shawn had yet to tell her, and she was content to wait him out. "I better head to class," he continued. "We're still on for Saturday?"

Sadie smiled, remembering the plans they had made when she announced she'd be traveling to his neck of the woods. Michigan was still several hours away, but closer than Colorado. He had school and some work meetings on Friday, but when he finished he would drive to Boston, probably arriving just a few hours after Heather and Jared got back from Dallas. They planned to all go to Salem on Saturday for a day of Haunted Happenings—an encompassing title of events hosted in the City of Witches every fall. Shawn and Sadie could then spend Sunday together before Shawn had to leave. She wished they could have more time together, but she didn't want him to miss school for it. She had developed a continual fear that he might drop out of college altogether and didn't want to tempt such thoughts.

"I am so excited to see you!" Sadie said. "It's simply breathtaking here this time of year. Remember when we came with Bre—what, seven years ago?"

"How could I forget?" Shawn said. "It was humiliating to tell people we'd gone all the way to Boston to see yet another zoo. I hated it when it was her turn to choose the family vacation."

Sadie laughed. "As opposed to your choice of Ohio so we could visit the Pro Football Hall of Fame?"

"Um, that's practically a religious study, Mom."

Sadie laughed some more. "You're a silly boy."

"But at least I'm not an animal freakazoid," he said, referring to the name he'd made up for Breanna when he was little. Sadie hadn't seen her daughter in months, not since she left for London on an internship with the London Zoo. It was hard coming to terms with the fact that Breanna might live the rest of her life in England. Sadie felt sad every time she thought about that, but now was not the time to feel sorry for herself. She was seeing her boy this weekend in the most beautiful place in the world this time of year—two reasons to celebrate.

"I got your e-mail with the MapQuest map, by the way," Shawn said. "You keep forgetting I have GPS on my phone."

"It's always nice to have a backup," Sadie said. She'd had her phone for months and could barely figure out how to set the alarm, let alone use the fancy-Nancy apps Shawn had downloaded for her. "I also signed us up for the after-dark Ghosts and Gravestones tour that goes over the famous haunting of the city. They talk about the North End tunnels and the Lady in Black; it sounded like something right up your alley."

"Sounds great," Shawn said. "You got us in the Saturday night before Halloween?"

Sadie smiled, quite pleased with herself. "It was the first thing I did once I knew we were coming. I'd heard about it from people who had taken the tour before and didn't want to miss it. I just hope it's not too scary for you."

Shawn laughed. "As long as you're there to protect me, I'll be okay. I better get going, though, I've got class in ten minutes. Enjoy those grandkids of yours!"

Sadie nearly corrected him but realized he was teasing her about how close she and Pete were getting. He also knew how much she wanted to be a grandma, rather than Aunt Sadie, and the thought that these boys might one day be *her* grandsons made her smile. "Alright, I love you, my boy."

"Love you too, Mom. I'll look for that e-mail about the long-lost boyfriend-father deal."

Sadie ended the call and put her phone in her coat pocket before pulling the collar up as a stiff wind came at her from the north. It had been nice weather when she and Pete arrived in Boston, but it had gotten colder every day since. Despite the temperatures, however, she loved autumn, loved New England, and was glad to be out of Garrison, Colorado, for a little while. Things had been changing for her over the last year, ever since the discovery of her neighbor's body in the field behind her house, and whereas she once felt perfectly accepted and comfortable in her small town, she now felt as though she were growing out of it. Most of her investigative work was from Fort Collins, an hour west of Garrison, but she'd even had a couple from Denver hire her; her world was so much bigger than it used to be.

She let out a breath and wondered where life would take her next. It wasn't that she regretted the changes—she'd always been open to adventure—but she missed the easy comfort she used to feel living in Garrison. It wasn't fair to give other people all the blame, though; she knew she approached them differently too, unsure what gossip they had heard or what decisions they'd made about her.

Cautious.

That's how she felt about even the people she'd been friends with for the last twenty-five years. Cautious was uncomfortable.

She looked up to see that she was only a few houses away from her destination. Instinctively her eyes moved to the house across the street from Jared and Heather's—Mrs. Wapple's.

The "Mrs." meant she was, or had been, married. Where was her husband? The yard was unkempt, the grass long and matted in places, and the front flower beds that bordered the small Cape Cod house were bare dirt—no flower stalks or landscaping remnants anywhere in sight. The hole from last night was filled, though a faint layer of dirt remained on the sidewalk. There were no Halloween decorations, and even from here, Sadie could see where real spider-webs clogged the corners of the recessed doorway and had caught stray leaves. A portion of rain gutter had broken away from the eaves on the east side and hung across the front window; the first heavy snow of the upcoming winter would likely rip it off completely.

The house was painted a medium-gray, but water stains had given it a mottled look. Jared and Heather's house, along with most of the houses on the street, had a hip-high chain-link fence. Mrs. Wapple's front yard was fence-free, though a six-foot-tall wooden fence with an additional foot and a half of latticework on top jutted out from the sides of the house and wrapped around the back half of the property, completely hiding the backyard from view. Sadie wondered what required *that* much privacy. She still stuck by what she'd told the boys last night, though—that Mrs. Wapple was just a silly old lady. She *was* intriguing, however, Sadie had to admit that.

The front gate of Jared's house creaked when she opened it, and she made a note to add "Oil the gate hinges" to Pete's list of household projects. All the houses along the street had an alley running behind them that led to single-car garages, or sometimes a carport. With garages in the back, the houses were even closer together. There was no street parking allowed overnight, which kept the street uncluttered.

Heather had decorated the front door with a ghost made of several layers of gauzy fabric. It had silent black eyes and an O-shaped mouth. As Sadie headed up the walkway, she watched it swing gently in the wind and had an idea about how to satisfy her curiosity about the witch across the street. That her plan involved baking—her favorite autumn pastime—was merely all the more reason to follow through.

CHAPTER 3

"I'm just trying to understand your motives," Pete said a few hours later as he snitched a ginger cookie off the cooling rack. Sadie had spent the morning cleaning up breakfast, getting the two younger boys bathed and dressed, getting herself ready, e-mailing Shawn the new case info, and double-checking that she had everything she needed for dinner. She'd forgotten how much work it took to run a house and take care of little kids at the same time. And she'd only had one boy, not three; they were a force of nature all their own. The boys were currently in the backyard playing and Sadie was busy transferring the last pan of cookies to the cooling rack and pretending not to notice the cookie theft taking place right under her nose—Pete's second.

"Do I need to give you Pete's Advice Number Three?" He took a bite of his cookie as though issuing her a challenge.

"Is that the one about not breaking the law or the one about not misleading you?" Sadie asked, clearing the pan. Pete's bits of "advice" were more like lectures, and they'd been repeated so frequently since Sadie started her business that she'd numbered them in order to make it easier for Pete to dispense his wisdom. It had become a bit of a joke between them now, or at least half a joke.

Pete leaned back in his chair and crossed his ankles. It was eleven o'clock in the morning and Pete was still wearing sweatpants. *Sweatpants!* Babysitting brought out a whole new side of Pete, or maybe just being out of Garrison was the secret ingredient. Either way, Sadie liked it . . . a lot. Not that she didn't always enjoy Pete's company, but it was fun to see Pete so laid-back. He kept talking. "Pete's Advice Number One is about lying to me—"

"Misleading," Sadie corrected, pointing her spatula at him. "I never lied to you."

"Okay, then," Pete said in a tone far too diplomatic to truly be agreeing with her. "Advice One is about misleading me. Advice Two is about breaking the law. Advice Three is about sticking your nose where it doesn't belong, isn't needed, or will create more problems than relief." He popped the last of his cookie into his mouth.

Sadie scrunched up her face. "Huh, it's funny that nowhere in any of your wisdom is there anything about taking cookies to a lonely woman."

Pete narrowed his eyes at her and finished chewing before he swallowed. "As I said, I believe that Advice Three covers that."

Sadie put a hand to her chest and widened her eyes with exaggerated horror at the suggestion that she had some kind of ulterior motive. "Quite frankly, Peter Cunningham, I'm offended."

He smirked at her, and Sadie smiled back, glad he found her so entertaining. She was totally taking these cookies across the street and he knew it. "Just to show you how *pure* my motives are, I've decided to take a plate to the houses next door as well. All the neighbors are getting cookies."

"Nice save," Pete said with a nod. "But I can still see right through it. This is all about Mrs. Wapple and satisfying your curiosity."

"He says as though he has no curiosity about the woman at all," Sadie muttered.

"I'm on vacation," Pete said. "I left my badge at home."

"No you didn't," Sadie said with a laugh. "It's in your suitcase."

"I was speaking metaphorically."

"I believe Advice Number One would fit this situation nicely," Sadie said. "And for your insubordination you get to do the dishes."

"No fair," Pete said, straightening in his chair and looking at the sink full of dishes. "You made the mess."

"Oooh," Sadie said, brandishing her spatula again. "You might want to take that back."

He looked from her to the spatula to the cookies. "Can I have another cookie?"

"You can have two," Sadie said. "*After* you do the dishes." She turned to the cupboard and took out a plate. She'd used paper plates for the other neighbors, but if Sadie used a real plate for Mrs. Wapple's cookies, she'd have an excuse to go back tomorrow in order to collect it—increasing her opportunity for observation 100 percent. She glanced out the window to check on the boys and then turned back to the table just as Pete stopped chewing another pilfered cookie, as though she wouldn't notice. "You're incorrigible," she said.

Caught, Pete shrugged and finished chewing. Sadie set down the plate and he helped her fill it with the soft brown cookies. She'd rolled the dough in sugar before baking, so they had the slightest shimmer when a melted sugar crystal caught the light just so. Once the plate was filled, Sadie covered it with plastic wrap, gave Pete a quick kiss, and headed out the door, curious to find out a little more information about the witch across the street.

When she pressed Mrs. Wapple's doorbell, she didn't hear anything inside. She pushed again. Nothing. Transferring the plate to one hand, she pulled open the screen door, cringing at the high-pitched squeak. You'd think the door hadn't been opened for years with the racket it made. Looking down, she startled to see a huge spiderweb she'd pulled free between the front door and the screen door—complete with a nickel-sized spider in the corner. She jumped away with a little scream, and the screen door slowly closed, creaking as it did so and giving her chills. She took a deep breath to calm herself and looked around to see if anyone was watching. Pete grinned at her from the picture window and gave her a thumbs-up sign that she pointedly ignored.

When she turned back, the screen door had closed. Did she dare open it again? If the spider came for her, she could easily smoosh it, right? When she'd been a little girl, her brother Jack had said he'd pay her a quarter if she'd kill one in his room. She'd taken the job, and then almost thrown up when she felt the exoskeleton crush beneath her shoe. Even thinking about it now made her shiver. Jack still owed her that quarter.

She reached out to grab the handle, but couldn't do it and quickly pulled back, wiping her hand on her pants. Instead, she knocked loudly on the Plexiglas screen door and waited. She couldn't hear footsteps, and after fifteen seconds, she knocked a second time, knowing the sound would be hard to hear inside. Twenty seconds passed before she accepted that no one was going to answer the door. Bummer.

However, the fact that the front door wasn't well-used simply meant that Mrs. Wapple had another entrance. Sadie went down the two porch steps and looked at the fence that stretched out from both sides of the house. How did Mrs. Wapple get in and out so quickly last night? There must be a hidden gate in the slatted fence. Maybe one with interior hinges. She walked to the right side of the house and began inspecting the longer section of fence, looking from top to bottom at each four-inch slat. They were snug against each other, but there had to be something. Before she knew it, she'd reached the far side of the fence where the wood butted up against the chain-link fence of the neighboring house. Undeterred, she retraced her path, taking even slower steps and looking even more methodically for anything that might betray a camouflaged gate. There were a few knotholes she was tempted to peer through, but that felt a little extreme.

She was halfway back to the front door when she realized that even if she found a gate, she couldn't enter the backyard of someone's home without permission—that would be in direct violation of Pete's Advice Number Three. Still, she'd like to know how Mrs. Wapple came and went so quickly.

Sadie scanned the ground up ahead to see if there was an area of worn grass that might indicate a gate, and nearly jumped out of her skin when she saw a pair of sneakers instead.

Her eyes snapped up until she was looking into the face of Mrs. Wapple. Or, rather, someone who looked like Mrs. Wapple. Only not so much like her, really.

The woman had her brown hair twisted up into a knot at the back of her head. Not a sloppy knot with pieces sticking out here and there, but a smooth bun-like twist. She looked to be a good fifteen years younger than Sadie, meaning she wasn't an old lady in any sense of the word, and had taken excellent care of her skin, which resulted in softer wrinkles and even coloring; Sadie would bet this woman always wore sunblock. The brown eyes behind the wire-rimmed glasses were inquisitive, and she was dressed in a light tan jogging suit not much different from a certain purple jogging suit Sadie had ruined last spring while involved in one of her unfortunate incidents.

"Can I help you?" the woman asked. She had polished, manicured nails that weren't long enough to be pretentious but weren't short enough to suggest a lot of time in dishwater. Her accent pegged her as a born and bred Bostonian, but the tones were rich, with firm emphasis and elocution. Schooled. The observations about her up-close appearance and tone of voice were small details compared to Sadie's confusion about whether or not this woman was the same one she'd observed last night. She didn't seem to recognize Sadie, which was strange since she'd stared so intently at her the night before.

Sadie gathered her thoughts and held out the plate. "I'm Sadie Hoffmiller. I'm staying with the Cunninghams' children while they look for a new home in Dallas and thought I'd come over and say hello to the neighbors. Are you Mrs. Wapple?"

The woman smiled, a very kind and natural smile, and accepted the plate with her delicate fingers. "Well, if you're visiting, then shouldn't I be the one to bring you cookies?"

Sadie decided to pretend that she hadn't seen a crazy lady outside last night at all. "I wouldn't turn them down," she said with a laugh. "But there's no need. For me, autumn means baking and I simply can't—or at least I shouldn't—eat them all myself. I thought it was a good excuse to get to know the neighbors even if I'll be here for only a few days."

"Well, thank you," the woman said, transferring the plate to one hand and extending her other one to shake. She did not have an impressive grip, but Sadie didn't hold that against her. "Pleased to meet you . . . oh, I'm sorry, what was your name again?"

"Sadie. Sadie Hoffmiller. I'm afraid I didn't catch your first name either."

"Oh, um, I'm Delores," she said, inspecting the cookies on the plate. "These look delicious, thank you."

They had run out of things to say pretty quickly, and Sadie fumbled around in her mind to think of a topic of conversation before settling on the weather. For all the jokes people made, the fact was that every person in the world was highly influenced by the weather. "I have to say, I think I picked the perfect time of year to come."

"Oh, indeed," Delores said, looking around. The street was peppered with trees, all of them varying shades of red, orange, and yellow. Breathtaking, really. "It's my favorite season, although I suppose most of us who live here would say the same thing." She looked back at Sadie. "Well, thank you for the cookies."

She was giving Sadie her exit orders. And Sadie would leave with nothing more than increased confusion. She could not allow that to happen! "Do you live here alone?" she asked before she considered her manners.

For an instant—no, not even that long—something crossed Delores's face. It wasn't anger or fear or even surprise, just . . . concern, maybe? "I do," she said quickly—not so fast as to appear suspicious but not so slow as to have the pause noted. But Sadie had seen the split-second reaction to her question. "Why do you ask?"

"Oh," Sadie said, forcing herself to relax. "I still have three dozen cookies across the street. If you were going to have to fight for your own share, I could bring you some more."

"This will be plenty," Delores said, smiling. "You're very generous. Thank you. If you can wait a moment, I'll put these on another plate and get this one back to you."

"Oh, no," Sadie said. "I'll just come back for it tomorrow." She started toward the walkway, stepping past Delores in the process, aware that she still hadn't found a gate. She reached the sidewalk and turned back to wave. Delores was standing in the same place, though she was facing Sadie this time. Her smile was just as pleasant as it had always been.

Sadie let out a sigh as she looked both ways before crossing the street. She immediately saw two redheaded boys jumping on the couch in front of the picture window, waving frantically to get her attention. She laughed and waved back with both hands, which only fueled their mania. It wasn't until she reached the front door that she looked back a second time. Delores was gone. Sadie looked at the grass but couldn't see an obvious pathway. Where had she come from, and where did she go?

Sadie went inside, and it was a full five minutes before Pete could ask her how it went; he'd only been able to watch for a minute before the boys came in from the backyard, throwing shoes and coats in every direction. The boys were playing Toy Story in the living room, giving Sadie time to cover the other cookies on paper plates with plastic wrap. By the time she finished recounting her exchange with Delores, Pete had that look on this face—that look that said he was thinking very hard about something.

"What?" she asked.

"She came from the other side."

"The other side?" Sadie said, immediately thinking about a book she'd read on near-death experiences that had the same name. She didn't think that was what he meant, though.

"Of the house—south. You were looking on the north side."

Sadie hurried to the picture window, dodging Woody's lasso in the process, and looked to the south side of the house. There was only about six feet of fencing on the south side, and it was farther from the front door. Why would there be a gate over there? But Sadie could see a rather faint path in the grass, arching from the fence to the sidewalk that led to the front door. Pete came up behind her and by the sound of it, he was eating yet another cookie. The man was going to make himself sick if he didn't show a little more restraint.

"Interior hinges," Sadie said, looking at the slats of the fence. "I knew it. But why not just use the front door?"

Pete nudged her. "Because she's a witch, remember? Witches do all kinds of crazy things."

Sadie elbowed him lightly, to which he responded with a dramatic "Ooof." She walked past him just as her cell phone rang. She pulled it out of her coat pocket and made a face when she saw it was Jane. She wasn't in the mood to talk to her right now; Jane was someone Sadie had to gear up for. She pushed the end button and turned around to face Pete. "We should take the boys to a park after Kalan gets out of school," she said, looking around for something else to think about. "Have you ever been to any of Olmsted's parks around here?"

"Whose parks?"

"Olmsted," Sadie said. "I read up on them when I came out here with the kids several years ago. Breanna and her passion for zoos pretty much set the pace for a lot of our vacations, and the Franklin Park Zoo is part of Franklin Park, which is part of Olmsted's Emerald Necklace chain of parks in the Boston area." She cocked her head to the side. "You've never heard of Olmsted?"

Pete shook his head. "You want to take the boys to the zoo?"

"No, just a playground or something. With all those parks, there's got to be a great playground tucked in there somewhere, right?"

Pete shrugged. "I guess."

Sadie nodded. "Good. I'll have the boys help me deliver the rest of the cookies after lunch, then they can take a nap. We can pick up Kalan from school and wear these kids out before bedtime."

"Now, *that* is something I'm up for," Pete said.

"I think it sounds like the perfect outing for today." The perfect outing to get her thoughts off Delores Wapple and the anxiousness of wanting to be working a case. Was that her problem? Was that why she was making cookies for neighbors? Was it a different kind of investigation since she'd sworn off actual work? She'd never thought about herself as a workaholic, but maybe she had simply never loved what she did enough to get addicted to it.

Sadie used the leftover yeast rolls from last night's dinner to make peanut butter and jelly sandwiches for lunch, looking forward to taking the other plates of cookies to the neighbors. Unfortunately, delivering the cookies was anticlimactic. The Middle Eastern man on the south side didn't speak much English, though he seemed quite pleased with the cookies. The people who lived on the other side weren't home, so Sadie went to the next house and woke up a middle-aged man who apparently worked the night shift. He took the cookies, but didn't look all that pleased to be woken up. The boys loved helping, though, and wanted to take more cookies to more houses until Sadie told them about the park after nap time. They were easy to redirect.

Jane called again when they were waiting in the line of cars to pick up Kalan. Sadie rejected that call too. When Jane called a third time, however, after they'd been at a playground called Mother's Rest for fifteen minutes, Sadie decided to give in and get it over with.

Laree's Ginger Cookies

¾ cup shortening
½ cup sugar
½ cup brown sugar
¼ cup dark molasses
1 egg
2 cups flour
¼ teaspoon salt
2 teaspoons baking soda
1 teaspoon cinnamon
½ teaspoon ground cloves
1 teaspoon ginger

Preheat oven to 350 degrees. Cream shortening and sugars. Add molasses and egg. Stir in remaining ingredients.* Roll into 1-inch balls, and then roll in sugar (about 4 tablespoons). Bake for 8 to 12 minutes, until edges are slightly darker than center.

Take them out when they are still soft. Allow to cool on pan 2 minutes before transferring cookies to a cooling rack. Store in an airtight container.

If you cook these too long, they will get a bit crispy (more like ginger snaps if you really cook them), but if you put the next batch in the container while the cookies are still warm, they will all soften up.

Makes 3 to 4 dozen.

*Shawn likes to add ½ cup white chocolate chips, and Neil liked ½ cup chopped walnuts. Bre always doubles the ginger.

CHAPTER 4

S adie took a deep breath before answering the phone. "Jane," she said in a careful tone as she signaled Pete that she needed a minute. Pete nodded and crossed his arms like a sentry as the boys continued to play with the two dozen other children enjoying the warmth of the afternoon, such as it was.

"How are you, dear?" Adding the endearment was something Sadie had read about in a magazine; if you said kind things out loud, you could sometimes help rewire your opinion of things. She left the fenced playground area and walked toward the stairs that led to the Boylston Street Bridge.

"I'm good," Jane said, as confident as ever. Her low voice, almost like a man's, was due in part to the cigarettes she smoked, but it also suited her personality. Jane was not feminine or understated. "So I was talking to Shawn and he says you're in Boston for the week." Sadie surmised from the background noise that Jane was driving. She hoped the younger woman was using a hands-free option to talk on the phone. After getting a ticket in Oregon for talking while she drove, Sadie had purchased a hands-free system and become a big proponent of the option.

"I am in Boston," Sadie said, noting that exactly five hours ago she'd specifically asked Shawn not to call Jane unless he absolutely had to. "I'm playing nanny for a few days." She'd reached the bottom of the stairs leading to the bridge and leaned against the railing.

"With Detective Cunningham, right?" Jane asked.

"Did Shawn tell you that?" Sadie asked, prepared to be even more annoyed with her son. Then again, Jane always seemed to know more than she should. When it came to the investigations, that was helpful, but it made Sadie uncomfortable when that extra knowledge was about her personal life.

"He didn't have to," Jane said smugly. "I knew you guys left town together last week. And I heard Jared matched in Texas somewhere—congratulations."

"How did you hear that?" Sadie said, standing a little straighter.

"You know better than to ask me," Jane said, her casual arrogance showing through. "Here's the weird part—I'm in New Haven."

"Connecticut?"

Jane laughed her throaty laugh that would fit perfectly in a smoky bar with insufficient lighting. "Of course Connecticut. I'm doing a freelance article on the number of Yale freshmen who drop out before the end of the first semester. I'm titling it 'Running Home to Mama.'"

"Oh," Sadie said. "Well, what a coincidence that we're so close to one another."

"No kidding, right? So, I was thinking I could come out there and you could make me dinner."

The girl had the social skills of an iguana. "Well, I'm not in my own home or anything, and we've got our hands full with the kids."

"Serious?" Jane said, and despite herself, Sadie was struck by the disappointment in Jane's tone. "I mean, of course I shouldn't be inviting myself over. Sorry. I just thought with both of us being in New England and all that, well, um, never mind."

"I don't mean to be rude," Sadie said, questioning what she should do. It was hard to keep up when Jane's attitude shifted so quickly. Yet one more way the younger woman kept Sadie on her toes. "It's just an awkward situation, what with us being guests and all."

Jane was quiet for a few beats. "That's right—you and Pete are staying there *together*, aren't you?"

"Not together like *that*," Sadie said, looking around when she realized her voice was a little loud. The sudden heat in her cheeks caused her to quickly duck her head. "I don't appreciate the implication that we're being improper."

"No, no, I'm not implying anything. Just looking out for a friend," Jane said in a tone too light for Sadie to take at face value. "And how's that working out, being in such close quarters?"

Jane had once tried to accuse Sadie of having less than high moral standards and it was still a sore spot between them, or at least for Sadie. She put her hand in her pocket and realized she was making a fist. "I'm not going to discuss this, Jane. Was there another reason you called?"

"Okay, okay, I'm done poking at you," Jane said with a laugh. "I guess that was all I needed to talk to you about. Just thought I'd check in; I haven't seen you since Portland."

Portland.

With that one word, Jane successfully triggered the sense of indebtedness Sadie usually managed to ignore. The fact was that Jane, whose job at the *Denver Post* had been shaky at the time, had found herself smack-dab in the middle of an amazing story when she had followed Sadie to Portland a few months earlier. To this day Jane had never printed the story. That was like Sadie developing the perfect recipe for something and refusing to bake it. And while Sadie continued to worry the story would show up somewhere, it hadn't. For three months it hadn't. The players in the drama that had taken place in Portland had moved on with barely a public whisper of the intricacies Jane knew about but had promised not to capitalize on. Sadie's name hadn't surfaced in anything other than the formal police reports.

Beyond that, Jane wasn't working for the *Post* anymore; even the column she had been writing for the last few years, "Ms. Jane," had been taken over by a new journalist. Sadie wasn't entirely sure what Jane was doing as far as employment was concerned other than helping Sadie out here and there with portions of a case.

And, still, Jane hadn't sold the story. Shouldn't that earn Jane some of Sadie's trust? Sadie sat down on the bottom step and took a breath as she changed her attitude.

"I'm fine, Jane," Sadie said, and she hoped Jane could hear the change in her voice. "Just a little high-strung, I guess. I really am sorry that despite being so close to one another there isn't room for a visit, but Pete and I really do have our hands full. It wouldn't be right to distract myself from the task at hand." Instantly Delores Wapple came to mind. Wasn't that a distraction? Sadie felt her shame deepen.

"I get it," Jane said. "Not a big deal. We'll meet up another time. Just know that I'm close by if you need me, okay? It's only a two-hour drive—shorter than Denver to Garrison."

"I'll remember that," Sadie said. "Thanks for calling."

They said good-bye, and Sadie shut off the phone and stared at it a moment before putting it back into her pocket.

"Aunt Sadie?"

Sadie lifted her head in time to get a huge armful of leaves thrown in her face. She was frozen in shock as not three, but four giggling voices erupted around her. Once she opened her eyes, she looked at Pete, the ringleader, who was quickly showing the boys how to scoop up armfuls of leaves with their hands. Fig's leaves kept going right though his arms, but he gathered as though the next assault depended completely on him.

"Oh, no you don't," Sadie said, running to the patch of grass where they were refueling and filling her arms with leaves for her retaliation. She threw the armful, which was rather paltry due to her haste, but caused the boys to squeal and drop their leaves. She grabbed a fistful of leaves and stood up, raising her hand high above her head. The boys screamed and started to run toward the playground. She cast a triumphant look at Pete, who was trying to get them to focus on gathering leaves again, and made chase, despite her being no match for the speed of three hyperactive boys.

As she chased them back to the playground, she was struck with the unexpected thought of whether or not Jane had ever played like this as a child. One day Sadie would find a way to learn more about what made Jane, Jane. Until then, she had a battle to win!

CHAPTER 5

It was nearly 5:30 when they got back to the house. Kalan and Chance ran around the yard while Pete got Fig out of his car seat and Sadie collected her purse and Kalan's backpack.

As she closed the door to the detached single-car garage, she saw that Pete had already reached the wooden steps that led to the back door of the house. He bent down and picked something up.

"What's that?" she asked as she came up behind him.

"The cookie plate." Pete stood up and turned toward her, the plate Sadie had given Delores in his hand. "There's a note with it," he said, holding them both out to her.

She took the plate in one hand and the note in the other.

"She must have brought it to the back porch to make sure you got it," he added before turning toward the door and digging the key from his pocket.

"Yeah, I guess so," Sadie said. She tucked the plate under one arm and opened the note.

"So much for your ploy to go back tomorrow, huh?" Pete said, smiling over his shoulder before opening the door. He winked at her and she scowled playfully. She didn't realize he'd figured out her plans for a second meeting with Mrs. Wapple. The three boys whipped past her, nearly knocking her off balance as they raced up the steps. It only slowed her reading down a little bit, though.

Dear Mrs. Hoffman,

Thank you for the cookies, they were delicious. I'm not around much and wanted to make sure to return your plate. I doubt I'll see you again during your stay but hope you enjoy the rest of your visit. Thanks again.

Delores

Sadie frowned and read the note again. By the end of the second read, Sadie wondered if Delores was trying to give her the brush-off—making it clear she didn't expect, or want, to see Sadie again. That made Sadie feel bad. She had hoped to befriend this woman, even if only for a few days. She also noted that while Delores said she wasn't around much, the boys watched her enough to have come to expect seeing her somewhat regularly.

Taking a breath in hopes it would help her shrug off her hurt feelings, she climbed the steps and let her mind turn to dinner—clam chowder. What could be a better dinner to make in Boston, especially at this time of year? She'd clipped the recipe from the newspaper several years ago when Garrison's most popular restaurant, Baxter's, had printed the recipes for three of its best dishes. Usually, when Sadie got a recipe from somewhere, she adjusted it to meet her own specifications. Not so with Baxter's clam chowder. It was perfect just as it was, and Sadie's attempts to improve it were pointless. She hoped the boys would eat it; Breanna had been fourteen before she'd attempted eating clams. And Shawn had only started to put up with them since moving to Michigan.

After dinner—which everyone but Chance had eaten without complaint—Sadie made a point to close the drapes over the picture window, not wanting to be tempted to watch Mrs. Wapple if she came out. Pete cleaned the kitchen while Sadie entertained the boys by reading *Where the Wild Things Are*—one of her favorites, never mind that the movie was disappointing. At 8:00, she kissed each boy on the forehead, grateful for their exhaustion. Apparently the plan to wear the boys out today had worked. In the process, she'd been able to experience another of the beautiful parks around Jamaica Plain. She wondered if all the Boston suburbs were this green and cozy; it almost felt like they were in a small town rather than in one of the largest cities on the East Coast.

After saying goodnight half a dozen times, she softly closed the boys' bedroom door behind her and returned to the kitchen. She stopped short when she realized Pete wasn't where she'd left him, but had moved to the living room. The lights were off and he had pulled the curtain open in the middle so he could look out the window.

Sadie took silent steps toward him. He was intent enough that he didn't notice her until she came right up behind him and said "Boo" in his ear. He startled, and she laughed before standing on her tiptoes to look over his shoulder.

"She's digging again," Pete said, stepping to the side so she could have a better view.

Sure enough, Delores Wapple was digging with the same shovel she'd used last night. Her hair hung loose down her back, and she wore what looked like a knitted bathrobe, or maybe one of those long sweater jackets, badly stretched out.

"How long has she been out there?" Sadie asked. In the faint streetlight, Delores looked nothing like the polished woman Sadie had talked to that morning.

"A few minutes," Pete said. "I heard scraping and looked out to see her dragging the shovel along the sidewalk. What do you think she's looking for?"

"Or what is it she's trying to hide," Sadie said. They were too far away and it was too dark for them to see exactly what she was doing—other than digging.

Suddenly, Delores leaned forward and lifted both hands to her head, dropping the shovel into the dirt. Sadie watched the woman's shoulders lift, hold, and then lower as though she'd taken a deep breath. A moment later, she bent down, slow and stiff, and picked up the shovel again.

"She's in pain," Sadie said, almost to herself.

"She's done that a few times," Pete said. "Almost looked like she lost her balance once."

"Poor thing," Sadie said as Delores went back to her digging.

"I wonder what's wrong," Pete said, his own concern evident. "And why digging is so important if she's not feeling well."

Sadie wondered those things as well and winced as Delores lifted a hand to her head again. This time the older woman kept hold of the shovel with her free hand, but stopped what she was doing until whatever was causing her trouble passed. When they'd brought the boys home at five thirty, it had been cold—not quite fifty degrees. It had to be much colder now that the sun had been down for a few hours.

Sadie watched for another minute while Delores continued to move slowly but determinedly. When she began trying to shovel with one hand while holding her head with the other, Sadie couldn't take it anymore. "I'm going to see if she's okay."

Pete looked at her, his eyebrows lifted. "You are?"

"Something isn't right," Sadie said, squinting. "She's obviously hurting." She moved toward the door then turned back to Pete. "Do you think it's a bad idea?"

Pete shrugged. "Not necessarily. I'm just wondering at your motive again."

"Okay, I admit it," Sadie said, holding up her hands as though surrendering. "I'm curious, but I'm also worried. Do you want to come with me?"

"And leave the boys alone?"

"Oh, right," Sadie said. She bit her bottom lip. "Well, why don't you watch from the window and ring a bell or something if you need to get my attention."

"I'll ring a bell and you'll come running?" Pete said, wagging his eyebrows. "I could get used to that."

Sadie smiled and shook her head as she pulled her jacket out of the living room closet. She shrugged it on and headed to the door. "Wish me luck," she said as she opened the door. The swinging ghost startled her, and she scowled before stepping past it.

"Luck," Pete said just before the door closed.

The cold air berated her for coming outside, and she hunched her shoulders against the frigid chill. At least it wasn't windy. She wondered if it was going to snow. Northern Colorado occasionally got snow before Halloween, but Boston was known for its winters, and she felt as though the weather might get an early start.

She quick-stepped across the street, hoping movement would warm her up. She kept waiting for the other woman to turn around at her approach, but she never did. Sadie stopped as Delores dumped a spadeful of dirt on the sidewalk between them. But even then, Delores didn't notice her. As she plunged the shovel back into the dirt again, Sadie glimpsed Delores's grip on the handle of the shovel. No polished fingernails caught the light, rather these nails were short and dirty and most definitely not manicured. Sadie felt a tremor rush through her. Something strange was going on here.

The gray hat Delores wore—the same one Sadie had noted last night—had a semi-floppy brim that ran around the circumference, but the cap was long and knitted from a coarse yarn, and came to a point midway down her back. Sadie realized that if the cap was stiff and starched, and if the rim was a bit wider, it would look just like a gray-knit witch's hat.

"Delores?" she said tentatively. It felt strange calling her by her first name. "Mrs. Wapple?"

Mrs. Wapple whipped her head to the side so quickly that the point of her hat arched out from her head, cutting through the moonlight. Sadie took a step backward despite herself.

"What do you want?" she said, her voice low and irritated with a gravelly quality Sadie didn't remember from this afternoon.

"I . . . uh . . ." She looked at the shovel in Delores's hand. "I saw you from the window across the street. Are you all right?"

"Of course I'm all right," she said, turning back to her shovel and mumbling something Sadie couldn't hear exactly but that sounded like "Angry birds," over and over again. Shawn had sent Sadie a link to a YouTube video about something called Angry Birds, but Mrs. Wapple didn't seem the type to be up on the latest online videos.

Sadie wasn't ready to take Mrs. Wapple at her word either and took a step forward. "Do you need help?"

Mrs. Wapple scowled over her shoulder, and Sadie noted more

differences between the woman she was talking to now and the one she'd spoken to earlier. This woman had a careworn face, and although the lines etching her skin didn't age her beyond her forties, it was not the skin Sadie had admired that afternoon. This woman also wasn't wearing glasses, though her squinting—and the deep wrinkles it created—betrayed that she probably needed them. She was thinner than the other woman too, not in a trim and healthy way, but in a tired and worn-out kind of way. Sadie couldn't think of her as Delores now that she'd noted the differences between the two women. Or were the weak light and cold temperatures playing tricks on Sadie's memory of the woman from this afternoon?

"I need potatoes," Mrs. Wapple said, turning back to the dirt. She lifted the shovel and drove it a couple of inches into the ground.

Sadie finally understood. "You're digging for potatoes?"

"That's what I said," Mrs. Wapple said, but she'd already lost some of the edge to her voice, and the next stab she took with the spade didn't go as far into the soil as before. She was tired. "They're rich in vitamin C."

Sadie reached for the shovel. "Let me try," she said gently. Once her hand closed around the handle, Mrs. Wapple let go of it, only to immediately raise her hand to her head as her forehead wrinkled in obvious pain.

"Are you all right?" Sadie asked, reaching out, but Mrs. Wapple turned away and pulled her arm from Sadie's grasp.

"I need potatoes," she said again.

Sadie cast a disbelieving eye at the flower bed, then lifted the shovel and stabbed the ground. The blade sunk about five inches, and she turned over the dirt and dug again. Next to her, Mrs. Wapple closed her eyes slowly, her hand still on her forehead as she muttered "Angry birds" again—Sadie was sure that was what she was saying. Sadie didn't want to annoy the woman so she waited until she'd actually dug down a good ten inches—having found no potatoes—before she spoke.

"You know," Sadie said casually, "I have potatoes at my house. Why don't I go grab some for you so you can get out of the cold?"

"I know there are some in there," Mrs. Wapple said, pointing at the dirt. She began drawing pictures in the air like she had last night. Her lips moved slightly, and then she turned her head as though talking to someone over her left shoulder. Sadie leaned in, hoping to hear anything she actually said out loud, but Mrs. Wapple suddenly snapped her head back, causing the point of her cap to swing over her shoulder. She dropped her hand and glared at Sadie. "I planted them myself."

Sadie knew that many Bostonians took great pride in their home gardens so she had no desire to argue, but it seemed unlikely that there were really potatoes planted here. "It's just so cold to be digging," she said. "I could run home and grab some—I'd be back in less than a minute, and then you could go inside and . . . perhaps take something for your headache."

"I don't need medicine," Mrs. Wapple said, but another wave of pain grabbed hold of her and she lifted her hand to her forehead again.

Sadie was concerned. Did Mrs. Wapple simply have a low pain tolerance, or was whatever she was feeling as debilitating as it looked? Lorna Labram—the music leader at church—often battled migraine headaches. Sadie had been with Lorna at a workshop once when one of her bouts had set in. When the pain became more than her friend could handle, Sadie had driven her home. The expression she remembered from Lorna's face on that drive back from

Fort Collins was very similar to the compressing pain twisting Mrs. Wapple's features. Lorna had stayed in bed for two days in a pitch-black room after that workshop.

Could it be pain alone that had changed Mrs. Wapple from the person Sadie had talked to that afternoon to the one digging for potatoes by the light of a three-quarter moon?

"I'll go get those potatoes," Sadie said a moment later when Mrs. Wapple didn't argue. She leaned the shovel against the house and hurried across the frozen grass. "Be right back," she called over her shoulder.

Pete was waiting for her and helped her locate the potatoes while she filled him in on the conversation. "You're not going inside her house, are you?" he asked.

"Um, I hadn't thought of that," Sadie said, lifting the grocery sack filled with six fist-sized potatoes. "It's probably not a good idea, though if I were in Garrison I wouldn't even hesitate."

"You're not in Garrison," Pete said, his tone sympathetic. "I know it's hard on that big ol' heart of yours to walk away, but I think giving her the potatoes is help enough for tonight. We can check on her tomorrow."

"I'm going to take her the rest of the clam chowder, too," Sadie announced, heading for the fridge with the grocery sack on one arm. While removing the Tupperware of leftover soup, she spied a can of Mountain Dew in the back—it had been there when Sadie and Pete arrived. She knew caffeine was often helpful for migraines, so she grabbed it as well. If Mrs. Wapple wouldn't take medication, maybe she would drink the soda and get some relief. Sadie put the soda in the bag with the potatoes and shut the fridge. "I won't go in," she said as she passed Pete on her way to the front door. "I promise." But she knew it would be hard not to help if Mrs. Wapple would just let her.

Baxter's Clam Chowder

2 cups potatoes, peeled and cubed
1 cup celery, chopped
½ cup carrots, chopped
½ cup onion, chopped
Juice from 2 cans chopped clams (reserve clams)
2–3 cubes chicken bouillon or 2–3 teaspoons granules
Water
½ cup butter
½ cup flour
Pinch of sugar
Pinch of salt
½ teaspoon oregano
¼ teaspoon thyme
¼ teaspoon curry powder
4–6 cups milk
2 cans reserved clams*

In a two-quart saucepan, combine potatoes, celery, carrots, onion, clam juice, and chicken bouillon. Add water until vegetables are covered. Simmer on medium heat until vegetables are tender. Mash slightly, but don't drain vegetables. (For a chunkier soup, mash only half of the vegetables.) Set aside.

In a large soup pan, melt butter over medium-high heat. Add flour and stir until a smooth paste forms. Add remaining ingredients except milk and clams. Simmer for two or three minutes to blend the flavors. Add milk one cup at a time, stirring constantly until mixture becomes a thick cream base. Add vegetables (the reserved liquid will thin the base) and clams. Mix together and heat through. (Be careful about cooking the chowder too long once the clams are added, as heat makes them more rubbery.) Thin to desired consistency with additional milk. Adjust spices, and salt and pepper to taste.

Serves 8.

*Shawn tried this once with chicken instead of clams and it turned out great. He also increased the curry by ¼ teaspoon.

CHAPTER 6

Mrs. Wapple didn't invite her inside. She didn't speak at all when Sadie returned with the sack of potatoes. Instead, Mrs. Wapple grabbed the bag and the Tupperware of soup and headed for the invisible gate. Sadie watched her push the gate open; it swung easily on well-oiled hinges, and then silently fell back into place, turning into fence again. Sadie returned home, pushing her hands into her jacket pockets and feeling unsettled.

She and Pete didn't talk about it much, but simply kissed good-night in the hallway. Pete went into his bedroom and shut the door while Sadie headed into the bathroom.

Is there any way that both women I interacted with today were the same person? she wondered as she took off her makeup.

Maybe the Delores she'd met that afternoon sleepwalked or had episodes of disassociation. But that didn't sit right. Would she un-polish her nails, cut them and dirty them in her sleep too? Her skin couldn't have flawed so quickly either—Sadie had seen both faces up close and while the features were very similar, they were not exact. That meant there had to be two women.

Sadie washed her face and applied her night moisturizer,

thinking hard. She shook her head. There couldn't be two women—at least not two *real* Delores Wapples. But there were two women who looked an awful lot alike. One had said she was Delores Wapple, the other had answered to the name.

Sadie brushed out her hair and put toothpaste on her toothbrush as she reviewed the conversation she'd had with the sane-looking Delores. Every moment she'd spent with either woman moved through her mind as she flossed, smoothed lotion on her hands up to her elbows, and tweezed a few eyebrow hairs that couldn't wait until her next waxing.

She let herself out of the bathroom and turned off the light. She could hear Pete's soft snores from the other room, and she hurried to her room to avoid the temptation to peek in on him . . . just because she could.

After setting out what she would wear tomorrow, she put lotion on her feet and pulled on her cashmere-and-shea-infused sleeping-socks. Sadie then laid in Jared and Heather's bed and stared at the ceiling. Today marked the end of the second day of her six-day stint as a babysitter. She was one-third of the way through and beginning to really worry about Mrs. Wapple. On the one hand, she knew it wasn't any of her business, but on the other hand, wasn't it her business in the big, broad spectrum of being a fellow human being who had identified a concern? Or was she justifying her thoughts to give herself permission to get involved? She sighed and rolled onto her side, clenching her eyes closed and willing her brain to stop. Hadn't she gotten herself into enough trouble by poking her nose into the wrong places?

That was a question she couldn't answer as easily as she would have liked. Yes, she'd gotten too involved in things she *could* have left alone . . . and yet that over-involvement had led to bad guys getting what they deserved, cold cases being solved, lost loves re-united, and justice obtained. In hindsight it was hard to see her mis-takes as actual mistakes. But she'd nearly been killed a few times, she'd been hurt *every* time, she'd put people she loved at risk, and she'd kicked sleeping dogs that some people might say would be bet-ter left to lie. Everything she'd done hadn't turned out roses—the truth wasn't necessarily painless—and she was worried that one day she would be the *cause* of something horrible, rather than the solu-tion. Part of her reason for opening up the investigation company was to satisfy her urge to solve a mystery here and there without so much personal risk to herself. Looking up skip traces and serving court orders was fun and seemed to be enough . . . for the most part. But she did miss the bigger mysteries—the kind that she'd found herself in by accident so many times over the last year. It made her feel guilty to even think that, but it was true. While she enjoyed the investigation work she'd been bringing in, it was different; satisfying, but not nearly as encompassing.

She pulled the pillow over her face and began reciting nurs-ery rhymes in her head, trying to drown out her thoughts. These thoughts were dangerous, and she knew it. She was only going to wear herself out for what was sure to be a busy day tomorrow. These little boys were relentless, and she needed to be at the top of her game if she was going to hope to keep up for day three.

Eventually, Sadie fell asleep to a rambling combination of "Jack Sprat" and "Ladybug, Ladybug" and didn't wake up until the room began to lighten the next morning. She got out of bed, did her morn-ing stretches, and then headed into the kitchen to make whole wheat pancakes for her boys—a good hearty breakfast to start the day.

As soon as she exited her bedroom, she saw something on the floor of the hallway, near the kitchen entrance. It looked like an article of clothing in the early dawn light. Even with all the adventures of the previous night, Sadie had still straightened the house and would bet a quart of her homemade syrup that the hallway had been clear when she'd gone to bed last night.

After turning on the hall light, she approached the item, wondering if one of the boys had gotten up in the night and dropped something. Had someone been sick and gone looking for his mother? She'd feel horrible if she'd slept through something like that!

The item looked like a bunched-up scarf or something, but it didn't seem familiar until she reached down to pick it up. With her fingers inches from making contact, her memory flashed to the coarsely knitted gray hat Mrs. Wapple had been wearing last night. She pulled her hand back and inhaled sharply.

Her mind was playing tricks on her.

She crouched down, inspecting the article up close. She told herself it *wasn't* Mrs. Wapple's hat—it couldn't be—but as she took in the details, she felt her pulse rate increasing.

The hat hadn't been carefully laid down and part of the brim was folded beneath it, the point of the hat twisting so as not to be readily obvious. The coarseness of the yarn and the shapelessness of the whole, however, were far too familiar for Sadie's comfort.

For several seconds, Sadie attempted to come up with another possibility—a duplicate hat, perhaps—but that did little to quiet her concerns. Finally, she took a deep breath and stood up, staring at the hat and trying not to panic about how on earth it had gotten here . . . in the house . . . in the middle of the hallway . . . sometime between ten o'clock last night and six thirty this morning.

"Pete," she said under her breath, realizing she didn't have to figure this out alone. She took long strides to his door. She knocked lightly, not wanting to wake up the boys in the next room, and then opened the door a few inches. She lifted one foot to enter before remembering their rule about staying out of one another's bedrooms. She pulled her foot back and stayed in the hallway.

"Pete," she said in a loudish whisper, leaning into the room and looking for something to throw that would get his attention but wouldn't injure him. Everything about the room screamed seven-year-old-boy except for the extra-large body in the bed and the fact that Pete had cleaned the room at some point. All the action figures were perfectly lined up on the dresser, tallest to shortest. "Pete, wake up," she said a little louder.

He shot up in bed and looked around the room, blinking rapidly. His hair stuck out in a dozen funny angles, but Sadie barely had time to notice how cute it was.

"What's wrong?" he asked, throwing back the covers and swinging his legs off the side of the bed. He was wearing only boxers and a T-shirt, and Sadie looked away for propriety's sake. She wasn't sure she was emotionally prepared to know his preference in under-garments.

"I'm really sorry to wake you so early, but you've got to see this." She held up her hand to block her view as he reached for a pair of jeans thrown over the footboard. "I'll, um, wait in the hall."

She shut the door and leaned against the wall, trying to ignore the heat in her cheeks.

Pete emerged a few seconds later. "What do I need to see?" he asked.

Oh, right. The hat.

"Over here," she said. She headed down the hall, stepping to the side so Pete would have a clear view. Pete did the same thing she'd done: crouched down and looked at the hat from all different angles.

"We can't be sure it's her hat," Pete said finally.

Sadie hadn't said anything about what she thought it was, and the fact that Pete jumped to the same conclusion was quite validating. "I know," she said, standing a few feet behind him with her arms folded. "But we *can* be sure it's not yours or mine or one of the boys."

"It wasn't here when we went to bed last night?"

"I'm certain we'd have noticed if we'd had to step around it."

"We were tired."

"Yes, we were," Sadie said, trying not to be annoyed by him playing devil's advocate but understanding why he was. "But I typically do notice things like that. For instance, the pants you're wearing are the same ones you had on yesterday; they've got a peanut butter smudge on the left leg from lunch. By the way, when you threw your pants over the footboard last night, your wallet must have fallen out of your back pocket because I saw it halfway under the bed."

Pete put his hand on his back pocket and seemed surprised to find it empty.

"Kalan took off one of his shoes in the kitchen when we got home from the park," Sadie continued, "but the other one didn't come off until he got to his room. I forgot to get it out of the kitchen before they went to bed so I decided to leave it there. There are only five glasses in this house; I'm assuming Heather had a set of six but broke one. Everything else is plastic, and there are three green ones and—"

"Okay, I get it," Pete said, standing. "You're observant."

Sadie accepted the compliment with a nod. "But for the sake of fantastical explanations, let's pretend the hat *was* there last night. We still have some of the same questions. Why? How did it get here? Mrs. Wapple had it on her head when she went back through her gate last night."

Pete let out a breath, a distinct wrinkle between his eyebrows. "Let's check the locks."

Sadie was closest to the kitchen so she headed for the back door. Pete crossed the living room to the front of the house. She heard him say "Locked," seconds before she twisted the knob on the back door. The knob didn't turn. "This one's locked too," she said, turning it a second time to make sure.

"So, how did the hat get here?" Pete asked when they returned to the hallway.

"Someone put it there." It almost seemed silly to say it out loud, it was so obvious.

"Why and how?" Pete asked, his voice tight.

Sadie had a brief movie play in her head of Mrs. Wapple picking the lock, putting the hat down, and then locking the door on her way out. It was like a cartoon—not real, not believable.

Sadie stared at the hat and felt a chill run down her spine as Kalan's words came back to her. She shook her head, trying to dislodge the words from her mind, but ended up saying them instead. "She's a witch."

"What?"

"Nothing," Sadie said, quick and sharp. "I . . . just . . . have no idea how the hat could have gotten here."

They stood for several seconds before Pete seemed to snap out of his thoughts. He ran his fingers through his hair and took a deep breath. "We should take pictures," he said. "Document the exact position of the hat. We should also look for anything else that might be out of place in the house."

"Good idea," Sadie said. She turned to look at the hat and startled to see Chance standing in the hallway, holding the limp hat by the point so that it hung nearly to the floor.

He wrinkled his nose and held it up another few inches. "Why is Mrs. Wapple's hat here?" he asked, scrunching up his nose. "It stinks." Chance threw it to the side of the hallway where it crumpled into a pathetic heap before he looked at Sadie expectantly. "I'm hungry."

Whole Wheat Pancakes

2 cups whole wheat flour*
⅓ cup sugar
2 teaspoons baking powder
1 teaspoon baking soda
1 teaspoon salt
2 eggs
⅓ cup oil (or melted butter)
2 cups buttermilk or sour milk (for sour milk, add 1 tablespoon white
    vinegar or lemon juice to 1 cup regular milk)

Heat griddle to medium. Combine dry ingredients and whisk together. Add eggs and liquids. Mix well. (Thin batter with water if consistency is too thick.) Drop by ⅓-cup portions on hot, greased griddle. Cook about three minutes on one side, until edges begin to look dry. Flip and cook one to two more minutes or until golden brown.
Makes approximately 16 pancakes.

*Shawn prefers white flour because it's not good for him. You can substitute the flour if you want, but you should really eat whole grains.

Homemade Maple Syrup

2 cups sugar
1 cup water
1 teaspoon Mapleine or maple extract*

<u>Microwave directions</u>: Combine all ingredients in a 3-cup capacity microwave-safe measuring cup or bowl. Cook 3 minutes. Remove from microwave and stir for 30 seconds for sugar to dissolve.

<u>Stovetop directions</u>: In a saucepan, bring ingredients to a boil on medium-high heat, stirring consistently. Boil 1 minute, stirring constantly.

Cool slightly before serving. Store leftovers in an airtight container. (Previously used commercial syrup bottles work great.)

*For a buttery flavor, add 1 teaspoon butter extract. For a vanilla flavor, add 1 teaspoon vanilla extract. For a tangy flavor, add ½ teaspoon lemon extract.

CHAPTER 7

Sadie distracted Chance with breakfast preparations while Pete put the hat back where it had been and attempted to recreate the state they'd found it in. He took a few pictures with his camera phone, but Sadie could tell he was frustrated that the hat had been moved. After that, he got dressed and went outside, doing a full perimeter check while Chance helped Sadie make her famous whole wheat pancakes with the whole wheat flour Sadie had bought at the City Feed and Supply yesterday. Sadie had thought it was a farm supply store from the name, but it was all about really good people-food. At home, she milled her own wheat, of course.

By the time she and Chance had finished mixing the batter, the electric griddle was hot and the syrup was cooling. She was helping Chance turn the first set of pancakes when Pete came in through the back door. He took off his shoes and rubbed his hands together to warm them up.

"Nothing," he said, removing his jacket and throwing it over the back of a chair. "No tool marks on the doorknob, no footprints, nothing out of place."

"What are tool marks?" Chance said, looking up at his grandfather.

Sadie and Pete shared a silent look.

"Those look done to me," Sadie said, turning her attention to the pancakes. "What do you think, Chance?" She took the spatula and lifted one up in order to peek at the bottom. It was barely brown.

"Not done yet," Chance said with an air of authority. "I think it needs ten more minutes."

"How about two?" Sadie said, returning the pancake to the griddle.

Chance shrugged as though giving in so that Sadie wouldn't feel bad. "Okay."

"And do you know what's really yummy on whole wheat pancakes besides homemade syrup?" Sadie asked.

"What?"

"Peanut butter."

Chance's big blue eyes went a little bigger. "I love peanut butter!"

"So do I," Sadie said, giving his shoulder a squeeze. "Let's find it and set the table while these pancakes finish cooking."

"Okay!" Chance nearly shouted, scrambling off the chair Sadie had pulled to the counter.

Sadie opened the cupboard under the sink and pulled out an empty grocery sack while Chance looked through another cupboard for the peanut butter; Sadie knew the peanut butter was in the pantry, but she needed him distracted. She handed the bag to Pete, who was standing at the edge of the linoleum with his hands on his hips still looking at the hat. "Why don't you bag it and tag it, Detective," she said, trying to lighten the mood.

He attempted a smile as he took the bag, but she knew better. "A little later—after the boys are up and Kalan is at school—I think we should head across the street, return the hat, and have a little talk with our neighbor."

"Do you think she broke in?" Sadie asked in a low voice so that Chance—who was still looking for peanut butter—wouldn't overhear.

"What else are we supposed to think?"

He held Sadie's eyes, and she said exactly what he wanted to hear—nothing. At least for a few seconds.

"Should we call the local police?" she asked.

Pete shook his head. "They won't take a stray hat seriously. But we should stop at the hardware store and buy an eyebolt."

"What's an eyebolt?"

"The chain-type locks like they have on hotel room doors. They're far more effective at keeping people out than they get credit for. A swing bolt would be even better."

"What's a—"

"I found it!"

Sadie turned around to see Chance holding up the jar of peanut butter from the pantry in triumph. "We better get those pancakes off the griddle," she said, hurrying back to breakfast. She looked at Pete over her shoulder as she helped Chance flip the now-overcooked pancakes. "I'll follow your lead," she said.

Pete attempted another smile, but his look was heavy. She turned back to the pancakes, spooning out another set when she realized she'd been able to read his expression perfectly. That meant he wasn't trying to block her from his thoughts and emotions as he had often done during the hard situations they had faced in the past. What she saw in his face, however, caused Sadie's throat to tighten. There were three little boys in this house—three vulnerable little boys—and something strange was taking place. The safety and sanctity of this home—the one place that should be the safest place in their world—had been violated. And Grandpa was in charge.

"I'm going to check on the other boys," Pete said as he turned toward the hallway.

"Good idea," Sadie said, watching him disappear and knowing he'd take the opportunity to have a look around the interior of the house as well.

Chance was ready to put a fresh batch of pancake batter on the griddle. Sadie gave him another squeeze, as much to borrow some of his naïve optimism as anything else, and helped him check to see if the pancakes were ready to turn—which they weren't. She took a deep breath to calm herself and wondered how a day that started like this would play out.

Pete returned to the kitchen with a sleepy-looking Fig and Kalan in tow; they'd obviously slept through the morning's excitement. When Sadie handed him a plate of pancakes, he whispered that nothing in the house seemed to be disturbed, which didn't surprise Sadie at all. Jared and Heather didn't own many valuables, and whatever intent had led to the hat being left in the hallway did not feel connected to theft—other than the theft of security. Sadie thought it might have been easier to have had something tangible taken.

Pete and Sadie acted as normal as possible throughout the rest of breakfast so as not to alert the boys—especially Kalan, who had shown the most interest in Mrs. Wapple from the start. Thankfully, Chance said nothing about the hat, going on and on about how wonderful peanut butter was on the "whole weed" pancakes instead. The other boys agreed; breakfast was a hit.

Pete drove Kalan to school while Sadie bathed the littler boys. After he got back, they cleaned up breakfast, made themselves presentable, and were just giving in to watching *Cars*—for the third time since they'd arrived—when the phone rang.

"Hey, Jared," Pete said when he answered the cordless phone, making eye contact with Sadie before heading down the hall where he could better hear his son on the other end of the line.

After a few minutes, he returned to the living room and held out the phone to Sadie. "Heather wants to talk to you and the boys."

Sadie paused the movie and ushered Chance toward the phone first. He stopped whining about the movie being interrupted when he realized it was his mom on the phone. Within seconds, Fig was trying to get the phone away from his older brother and calling "Mommy! Mommy! Mommy!" while Chance turned by degrees, always keeping his back to his little brother.

"I think we ought to keep everything to ourselves for now," Pete whispered to Sadie while Chance said good-bye and handed the phone to Fig, who ran into the kitchen as though someone might take the phone from him. Sadie nodded her agreement, though she had hoped Heather might have been able to fill in some blanks about Mrs. Wapple. It would be more difficult to get the information without telling her exactly why she needed it, but she agreed with Pete that it wasn't worth the parental panic that would most certainly take place if they revealed what had happened.

When Fig finally said good-bye, Sadie put the phone to her ear and signaled Pete to start the movie.

"Hi there," she said, going into the kitchen and sitting at the table. "How are things going for the two of you?"

"I should be asking you that question," Heather said. "How are my boys treating you? Are they behaving okay?"

Sadie was glad to have struck such an easy friendship with Pete's daughter-in-law from the very first phone call, and she caught

Heather up on the antics of her three sons since they'd last spoken yesterday morning. Heather mentioned that they'd found a nice complex closer to the hospital—and the urban area around it—than they'd originally planned. It had a playground and a swimming pool that the young parents hoped would make up for the fact that they wouldn't have their own yard—something they had considered essential when looking for a place in Boston that had eventually led them to the Jamaica Plain rental. Heather also commented on the weather, though it was hard for Sadie to believe the temperatures were in the eighties in Texas when she was wearing her warmest, thickest, fuzziest socks.

"I bet you won't miss another New England winter," Sadie said.

"Not one bit," Heather said with emphasis. "I grew up in Arizona, and if you ask me, snow shovels are medieval torture devices."

They both laughed and talked a little more about when Jared would actually start his residency and how the family would facilitate the cross-country move. During a brief lull in the conversation, Sadie asked about Mrs. Wapple as casually as possible.

"Why? What's the Witch of Browden Street done now?"

"The Witch of Browden Street?" Sadie repeated.

"Well, that's what the neighbors called her, and it kinda stuck—she's *that* weird—and Salem's only half an hour away, you know." She laughed. "So you must have seen her. What did she do?"

"Oh, nothing really," Sadie said, perhaps too quickly. "I'm just wondering what you know about her."

"Not much," Heather said. "She's only lived there a few months and mostly keeps to herself, but now and then she comes out and hollers at people or starts chanting and stuff. Someone told me that she steals other people's mail, but Jared and I have a PO Box."

"Have you ever talked to her?"

"No," Heather said. "I don't think anyone talks to her. There are a few knotholes in her fence that she looks out of. Sometimes she yells at people when they pass by her house. Creepy. Why do you ask?"

"Well, I talked to her last night."

"You did!" Heather said with a laugh. "What happened? What did you talk about?"

Sadie kept the details scarce, focusing only on the Mrs. Wapple that the boys seemed to know and the woman in pain she'd given potatoes to. She hadn't figured out how the woman she'd given the cookies to factored in, so she left her out of it.

"Wow," Heather said, her voice soft and humble. "I've never seen her act like she's hurt or anything."

"Does anyone else live with her?"

"No, she's alone."

"Does she have a caretaker of any kind? Family? Church connection?" Maybe the woman she'd given the cookies to was a family member—a sister perhaps.

"Not that I know of," Heather said. "I suppose someone could enter through the alley—I wouldn't see them if they did—but I've never seen anyone visit other than some Mormon missionaries who got an earful over the fence a few weeks after she moved in. She's *not* interested in religion, in case you were wondering."

Sadie struggled with how to move to the next subject and finally used Kalan to introduce it. "Kalan said she cast a spell on someone's dog and it got hit by a car."

"Oh," Heather said, sounding embarrassed. "I didn't know he'd heard Jared and me talking about that."

"What happened to the dog?"

Heather was quiet for a few seconds. "Mr. Forsberk's dog pooped in her yard, and she came out from behind the fence, screaming. He started yelling back and she told him his dog would die within a week and did this weird waving thing in the air with her hand—the boys and I saw the whole thing. The dog was hit by a car two days later right in front of her house. I didn't make a big deal about it to the boys, but Kalan did ask a lot of questions."

"And you think she has . . . supernatural powers that caused the accident?"

"Yeah, I guess I do," Heather said as though apologizing. "I grew up close to the reservation and there was always a lot of talk about spirits and hexes and black magic, or bad medicine. I've never had the luxury of not believing in another realm, and Mrs. Wapple is exactly the kind of person who would invite that type of energy. The fact is, she said the dog would die and it did."

"Hmmm," Sadie said, vastly uncomfortable with Heather's thoughts on the subject. "Well, that's certainly something to think about. I haven't seen the angry side of her, or the . . . uh, witchy side, but I am worried about her."

"Well, maybe it's worth calling social services or something. I'm the last one to say she doesn't need help—witch or not."

"That's not a bad idea," Sadie said, nodding to herself while the boys laughed at something in the other room. "Thanks for the information. I'm glad you've had a good trip. Like I said, the boys are doing great, so don't worry about them a bit."

"Oh, I'm not worried," Heather said. "I miss my little men, but it's the first time Jared and I have gone anywhere just the two of us since he started medical school, and we're enjoying that an awful lot."

She thanked Sadie for helping out; Sadie humbly refused the

thanks, insisting it was her pleasure—which it certainly was. Heather promised to call tomorrow after Kalan got home from school, and a few minutes later, they said good-bye. Sadie hung up, her eyes finding the bag with the hat hanging on the back door.

Pete's hand on her shoulder startled her. "Somebody's jumpy," he said, passing her on his way to the cupboard by the phone. It held the local phone book, pens and pencils, and a few different pads of paper. Pete grabbed one of the notebooks and flipped through it until he came to a blank page.

"What are you doing?" Sadie asked, noting that he seemed lighter . . . no, he seemed determined. He pulled his cell phone out of his pocket and smiled at her.

"Making a few calls," he said as though she would be satisfied with such a paltry explanation.

"About Mrs. Wapple?"

Pete shrugged. "It wouldn't hurt to know a little more about what we're dealing with. A guy I used to work with in Colorado Springs was from the Rhode Island PD originally. He might know someone who could do a little research for me—off the record, of course. I mentioned to Jared about putting in some eyebolts, but he said he has to clear it with his landlord and he thinks I'm being cop-dad." He shrugged off the comment. "Anyway, I hope he'll get back to us on that soon. It would sure make me feel better."

Sadie nodded and relaxed, relieved that Pete was doing something real, something solid, something logical. Why couldn't she do the same thing? She thought about her cute little laptop in her room. She didn't have Pete's connections, but that didn't mean she didn't have some tricks of her own. The house was run-down and the furniture was used, but Jared had excellent Internet service and a wireless router that Sadie very much appreciated.

"I'll race ya," she said, glancing at the clock. "The movie has an hour to go and then the boys will need lunch. Let's meet back here in forty-five minutes and compare notes."

Pete smiled, a genuine smile this time. They were on the case, together. This was Pete's comfort zone and Sadie was now a part of that. She liked that very much.

He started toggling through his phone and gave her a wink. "You're on."

CHAPTER 8

O kay," Sadie said, popping a Froot Loop in her mouth as she and Pete reconvened at command central—i.e., the kitchen table—fifty minutes later. There wasn't a more dignified snack food available so she'd had to make do with dry cereal. She needed fuel of some kind to keep her brain working; the pancakes were beginning to wear off. She settled in on her side of the table with her laptop open in front of her. Pete sat opposite her and had filled up two pages of the notebook, which had her worried. It wasn't a competition, but she really wanted to win. "What have you got?" she asked, officially beginning the meeting of minds.

"Well," Pete said, turning back to his first page. "I'm still waiting for one more call to come back verifying a few details, but she doesn't have a criminal record."

"That's good news," Sadie said, relieved. She hadn't bothered looking for criminal information since she figured Pete had that market cornered.

"Yeah," Pete said. "But she had her driver's license—Vermont issued—revoked back in '97. Her doctor said the medication she was taking impaired her ability to operate a car."

"Which means at some point she was able to *have* a driver's license, and she had residency in Vermont," Sadie said.

Pete nodded and wrote something in the margin. "I couldn't find details about her medication, but I found reference to some hospital stays. One in '96, one in '98, and another one in '01. They were all three to five days long—I'm guessing it was a psych ward." He grabbed a handful of Froot Loops and put them all in his mouth.

"I found the '96 and '01 stay, but not the '98," Sadie said, adding "1998" next to item four on her list of twelve details she'd put at the top of her list for organizational purposes. "The first stay was in Vermont, right?"

"Right," Pete said. "It looks like she lived there for about five years before that. The next two stays were here in Massachusetts."

"The last stay was in Belmont. Where was the other one?"

"Not sure."

"Family members," Sadie said, moving on to the next topic.

"Mother died in the early nineties in a car accident. Other than that, there's her father and a younger sister."

"The sister's name is Gabrielle," Sadie said, nodding. That was item eight on her list, and an important discovery. "I think she lives here in Boston. I wonder if she's the person I talked to yesterday. Maybe she pretended to be Delores, though I don't know why she would."

Pete nodded. "I figured that must have been her, too."

"Her dad's dead," Sadie said—item six.

"He is?" Pete asked, reading through his notes.

"Yep, four months ago."

"How do you know that? I didn't find it."

"Okay, I admit it—I asked Shawn for help. He discovered in one of our other cases last month that while it sometimes takes time for official records to be updated, the obituaries are immediate. Anyway, he found the dad's obituary—it was run in Lowell, north of here. It requested that in lieu of flowers, donations be sent to Eastridge Hospice in thanks for the care he'd received, so that means he knew he was dying. There was only a graveside service, but Delores and Gabrielle were mentioned by name in his obituary—Delores first, which would make her the oldest. Delores's mother's obituary stated that she and Timothy Wapple had divorced but remained friends, and there was no mention of any other marriage. I'd guess Dad didn't remarry either, since no other wife was listed in his obit. He gave generously to the Veterans of Foreign Wars—that wasn't in the obituary, though, I found that by happenstance when his name came up in an old record of donors for an event back in the early nineties."

Pete stared at her. "You found all that in less than an hour?"

Sadie shrugged. "Like I said, I had help."

Pete tapped his phone. "So did I," he said. "It's still impressive that you found so much."

"Finding stuff was the easy part," Sadie said. "The tricky part was putting the pieces of information together. For instance, Mrs. Wapple receives disability, but she doesn't have a phone, and her mail is forwarded. Shawn's going to look into her former address in between his classes today, so we might get some more information from that sector."

"She's a registered Democrat," Pete chimed in. "But she hasn't voted for several years."

"Good job," Sadie said with a smile, not telling him she'd found that too.

Pete had found a complaint filed by one of the neighbors in Jamaica Plain six weeks ago—not long after Delores had moved in; she'd been yelling over the fence. Three complaints had been filed over the years in Lowell too, where Sadie assumed Delores had lived with her father. In high school, Delores had set a swimming record in the freestyle back in the late eighties—her freshman year. Sometime between that accomplishment and the first hospitalization in '96, things had changed for her dramatically, but there was little information available. She was currently forty-two years old and her birthday was January 6.

"That makes her a Capricorn," Sadie added as an interesting side note. "They're usually very goal-oriented but can be aloof and distant before they really come to trust someone."

Pete smiled at her.

"What?" she said, feeling self-conscious. This was serious business. She didn't expect or necessarily want a smile. Was he making fun of her for being familiar with the zodiac? That was uncalled for.

"You're good at this."

Sadie waved the compliment off, but in her heart she locked it away to enjoy later. "I wish it were more than bits and pieces," she said. "Before all these privacy acts were put into place, the nursing home I used to volunteer at would let us read up on patients' histories, so that we knew where the residents had been in their lives. They would often have pages and pages of history, gathered from the patient, their families, and the doctors. I wish we had something like that."

"There are good reasons those things aren't part of public record," Pete said. "Say Mrs. Wapple has some kind of remission, she'd have a very hard time reestablishing herself in this information age if everything about her life was so widely available. It's too bad you and I both found her hospital stays."

"I understand all that," Sadie said. "I'm frustrated because there is a history that could help us figure out what exactly we're dealing with but we can't get our hands on it. I hate that."

"Well, we have found quite a bit," Pete said. "We know she has a medical history with strong indicators that point us toward mental illness. Yet, based on the swim team record you found, that didn't hold her back when she was young. She's not in an institution—which says a lot—but we know from our own observations that she isn't well. She's reclusive, but not criminal. Annoying, but has never hurt anyone. She's also a native of Boston who lived out of state for a little while but came back. Both of her parents are deceased, leaving her in the care of her sister, most likely."

"When you say it like that, it does seem like a lot of information," Sadie said. "Did you find out why she's called Mrs. Wapple? Wapple is her maiden name."

"I didn't find any marital history, so I don't have an answer for that. However, with what we do have, I feel better approaching her about the hat," Pete said, leaning back in his chair and putting his hands behind his head. "I don't think she's dangerous."

"She did come in the house," Sadie said. "That's disturbing."

"Yes," Pete said with a conciliatory nod. "That's very disturbing."

They looked at their notes for a minute. "So, is that what we're going to do? Confront her about the hat?" Sadie ate another Froot Loop.

"Yes, but I think we should call the sister first, now that we know Mrs. Wapple has an unstable history," Pete said. "She might have some valuable insight, not to mention that Mrs. Wapple might not have the ability to get help on her own. Her father died, and she's recently moved. Those are two very difficult things for anyone to cope with, let alone someone with a history like hers. I think we'll need the sister's involvement to make sure she gets the help she needs."

"Gabrielle's not listed in the phone book," Sadie said. "I looked. In fact I can't find a Gabrielle Wapple anywhere online. Maybe she's married."

Pete smiled. "Well, it's good to know I have a few tricks you haven't tapped into yet." He slid his notebook around so Sadie could see the ten-digit phone number written in the upper section of the paper. He'd circled it three times, showing his pride in the discovery. "She must have married at some point, though she listed herself as single on her tax returns last year. She goes by Gabrielle Marrow."

"An unlisted number?" Sadie said. "What's she hiding from?"

Pete shrugged. "Let's give her a call and find out." He dialed the first couple of numbers and then looked at Sadie. After a few moments, he held the phone out to her. "Do you want to call?"

Sadie kept her hands in her lap. She did want to talk to this woman and get the information herself. But . . . "I think you should," she heard herself say. "She lied to me about who she was; she might be defensive."

Pete nodded and finished dialing the number. He put the phone to his ear.

Sadie waited anxiously, watching Pete's face. After several seconds passed, he said quietly, "Voice mail."

Sadie felt herself deflate as disappointment replaced her eagerness. No answers—not yet. Pete left a message saying he wanted to talk to her about her sister. He didn't refer to himself as a detective, and yet his voice was still strong, warm, and authoritative—not to mention very attractive. Any woman would be a fool not to call back a voice like that.

He hung up and set his phone on the table.

"I hope she'll call back," Sadie said. She slumped in her chair, then sat up straight as Pete reached across the table, taking her hands in both of his.

"She will," he said with confidence. "She's obviously filling the caretaker role to some extent. She'll call back."

Sadie looked into his eyes for several seconds and felt everything melt away as the air between them became warm. "I could get used to this, you know," she said, her voice almost a whisper.

"What? Working a case together?"

"Well, that too," Sadie said with a smile. She leaned forward, resting her elbows on the table but letting him keep hold of her hands. "I meant sitting across the table from you and finding it so *fabulously* comfortable."

"How about making dinner for me every night?"

"Every night?" Sadie asked, lowering her chin. "You won't eat leftovers?"

"I'd eat *your* leftovers," Pete conceded. "Would you iron my shirts?"

Sadie smiled sweetly but shook her head. "You iron your shirts; I'll iron mine."

"Shoot," Pete said, pulling his eyebrows together as though re-considering the entire arrangement. "What about the rest of my laundry?"

"I'd wash every blessed sock with love," Sadie said, batting her eyelashes. "Would you take my car to the repair shop for me?"

"You bet," Pete said, leaning in as well so that only a few inches separated them—it was a very small table. "I'd even scrape the frost off the windshield of your car."

"I don't get to park in the garage?"

"Um, with my tools and things there's only room for one car."

"So you assume all this would take place at your house?" Sadie asked in a crooning voice, leaning forward even more. She could smell the Froot Loops on his breath.

"I have better closet space."

"Ooooh, you know how to drive right to the heart of the matter, don't you?"

He moved another inch closer, and she could feel the feather-light brush of his lips against her own when he spoke. "Don't forget the extra-large laundry room, the double ovens, and the skylight in the master bath."

Sadie lowered her voice. "You had me at closet space."

"Ew! They're kissing!"

Sadie and Pete split apart, laughing at themselves and at the two boys who were making exaggerated throwing up sounds. Luckily, it didn't take much to distract them. Lunch came and went, then more play time outside, then naps, which really only consisted of quiet play time in the boys' room. Whenever Sadie entered the kitchen and saw the hat hanging on the back door, she was reminded not only of the hat incident, but of her concern for Mrs. Wapple and the fact that Gabrielle hadn't called back yet. After cleaning up lunch, Sadie prodded Pete to call Gabrielle a second time. He ended up leaving another message.

"Two messages," Sadie said, shaking her head and looking at the hat again. "Now what?"

Pete regarded the bag. "Maybe we're making this harder than it needs to be," he said, sliding his phone into his pocket. "We can still talk to Gabrielle when she calls, but maybe we should take the hat back and get it over with."

Sadie lifted her eyebrows, feeling conflicted at the suggestion. It made sense to cut to the chase and see what Mrs. Wapple had to say about the hat being in their house—especially now that they knew she didn't have any kind of dangerous history—and yet, Sadie had a strong feeling that whatever information they got from Mrs. Wapple would be incomplete. "We *definitely* need to get ahold of the sister."

Pete nodded. "I agree, and hopefully she'll call back, but if we return the hat, we might have even more questions to ask when she does call. Besides that, having this hat around is . . . distracting."

"I can't argue with that," Sadie conceded. Regardless of the demands the boys put on their time and attention, the hat was taking center stage. "Why don't you take it. I'll keep cleaning up." She'd already spoken to Mrs. Wapple once; it was only fair to give Pete a chance.

Pete nodded, took the bag, and let himself out the front door. Sadie didn't clean up, though. Instead she stood at the window and watched him cross the street and approach Mrs. Wapple's house with long, confident steps. He went to the front porch and Sadie made a face—she should have reminded him that the front door wasn't well-used. He opened the screen door and knocked, waited, then knocked again before hanging the bag on the handle of the screen door and heading back.

"You're just going to leave it there?" Sadie asked when he returned.

"We'll keep an eye on it and see if she picks it up. Bait."

"Bait?" Sadie repeated, looking at him with confusion. "We're not trying to catch her."

"But we do want to observe her."

"But she doesn't use the front door," Sadie said. "Surely you noticed the rusted hinges and spiderwebs."

Pete shrugged. "She's missing her hat; I'm sure she'll come out at some point and see it there. Tonight if not sooner. At least we got it out of here."

Sadie chose not to argue, even though this hadn't been what she'd expected when he said he wanted to take the hat back and get more information. When the boys gave up pretending to nap, she and Pete walked with them to pick Kalan up from school, then took the long way home by way of a local park. It was after 4:00 when they returned home, and the afternoon breeze had picked up, making going home a welcome reprieve.

The bag was still on the door handle when they returned. Sadie realized that if they'd really wanted to use the hat as bait they shouldn't have left. Oops. The bag swung back and forth in the wind. They didn't talk about it. Instead, Pete called Gabrielle a third time but decided not to leave a message when it went to voice mail again.

Sadie justified her growing concern about Gabrielle's silence by telling herself that this was Gabrielle's home number and she was probably at work. Perhaps she could find where that place of work was. Nearly an entire day had passed and Sadie was anxious to determine what they should do next. She also worried that Mrs. Wapple might be in more pain than she'd been in last night. They weren't treating her pain as though it was urgent, but what if it was?

"I think I should go over and check on her," Sadie said once the boys were settled into a rousing game of Legos, if you could call Legos a game. With these boys everything was a game or competition of some kind.

Pete looked at her, a questioning expression on his face.

"It's been a whole day," she said, glancing out the window at the bag hanging on the front door. "And she was really hurting last night. What if she's worse?"

"She broke into our house."

Sadie sighed. "I won't go inside or anything, and your research proved that she doesn't have a criminal or dangerous past. I just want to make sure she's not passed out on the floor or something." He didn't seem convinced, so Sadie quickly suggested an alternate plan. "Or we could just bypass her sister and call social services. Heather suggested that this morning, and the idea's been growing on me. That said, it's after four o'clock, and I'd be surprised if they'd be able to come right out. My friend Diane called Adult Protective Services on her neighbor, Ruth, because she suspected that the woman's niece who'd moved in with her wasn't taking care of her. It took almost a week for them to come see her, and by then Ruth was eating stale bread with Crisco instead of butter because the niece hadn't gone to the store. True story."

"I don't like you going alone," Pete said. He glanced into the living room, where three little boys were sprawled out on the floor fighting over the blocks.

Sadie cut him off at the pass. "We're not leaving them here alone. Not even for a few minutes. I'll have my phone, and I won't be long, okay?"

Pete sighed, then shrugged. "Okay, but be quick."

Sadie put her coat back on before giving Pete a quick peck on the cheek and slipping out the front door.

She was triumphant as she crossed the street and cut across the lawn, heading for the gate in the fence. She was doing something, and she felt very good about that. As she reached the curb in front of Mrs. Wapple's house, something caught her eye and she looked to the right in time to see the front door of the house on the corner shut. For a moment she wondered if it was important, but then shrugged it off, refocusing on her goal—checking on Mrs. Wapple to see if she needed some kind of intervention.

CHAPTER 9

The wind blew Sadie's hair in every direction possible; she had to keep a hand beside her face to keep it out of her eyes. Good thing she had no plans to go anywhere tonight and thus didn't have to be too stressed about the havoc being waged against her coiffure. At the front porch, Sadie stopped and considered proper etiquette. It only made sense to go to the back door since the front door was unused. But the back door was kind of like Mrs. Wapple's *front* door, except that the fence enclosed it, which made Sadie wonder if it were proper to go back there without cause. Hmmm.

After a few moments, she retrieved the hat hanging on the front door. Pete had wrapped the handle of the bag around the doorknob twice, which explained why the wind hadn't had its way with it yet. On her way to the gate, Sadie glanced across the street to see Pete standing in the window. She gave him a smile and thumbs-up sign. He nodded but looked rather grim.

At the gate, Sadie ducked her head to turn her face out of the wind, took a breath, and knocked as loud as she could on the wooden fence. "Mrs. Wapple?" She hoped her voice was loud enough to be heard over the sound of the wind through the trees. She could see one of the knotholes Heather had told her about; it was five feet up from the ground, the perfect height to spy through. Sadie was tempted to look through it herself, but didn't want to be caught doing so. Last night Mrs. Wapple had simply pushed on the gate to open it, so when Sadie didn't get an answer, she did the same. It swung open easily.

"Hello?" she said as she slowly walked into the backyard. "Mrs. Wapple?"

The gate closed behind her. Being hidden in Mrs. Wapple's private space made her feel a little reckless, and she took a breath to calm herself down. An oak tree stood in one corner, half of its brown and auburn leaves still on the tree and the other half blowing across the lawn. The upper branches moaned in the high wind.

Opposite the tree was a single-car garage set in the corner of the yard. The tall wooden fence kept the yard very much contained and blocked most of the wind. The grass was dormant, but had been mowed rather recently, and the edges went right up to the tall fence and the house—no flower beds to dig in back here. There was a container garden, however, in one corner of the cobbled patio filled with what was left of some pink chrysanthemums. A sturdy-looking wrought iron table was flanked by two matching chairs on the patio; an empty flowerpot sat in the center. Sadie could envision Delores— the woman she'd met yesterday—sipping coffee while she watched the leaves fall. She couldn't picture Mrs. Wapple doing the same thing, though.

The patio was flanked by a sliding glass door, and Sadie approached it carefully, hoping to see inside the house. Was the inside of the house as well-kept as the backyard, or was it in disarray like the front of the house? It was uncomfortable to see such dichotomy.

Once Sadie reached the door, she knocked and took a few steps back for the sake of her manners. She attempted to smooth her hair, though it was a losing battle; no doubt she looked like an Albert Einstein impersonator about now. It was dark inside the house, as though all the curtains were drawn except for the one by the sliding glass door. Sadie could see into what looked like an enclosed patio or maybe a sunroom of sorts. It had a basic set of white wicker furniture with simple gingham cushions and a terra-cotta tiled floor. There were empty plant pots, piles of newspaper, and a dirty-looking pet carrier within view as well. Mrs. Wapple had lived here only a couple of months, which led Sadie to conclude that either she'd not finished unpacking and organizing her own space, or she'd become very comfortable very fast.

Sadie knocked again and considered what she would do if there were no answer. She'd come over to make sure Mrs. Wapple was okay. If she didn't get some kind of proof that was the case, she was no better off than she'd been before she'd come.

Suddenly, movement inside caught her attention. She leaned forward and squinted to better see into the dark interior; for the first time she picked up on the ripe smell of garbage not taken to the curb in a timely manner. "Mrs. Wapple?" Sadie said, her face nearly touching the glass as she tried to see past the cluttered room. "It's Sadie Hoffmiller from—"

Something slammed into the glass right in front of her face. Sadie let out a squeaky scream, jumped backward, and looked at the bottom of the glass to see what it was. A book? Someone had thrown a book at her face?

She looked back up and nearly screamed a second time as she stared into the wide-eyed face of Mrs. Wapple staring her down from the other side of the glass. Sadie's hand went to her throat, which had gone dry, and she tried to get her heart rate back in check. Mrs.

Wapple didn't move, didn't even blink, she just stared at Sadie in a way that made Sadie glad the book hadn't broken through the glass between them.

"I, uh, I . . . I found your hat!" Sadie stammered, then realized how stupid that sounded. She'd found the hat in the hallway of Jared and Heather's house that morning and thought Mrs. Wapple had put it there somehow. But she held up the bag anyway.

Mrs. Wapple watched it without changing her expression. After a moment, Sadie opened the sack and pulled out the hat.

"My hat!" Mrs. Wapple screamed—really screamed—from the other side of the sliding glass door and smacked her open hand onto the glass, causing it to vibrate. Sadie jumped again and took another step back. "You stole my hat!"

"No, I didn't steal it," Sadie said. "It was—"

"Thief! Thief!" Mrs. Wapple raised her hand and punched at the sky.

Sadie ducked as though lightbulbs might start bursting again, but nothing happened other than a significant burst of wind that made the oak tree behind her creak ominously. She looked around and then hurried toward the wrought iron table.

Mrs. Wapple continued to scream, "Thief! Thief!"

Sadie put the hat on the table and set the flower pot on the edge of the brim so it didn't blow away. Then she balled up the grocery bag and began taking long strides toward the gate, unable to think of anything other than getting out of there. She heard the sliding glass door slide along its track behind her and nearly broke into a run for fear that Mrs. Wapple was coming after her.

"Thief!" she heard, louder this time since the glass was no longer a barrier. Sadie sped up, worried that Mrs. Wapple would follow her home, screaming at her the entire time. Instead, Mrs. Wapple fell silent.

At the gate, Sadie grabbed the handle and looked over her shoulder. Mrs. Wapple's back was to Sadie as she picked up the hat, almost reverently. She put it on her head and turned to stare at Sadie, lowering her chin and scowling. Sadie had to fight the wind to open the gate, but she couldn't take her eyes away from Mrs. Wapple.

"Go away from here," Mrs. Wapple said in relatively normal tones. She turned back to her house and stomped away as Sadie pulled hard on the gate, to which it responded too well, blowing wide open and wrenching her arm in the process.

Sadie didn't need to be told twice, and she didn't look back to see if the gate closed after she darted through it. Instead, she practically ran across the street, up the porch steps, opened the door, and then shut it too loudly, causing all three boys to look up at her from their Legos.

"What happened?" Pete said, crossing to her and touching her shoulders. "Is she okay?" He paused. "Are *you* okay?"

"I'm fine," Sadie said, swallowing hard and running a hand through her hair as though the state of disarray up there was her biggest worry. "And she's okay. Just . . . freaky."

"Freaky?" Kalan repeated.

Sadie looked past Pete to see three sets of eyes watching her closely. She forced a smile, though she sensed it was twitching slightly. "I meant . . . creaky. Mrs. Wapple's fence needs a good ol' dose of WD-40."

"What's double D forty?" Kalan asked, a soft little wrinkle on his forehead.

"Never mind," Pete said. He gave Sadie a look and said loudly, "Were you, um, going to get dinner started in the *kitchen*?"

Dinner. Cooking. Solace! "I was," she agreed with a nod.

"I'll come help you in a minute," Pete said as he lowered himself to the floor, intent on distracting the boys from Sadie's unusual entrance.

Sadie went into the kitchen. She put both hands on the table and closed her eyes, breathing deeply several times until she felt more like herself. The wind whistling across the kitchen window did very little to calm her down. Holy moley, that had been scary. After she pulled herself together, she took out the chicken breasts from the fridge and mixed up the marinade before combining the two and returning them to the fridge. She washed her hands and stared out the window as she replayed the scene in Mrs. Wapple's backyard. Chills broke out across her chest and shoulders as she remembered Mrs. Wapple's crazy face up against the sliding glass door.

"So what happened?"

She startled and turned to see Pete watching her with concern. She shook her head, not sure of the right words, but then she just opened her mouth and found herself telling him everything. When she finished, Pete's eyebrows were up. "Maybe she *is* a witch," he said.

Sadie shook her head, hoping he was making a joke. "She needs help," she said. "The house is a mess, and I could smell garbage. She's just not . . . normal. I . . ."

"What?"

"Can you handle things for a little while so I can try to figure out where Gabrielle works?"

Pete hesitated before he spoke. "Yeah."

"Thanks. Mrs. Wapple didn't seem to be in pain just now," she said, realizing she also hadn't been mumbling about angry birds. "But I'd like to make one more attempt to contact her sister. Having a family member involved is the best way to get her help sooner rather than later, and since you found her correct last name, I think I can do a better job researching her this time."

Pete considered that and nodded. "Okay. But if you hear me crying uncle, come save me, okay?"

Sadie smiled and headed back to her room. She sat on her bed and pulled the laptop close but noticed she was still shaking from the Mrs. Wapple-induced adrenaline rush.

"I *will* figure this out," Sadie said to herself as she opened an Internet browser and typed in the URL of the first website designed to find any and all mentions of *Gabrielle Marrow* on the World Wide Web. From there, she'd simply follow the information until she knew everything she needed to know.

CHAPTER 10

As it turned out, Gabrielle Marrow was not what Sadie expected. There was very little to find about her until the last few years, when she'd risen quickly through the social circles of upper-class Boston society. She was the director for an art gallery that often hosted fundraisers heavily attended by what Sadie would call the Boston aristocracy. The Bastian Gallery was closed Sundays and Mondays, which explained why she was at Mrs. Wapple's house on Monday afternoon.

Gabrielle didn't appear to have any children, but Sadie had found two mentions of her on a website deemed the "expert" on socialites in the Boston area. Both times Gabrielle had been on the arm of the Boston Brahmin, a Mr. Bruce Handell. The Handell family, according to an article Sadie found, could trace their ancestors directly back to the original settlers of New England and were considerable real estate moguls and philanthropists. Bruce had two teenage daughters from a previous marriage and, though the articles weren't focused on his relationship with the new woman in his life, Sadie noticed a flashy ring on Gabrielle's hand in the photo from a benefit in September, despite the fact that her finger had been bare when Sadie met her at Mrs. Wapple's on Monday.

After educating herself about Gabrielle and finding out where she worked, Sadie was ready to act. She considered talking it over with Pete, but she didn't want to waste time. She knew Pete wanted this situation over with as much as she did so she just jumped in with both feet and called the Bastian Gallery on Newbury Street in downtown Boston. A man's voice answered the phone with a mono-tone, "Bastian Gallery. This is Hansel."

Hansel? Really?

Sadie paused before asking for Gabrielle, only then remembering that Pete had made the previous calls due to Sadie and Gabrielle's strange meeting yesterday—this might be awkward. Sadie braced herself when Gabrielle picked up the phone.

"This is Gabrielle," she said in an airy, slightly British-sounding accent that spoke of good upbringing and cultured tastes. From the information Sadie had found about Delores Wapple, however, nothing seemed to indicate that the family itself was so well-appointed.

"Hello, Ms. Marrow. My name is Sadie Hoffmiller. You and I met yesterday at your sister's house." There was no reason to not be direct at this point, she figured.

There was a pause. "Yes, Mrs. Hoffman, how may I help you?"

She offered no apology or explanation for posing as Delores? Interesting. Sadie decided to follow Gabrielle's lead and ignore their meeting, for now. "I'm very concerned about your sister," Sadie said, jumping straight to the heart of the subject. "We've had a few . . . incidents and I feel that she needs some kind of help—medical help, probably—and as soon as possible."

"Thank you for your concern. I'll make sure it is taken care of."

Sadie pulled her eyebrows together. Gabrielle's tone was as even and poised as it had been when she'd said hello. Sadie heard a voice in the background, and Gabrielle must have covered the phone since it went silent for a few seconds. As soon as the background noise reappeared, Sadie spoke again, not wanting to lose her opportunity. "I think she's in a great deal of pain," she said. "And she doesn't seem to be mentally stable and—"

"Thank you, Mrs. Hoffman. As I said, I'll see to it."

"It's Hoffmiller," Sadie corrected her without thinking. She shook her head in frustration and forged ahead. "You'll see about getting her to a doctor?" she asked, needing specifics. "I'm also concerned about her home. It's a mess and—"

"Thank you for calling."

"I'm sorry, Ms. Marrow, but I'm not sure you understand what's going on. I know you were here yesterday, but last night—" There was a click and the line went dead. Really? Gabrielle had hung up on the woman trying to help her sister?

Sadie took a deep breath as she regarded the phone, but could feel her frustration percolating. She hit redial and put the phone back to her ear. Hansel answered again. "Yes, I'd like to speak with Gabrielle Marrow, please."

"I'm afraid she's not taking any calls. Would you like me to take a message?"

"She took my call a minute ago."

"She is no longer taking calls. I'm happy to take a message." His monotone made it impossible to read his mood or guess what Gabrielle might have told him.

"Okay," Sadie said, wriggling a little as she sat on the bed. "Tell her that . . ." There were several things Sadie wanted to say, but she had to consider the whole catching flies with honey advice and asked herself what was most likely to get the right kind of attention.

"Tell her that I would really appreciate talking to her, that I'm trying to help."

Hansel paused. "That's the message you'd like to leave?"

"Yes," Sadie said. "Word for word." She waited until he repeated it back to her, then she gave him her cell phone number. "Please see that she gets it immediately."

"I will," Hansel said, but his tone sounded . . . confused.

Sadie's intent was to prick Gabrielle's conscience and so she drummed her fingers on her thighs, waiting for Gabrielle to call back, contrite and humbled by Sadie's sincerity. Three minutes passed. Then five. Sadie's hopeful expectations of a display of sisterly love and affection gave way to irritation. Sadie had never been good at waiting in the first place, and when someone's health and safety was on the line, it was nearly impossible. While she waited for Gabrielle to call back, she kept digging into Gabrielle's life.

On the art gallery's website were biographies of the key employees. Like the others, Gabrielle's bio talked about her education—substantial and impressive—and group affiliations, which had hyperlinks connecting to their websites. Sadie clicked on each link, going to the home pages and updating herself on the groups' purposes so as to get a more dimensional look at this woman. Art Project was an art program for underprivileged children. Scavenger Files used recyclable materials to create sculptures and encouraged the green movement and personal creativity; some of the artwork had been displayed at the courthouse last spring. Boston Women for Education was self-explanatory; the website was saturated with pictures of fancy ladies reading books to poor children. Sadie clicked on the link for Global Initiatives. The home page brought up an announcement about their semiannual banquet. Sadie was just about to click on the ABOUT US link when her eye caught the date of the upcoming meeting: Tuesday, October 21.

That was tonight!

Sadie leaned forward and read the date again before eagerly reading the rest of the information. The banquet was being held at the Marriott at Copley Place, which Sadie had seen when she and Pete took the T downtown last Saturday.

On an impulse, Sadie called the art museum again, but from Heather and Jared's phone on the nightstand instead of her cell this time. Hansel answered.

"Yes," Sadie said, disguising her voice with her best impression of a Boston accent—not the Bronx of Boston, though. She was going for something a little more highbrow like Gabrielle had used. "I'm calling to confirm that Gabrielle Marrow will be attending tonight's dinner at the Marriott for Global Initiatives." She worried she'd gone too British in her enunciation and cleared her throat in anticipation of having another go at it.

"Hold on one moment," he said and put Sadie on hold. She felt her heart rate increase as she waited. Less than fifteen seconds later he got back on the line. "She said that, yes, she received her e-mail confirmation. She wanted me to double-check that she was on the guest list."

"Oh, yes," Sadie assured him—her accent was much better this time. Very Boston. "She's on the list, we're just verifying."

"But she got her confirmation," Hansel said. Sadie heard Gabrielle's voice in the background telling him that she'd almost pulled the e-mail up on her computer to verify she had it. She sounded quite concerned that there could be a problem. Far more concerned than she'd been about her sister. "She wants to make sure—"

"Rest assured, she's on the list. I simply wanted to make sure she was still planning to attend. Thank you for your help."

Sadie hung up and scowled. Mrs. Wapple deserved better. For a few minutes, Sadie updated the notes she'd been taking on the research she'd done throughout the day. When she finished, she took a deep breath and knew she'd be unable to shake the unsettled feeling in her stomach until she was certain that Gabrielle Marrow knew the full spectrum of Sadie's concerns. Based on the dates of the obituary and when Mrs. Wapple moved into the neighborhood, it was easy to see that Mrs. Wapple had probably lived with her father until he passed away. Her care, such as it was, must have then transferred to her only living relative, her younger sister. Was Gabrielle overwhelmed by the responsibility? Did she not understand the extent of Mrs. Wapple's problems? Regardless of the reasons, Gabrielle had to be *made* to understand. She had to become an advocate for her sister.

When Sadie reentered the fray of the household a few minutes later, she immediately began cutting up broccoli at the counter while updating Pete on what had transpired over the last hour. She hoped the boys would like the broccoli in brown butter she was making for dinner; it complemented both the broiled chicken breasts and chicken nuggets. She was calling it Snowy Trees for the boys' benefit; she intended to see them eat green vegetables.

When she finished telling Pete about the phone calls, silence hung between them. Pete didn't ask if Sadie was going to the dinner at the Marriott, and she didn't ask his opinion as to whether or not she should crash it. Sadie put the broccoli in the steamer basket where it would wait its turn, and then preheated the oven before pulling out the pots and pans she needed to cook the rest of dinner. It was almost five o'clock.

"The banquet starts at six thirty, but I need to be there by six to make sure I can intercept Gabrielle," she said, thinking out loud. "I can take the T and be there in twenty minutes." She and Pete had taken the subway to the Boston Common on their first day to tour the monuments and historical sites spread throughout the park—another jewel on the Emerald Necklace of parks designed by Olmsted—and Sadie had used the subway to travel between Jamaica Plain and her hotel in Brookline before Heather and Jared left town. She was practically an expert.

"By yourself?" Pete asked with a concern Sadie chose to ignore.

Sadie nodded. "I adore mass transit," she said brightly. "It's like a whole other society." There had been a man dressed like Santa Claus singing Irish drinking songs when she and Pete had gotten on at the Haymarket station for the ride home. They'd kept their distance, but it was a delightful show.

"Yeah, I know," Pete said, looking at her curiously. "That's not always a good thing."

"I'll be fine," Sadie said. "Besides, it'll be much safer than trying to drive around downtown by myself. I have my baton and my mace and that laminated street map. You weren't worried when I was going back and forth to the hotel."

He still looked skeptical. "The hotel wasn't in downtown Boston."

"The Back Bay station is connected to Copley Place. I'll be fine, and it will be much easier than navigating the streets in that minivan."

She looked at the clock. She would need to leave here by at least 5:30 in order to get to the Forest Hills station on time. Dinner wouldn't be done by then, but she should be able to cook the broccoli and start the chicken baking. Darn, she hated missing a meal.

"I have to be careful about what I get myself involved in," Pete said, interrupting her planning. His tone was deceptively even. Sadie looked over at him and when he didn't look away, Sadie understood. He wasn't going to tell her not to go, but he wasn't going to be a part of it either. She could live with that—it was part of the agreement they'd made when they had both accepted the new level of their relationship. He wasn't going to try to change her, even when he really, really, wanted to. It still made her feel like she was doing something wrong, however.

Chance ran into the kitchen and attempted to hide behind Pete as Fig chased him, sufficiently interrupting them before their discussion could continue. The boys circled Pete three times before Pete grabbed Chance around the middle and threw him over his shoulder. He then flipped him back down and tickled him until both boys screamed with laughter. Kalan heard the laughter from the living room and joined his brothers as they bolted down the hallway, slamming the door to their bedroom closed against the "tickle monster."

Pete leaned against the wall, taking a deep breath and stretching out his back with a grimace. "They're going to send me to an early grave," he said, pushing back his hair with one hand. "I'm sure of it."

Sadie smiled and took the bag of chicken nuggets out of the freezer. After hesitating a minute, she picked up the topic of Mrs. Wapple again. "I was thinking maybe we could set a deadline. Do all we can for Mrs. Wapple until then before we let ourselves off the hook."

"I like that idea," Pete said with a nod. "How about ten tomorrow morning?"

Sadie felt a huge weight lift from her shoulders. If she did all she could do, she'd be at peace turning the problem over to someone else. Once she passed the baton, she could focus back on the boys and this trip. She and Pete had talked about renting a rowboat on Jamaica Pond, or visiting some of the colonial graveyards that housed some of the gatekeepers of the nation's history. To do those things, and fully enjoy them, she needed to be at peace with having done the best she could by Mrs. Wapple. But in order to feel like she'd exhausted every option, she had to make one more attempt to contact Gabrielle Marrow; it would be better for everyone if Gabrielle were involved, and it seemed that the only option left was a face-to-face meeting.

"Ten o'clock is good," Sadie said. She opened the bag of chicken nuggets and dumped the frozen chunks of chicken puree onto a jelly roll pan, trying not to feel bad about feeding the boys processed food. She pulled the marinated chicken out of the fridge and transferred two pieces to a baking dish. "It will be so nice to think about something else."

The boys were still laughing in their room, distracted from the tickle monster for the moment. Pete stretched out his hand. "Deal?"

Sadie washed her hands before taking his and giving it a good, firm shake. "Deal."

Instead of letting go, however, Pete pulled her toward him and wrapped her in his arms. He kissed her on the cheek and held her against his chest.

Sadie closed her eyes and sent up a little prayer of gratitude that Pete wasn't trying to make her ignore the instincts pulling her in a direction she knew he didn't necessarily agree with. It was a big step for him, and an important step in their relationship that she did not take lightly.

They had only a few seconds to steal before the boys would start wondering where the tickle monster was. Pete gave her a look of surrender as he lifted his hands over his head in monster-like claws and roared a terrible roar while stomping down the hall.

Sadie put the two chicken options in the oven and began grating the Mizithra cheese for the Snowy Trees while planning how she was going to approach Gabrielle without coming across as a stalker. It was going to be tricky.

Broccoli in Brown Butter

4 cups fresh broccoli florets (about 2 lbs. of broccoli crowns before trimming)
4 tablespoons real butter (margarine does not substitute)
¼ cup grated Mizithra cheese*

Steam florets until tender crisp. While broccoli is steaming, heat butter on medium-high heat, stirring constantly to keep it from burning. (The longer it browns, the nuttier the flavor.) Add steamed broccoli to browned butter and toss until broccoli is well-coated. Spread buttered broccoli in a single layer onto a platter or large plate. Sprinkle with Mizithra cheese. (Breanna prefers freshly grated Parmesan cheese to Mizithra.) Serve hot.

Serves 6. (This is the perfect side dish for any pasta dish or grilled chicken.)

(Shawn would only eat these if I called them Snowy Trees or Dinosaur Food when he was little.)

*Mizithra is a dry, white cheese sold in the deli area of most grocery stores and shrink-wrapped in four 10-ounce portions. It does not melt, but has a mild, salty flavor. Add more or less to taste.

CHAPTER 11

Pete agreed to keep an eye out for Mrs. Wapple while Sadie "went to the store," never mind that she had fixed her hair and makeup in record time before changing into her khaki slacks and dress boots that matched the black peacoat of Heather's she'd borrowed from the hall closet. The website gave every impression that this was a posh event, so she did her best to dress accordingly, and she was glad to have come prepared—Pete admitted he'd packed only jeans and sweatshirts. Men never prepared for such contingencies.

Sadie kissed Pete good-bye before heading to the minivan. She held a scarf over her head, determined to not let the wind get the better of her hair reparations. She arrived at Forest Hills station and boarded the train almost immediately. Her companions were not singing Irish drinking songs, unfortunately, but there was a group that looked like a four-generation family—a great-grandmother in her seventies, Sadie guessed, a grandmother, a mother, and a four-year-old girl sitting on her grandmother's lap. Their features were so similar Sadie couldn't help but think what a great portrait it would make. She wondered if the matriarch had been born and raised here, only to set a precedent for all these girls coming of age in Bean Town.

The ride was about ten minutes; Sadie doubted she'd even be on the turnpike by now if she'd chosen to drive. She poured out of the doors with her fellow patrons and followed the signs through the Dartmouth tunnel to the Copley Place Mall. At that point she consulted one of the mall maps to find her way to the Marriott and only stopped twice—once to drool over shoes at a high-end store she had no business entering.

Eventually she found herself in the sleekly designed main lobby of the hotel, and only then did her nerves begin setting in. Exactly how was this little meeting she was so intent on having going to pan out?

She inhaled deeply and followed the signs pointing to the Global Initiatives banquet being held in the Boylston room. The hotel was huge—thirty-eight floors of rooms, suites, and conference areas. Astounding. Sadie imagined the view of the St. Charles River was breathtaking from the upper levels, but she was glad the Global Initiatives event was on the main floor so she didn't have to navigate vertically as well as horizontally. She entered the area outside of the Boylston room and realized that posh in Boston, Massachusetts, was very different from posh in Garrison, Colorado. The women fairly sparkled with their perfectly highlighted hair, shimmering jewelry, and translucent-looking skin. Sadie didn't fit in as well as she'd hoped, and her insecurity about her hair tripled, but she stood up straight and hoped no one was assessing her as closely as she was assessing them.

Sadie unbuttoned the peacoat and tucked her scarf under the collar while she looked around. Two women sat at a table labeled Registration; one of the women was wearing a mink-collared vest. As women approached the table and gave their names, they were checked off a list and allowed to enter the banquet room. Sadie avoided the table, but she did walk by the doorway and estimated there were seats for about sixty. Only a dozen women sat or stood by the tables—none of them Gabrielle. Other guests were talking in small groups in the foyer area, which was really just an extra-wide hallway. Sadie had sent the photo of Gabrielle from the art gallery's website to her phone for reference and double-checked it as she scanned faces. It took only a few minutes to wind through the groups of chattering women who hadn't gone in yet for Sadie to assure herself that Gabrielle wasn't among them.

She imagined Pete back at the house, spending the evening with the three little boys, and felt a lump rise in her throat at missing it. Gabrielle better realize how serious Sadie was now. The deadline she and Pete had decided on for tomorrow morning helped reassure her that one way or another she was getting closer to being finished with this. But she still hoped she wasn't wasting her time at this event that made her feel frumpy and anxious.

She wandered for the next ten minutes, feigning interest in the art on the walls and overall design of the hotel—which really was lovely—while avoiding eye contact, which wasn't difficult since no one seemed to notice her. She continued to notice them, however, and coveted a few of the particularly striking brand-name handbags and designer shoes she couldn't afford. Definitely not Garrison.

Finally, she saw a profile she recognized in a group of women who'd just come around the corner from the direction of the registra-tion desk. Sadie moved closer and consulted her phone to make sure that the woman was, in fact, Gabrielle Marrow. She didn't look much like the woman she'd seen at Mrs. Wapple's yesterday, which only meant that she'd put a lot into getting ready for tonight's dinner. She was dressed in high-heeled boots, trim tweed slacks, and a burnished red leather blazer that brought out the red tones in her golden-brown hair. The big diamond ring on her finger caught the light when she tucked her hair behind her ear. Her makeup was flawless.

Sadie quickly slid into line behind Gabrielle, then took a breath and tapped her on the shoulder.

Gabrielle turned, freezing when she saw Sadie standing there instead of the acquaintance she surely had expected. Sadie gave her a few seconds to let the recognition set in. Probably like a toothache if the expression on Gabrielle's face was any indication.

"Hi, Gabrielle," Sadie said when she was certain Gabrielle knew who she was. "I wonder if I could have a word."

Gabrielle glanced at the woman closest to her and then plastered a smile on her face when the woman turned to see what was going on. "Um, will you check me in?" she asked her friend. "I'll be right back." She continued to smile at Sadie. "Over here?" she asked, pointing toward the far end of the gathering area as she adjusted her purse strap nervously.

Sadie nodded, but caught the darting looks Gabrielle cast around the group as they moved away, as though hoping no one was noticing her. The woman Gabrielle had been standing next to in line pulled her eyebrows together as much as her Botox would allow and lifted a hand to her hair—too much hair to not have extensions. Sadie smiled politely and then hurried to keep up with Gabrielle, who was several steps ahead. When they were far enough away to suit Gabrielle, she turned Sadie so that Sadie's back was to the group of people. Her expression was as pleasant as ever. Her tone, on the other hand, was not. "What are you doing here?"

"Trying to get your attention," Sadie said.

"I assured you that everything was being taken care of."

"I know that's what you said," Sadie agreed. "But I did not feel as though you were . . . listening to what I had to say. I am very—"

"Of course I was listening," Gabrielle cut in, folding her arms. "But I can't drop everything at a moment's notice." Sadie watched Gabrielle wrestle with what she'd said behind her perfectly polite, if not plastic, expression.

"If you understood how concerned I was, you *would* drop everything to look in on your sister. She is—"

"I know." Gabrielle looked past Sadie's shoulder, irritable and impatient.

Sadie followed her glance to see the blonde woman Gabrielle had come with chatting with a few other attendees of tonight's banquet. Gabrielle obviously wanted to join that discussion rather than have this one.

"You know, Gabrielle, it's very hard for me to believe you're listening when you keep cutting me off," Sadie said, unimpressed with Gabrielle's reaction. "I need to be assured that you understand my level of concern for your sister. Is she under the care of a doctor?"

"She hates doctors," Gabrielle admitted, finally participating in the discussion. "She won't go."

"You might have to make her go, then," Sadie said. "She's in a great deal of pain, and while I don't know what her typical behavior consists of, she's coming out at night, yelling at the neighbors, and talking to people who aren't there."

Gabrielle's jaw tightened even though she continued to smile. She leaned forward, although her expression barely shifted. It was strange to hear the tone of her words and yet see her smiling at the same time. "This is not the place—"

"Then when?" Sadie said, disappointed that Gabrielle was still worried only about causing a scene. If Sadie had only wanted to embarrass Gabrielle there were far better ways to do it. Sadie's phone chimed, indicating a text message, but she ignored it for now. "And where? I already tried calling you and—"

"How did you even find me? How did you know I would be here?"

Still about Gabrielle. "You're her *sister*," Sadie said, hearing the sorrow in her tone as she tried to redirect the conversation back to Mrs. Wapple. "Look, I really don't play hardball very well," she said, "but there is something wrong with your sister."

Gabrielle glanced over Sadie's shoulder again, a wave of fear crossing her face. "Can you give me twenty minutes? Let me get settled in, and then I'll meet you in the Connexion Lounge—not here."

Not where anyone she knows might see us, Sadie mentally translated.

"I can wait twenty minutes," she said with a nod, quick to agree to any terms that would give her what she'd come for.

Gabrielle nodded and took a few steps away before turning back and giving Sadie a look that was either repentant or embarrassed, Sadie wasn't sure which. "I'm not a bad person," she said quietly.

"Then do the right thing by your sister."

That brought Gabrielle up short, but after a brief pause, she turned and hurried back to her friends. As soon as Gabrielle rejoined her group, the other women leaned into her while glancing at Sadie. Did Sadie really look so out of place that she warranted being such a furtive topic of discussion? She smoothed her shirt front and headed toward the lobby. Sadie had already passed the Connexion Lounge, so it wasn't hard to find her way back to it.

She situated herself on the surprisingly comfortable chairs in such a way that she would be able to see Gabrielle when she appeared in the lobby area below her. Then she was left with one of her least favorite things to do—wait. It was a beautiful lounge, complete with mini fire pits on some of the tables. You didn't see indoor flames very often these days. The warmth was nice, and she hoped it would help take the edge off the wait before her.

She let herself relax for a few minutes as the warmth and dancing fire worked their magic, then she remembered the text message that had arrived while she and Gabrielle had been talking. Grateful for the distraction, she retrieved her phone from the inside pocket of her purse that looked like a Kmart special compared to what the other women were carrying. Oh yeah, it *was* a Kmart special.

The text was from Shawn, checking in. She quickly texted back that she was waiting to talk to the sister. His reply asked her to call when she was done, and Sadie couldn't help but smile at his determination to be involved. Oh, but to have even a little bit of his enthusiasm. As it was, Sadie's drive was waning since so little of what she'd discovered or encountered was positive. No one seemed to want Sadie involved in this . . . well, except Shawn, but he wasn't here so it didn't feel fair to count him. With a little luck, talking to Gabrielle would end Sadie's involvement. After assuring Shawn she would let him know how it went, she ended the conversation and began writing down a list of what she *wanted* to talk to Gabrielle about.

A large man suddenly appeared at the right side of her chair, startling her.

He was Caucasian, with a square face, square jaw, and expansive chest and shoulders. His crew cut made his hair look like freshly mowed grass, except it was blond, not green. He looked down at her with a steeled expression, and Sadie tried not to cower under the weight of his glare. "Are you Sadie Hoffmiller?"

She recovered from her surprise enough to register the security guard uniform and slowly closed her notebook before standing up in order to be at his same level. Unfortunately, he was still nearly a foot taller than she was, and she continued to feel intimidated.

"Yes, I'm Sadie Hoffmiller. Can I help you?"

"I'll need to ask you to leave the hotel, ma'am."

"Leave?" Sadie asked, raising her eyebrows. "Why?"

"A guest at the hotel has reported that you've been harassing her. Management has asked that you leave, since you're not a paying guest or on any of the guest lists of tonight's closed events."

Sadie felt heat creeping up her neck. "I'm not harassing anyone. I simply came here to talk to her."

"And she has requested that you be removed from the premises."

Sadie scanned his face in hopes of finding some sympathy, but she saw none. This obviously wasn't the first time he'd had to do this, and Sadie was embarrassed to be treated as though she were doing something wrong. But right now embarrassment was weakness and she needed to appear strong so she tamped it down and drew together all her confidence.

"There's simply been a misunderstanding," Sadie said calmly. "She asked me to meet her here in the Connexion Lounge in"—she turned her wrist to see the time on her watch—"about ten minutes."

He blinked at her but was not swayed. "I need you to exit the hotel and vacate the premises."

"But I am not harassing her!" Sadie said, incensed by the injustice. A couple seated a few tables away turned to watch the scene, and she felt her cheeks heat up even more as anger mingled with her embarrassment.

The security guard pulled himself up even straighter, adding two more inches to his already imposing frame. "If you refuse to cooperate, this will get a lot more complicated. I'll ask you one more time to vacate the premises."

CHAPTER 12

The security guard walked her back to the mall and watched until she turned a corner out of view. Her cheeks were still on fire as she hurried into the subway car and took a seat in the corner, heading back to Forest Hills. The vapor of defeat surrounded her in the capsule, which smelled like stale exhaust and wet cement. A group of teenage girls occupied the other end of the car, and she ignored them, glad that they did the same to her as she stared out the window at the dark subway tunnel, trying to decompress from what had happened. She couldn't believe Gabrielle had turned her in to security! Why was she so against Sadie's help? Was she hiding something? Should Sadie be *protecting* Mrs. Wapple from her sister?

Thinking about Mrs. Wapple stirred up a whole list of questions: Was she digging for potatoes again tonight? Was she hurting? Mumbling about the angry birds in her head? No. First thing tomorrow, Sadie would call social services and wash her hands of the whole situation. She'd done enough—too much, perhaps—but at least she knew she'd done her very best. Gabrielle couldn't say the same thing.

After marinating in her embarrassment for a few minutes, she dialed Shawn's number, turning away from the girls, who were, like, totally having a great time.

"Hey," she said. "I'm on the subway so if my call drops or it gets too loud, I'll call you when I get to Jamaica Plain."

"Okay," Shawn said. "So, what happened?"

Sadie laid out all the gory details.

"I can't believe she had you kicked out," Shawn said when Sadie finished unloading the events of her evening. "Are you okay?"

The question unhinged her a little bit, and a wave of unexpected emotion caused tears to rise in her eyes. "I'm okay," she said, but her tone sounded vulnerable even to her own ears. The fact was she could really use a hug right about now. It was a good thing Pete was so huggable and waiting for her at Jared's house. "I'm just . . . embarrassed." She blinked several times to clear the tears.

"Yeah, I bet," Shawn said. "Are you going to try to talk to her again?"

"No," Sadie said, shaking her head for emphasis. "We'll call social services in the morning and let them take it from here. Gabrielle knows how her sister is living, and she's chosen to do nothing about it. I don't know why I thought talking to her would change anything, but I no longer believe Mrs. Wapple's sister is her best option."

"Well, you've sure gone the extra mile, Mom, you can feel good about that."

More tears. He was such a good son.

"*And* you have all the luck," Shawn said. "Always stumbling into adventure."

Sadie frowned. "You make that sound like it's a good thing."

Shawn laughed, and Sadie tried to see it from where he stood, removed and intrigued.

"Do you still want the landlord info? I found the one in Lowell as well as the current owner of the rental house on Browden Street. It was rented in the sister's name, though."

Sadie had forgotten Shawn was researching Mrs. Wapple's housing and for an instant she was excited to get the information. The instant passed quickly, however, and was replaced with regret. "I don't need it anymore," she said. "I'm sorry I wasted your time."

"Nah," Shawn said. "It's fine, and it didn't take me long to find—bless public information databases and Google Earth. You're sure you don't want to make these two final calls?"

Sadie *was* tempted, but the humiliation and frustration of her dealings with Gabrielle were still fresh enough that she was not swayed. "No. It's done."

"All right," Shawn said, but he didn't seem to agree. They both sat in silence—well, as silent as a subway car could be—for a few beats before Shawn spoke again, changing the subject dramatically. "So, I talked with Jane today," he said casually. "She said you told her you couldn't see her while you're in Boston. She's not far away, ya know."

Jane again? That woman was so removed from Sadie's thoughts that it was annoying to have to make room for her. "I'm not at my own home, Shawn," she said, repeating what she'd told Jane. "And I'm already feeling horribly guilty for being so distracted by Mrs. Wapple. Pete and the boys deserve more from me. I actually fed the boys chicken nuggets tonight. I'm so disappointed in myself."

Shawn laughed. "Okay, I can see your point. What do you think about inviting her to come to Salem with us on Saturday instead? You'll be done playing grandma by then."

Sadie frowned. The thought of inviting Jane after the baby-sitting job was complete had crossed her mind—she was too efficient to have not considered the option—but she'd also looked forward to having time alone with the two men in her life: Shawn and Pete. The two of them hadn't spent much time together—

Wait—why was Shawn working so hard for her to meet up with Jane in the first place?

The thought brought an unwelcome realization that Shawn had brought up Jane during nearly every phone call they'd shared this week. He'd also asked for Jane's help in one of the PI cases almost immediately after Sadie had asked him to use her only if he absolutely had to. And hadn't he told Sadie she should try to form a new opinion about Jane? Beyond that, Sadie had been waiting weeks for Shawn to tell her he'd changed his major. That he hadn't confided in her yet—not to mention that he hadn't discussed it with her before he actually made the change—was a sign of his growing independence. Another perspective on that independence, though, was that he was keeping secrets from her. Or at least he thought he was.

Shawn didn't . . . *like* Jane, did he?

Sadie's stomach dropped, only partially due to the subway car slowing down. She checked to make sure it wasn't her stop; it wasn't. There were a few more to go.

Jane? Sadie thought again. Why Jane? She was hard and masculine and . . . strange. Sadie pictured her teddy bear of a son, huge, but soft and kind, with a quick wit and a big heart. Jane, on the other hand, was sharp—both with the angles of her body and that tongue of hers. She was rough around the edges, sarcastic, cynical, and worldly. She was also in her late twenties, by Sadie's estimation. Shawn was barely twenty-one years old. The two of them as a couple was impossible to imagine. And yet, the signs that Shawn might be thinking in that direction were all there.

If she could get the two of them together in one place she had no doubt she could find out exactly what Shawn's feelings for Jane were. "I suppose she could join us for the trip to Salem," she said carefully. "She'll still be around come Saturday?"

"She's staying in Connecticut for another week. She's digging into some additional article ideas. I know she'd love to hang out with us. She's never been to Salem."

Sadie allowed herself a few moments to mourn the lost chance for Pete and Shawn to bond. Would she and Shawn still take the Ghosts and Graveyard tour Saturday night? Would Jane stay for Sunday, too, the day she and Shawn were planning to spend together, just the two of them?

"Well, then, by all means, invite her to come along, though I'd understand if it doesn't work out with her schedule." *Please don't work out, please don't work out, please don't work out.*

Sadie's cell phone beeped, indicating that the battery was low.

"It'll work," Shawn said, sounding more excited than Sadie wanted him to. "She really thinks highly of you, Mom. She had a rough childhood, and I think she looks up to you almost like a mother figure, ya know?"

"Oh, well," Sadie said humbly. "That's . . . um, nice to hear." She paused, not liking that Shawn and Jane were close enough to share stories about their childhoods, but curious as to what Shawn knew all the same. "She had a rough childhood?"

"I don't know the details, but she mentioned her parents' divorce and living with her grandparents for a few years. I think you've kind of shown her what a normal parent is like, and I think she's trying really hard to be a better person, ya know?"

"I don't mean to have such a harsh opinion of her," she said, feeling guilty. "I'll be more open-minded, okay?"

"Awesome," Shawn said. They small-talked for a minute longer before Sadie's phone beeped again and she begged off. Shawn promised to check in again tomorrow, and Sadie promised to charge her phone all night so she wouldn't have to cut their next conversation short. "Oh, and, Mom, I know you said you're done with this lady and figuring out her story, but keep Jane in mind if for some reason you decide to work on it a little more. I know she'd love to come up there if you needed her, and she told me there isn't anything she's doing that can't be adjusted to make room for you, okay?"

"I'll just be making a phone call to social services," Sadie said. But there *was* the possibility that Jane could find out more details than Pete and Sadie had been able to uncover. The thought was momentarily tempting, just as the landlord information Shawn had found had been tempting, but Sadie didn't need those kinds of details anymore. "But thanks for the info," Sadie said. "I'll keep it in mind."

They said good-bye, and Sadie spent the rest of the ride, and then the subsequent drive back to the house from the Forest Hills station, with her thoughts bouncing between concern for Mrs. Wapple and curiosity about Shawn's *situation* with Jane—she couldn't allow herself to think about it as a real *relationship*. "Oh, please don't let him fall in love with that girl," she whispered under her breath as she pulled onto the alleyway behind Jared's house and parked in the single car garage.

Her phone beeped again, and she found it more aggravating than usual. There were many things Sadie could handle—three-inch heels when the occasion demanded formal attire, eating canned green beans when someone else made dinner, a beeping cell phone—but Jane Seeley as Shawn's girlfriend was not on the list. She certainly wanted good things for Jane, but did that have to include Sadie's only son?

Pete was watching a basketball game when she let herself in the back door. She hadn't bothered with the scarf over her head and her hair had suffered for it. She put her purse on one of the kitchen chairs and locked the door behind her before taking off her coat and heading for the living room. Whispered voices from the boys' room told her that while Pete may have put them to bed, they weren't asleep. As soon as they realized Sadie was back, they sent Fig out to beg for a "stowy." Pete assured her he'd read to them already, but Sadie knew they liked the voices she used for different characters. For all of Pete's talents and abilities, taking on the sweet voice of a bunny rabbit or the gravely yell of a crocodile was something he still needed to work on. After she hung up her coat and plugged her cell phone into the charger in the bedroom, she consented to one more story, losing herself in the world of make-believe for what didn't feel like quite long enough.

When she returned to the living room, Pete had the curtains wide open. He was still watching the game, but he glanced out the window on a regular basis. For all his talk about needing to keep a distance from this situation, he was still suspiciously involved in it.

"You didn't get mugged, beaten, or kidnapped?"

Sadie smiled. "Not today."

"She hasn't come out," he said.

Sadie stepped to the window and looked up at the sky. There was a thick cloud cover, so she couldn't see the moon, but the night was lit with a foggy silver light. Gabrielle would be leaving the dinner soon. Would she feel any regret for handling this opportunity the way she had? Would she reconsider once she was away from her ritzy friends?

For a moment Sadie thought of her own sister, Wendy. Wendy was the oldest of the three siblings, and she and Sadie had always been at odds with each other. In truth, Wendy had been at odds

with their family most of her life for reasons Sadie had yet to figure out. At eighteen she'd left home for college in Illinois. A few
years later she got married, without inviting anyone to the wedding;
Sadie's parents had been deeply hurt. A few years later, Wendy got
divorced, then married again, had a child Sadie had seen only once,
and divorced a second time. Sadie hadn't spoken to her since their
father died; Wendy hadn't come to the funeral.

It was strange to even think that she had a sister. Sometimes
Sadie felt bad that she didn't miss Wendy. And yet, even after so
many years of estrangement, if Wendy were in trouble and needed
help, Sadie would be there. Gabrielle should be that kind of sister
even if she didn't want to be, even if her sister threatened her social
aspirations. Sadie had little doubt that was at least part of Gabrielle's
issues. She thought back to how Gabrielle had acted when she'd been
forced to talk to Sadie in front of her friends. How would her friends
react if they knew her sister was the Witch of Browden Street?

Sadie turned away from the window and her uncomfortable
thoughts and sat down next to Pete on the couch. He muted the
basketball game and asked her how it went.

"At the *store* or at the hotel?" Sadie asked, not sure where his
line was exactly.

He smiled. "Hotel."

Good. She told him everything that had happened, and he
rubbed her shoulder when she explained about getting kicked out.

"On to social services in the morning, then?" he said when she
finished.

Sadie nodded and took a deep breath, held it, and then let it out,
trying to blow out the negative energy the way they taught her to do
in her weekly yoga class. Pete gave her hand a squeeze, then leaned
in to kiss her temple.

"You're a good woman, Sadie," he said. "And you've done the right thing."

"Thank you," Sadie said, pulling her feet up onto the couch and curling into Pete as he turned the sound on the TV back on. Basketball held no interest for her, but being close to Pete made it worthwhile. She tried to unwind, tried to let go of the worry and anxiety in her chest, but her eyes kept going to the window, and she realized she was hoping to see some sign of Mrs. Wapple. After fifteen minutes, she excused herself to clean up the kitchen. Pete offered to help, but cleaning was relaxing for Sadie and she wanted him to watch his game. She also realized she was starving and fixed a passable meal from the leftovers.

After the game was over and Sadie had the kitchen gleaming, they locked up—checking the locks twice. Sadie moved to the front window in order to pull the blinds closed, but hesitated as she looked at Mrs. Wapple's house, completely dark and empty looking. Would alerting social services mean that Mrs. Wapple couldn't live in her home? Perhaps she'd end up in an institution of some kind and lose her independence completely. Sadie supposed that having her being cared for properly was the most important thing, but she also hoped that perhaps being under the supervision of a doctor would be enough to make Mrs. Wapple capable of caring for herself.

Pete came up behind Sadie as she moved the curtain aside, revealing a section of the window normally blocked by the heavy drapes as well as the pull cord that would close them. He put a hand on her shoulder.

"I wish we'd accomplished more today," she said, holding back the curtains. She wrapped her fingers around the pull cord. "We were so intent on getting Gabrielle involved that—"

Pete's hand tightened on her shoulder at the same instant Sadie caught sight of a pale white face staring at her from the other side of the glass only inches above the bottom pane of the window. In the split second before she jumped back, she registered dark eyes, bright pale skin, and long tangled hair. She dropped the curtain over the face, quickly slapping her hand over her mouth to keep her gasping scream from waking the boys. She stepped backward, tripping over Pete's foot. He steadied her, then immediately grabbed the curtain, pulling Sadie out of the way as he stepped forward to look at where the face had been in the lower corner of the window. The face was gone.

Pete leaned forward to look out the window before stepping to the side and grabbing the handle of the front door.

"Pete!" Sadie said. "Don't—" She cut off when he looked at her, and she realized there was no way he wasn't going out there. He flipped on the porch light, turned the dead bolt, and threw open the door. The gauzy ghost made them both jump, and Sadie clamped her hand over her mouth a second time. Pete scowled as he disappeared through the doorway and down the steps. The wind sent the wispy tendrils of the ghost decoration dancing wildly, and Sadie grabbed the decoration off its hook. The wind caught the door and Sadie had to wrestle it closed. As soon as the door was shut, she stuffed the ghost behind the couch—she'd had enough!

She moved to the window and watched Pete walk cautiously, but intently, toward the corner of the house that was flanked with thick bushes bent over by the wind. His gun was locked in his suitcase, and Sadie wondered if he should have grabbed it. She put her hand on her neck and moved the curtain in order to glance at where the face had been. It wasn't there, of course, but she couldn't get the image out of her head. Long face, almost skeletal, and tangled hair that was long and dark. Was it Sadie's overactive imagination that made her think she had seen a gray knit hat? Had the face really looked like Mrs. Wapple, or was that another figment of Sadie's traumatized imagination?

Within a few minutes Pete was back. She knew he hadn't found anything by the look on his face when he came in. He locked the door behind him and ran his fingers through his hair, though the action seemed more anxious than vain.

"There's nothing there, and the ground is too hard for there to be any footprints."

"Do you think it was Mrs. Wapple?"

"If it was, she's faster than she looks."

Sadie looked again at the place where the face had been. "If someone were crouching below the window, waiting for us to pull back the curtains, they could pop up and then run as soon as I dropped the curtains."

"Possible," Pete said. "But, again, fast. I didn't see or hear anything while I was out there. No retreating footsteps or starting engines."

"Though with the wind, would you be able to hear much?"

Pete nodded his acknowledgment of that possibility but didn't seem to like it.

Just thinking about someone waiting outside the house, watching them, sent a chill down Sadie's spine. How the person got away was not as important as why she had been there in the first place. "What is going on here?"

"I don't know," Pete said, looking deep in thought, his eyes fixed on the window where they'd seen the face.

"Should we call the police?"

Pete hesitated. "And tell them what?"

"About the hat and the Peeping Tom."

"There's nothing to tell but an unbelievable story without any evidence to back it up."

Sadie didn't want to sound like she was questioning his expertise, but she would feel better if they called the police. Then again, based on her own experience, involving the police was not always helpful. More than once the police had made an already difficult situation an extremely complicated one.

"It looked almost . . ." It was hard for her to say it out loud, but silly not to. "Like a ghost," she finished.

Pete took a breath and let it out, then scrubbed his hand over his face. "It's been a long day," he said. "Let's go to bed."

"And not talk about what we just saw?" Sadie pointed to the window.

"I don't want to talk about it right now," Pete said, turning away.

"I understand, but that doesn't change what we—"

"I don't believe in ghosts, Sadie," he said sharply, not turning around. "I believe in facts, evidence, and reality."

"So it's not a ghost," Sadie said. "But something has happened two nights in a row now, and we need to discuss it."

Pete turned the dead bolt on the door as Sadie tried to find the words she needed to bridge this unexpected gap. She'd just opened her mouth to say something when all the lights in the house went out, plunging them into eerie darkness and causing Sadie's heart to race all over again.

CHAPTER 13

Sadie startled at the feel of Pete's hand on her elbow. "Go to the boys' room," he said in a low, controlled whisper.

"Where are—"

"I'm going to check the fuses," he said, releasing her. "There's a flashlight in the pantry; I'll get it." He headed toward the kitchen.

Sadie swallowed the fear billowing up in her chest and put out her hands, moving carefully in the direction of the boys' room while her eyes adjusted to the darkness. The wind must have blown down a power line, though the timing was . . . scary. She found the corner of the living room and hallway just as a light flared up behind her. She looked over her shoulder to see Pete coming toward her with a flashlight he kept pointed at the floor. "Are you okay?" he asked.

"I'm fine," she said. She'd reached the boys' room and put her hand on the knob. Pete moved past her and though he didn't say anything, she knew he was getting his gun. Sadie took a deep breath and carefully opened the door to the boys' room. Normally they had a night-light plugged in, but with the power out, their room was as dark as the rest of the house. Through the partially open slats of the mini-blinds on their window, however, Sadie could see lights from the neighbors' homes. *Their* power hadn't gone out.

Pete returned to the hallway. "I'm going to check around outside again—just in case."

"All right," Sadie said. "Be careful."

He didn't answer, but she listened to his retreating footsteps for a few moments before turning her attention back to the boys. She almost hoped Pete *would* find a Peeping Tom hiding in the bushes so that they could explain all this.

Sadie didn't dare step into the room very far for fear of running into something and waking up the boys, but she made sure to listen for three distinct sounds of breathing that assured her they'd slept through everything so far. She began feeling around for a place to sit down when she remembered the candle she had in her suitcase. She liked to bring a scented candle with her when she traveled in case wherever she stayed didn't smell as nice as she'd like, but it was the option of light—constant, comforting light—that had her moving toward the doorway again.

Her room was across the hall from the bathroom, which was next to the boys' room, and she carefully felt her way across the hallway and into the open doorway. The wind whistled around the window frame and the muted moonlight outlined the shapes of the furniture. Sadie moved toward her suitcase set on top of Heather's cedar chest at the foot of the bed. She'd wrapped the votive in an extra pair of pajamas and tucked them into the left side of the suitcase. She found the suitcase and within a minute had found the candle as well. She always packed her bags in the same basic organization so that she had the placement of each item memorized.

But what about matches? She knew Heather had some in the pantry in the kitchen, but Sadie wasn't sure she wanted to venture back into that part of the house. Then she remembered the book of matches she had picked up from Abe and Louie's steakhouse. Pete had taken her to a special dinner their first night in Boston, and Sadie had picked up the book of matches to remember the evening.

She stepped to the dresser and put the candle down so she could feel for the matches.

As soon as her fingers touched the book of matches she heard something.

"Sadie."

She snapped her head to the side as a chill rushed through her. She couldn't tell where the throaty whisper had come from; she wasn't sure she'd heard it at all. The shapes in the room were dark, silent, foreboding, and the far side nearest the door was completely black. She was hearing things. After pausing for only a second, she turned back to the candle and fumbled even quicker with the matches. Her hands were shaking. She lit the match and quickly put it to the wick of the candle, telling herself to calm down, take a deep breath. The wick caught and the warm glow of candlelight fanned out around her as she shook out the match and dropped it in the trash can.

Her cell phone was dark and silent on the dresser, and she quickly unplugged it and shoved it in her pocket, not ready to call the police without Pete but not wanting to be without means of communication either. The smell of cinnamon and mulberries tickled her nose, and she took another deep breath. Nothing bad could happen when scents like this were in the air, right? The throaty whisper had been her own imagination, or perhaps one of the boys had called for her. She needed to get back to them in case they woke up.

With the candle in one hand, she turned as her bedroom door suddenly slammed shut, rattling the walls and windows.

Sadie nearly dropped the candle and had only just recovered when she heard one of the boys call out. Without a moment's hesitation, she crossed the room and grabbed the doorknob while attempting to push the door open before realizing it pulled into the room. She refused to look around as she hurried down the hall and through the still-open door of the boys' bedroom, where Fig's call for his mother had turned to crying. The candle cast an eerie yellow light for a few feet around her; Sadie tried not to think about what was hiding in the darkness outside the light's glow.

"It's okay," she said as she hustled across the room. Kalan was sitting up in his makeshift bed in the corner and she hurried toward him. The other boys were awake too, but not as alert. "I'm right here. The power went out, everything's okay."

"What was that crash?" Kalan asked. His voice was scared and it tugged at Sadie's heart.

"Um, the door slammed," she said. "It's . . . windy." She put the candle on the dresser before sitting on Fig's bed. He snuggled into her and soon Chance and Kalan had both joined them. She was making shushing noises and taking turns smoothing their hair when she saw a beam of light coming down the hallway.

She knew it was Pete, but she tensed anyway and pulled the boys a little closer.

"Sadie?"

Just hearing his voice relaxed her. "I'm right here," she said.

He stepped into the room and pointed the flashlight at the floor while he moved toward her, kneeling in front of them and putting his hand on Chance's back. "What was that?" Pete asked.

"The wind slammed the door," Kalan said.

"I wan' Mama," Fig whined. Sadie pulled him closer and kissed the top of his head.

"The wind?" Pete asked. He looked at Sadie quickly, and she simply held his eyes to communicate that now wasn't the time to discuss the probability of wind blowing an interior door closed.

Pete looked back at the doorway, flashing the beam of light into the hall.

"What?" Sadie asked. Had he heard something? She hadn't, but she had the three boys right next to her.

"Nothing," Pete said, but he kept the light trained on the hall for a few more seconds before turning back. "It's not the fuses, and the neighbor's lights are fine. I was looking for the power box on the outside of the house. It's the only thing I can think of to explain—"

The lights came on.

All of them. Even the ones that had been off when the power went out.

The boys shielded their eyes from the sudden brightness, and Pete moved to the doorway to flip the switch off. The rest of the house was fully lit. He forced a smile as he faced them and shut off the flashlight. "There," he said in what Sadie knew the boys would find a reassuring tone but which she did not. In his own way, he was as scared as she was, taking note of all the details that didn't fit. "The power's back on. Nothing to be worried about."

But there was a lot to worry about. What was going on here? "Guess what?" Sadie said, making an instant decision and turning to Kalan.

He looked up at her expectantly.

"We're going to have a slumber party," she said with a big smile.

"Swumber pawty?" Fig said, looking adorably confused with his red hair sticking up and his sleepy eyes.

"That's right," Pete said, picking up Sadie's train of thought. "A slumber party, where we all get to sleep in the same room. It'll be fun."

"Where?" Kalan asked.

"In your mom and dad's room," Sadie said. Their bed was big enough for her and the two littler boys. "Grandpa's going to sleep on the floor, and Kalan gets to sleep by him."

"Yep," Pete said. "A great big slumber party. How does that sound?"

It was hard to drum up much enthusiasm this time of night, but the boys went along with it, giving Sadie and Pete the benefit of the doubt that this slumber party thing was worthy of their interest.

Pete moved Heather's cedar chest from the foot of the bed to the space between the bed and window. He then double- and triple-checked every door and window in the house while Sadie got the boys situated. Once assured everything was secure, Pete pulled the mattress off Kalan's bed and dragged it into Jared and Heather's bedroom. It barely fit between the foot of the bed and the dresser. Neither Pete nor Sadie talked about breaking the bedroom rule as Sadie settled in with her two wiggly bedfellows and Pete situated himself on the floor with Kalan. She wished she could talk to Pete about the door, or the voice she may or may not have heard, but there had hardly been an opportunity.

One by one, the boys drifted off to sleep. Sadie tried, but each time she closed her eyes, the face from the window would appear and her eyes would snap back open. After several minutes, and not having heard Pete's soft snoring, Sadie whispered. "Pete?"

"Yeah," he whispered back.

"Should we have called the police?" Years of believing the police were the answer to every bad thing was apparently stronger than the less-than-positive run-ins Sadie had had with police in the recent past.

He was quiet for several seconds. "I don't think they'd take it seriously."

Sadie could imagine what they would say about a ghostly face, unexplained electrical issues, and a hat showing up where it didn't belong. Would she take it seriously if someone tried to convince her?

Pete's voice came to her through the darkness. "I never heard back from Jared about the eyebolt," he said. "I'll make sure to get one put in tomorrow. I'll pay the blasted deposit if the landlord takes issue with it."

Sadie nodded, then realized he couldn't see her. "That's a good idea."

Pete spoke again. "Let's talk about things in the morning. I don't want to wake the boys."

"Okay," she said out loud, but she still wondered about calling the police. Chance snuggled into her, and she wrapped her arms around him as tight as she dared, inhaling the scent of little boy mixed with the remnants of this morning's shampoo, and said a little prayer of her own, asking that morning come quickly and with it, some answers and some peace.

CHAPTER 14

Pete had said they would talk about it in the morning, but they didn't. The tension seemed brittle and the topic fragile in the morning light. Continued cloud cover threatened snow, revealing that the cold snap gripping New England was not letting go just yet. The events from last night seemed hard to believe now. If not for Pete having been there, Sadie might have wondered if she'd really seen anything at all. But he *had* been there, and by the lines between his eyebrows and the force of his smile, Sadie could tell the burden of it was sitting heavy on his shoulders.

Instead of discussing what had happened during the night, they were careful as they executed the morning routine: careful to appear normal, careful to stay on schedule, and careful not to give the boys anything to worry about. The boys, for their part, were whinier than usual, probably due to the late-night awakening, but they didn't ask any questions—thank goodness, since Sadie and Pete had no answers.

Pete drove Kalan to school while Sadie combined ingredients in the slow cooker for dinner—Boston baked beans—and the boys got dressed, an activity that involved lots of laughing and yelling and a few half-naked chases through the house. The baked bean recipe was one of Heather's Sadie had added to the week's menu and grocery shopping list on Saturday. She'd been eager to see how it measured up against the bean recipe she made every Fourth of July—right away she was intrigued with the Worcestershire sauce and the variety of beans. She'd never cooked with butter beans before.

As she measured and stirred, she lined up the details of last night's events—double-checking them in her mind to make sure she wasn't missing anything. Once the ingredients were simmering, she found Pete's notebook, flipped to a clean page and wrote down everything in a bulleted list. Pete came home and wrestled the other boys into coats, gloves, and hats before taking them outside to play in the backyard. It took Sadie three drafts of her list before she had the proper chronological order of events. She felt better about having it on paper, even if seeing the intricacies made it seem even harder to believe. Could one person do all of that with such expert execution? How could they not get caught with such intricate timing? What other explanations could there possibly be?

She was just finishing up when Pete came back in and asked if he could use her laptop—he'd keep an eye on the boys through the window—while Sadie showered and got ready for the day. Sadie didn't like how it felt as though they were circling each other, and although she was eager to talk about last night, she handed him her laptop instead and took a long hot shower.

Once she was dressed, with her hair done and her makeup in place, Sadie felt ready to conquer the day. She returned to the kitchen to check on the beans and trailed her hand across Pete's shoulder blades as he sat at the table. The boys were still outside; she was cold just thinking about it but assumed since they were running around they must be staying plenty warm.

"So," she said, lifting the lid of the slow cooker and inhaling the sweet aroma.

"So," Pete said, his back toward her.

"I've been thinking," she said as she stirred the beans. "We both agree it's nothing supernatural, which means someone is working really hard to make us think that it is." She paused. "I thought I heard a voice. Last night. When you were outside."

Pete turned in his chair and gave her his full attention. "A voice?" he said—perfectly even, perfectly calm. Strangely, she found herself feeling an unexpected rush of defensiveness.

"When I went into the bedroom to get the candle," she explained. "I thought someone called my name just before the door slammed shut. That's what woke the boys."

"But you're not sure?"

"I wish I were," Sadie said, frustrated that she didn't have a definite opinion. "But my adrenaline was rushing, and it had been an overwhelming night."

Pete nodded thoughtfully. Sadie continued. "Anyway, I made a list of the order things happened last night," she said, retrieving the notebook from the counter and handing it to him. She pointed at the fourth line. "I think whomever we saw in the window shut off the power to the house via the power box on the outside of the house. My parents' house had one, so I'm assuming this one does too, since it's an older home."

"It's on the west side," Pete said. "It's not secured. I found it this morning."

Sadie nodded, emboldened by having supposed correctly, and continued her hypothesis. "So, if they turned off the power and then came inside after you went *outside*, they could have flipped all the light switches on. There are only six rooms; it wouldn't be hard.

They could have come into my bedroom. My back would have been to the doorway when I was lighting the candle. They said my name and then slammed the door before hiding in the bathroom, or maybe in your bedroom. When you came back inside, they would have known you'd check on me and the boys, which would give them the chance to get out of the house. You heard something in the hallway, didn't you? That's why you shined the flashlight out there when we were in the boys' room."

Pete paused, but finally nodded. "I thought I saw something out of the corner of my eye. A shadow maybe."

"But you were more intent on making sure we were okay than following what you didn't consider possible—that they could have come inside while you were doing the perimeter check."

Pete looked at the timeline without commenting.

Sadie continued. "They got out of the house and turned the power back on."

She could feel that Pete was trying to come up with an argument but when he looked up, there was the slightest look of resignation on his face. "There's no way to tell if the power box had been tampered with. I checked it when I went outside. It's not hard to turn off or on."

Sadie felt the thrill of victory. He was agreeing with her, but she needed to hear him say it. "So you agree that what I'm suggesting is plausible?"

"But not probable," Pete said, unable to give in so easily. "Everything would have to go perfectly, with precise timing. They would have been within a few feet of us much of the time and moving around without a sound." He was hesitant to draw a conclusion, and Sadie let him continue processing for another thirty seconds, but her patience was wearing thin. If he could accept this possibility, then it gave them something solid to consider, to build on. He shook his head. "I don't see how it could be possible."

Oh, he was stubborn! "If not that, then the only explanation I can come up with is that there is something spectral going on." She knew he was not open to that idea—neither was she—but she hoped presenting him with that alternative would encourage him to give her suggested chronology more consideration.

It worked. He straightened his shoulders and folded his arms. He looked her in the eye as though challenging her. "So assuming someone knew the exact layout of the house, orchestrated every-thing perfectly, *and* slipped out without us seeing them, who was it?" Pete asked.

"The only person I can think of is Mrs. Wapple," Sadie said, though that wasn't true. She took a breath and decided to lay it all out. "Or her sister, Gabrielle."

"Why would her sister do this?"

Sadie hated being questioned by him, hated the detective-face that had taken over his features. "All I know is she's determined not to listen to my concerns about Mrs. Wapple. Maybe she's hid-ing something. Maybe there's something about her sister she doesn't want us to know and she's trying to scare us away."

"It's like the plot of a stupid *Scooby-Doo* episode," Pete said, pushing both hands through his hair.

Sadie tried not to be offended; she liked *Scooby-Doo*. At the same time, this wasn't the first time the sleuthing dog and his friends had been brought into discussions about her mysteries. She didn't appreciate the comparison, even if she found the cartoon relatively entertaining. It had been one of Breanna's favorites, and Sadie had felt a renewed kinship to Velma over the last year.

"Except that leaving the hat in the hallway Monday night was more like an invitation than a skull-and-crossbones," Sadie added, just to keep things complicated. "There's no *Scooby-Doo* episode with that plot point in it."

"So maybe Gabrielle is as crazy as her sister, but can play the part of a normal person better than her sister."

"A psychopath?" Sadie asked, connecting the dots to the conversation they'd had Sunday night. She sat down in the chair across the table from him. "You're more familiar with the characteristics than I am. Is there anything else about the sister that fits?"

"Justifying bad behavior," Pete said reluctantly. "And psychopaths hate to be questioned because they assume whatever they do is right."

"Gabrielle fits that," Sadie said. "She refused to listen to my concerns about her sister but agreed to meet me before kicking me out."

Pete nodded and stared at the tabletop, deep in thought. "Psychopaths often have a difficult time anticipating the consequences of their actions because they assume that they are too smart. The rules don't apply to them, so why should they fear the punishments?"

"I could keep chasing her down, if I wanted to. Kicking me out of the hotel wasn't the most effective way to get rid of me."

"It's impossible to diagnose a person based on such limited information," Pete added. "It can take years, and a long behavioral history, before trained psychiatrists can determine psychopathic patterns."

"We're not diagnosing," Sadie said with a shrug. "We're just considering possibilities. And, quite frankly, Mrs. Wapple doesn't really seem . . . capable. The sister's the only other person involved in this situation, and she has not been reasonable to deal with on any level."

Pete didn't say anything for a few seconds, and when he did speak it wasn't what Sadie was expecting to hear. "I'm going to call social services," he said, pushing back from the table. "Whatever—*whoever*—is behind this might back off when we stop being involved and turn it over to people who can really do something for Mrs. Wapple. We'll let them figure out what Mrs. Wapple or her sister is trying to hide. This is bigger than us, and we need to get out of it."

Pete left the room, and Sadie kept her disappointment in his quick decision to herself. A moment later, she heard him shut the door to his bedroom. While waiting for Pete to return with an up-date, she alphabetized the canned vegetables in the pantry, and then decided to organize them by expiration date instead. She looked out the window every minute or so to make sure the boys were still playing, glad they were working out so much energy. A part of her wished she could do the same. She could feel her frustration build-ing. Frustration with what had happened last night, frustration that the trip was going this direction, and even frustration toward Pete. She felt like he was leaving her out, or trying to protect her. Whatever his motive, he wasn't sharing all his thoughts the way she was sharing hers. She didn't like it.

Thirteen and a half minutes later, give or take a few seconds, Pete returned to the kitchen, notebook in hand.

"So?" she asked, meeting him in the middle of the tiny kitchen and looking at him expectantly.

He looked up as though surprised to see her there. "Oh, yeah, I talked to a case worker and gave them the information. They said they'd send someone over in the next few days."

"Days?" Sadie said. "That's too long."

Pete shrugged, an entirely too casual gesture for Sadie right now.

"The wheels of bureaucracy move slowly, especially in a big city like this. We already knew that would probably happen."

"And you're not bothered by that?" Sadie asked as her frustration broke through the surface. "This woman is sick, and she's in pain. We're just supposed to sit back and twiddle our thumbs?"

Pete's jaw tightened, but he quickly reset his neutral expression as he tossed the notebook on the table. "We need to go somewhere for a few hours," he said, shoving his hands in the pockets of his jeans. "Get out of the house and clear our heads. Where should we go?"

"That's it?" Sadie asked, not wanting to change the subject. "You're not going to dialogue this with me?"

Pete blinked at her. "We're trying to make sense of things that don't make sense. It's an exercise in futility."

"And we'll never make sense of them if you shrug your shoulders and pretend it didn't happen." She paused, not wanting to lose her temper. "Maybe we need to call the police about last night. Maybe they can help us make sense of things."

"I *am* the police," Pete said, sharply enough that Sadie startled a little. He must have heard the edge too, because he shook his head. "We're not calling the police," he said evenly. His jaw tightened again.

"You're in the middle of this, Pete. They might be the objective perspective we need to figure this out."

She was upsetting him and she watched his chest expand as he took a deep breath. He pointed out the kitchen window to where the boys were playing in the backyard and lowered his voice while taking a step toward her. He didn't sound angry and the edge in his voice had softened, but his words were sincere. "I have three little boys I'm supposed to be taking care of, Sadie. My son's children. And there is something really scary going on in their house. I don't know what to do; I don't know what to believe. I don't know if we should leave the house and go to a hotel, or if I should call Jared and tell him to come home." He crossed his arms over his chest and looked at the floor while shaking his head. He took a deep breath before meeting her eyes. "Calling the police about hats and lights going off and on will have them rolling their eyes. Nothing has been taken, no one's been hurt or threatened, there is no proof of a crime, and things are just weird enough to make us look like a bunch of overzealous hicks caught up in pre-Halloween fantasies." He stopped for a breath. "More important than that, however, is that at some point Jared and Heather *are* going to come home, and I'll need to tell them what's going on—and I have no idea what that is. You want to discuss every possibility, but I don't see anything that makes sense. I can't believe something paranormal is happening, but I can't believe anyone would set this up either. I just don't know, okay? I don't know. And that's the scariest thing that could ever happen to me."

Sadie felt her frustration fade in the wake of his vulnerability. He must have read it in her face because he seemed to relax too.

Pete continued. "I just want to keep things as normal as possible for the boys, okay? I don't want them to get upset. That's all I really care about right now. We'll buy an eyebolt for both doors and maybe have another slumber party. I just want to know the boys are safe, okay? That's all I can really focus on right now."

Sadie nodded her understanding, realizing that part of what Pete meant, but didn't say, was that he felt he could protect them from whatever was happening. That's what he did—he kept people safe—and yet his foundation must feel unstable under his feet right now. He wore a zippered jacket over his T-shirt, and Sadie wondered if the jacket was concealing his shoulder harness and gun. She held his eyes for a couple of seconds, reading the fear, anguish, and discomfort there. It was the pleading in his expression that helped her make the decision to follow his lead. These were his grandchildren, it was his son's house, and she was here to support him.

She still didn't understand why he didn't want to call the police—so what if they thought it was silly; they might be able to help—but it was obviously something Pete didn't want to do. Maybe his being a cop made it complicated somehow, or maybe there was something else holding him back. She amended the thought as soon as it entered her head. There was nothing suspicious in Pete's behavior. He understood law enforcement better than she ever could, which meant that not calling the Boston PD must be the right decision. She would support him in dealing with the situation this way, even if she didn't understand why he was so determined. At least for now.

"I bet the boys would like the Franklin Park Zoo," Sadie suggested, willing to change the subject now. "I know Kalan would be disappointed not to go, but maybe we can make it up to him. Breanna told me the zoo has a new baby gorilla."

Pete put his hands in his front pockets, his expression unreadable. She sensed that he was embarrassed by his monologue; it wasn't like him to share his insecurities so easily. She moved toward him and hugged him, rubbing his back in order to comfort him while at the same time verifying the strap of his shoulder harness. She wondered if the zoo allowed concealed handguns and could only assume he'd gotten the proper clearance to carry a concealed weapon in a state other than the one his license was issued in. She reminded herself again, *He's a police detective. He knows how to handle these things.*

"I like gorillas," Pete said dryly when she pulled back.

Sadie laughed and kissed him quickly on the lips. "Let's feed these boys a quick lunch and get out of here, okay?"

Whitty Baked Beans

½ pound diced crispy bacon
½ pound ground beef, browned and drained
1 medium onion, chopped
1 (15-ounce) can butter beans, drained*
1 (16-ounce) can kidney beans, drained
1 (16-ounce) can pork and beans, undrained
⅔ cup packed brown sugar
½ cup ketchup
1 tablespoon prepared mustard
2 tablespoons apple cider vinegar
2 tablespoons molasses
½ to 1 teaspoon Worcestershire sauce

Fry bacon, remove from pan, and drain. Add ground beef to the same pan and brown with onion. (You can also use extra bacon or kielbasa in place of hamburger.)

Combine all ingredients in a slow cooker. Mix well and cook 1 hour on high or 3 to 4 hours on low. Turn cooker to low or "keep warm" until ready to eat. Refrigerate leftovers.

Serves 10 as a side dish, or 6 as a meal.

*Butter beans are large, flat, yellow beans that give this recipe a nice variety. Feel free to substitute another type of bean if you don't like the texture of butter beans. Great Northern beans or black beans make a good substitution. For a less saucy dish, add an additional can of drained beans of your choice.

CHAPTER 15

The zoo was cold but fun—or at least it was as fun as possible for two people feeling as burdened as Sadie and Pete were. Like the rest of the city, the zoo was decked out in Halloween paraphernalia—spiderwebs stretched across buildings and hundreds of pumpkins, cornstalks, and creepy characters peeked through windows. Sadie updated Shawn on the latest news while Pete took the boys through the reptile house. She and Shawn were just getting to the brainstorming phase of the discussion when Shawn realized he was late for class.

The boys ran from one exhibit to another for almost two hours before the cold, the wind, and sheer exhaustion took their toll. Sadie took several pictures of the baby gorilla for Breanna, and Pete bought both boys a four-inch plastic replica from the gift shop. He purchased a larger one for Kalan, who would not be happy to have missed the field trip.

On the way home, they stopped for hot chocolate at a little mom-and-pop diner, and then Sadie and the boys waited in the parking lot of a hardware store while Pete bought two eyebolts, one for each door, and five pumpkins for a carving contest when Kalan got home from school. Taking steps toward the boys' safety seemed to lift Pete's spirits—and Sadie's. They would be safe tonight, Sadie was sure of it, and the pumpkins would be a good distraction, even if pumpkin guts were one of Sadie's least favorite things to handle.

Both Chance and Fig fell asleep on the ride home from the hardware store. Sadie looked out the passenger window and watched Boston come and go between the trees that were bending under in the wind, wishing she felt more settled than she did. Loose ends drove her crazy, and there were so many loose ends snapping in the breeze that she found it hard to concentrate on anything else. They pulled into the garage and Sadie reached down to undo her seat belt. Pete's warm hand on hers made her pause.

"I'm sorry," he whispered.

"For?"

"For being distant. It's a problem I have when a simple solution isn't simple. I just have to keep things . . . logical."

Sadie stared at him. "I can understand that," she said, relieved. He gave her hand a squeeze and pushed the button to release her seat belt just as her cell phone rang.

Pete let himself out of the van while she dug through her purse and pulled out her phone. She didn't recognize the phone number but the area code was local, which piqued her curiosity. "Hello," she said, opening the passenger door just as Pete rolled back the side door of the minivan.

"Hello? Is this Mrs. Hoffman?" a woman asked.

Why did everyone mess up her last name? It wasn't hard. "This is Sadie *Hoffmiller*," she said with emphasis.

"Oh, sorry, Mrs. Hoffmiller. This is Gabrielle Marrow."

Sadie sat upright, one foot out of the car and one still in. She couldn't think of anything to say before Gabrielle continued. "I'm sorry I missed you at the hotel last night, and I've been—"

"Missed me?" Sadie said automatically, putting both feet back into the car so that she could properly focus on the phone call.

"I looked for you in the lounge for a few minutes before returning to my dinner." Her tone was accusatory, as though determined to see Sadie as having complicated her evening. This woman had some serious issues, and Sadie thought again of the definition of a psychopath: someone who was willing to do anything for what they wanted. What did Gabrielle want? How was Sadie in the way? Why was she calling?

"Really," Sadie said carefully, trying to figure out the game this woman was playing. Maybe she didn't know the security guard told Sadie *why* she was being kicked out. Or maybe she had too much wine at her banquet and was making something up to fill in the blank spaces. Or maybe she was just plain crazy.

"Look, I know we got off to a rough start," Gabrielle said before Sadie could think of a response that didn't involve screaming. Gabrielle's voice sounded professional but tired, as though she *had* to make this call but wished she didn't and wanted it to just go away. "I've got an artist reception at the gallery tomorrow night," she continued, "and I'm not at the top of my game right now. Actually, I haven't been at the top of my game for several weeks and—"

"I know you had me kicked out of the hotel." Sadie was running out of patience and tired of trying to come up with a politically correct way to have this conversation. "And I don't appreciate you pretending it was otherwise."

"Kicked out?"

"Yes," Sadie said emphatically. She looked over her shoulder as Pete released Fig from his car seat. Chance was walking on his own, but Fig was not so easily roused. Pete caught Sadie's eye, and she held up one finger to signal she'd be there in a minute. Pete adjusted a limp Fig to one shoulder and nodded.

"Uh, I don't know what you're talking about Mrs. Hoffman." The edgy tone Sadie remembered from yesterday was back.

"*Hoffmiller*," Sadie corrected her again. "I took the T all the way to the hotel last night to try to get you to listen to me. Why would I leave?"

Gabrielle was silent for a few beats before saying, "I don't know what you're talking about." She sounded annoyed. "I went to meet you in the Connexion Lounge, just as I said I would, but you weren't there. I've worked very hard to find the time to call you today and clear the air between us."

Sadie was tempted to keep arguing, knowing she had an arsenal of weapons at her disposal. This woman had lied to her when they first met, and then followed up with a cold and pompous attitude. But that would not get her answers. She thought back to Pete's question about Gabrielle's motive, assuming she was the one behind all the strange things happening. Sadie had surmised she was hiding something, or trying to keep them away from Mrs. Wapple. So why was she calling now?

Pete closed the door of the minivan and headed out of the garage with Fig over one shoulder and leading Chance with his other hand.

Sadie took a breath and kept her voice calm when she spoke, changing her tactics completely. "I would like to have things resolved between us as well."

Gabrielle paused, perhaps surprised by Sadie backing down. "Um, good," she said. "I guess we should start at the beginning, when I met you in front of Dee's house."

Dee? A nickname? Sadie hadn't expected that type of endearment. "Right, and you said you were her."

"I'm sorry about that," Gabrielle said, sounding contrite. "Dee's only been there a couple of months, but there have already been a few problems with the neighbors, which is why I sealed the front door. I hoped that would keep her in the backyard, away from people, at least until she settled in. When you asked if I was her, it just seemed simpler to play along."

The front door was sealed? Was that even legal? "Was she living with your dad before moving here, then?"

Gabrielle paused. "How do you know that?"

"I don't *know*," Sadie said. "But I found your dad's obituary in the newspaper and assumed your father was taking care of her until he . . . died." She grimaced. Her own father's death was still a painful memory; she missed him so much.

"You read my dad's obituary? Who are you?"

"Just someone trying to help your sister. I'm sure it's been hard to suddenly become your sister's caretaker."

"I'm not her caretaker," Gabrielle said, defensive. "She can take care of herself."

"No, she can't," Sadie said. "Maybe because of losing your dad, or maybe because of the new location—I don't know—but she's not settling in, and she's not well."

Gabrielle didn't respond for a moment. "I'm doing the best I can."

"I've been here only a few days, but I can already tell something is very wrong with your sister. She needs help."

When Gabrielle spoke again, her icy tone had returned. "Well, it's obvious you've already made your mind up about me," she said. "But you really have no idea what's going on here so don't—"

"Wait," Sadie jumped in, trying to save the conversation. "I'm not trying to be judgmental, Ms. Marrow, just lining up the facts. I've already called social services, but—"

"You called them?" Gabrielle said, shocked. "Why would you do that?"

Oh, this was not going well. Gabrielle was obviously on edge and her mood was twisting like a windmill. "You wouldn't talk to me on the phone," Sadie reminded her. "You had me kicked out of the hotel, and you were—"

"I did *not* have you kicked out!" Gabrielle said. "I left a very important meeting to talk to you, and you were not there."

Argh! This was so aggravating. Was Gabrielle psychotic *and* delusional? Sadie tried to get the conversation back on track. "Look, Ms. Marrow. I want to help your sister, and help you if I can. Really, that's all I want to do."

"Help me?"

"If I can, yes. That's why I called you, why I went to the hotel, and why we called social services this morning. We are concerned. We want to—"

Suddenly Pete appeared in front of the minivan with Fig still sleeping over his shoulder. He was gesturing for Sadie to get out of the car. She furrowed her brow as he pulled open her door. She looked up at him.

"I need your help," he said.

"Just a minute," Sadie said to Gabrielle, pulling the phone from her ear and stepping out of the car. She covered the mouthpiece. "It's Gabrielle," she said to Pete in an urgent whisper. "She's finally called me back, and I think we're getting somewhere."

"The back door was unlocked," Pete said. "Someone's been in the house again."

CHAPTER 16

Sadie felt her stomach drop. Pete gave her a strong look and then headed out of the garage while Sadie waged a battle inside herself.

"Gabrielle, I'm really sorry, but can I call you back? I've got a bit of a situation here that demands my immediate attention."

Gabrielle let out a heavy groan on the other end of the line. "There are a hundred things I need to take care of before tomorrow's reception." Something in her voice, however, sounded as though she regretted that; she wanted to talk to Sadie.

"I'm sorry. Um . . . what if we met in person later tonight? Whatever time works for you." Meeting in person was always much more effective than talking on the phone anyway. She'd make sure it was a public location so that she'd be safe.

"I'll have to call you back when I have a better idea of how the rest of my day is going to come together."

"That's fine," Sadie said, the urgency to join Pete pressing in on her. "Anytime would work for me."

"I'll call you as soon as I have a time," Gabrielle said. They said good-bye, and Sadie hung up, trying to shut out the regret of missing an opportunity to finally connect with this woman. She hurried toward the house. Pete was standing outside the open back door, Fig still asleep on his shoulder. He pushed a final button on his cell phone with his free hand and put it to his ear as Sadie approached. With his head, he motioned toward the open back door and stepped out of her way.

Chance sat on the wooden step, looking tired and a little confused. Sadie ruffled his hair as she passed him and looked inside the house, lifting her eyes as she surveyed the small section of kitchen she could see from the doorway. Plates and bowls lined the floor, each one placed carefully in a pattern. Plate, bowl, plate. There were three or four rows of them near the door, then a row of forks. Next to that was a row of spoons, and next to that was a row of butter knives. All the cabinet doors as well as the drawers had been pulled open.

Sadie swallowed and looked past the kitchen into the hallway. What looked like Mrs. Wapple's hat was back in the same place where it had been yesterday morning. All the curtains had been closed, lending a pale darkness to the interior of the house. A gust of wind blew from behind her and points of cold pricked against Sadie's cheek. She looked up at the gray sky as the first snowflakes began to fall. Pete was giving the address to what Sadie could only assume was a 911 dispatcher. His determination not to call the police had been exhausted.

"What's the matter, Aunt Sadie?"

Sadie looked down at Chance. His sleepy eyes looked up at her dolefully. She sat down next to him on the porch, turning her back to the disturbing state of the house and put her arm around his shoulder, pulling him closer in the guise of keeping him warm.

"Someone's playing a game with us," she said, trying to keep her tone from showing how scary the game had become.

"What kind of game?" Chance said, stifling a yawn.

"I don't really know," Sadie said. What she did know was that she didn't want to play anymore.

"We're okay to clean it up?" Sadie said in surprise, standing up from where she'd been sitting on the couch twiddling her thumbs for the last hour. Pete closed the front door behind him—the snow was really blowing now—and Sadie watched the last police car drive away. Luckily, the police had cleared the house pretty fast and allowed Sadie to put the boys down for their naps; they actually fell asleep too.

"They took pictures," Pete said, his tone flat. "And filed a report."

"Are they taking it seriously?"

Pete shrugged, put his hands in his pockets, and looked out the front window. It was becoming a habit for both of them to stare across the street. The snow was falling at a forty-five-degree angle and a wispy sheet already lay over the grass. The wintry light coming through the window accentuated the lines around Pete's face and the furrow in his brow, making him look older while also emphasizing how concerned he was. "Mrs. Wapple didn't answer the door, and there wasn't cause for forced entry."

"The front door is sealed," Sadie said. Pete turned to look at her. "Her sister told me that on the phone. She hoped it would keep Mrs. Wapple from bothering people."

Pete turned back to the window.

"Did you tell them we'd called social services?" Sadie asked.

Pete nodded. "They said they'd follow up with them and make sure she was a top priority. They'll also come back this evening and try to talk to Mrs. Wapple once she's home."

"She's there," Sadie said, moving to stand beside Pete. He took one hand out of his pocket and draped it over her shoulder, pulling her toward him.

"I know," he said with a sigh. "But they're just following procedure. At least we have a report on record with them now. If anything else happens, that creates a foundation."

Sadie nodded and watched the snow fall for another minute. "Maybe we should stay at a hotel," she said. "The boys could swim. We could make it an event."

"I thought about that," Pete said.

"But?"

"I'd like to be here when the police come back to talk to her tonight."

Sadie leaned into him, wishing she could be more help. He gave her shoulders a squeeze and kissed the top of her head. "I need to call Jared," he said when he pulled back. Sadie's stomach dropped. What a miserable phone call to make. He removed his arm from her shoulders and reached into his pocket for his phone. "And then I'll install the bolts."

"I'll clean up the mess," she said, turning toward the kitchen. She glanced around and noticed there were no gray patches on the doorknobs or walls like on TV after police had investigated a crime scene. "Did they dust for prints already?"

Pete shook his head. "Dusting for prints is a waste of time. They know I'm a cop so they didn't bother putting on the show."

"A waste of time?" Sadie's crime-TV-watcher sensibilities were at instant attention.

"Running fingerprints is laborious and not highly effective without a significant crime having been committed."

"That's so disappointing."

"I know. It ruins the romance a little bit, doesn't it?" He smiled and Sadie smiled back, though neither of their smiles were happy ones.

Pete headed down the hall, phone in hand. Sadie stopped at the threshold to the kitchen and studied the strange pattern of dishes, wondering if the pattern meant something. After several seconds, she took a few pictures with her phone and started gathering up the dishes.

The beans in the slow cooker smelled amazing, and she stirred them again and turned the heat to warm. She'd already cooked them too long as it was, but beans were pretty easygoing. She closed all the cabinets and drawers before putting the dishes from the floor into the dishwasher, easily a full load, and running it on the pots-and-pans cycle. Then she filled the sink with hot water, added some Pine-Sol, and gave the kitchen a good mopping, which didn't take long since the whole patch of floor was only about twenty square feet. As she was draining the dirty mop water out of the sink, Pete appeared in the doorway.

"How'd he take it?" Sadie asked, rinsing out the mop.

"Jared has a meeting with the chief resident at nine o'clock tomorrow morning and an orientation dinner tomorrow night," Pete said without looking at her. "Heather's going to see if she can find a flight home."

"Were they upset?" Sadie asked, leaving the head of the mop in the sink to drain as she dried her hands on a dish towel.

"The police called Jared before I did. I gave them his number, but didn't think they'd act so fast. He feels like we kept things from them."

Sadie crossed the newly cleaned floor on her toes so as not to mar the finish and followed Pete into the living room, where they both sat down on the couch. "We kinda did keep things from them," she said, tucking her feet beneath her. Pete finally met her eyes. "At the time it made sense not to worry them needlessly," Sadie added. "And I stand by what we chose to do, but I can understand their perspective. I'm sure when they get here and we can talk about it face-to-face they'll calm down."

Pete gave a noncommittal shrug and tipped his head back on the couch so he was looking up at the popcorn ceiling. "It's been really hard for me to keep my children close since Pat died," he said, his voice soft and vulnerable. He didn't put his arm around Sadie as he spoke. Instead, he fidgeted with a loose thread on the couch cushion and lowered his head to stare through the window at the house of the woman who seemed to be the one causing so much havoc. "Pat really was the glue for all of us. She kept up with what was going on in the lives of the kids and grandkids. She sent birthday presents, planned the holidays, and went to recitals and baseball games—all that stuff. She came out for a week when Kalan and Chance were born. Fig wasn't born until . . . after."

Sadie wanted to put a hand on his knee or give some kind of comfort, but talking about his late wife was still a fragile topic between them and she feared upsetting the balance. She understood how hard it was for him to make room for her, with Pat so dominant in his heart, but trusting Sadie with Pat's memory was also an important part of their relationship.

"It's been so hard for me to try to be her," Pete said, his voice almost a whisper. "Hard for me, hard for the kids. I've tried to be more involved and make up for her absence, but it's not the same. This . . . this trip here felt like a . . . a new start of sorts. Jared inviting me into his life, trusting me to take care of his children, wanting me to be more to them—and to him—than I've been in the past." Sadie watched his hands rub absently on the thighs of his pants. "Not to mention welcoming you."

He paused and looked at the floor. "I hate failing him," he finally said.

Sadie sensed he wanted her reassurance now, so she took his hand in both of hers and held on. "This isn't your fault," she said. "And Jared will see that. You've done the best you can with a very strange situation; he'll see that, too. And maybe you're not giving yourself enough credit. Your children lost their mother, and there are few things as painful as that, but I think everything you do to try to keep them together makes a huge difference. Pat sounds like a wonderful woman, an excellent mother, but she wasn't the *only* thing holding your family together. The fact is that Jared *did* invite you here to watch his children; he *does* want you in his life and once he gets here and realizes that no one's been hurt, that the boys are not traumatized, and that you've done everything you can to deal with this situation, he'll calm down and be okay."

Pete nodded, but Sadie could tell he didn't believe her. Not really. After another minute, Pete's phone rang. He seemed grateful for the interruption and gave Sadie a quick smile before answering the phone. "This is Detective Cunningham," he said as he stood up from the couch and headed down the hall toward his bedroom.

Sadie returned to the kitchen to finish cleaning up and thought about the interrupted phone call she'd had with Gabrielle. With the police involved and morale so low for Pete, she wasn't sure talking to Gabrielle was the right direction. Sadie hadn't said anything to Gabrielle about Mrs. Wapple's hat or the face in the window that looked like it could have been her, but it seemed now as though she should have. The police might get in touch with Gabrielle, adding a whole new dynamic to the conversation they didn't get to finish. Sadie stressed about it for another minute and then decided to take things with Gabrielle as they happened.

Sadie needed to distract herself with something, and she was in serious need of some comfort food, which made her think of the cinnamon twists her mother-in-law would make for special occasions. It was a recipe adapted from cinnamon rolls, but with a twist . . . literally. Rather than buns, the twists looked like little bow ties about the size of a cookie. They had all the same spices and texture as cinnamon rolls, but were dipped in icing instead of coated with it. She imagined the boys would love them, and so while Pete continued his phone call, she mixed the dough, covered it, and put it on top of the fridge where it was warm so that the dough would rise.

By the time Sadie finished cleaning up the new mess, it was 3:15 and nearly time to pick up Kalan from school. She headed down the hallway to ask Pete if he wanted her to go to the school, but she slowed down when she heard him on the phone. The door wasn't closed all the way. He'd been on this call for over half an hour unless he'd made or received other calls as well.

"Yeah, I've called everyone I know who they might contact directly. . . . I don't think the Boston PD has looked at my file yet, but it has me worried," Pete said.

Sadie furrowed her brow while Pete paused to listen to whoever was on the other end of the line. Who was he talking to?

"Believe me," Pete said. "Bringing this up is the last thing I want to do. . . . Right. . . . I just wanted everyone to hear my version of this situation before they started asking questions. I'd appreciate it if you'd let me know if they contact you. I want to be ready if they . . . I know. . . . You'd think Michaels wouldn't still be haunting me fifteen years later. . . . I know. . . . I was also going to . . ."

Sadie turned and was halfway down the hall before she realized she'd chosen not to eavesdrop. But she hadn't turned away soon enough. Michaels? Haunting? And who was Pete talking to? Obviously Michaels was someone from Pete's past and something the police would find if they looked at his file. Michaels was also something Sadie knew nothing about. Fifteen years ago Pete was married to Pat and working in Fort Collins, or had he still been in New Mexico then?

"Don't do this," she whispered to herself as she found herself in the kitchen again. "Don't start inventing things from pieces of information you can't understand." Was this why he hadn't wanted to call the police before this afternoon? But how bad could this Michaels thing be if Pete were still a police detective?

She dished herself up some beans—there was no better distraction than food—and nearly groaned out loud at the perfect blend of spicy sweetness. Heather's beans were much better than her own recipe. She heard Pete's footsteps approach a few minutes later and turned to face him, gathering up her newly awakened concerns and shoving them into a closet. She trusted him. She would just ask him about it and get it over with. But when she opened her mouth, that's not what came out. "It's about time to pick Kalan up from school," she said.

"Do you want to go or should I?" He didn't look particularly guarded, just tired. But then again, he didn't know Sadie had overheard anything.

"I can go," Sadie said, eager to get out of the house for a minute.

She grabbed the keys to the minivan and headed out the back door, deep in thought. She made her way to the school, driving carefully due to the snow that was still falling, though it was lighter than it had been earlier. While waiting in line behind all the other parents waiting to pick up their children, she called Shawn, but it went to his voice mail. She left a message about the kitchen incident and the police involvement, ending with a caution that she didn't know if they were going to stay in the house or not tonight and asking him to call when he could. She'd been thinking about the information he'd found out about Mrs. Wapple's former landlord. Maybe it *would* be worthwhile to talk to him. Sadie assured Shawn in the message that everything was fine, told him not to worry, and then ended the call.

When he called back, maybe she'd ask if he could look into Pete's history fifteen years ago. If there had been a public mention of this Michaels person, Shawn would find it. Or he'd ask Jane to find it. The idea made her uncomfortable, however, as though she'd be opening a can of worms she might never get the lid back onto. This was Pete's secret, and she didn't want to involve anyone else in figuring it out. The next question, however, was if she wanted to figure it out herself.

Kalan came out of the front doors of the school, and Sadie waved when he spotted her, gratified by the way his face lit up with recognition. He looked like a turtle, with his big backpack perched on his back while he leaned forward in order to keep his balance as he ran. He pulled open the sliding door of the minivan and as soon as it was closed, he began chattering about his day. He was excited for the upcoming Halloween Carnival next Wednesday—they'd sent home flyers today. Sadie listened, nodding and asking questions as necessary. He was going to be a ninja for Halloween, and Sadie exclaimed what a perfect ninja he would be because he was really fast. He liked that.

When Sadie and Kalan returned home, it was obvious Pete had made the choice to pretend to be in a far better mood than he actually was. He went through Kalan's backpack, looking over his work from school, and when the younger boys woke up and wanted to make a snowman, Pete acted as though there was nothing he would rather do.

Sadie bundled up and went outside with them, trying to think of how to tell Pete she'd overheard part of the phone call, but he seemed to be having such a good time that she hesitated ruining it. She stood on the covered porch, amused with their amusement for a little while but wanting to spare her hair from the snow. Five cold minutes was all she could stand. Once her nose started tingling, she was ready to go inside.

Sadie pushed her hands deeper into her pockets. "Well, you guys keep working on your leaf-grass-snowman. I'm going to make dinner and get some cocoa ready for when you come to your senses."

Pete nodded but he was intent on proving a snowman was possible even with less than an inch of snow. She shook her head and hurried up the back steps, glad to have an excuse to go inside.

She shut the door behind her and rubbed her hands together to warm them up on her way toward the pantry. She pulled out the hot cocoa mix she'd put together a few days earlier; Heather had wanted to know how to make hot cocoa from scratch, and Sadie was more than happy to give a demonstration.

Within a few minutes, five plastic cups were waiting with just the right amount of cocoa powder in the bottom. She filled Heather's cute little red teapot and put it on the stove; it was much more romantic boiling water on the stove than in the microwave. When the boys came in, she could turn on the burner and have hot water by the time they got their snow gear off.

Despite being busy and focusing on details, Sadie was still anxious. She tried to take comfort in the fact that they had done all the right things. The police were involved, and everything was silent across the street. There was every reason to believe this was over and done. But why was Pete worried about the Boston PD looking at his file? And was it realistic to think Mrs. Wapple would leave them alone now?

The dough for the cinnamon twists had finished its first rise, and it took only ten minutes for Sadie to roll out the dough and top it with the butter and spice mixture. She used a pizza cutter to cut the rectangle into four horizontal strips and then cut the horizontal strips into one-inch sections vertically. Before placing the strips on the cookie sheet, she twisted each one into a little bow tie. She'd halved the recipe so it fit perfectly onto one pan. It helped that she had made the recipe so many times that it was easy; the first few times she had made them, she'd wondered if they were worthy of her Little Black Recipe Book. All it had taken was practice, though, and now they seemed downright simple to do.

She covered the pan with a dish towel to let the dough rise for a few more minutes and was washing her hands when the home phone rang. Sadie looked at it on the wall with annoyance as she held up her freshly washed arms like a doctor waiting for sterile gloves. Her annoyance quickly turned to trepidation, however, when she realized it could be the police. It could also be Jared or Heather, and Sadie didn't feel up to talking to them right now. She hated it when people were mad at her. If only Pete weren't outside.

It rang for the second time, and Sadie hurried to answer it, all her internal arguments moot. It was simply irresponsible to ignore a ringing phone—it might be important—and she could wash her hands again when she finished.

"Hello?" Sadie said into the phone, wiping her left hand on the front of her pants before realizing what she was doing and reaching for a dish towel. The kitchen was small enough that she could reach every corner with the phone still against her ear.

Silence.

"Hello?" she said again.

A garbled voice said something—two words Sadie couldn't understand but that caused a shiver to run across her shoulder blades. The voice was familiar.

"Excuse me?" she asked.

The voice spoke again, and this time Sadie thought it said, "Help me."

Cinnamon Twists

4 cups flour, divided
½ cup sugar
2 teaspoons salt
1 tablespoon instant yeast
½ teaspoon cinnamon
¼ teaspoon nutmeg
1¼ cups warm milk
⅓ cup butter, melted
1 egg

Filling
½ cup brown sugar
2 tablespoons cinnamon
½ teaspoon cloves
⅓ cup butter, softened

For the dough, mix 2 cups of flour with the remaining dry ingredients. Stir to combine. Add all liquid ingredients and mix well.

Add remaining flour until dough is tacky to the touch, but not sticky. Knead 6 to 8 minutes or until dough is smooth. Grease a bowl and let dough raise, covered, until double (about 40 minutes). For filling, mix together brown sugar and spices. Set aside.

Sprinkle flour on the countertop and roll out dough into a 16x12-inch rectangle. Spread with ⅓ cup soft butter. Sprinkle butter with sugar-spice topping all the way to the edges. Let dough sit for 10 minutes.

Use a pizza cutter to cut dough lengthwise into four 3x16 inch strips. Then cut every inch vertically so that you have sixteen 1x3-inch strips. Lift each strip from the counter and twist 360 degrees before placing it on a greased cookie sheet. (Twists should look like a bow tie with the spice mixture facing up at both ends.) Place twists about ¾-inch apart. Cover shaped dough and let raise until double (about 30 minutes). Bake at 350 degrees for 8 to 10 minutes or until golden brown.

Makes 4 dozen twists.

Optional Icing*
4 ounces cream cheese, softened
2 cups powdered sugar
¼ cup evaporated milk (regular milk works too)
¼ teaspoon vanilla

Mix softened cream cheese until smooth. Add powdered sugar and mix until smooth. Add evaporated milk and vanilla; mix until smooth. Add more milk or powdered sugar until icing is slightly runny.

*Pretty much any leftover frosting could also work as the icing. Simply warm frosting to room temperature and add milk until "dippable."

Note: Breanna feels the recipe is fussy, but she'll still eat them ☺.

CHAPTER 17

Sadie stood up straight and spun around to get Pete's attention, but of course he was still outside.

"Help me," the voice said again, this time clearer.

"Who is this?" Sadie said, her heart rate increasing as a rush of heat overcame her.

"It's me," the voice answered.

"Who?"

"Delores."

Sadie froze. "Delores Wapple?" Mrs. Wapple didn't have a phone, did she?

"Help me," the voice said again.

"O-okay," Sadie said, walking to the living room to look out the front window. The house appeared just as it always did, gray and dismal. The snow was still falling, whitewashing everything. "What do you need help with?"

The line went dead.

"Hello?" Sadie said into the phone. "Mrs. Wapple? Delores? Hello?"

There was no one there. Sadie pulled the phone from her ear

and scrolled to see the most recent number on the caller ID. The screen said NO DATA.

She ran to the back door. Pete looked up when the door opened. He must have read the alarm on her face because he stood quickly and took a step toward her. She met him halfway across the yard.

"Mrs. Wapple just called me," she said as snowflakes landed on her hair. She held out the cordless phone as though that alone was proof. "She said she needed help, and then the line went dead."

Pete stared at Sadie, then past her shoulder and into the house. The situation was wearing on him, and in that moment Sadie realized how affected he was by all of this and decided she wouldn't put more on his shoulders; she'd do this one herself. Her decision was encouraged by the fact that he was keeping something from her. She was trying hard not to judge him for that, or overanalyze it, but it showed that they were still two individuals. He was entitled to deal with things his way, and she was entitled to deal with things her way.

"I'm going over there," she said, turning back to the house.

"What?" He put a hand on her arm. She'd forgotten to grab her coat, and his wet glove made her take a sharp breath.

"She called for help. You stay with the boys, and I'll be right back, okay?"

Pete shook his head, but she pretended not to notice. She didn't have time to consider his opinion on this. "I'll be right back," she said again before she pushed through the back door and hurried through the house and down the front steps, careful not to slip on the snow-slick pavement.

She grabbed her phone on her way through the house but was crossing the street before she realized she still hadn't grabbed her coat. No way was she going back inside and opening herself up to discussing this with Pete.

She didn't even attempt the front door this time, knowing it was sealed, and went straight to the nearly hidden gate. In an instant, her last visit to Delores's backyard came back, and she relived the heart-stopping panic she'd felt when Delores's face had suddenly appeared on the other side of the glass. She did not relish encountering anything like that again and questioned why she was here after the break-in that afternoon. But the voice on the phone had asked for help. Sadie simply couldn't ignore that, so she carefully entered the backyard and made her way to the patio. Snow clung to the grass but had melted over most of the bricks of the patio, making it wet and slippery.

Sadie took a breath and was about to knock on the sliding glass door when she noticed that it wasn't closed all the way. The edge of the doormat inside the house had come up just enough to prevent the door from sliding the last quarter of an inch. A wave of trepidation raced down Sadie's spine. It seemed someone had closed the door in a hurry, and yet there were no footprints in the dusting of snow that would indicate a recent exit or entrance to the house—at least not on the grass.

She knocked. "Delores?" she called loudly. It felt strange to call her by her first name, as though they had a basis for that kind of familiarity. After a moment, she called again, "Mrs. Wapple?"

No one answered and Sadie glanced toward the gate. Should she get Pete? Urgency took her forward instead of back, and she slid the door open, smooth and fluid in its tracks. "Delores?" she called again, leaning inside. "Mrs. Wapple? It's Sadie Hoffmiller. What's wrong?"

No answer.

All the blinds were closed, as they'd been yesterday, and as she took a step onto the tile, she squinted in an attempt to help her eyes adjust to the dim interior. The sunroom area, if that's what it was, went back about eight feet. Two tiled steps led up to a small kitchen, with a hallway shooting off to the left. Everything was as cluttered as the sitting area was. She could see part of one doorway down the hall that had a light on—the only light on in the house. A den, perhaps? With her eyes on the lit room, Sadie dodged clutter and followed a thin trail that headed toward the tiled steps.

"Mrs. Wapp—" Her shoe hit something, and when her foot hit the ground, it slid across the floor. She stumbled, catching herself on the back of the wicker settee and sending a pile of magazines and papers that had been balanced there to the floor. Once she righted herself, she looked down at whatever she'd kicked over and gasped at the pool of red oozing liquid quickly overtaking the magazines at her feet.

Blood?

She scrambled backward, realizing her shoes were covered in it, and clamped her hand over her mouth to keep from screaming before she noted the pungent, chemical smell. Her eyes were adjusting to the darkness, and she could make out an overturned can not far from the puddle and partially concealed by an old tablecloth thrown over an end table.

Paint?

She fumbled for the light switch on the wall. The three steps to the switch were sticky and slick with her shoes covered in paint. Once the lights were on, she bent over enough to assure herself that it was red paint, not blood. The face of a Labrador retriever on the front of one of the magazines was slowly being engulfed by the growing red pool. Sadie could just make out the white address label in the bottom corner before it disappeared completely.

Her relief at not having stepped in a pool of blood was short-lived when she realized she'd just tracked wet paint across half the room. Her face heated up as she imagined how she was going to explain this horrendous mess. Then she wondered what a spilled can of paint was doing on the floor anyway. Had she kicked it over? Was that what her foot had hit? But a can of paint would be heavy. She hadn't hit it very hard, and yet the puddle was still expanding, proof that the paint hadn't already been there when she came in. A look at her hands caused her to jump again when she discovered paint on her fingers as well. The whole wall just inside the sliding glass door had been freshly painted red. Since she'd fumbled for the light, the paint was all over her hands too.

She felt horrible about the mess and confused at what was happening. Mrs. Wapple was painting? Then she remembered Mrs. Wapple's call for help. Was this some kind of setup? Her spine prickled and her stomach tightened. What was going on here?

"Delores!" she shouted. "Mrs. Wapple!"

She turned her attention toward the lit room again, able to see a portion of the doorway from where she stood. What should she do? She could leave and tell Pete what happened, or she could take off her shoes and investigate the room. The fear that she wasn't safe here was strong, but she had faith in her abilities to deal with that. What she didn't have faith in was anyone else finding the answers if she left this undone right now.

After a moment's hesitation, she bent down and began pulling at the laces of her wet and paint-covered sneakers, her adrenaline pushing her forward. Her heart rate sped up as questions began colliding into one another in her mind. There wasn't any other painting paraphernalia scattered about, so why the paint can? And why was the house so dark? It was four thirty in the afternoon. Once Sadie had unlaced her shoes, she stepped out of them and left them where they were as she hurried toward the stairs, being more careful where she put her feet this time.

"Mrs. Wapple," Sadie yelled, in a voice louder and more concerned than she'd been using so far. "Mrs. Wapple, are you there?"

As she passed through the kitchen, she looked around. Like the sitting area, the kitchen was not tidy. There were piles of papers, empty cans, and a sink full of dishes. It smelled like overripe fruit, something Sadie had smelled yesterday. She crinkled her nose and turned back to the hallway. "Mrs. Wapple," she called again. "What's going on here? What's—" She stopped short, almost skidding to a halt on the kitchen linoleum.

She could see into the doorway of the lit room. There was some clothing strewn around the floor, but her attention was fixed on a single shoe poking out from behind the bed. Just one. It wasn't on its side as though flung aside; rather, the toe pointed toward the ceiling like the Wicked Witch of the East's feet did after the farmhouse fell on her in *The Wizard of Oz*. Sadie's heart began to race with the implications. Was there a foot in that shoe? A foot connected to a body hidden from her view by the bed?

"Mrs. Wapple?" she said, her voice almost a whisper. She took a single step into the room before stopping. She stared at the shoe and tried to swallow the lump in her throat as a quick reminder of all the bodies she'd seen over the last year played through her head. *It isn't another dead body,* Sadie chided herself. *You're overreacting.* But she couldn't make her feet move forward. What if it *was* a body? Mrs. Wapple's body. The title of the article Jane had written about her last summer came to mind: "Modern Miss Marple: A Magnet for Murder." It was a clever alliteration, she knew that, but it wasn't normal how many cases of homicide she'd stumbled into lately. Was she prepared to find Mrs. Wapple dead in her bedroom?

"You just spoke to her," she said out loud. Her words felt weighed down by the walls that seemed to be moving in on her.

"Help me."

Sadie whipped her head around. The voice hadn't come from the bedroom, but from further down the hall, where the boxes stacked along both sides of the hallway blocked any light.

"Who's there?" Sadie asked into the heavy darkness, her voice shaking. She looked back at the shoe, still trying to decide what to do.

"Help me, Sadie," the voice said again—the same voice Sadie had heard on the phone and the same voice she thought she'd heard in her bedroom last night right before the door had slammed shut. Suddenly a burst of air came from the direction of the hallway like a gust of wind: chill and . . . wet?

Fear streaked through Sadie like a lightning bolt, and she ran into the lit room, slamming the door closed behind her. Then she turned and felt the room begin to spin as she looked at Mrs. Wapple laying on her back between the bed and the wall, peaceful in her repose other than the deep red blood, the same color as the paint, that was matted to the side of her head and pooling into the carpet.

CHAPTER 18

The scene didn't make sense, or, rather, Sadie couldn't make sense of it as her thoughts became suddenly sluggish. Why was Mrs. Wapple lying there like that? An uncharacteristic darkness pulled over Sadie's eyes, and she felt herself falling backward against the wall. Her breathing was coming in jagged clumps, and she gripped her chest as though she could force her lungs to fully inflate. She blinked several times, ordering herself to retain her senses, and after a few seconds the air began to clear. She could see again, but the scene before her hadn't changed. Sadie swallowed, still gasping for air as though she'd run a mile.

"Mrs. Wapple?" she croaked, taking a step forward as tears filled her eyes. "Oh, please . . ."

Mrs. Wapple didn't move, but as Sadie lowered herself to her knees, knowing she needed to check for a pulse, she noticed Mrs. Wapple's chest rise and fall. Sadie was finally able to take a full breath of her own. Mrs. Wapple was alive!

To make certain, Sadie carefully took Mrs. Wapple's wrist; it was cold and limp in her hand, but she checked for a pulse, relieved when she felt the slight expanding of Mrs. Wapple's artery beneath her fingers, weak but apparent.

She isn't dead, Sadie said to herself as tears overflowed and ran down her cheeks. *She isn't dead.*

But she was in serious need of help.

She stood up, reaching for her phone in her pocket. She turned on her sock-clad heel, pulling open the door of the bedroom and running for the sliding glass door.

In her haste she forgot about the paint and slid across the tile in her socks. A pile of boxes was the only thing she could grab for, but they weren't steady and she pulled them down with her as she fell. She landed hard on her side with an "oomph" as the contents of the boxes spilled all over the paint-covered floor. Spools of thread, some pens, and numerous papers went everywhere. Sadie's phone was somewhere in the midst of the new mess she'd made, and she got on her knees, scrambling to find it in the debris. She was moments away from abandoning the phone completely when she found it partially covered in wet paint. She tried to wipe off the paint with the clean tail of her blouse as she ran into the backyard.

The run across the yard wasn't very long, but as soon as she was out of the house she began to doubt everything she'd seen. Paint on the wall. Spilled paint on the floor. Dark house. A single light in a single room. The strangeness made Sadie want to go back and verify all the details before she pulled Pete in, but then she pictured Mrs. Wapple unconscious on the floor and she sped up. A car honked as she ran into the street; she hadn't looked both ways. She waved her apology but didn't break her stride. She ran up the front steps of Jared and Heather's house and threw open the door.

"Pete!" she called out breathlessly. Was he still outside? "Pete!"

He looked up from the table, where he was helping Fig stir some mini-marshmallows into his hot cocoa. As soon as Pete saw her, he straightened, dropped the spoon, and hurried toward her.

"What happened?"

Confused by his intensity, Sadie looked down and saw the red paint on her hands and smeared down the left side of her pants and shirt where she'd fallen on the tile. She hadn't even registered the pain from the fall when it happened, but now it caught up to her as her hip began to burn and her shoulder throbbed. She hurried back to the parquet wood by the front door, not wanting to get paint on the carpet.

"Blood!" Kalan blurted out.

Sadie looked past Pete to see Kalan staring at her with wide eyes. Fig sipped his cocoa with his spoon, and Chance spun around in his chair to look at her.

"It's not blood," Sadie hurried to assure them. "It's—"

"Paint?" Pete said, leaning closer and sniffing. He lifted his hands as though he wanted to put them on her shoulders and hold her still, but inches away from her, he changed his mind and took a step back while looking her over.

Sadie nodded, feeling oddly vulnerable beneath his inspection. "Yes, it's paint." She gave the three boys a fake smile as she reached for Pete's hand. "Everything's fine," she said in a high-pitched voice. She could feel herself beginning to shake as the shock set in. "Keep drinking your cocoa."

Pete pulled his hand out of reach, and she looked down to see the paint on her fingers. "What's going on?" he asked quietly, looking at her with an intensity she didn't like. It felt accusatory somehow.

Sadie took a breath and explained it all in two sentences, finishing with, "We need to call 911." Her phone! She held it up in both

PUMPKIN ROLL

hands and realized the 911 call she'd attempted at the house had been dropped at some point. Pete headed down the hallway toward the bedrooms.

"Where are you going?" Sadie said, stepping toward him before remembering the carpet and moving back to her square of fake wood.

"You'll need to stay with the boys," he called back to her.

Sadie bent over and peeled off her paint- and snow-drenched socks and balled them up by the door before hurrying to the doorway of his room, careful not to touch anything. She watched as he dug into his suitcase and pulled out the leather clip with his badge attached. Then he punched in the code to his portable gun safe and grabbed another magazine; he'd been wearing his shoulder harness all day.

"Why are you taking your gun?" Sadie said, scared that he was armed for some reason. Maybe it just made it that much more serious. She held her phone in both hands, knowing she needed to call 911, but . . .

Pete glanced at her, and she immediately recognized his detective-face expression. "Promise me you'll stay here." He put the magazine in his front pocket. "Don't change your clothes. And don't wash your hands either. Call 911." He nodded toward the phone she was still clutching.

"Of course," Sadie said. He pushed past her, causing her to lean against the wall, but she stepped away quickly for fear of painting the doorway.

Sadie followed Pete down the hall, wishing she was going with him, but then feeling glad she wasn't. "Go through the backyard, and mind the paint inside the sliding glass door."

Pete headed toward the front door while Sadie punched in the

163

numbers for 911 a second time. Kalan was watching her carefully—scared—and Sadie tried to give him a reassuring smile as she went into the living room and watched Pete disappear through the gate leading to Mrs. Wapple's backyard.

It was all so surreal, and she found herself still questioning what she'd seen as she put the phone to her ear and listened to it ring on the other end. What if she'd somehow created this in her mind? What if it wasn't real? The heavily accented voice on the other end of the phone brought her back to reality with a sharp sting. "This is the 911 dispatchah. What's ya emahgency?"

CHAPTER 19

For the next hour and a half everything was sheer chaos. Sadie put a movie on for the boys while she answered the dispatcher's questions, but it only diverted their attention until the first siren came blaring down their street. There were two more patrol cars, an ambulance, and a newspaper reporter within minutes of the first responder. Pete stayed at Mrs. Wapple's house, which meant Sadie had no idea what was going on. She closed the curtains and tried to keep the boys distracted from what was happening outside, finally resorting to letting them eat chocolate chips straight from the bag and turning the sound on the movie way up.

Per Pete's instructions, she didn't change her clothes, but she could feel everyone staring at her when an officer came to the door and invited her outside so she could talk to him without the boys overhearing. She put on her clogs but didn't dare grab a coat for fear that the paint might still be wet in some places. The left side of her body was saturated with it; she could feel her clothing sticking to her skin.

It was nearly dark outside and she shivered on the porch amid the lightly falling snow, though no one else seemed bothered by the weather. Another officer stood inside the front door, keeping an eye on the boys. The ambulance was already gone.

"Had you evah been in Mrs. Wapple's house before this aftahnoon?" the officer asked.

"No," Sadie said, trying not to notice the reporter standing on the sidewalk writing frantic notes as he looked at her, covered in red paint. "I hadn't been inside—just in the backyard yesterday. Is she okay?"

"She's stable, if that's wha' you mean," the officer said, skimming his notes. "She'll be fully assessed at the hospital."

"Thank goodness," Sadie said, bouncing on the balls of her feet in an attempt to warm up.

"You went ovah to her house today because of a phone call whe' Mrs. Wapple asked for help?"

"Yes," Sadie nodded and shifted her weight. She was freezing.

"How did you know it was Mrs. Wapple?"

"She said she was Delores."

"What exactly did the callah say?"

"She said 'Help me' over and over, and when I asked who it was, she said Delores."

"And yet you also believed this to be the same woman who broke into your house ahlier today. Why did you go ovah?"

"Because she said she needed help."

"Why not call the police?"

"Because it felt urgent."

"Were you, perhaps, angry with hah and wantin' a confrontation?"

Sadie stared at him and could no longer ignore the trap being spun around her. Anger began rising in her chest and neck. They could not think she had done this. "I know it looks bad," she said, waving toward the paint that had dried solid on her clothes. "But I did not hurt her. Why would I? I went over there to help her. Trace the number—whoever made the call set me up."

He didn't answer her but kept taking notes.

She noticed Pete and another officer exit the gate at Mrs. Wapple's. Someone had let him get his coat at some point, or had he grabbed it on his way out the front door? For a moment she thought he was coming back to the house, but the officer stopped and the two of them continued talking on Mrs. Wapple's sidewalk, Pete glancing up at her every so often. Sadie wondered if he was answering the same type of questions she was.

After another volley of accusations meant to sound like questions from the officer she was talking to, Sadie watched as Pete crossed the street, only to be stopped by yet another officer. She wanted so much for him to be next to her, supporting her, not looking at her like she was a criminal.

"I undahstand you called social sahvices this mornin' to report a problem with Delores Wapple," the officer said.

"Um, no, I didn't place the call. Pete Cunningham did." She inclined her head toward Pete, who was standing just outside the chain-link fence surrounding Jared and Heather's yard. An officer opened the gate and Sadie noted that it didn't squeak. When had Pete oiled it? Had she remembered to ask him to? "When we saw her outside a couple of nights ago she seemed to be in a lot of pain. Our attempts to contact her family were unsuccessful."

"Why, exactly, were you so detahmined to involve yourself with this woman who you don't know and who you felt was harassing you?"

Pete was suddenly beside her. Finally. He took her elbow and steered her away from the officer, explaining he'd return her in just a moment. His voice must have held the right amount of authority, since the officer didn't try to stop him and instead turned his full attention to the notes he'd been taking.

When they were a few feet away, Pete let go and leaned toward her, lowering his voice. "They want you to go to the station."

Sadie's heart jumped. "Why?"

Pete simply looked down at her paint-covered clothes. "They say they need pictures."

"They say?"

"They are being very careful about what they tell me, probably because I'm with another department and they feel like I'm critiquing their investigation. I don't know. I've never dealt with a case outside of my own jurisdiction."

Panic began setting in. She didn't want to go to the police station. She didn't want pictures taken, questions asked. "But why would they have me come down? Do they think I attacked her?"

"It's a reasonable conclusion for them to reach," Pete said, looking past her and scowling at the reporter who was talking to one of the other officers. "But we're in a bit of a catch-22. If you don't go, they'll think we're hiding something. If you do go, however, you'll likely be subjected to further questioning and . . . I can't be there with you." His voice fell for the last part of his explanation. Sadie nearly asked why he couldn't be there, but then realized that if they were going to question her officially, the only person she could ask for was an attorney. She didn't know any attorneys in Boston! Heck, she didn't know any attorneys in Colorado except Frank Barton, who went to her church. But he handled divorce cases, not criminal accusations.

"Heather couldn't get a flight out of Dallas until early tomorrow morning," Pete continued.

"Does she know what's happened?" Sadie asked, her stomach in knots. It didn't take much imagination to picture what it would feel like to be thousands of miles away from your children when something like this happened. Even as easygoing as Heather seemed to be, this was way up on the list of things to panic about while out of town.

"Jared called to give me the flight information about twenty minutes ago and I updated him on what's happened since we last spoke." Pete shook his head and pushed his hand through his hair. "I can't just leave the kids with a neighbor."

"No," Sadie said, pulling herself up by her emotional bootstraps. She'd met the neighbors and none of them were the type she'd trust with Pete's grandchildren. "You can't leave them, especially now. I'll be fine."

"You're sure you're okay?" Pete asked, his eyebrows pulled together with concern.

"I have nothing to hide, and I know how to handle myself," she assured him, which reminded her that he *did* have something to hide: Michaels.

Pete nodded. "I'm so sorry, Sadie," he whispered, lifting a hand and running the backs of his fingers down her cheek.

Sadie's entire body reacted to his touch, warming up instantly. She reached up and took his hand in her own. "Sorry for what? This isn't your fault." But had he made it worse by not calling the police sooner? Was she jumping to conclusions? She wished they could talk about it right now. With the police around, though, that wasn't going to happen.

"This isn't how I wanted this trip to go," Pete said.

Sadie smiled reassuringly. "I know that," she said, taking a step closer so that their foggy breath blended together. "And I'll be fine, okay?"

Pete nodded. "If you start feeling like they're painting you into a corner, stop answering their questions."

Sadie raised her eyebrows. "Really?"

"They need to find someone to blame this on—nothing's as unsettling to a cop as a crime without a perpetrator—and you're the most logical assumption. Until or unless they find someone else who makes a better suspect than you do, you're in the hot seat."

"Well," Sadie said, trying to sound strong as she attempted to lighten the heaviness that had quickly descended. Her smile, however, was shaky at best. "My feet are numb, and I can't feel my nose, so maybe a hot seat wouldn't be too bad right about now."

CHAPTER 20

They did, indeed, take pictures of Sadie at the police station. Pictures of her hands, feet, hair, and clothing. After they'd had her stand and turn and pose two dozen different ways, they handed her some gray hospital scrubs and asked her to change. Sadie suspected this was standard dress code for the inmates they booked into jail and didn't like the idea of looking like one of them.

"What will happen to my clothes?" Sadie asked the female officer, Officer Gall, who had accompanied her through the police station.

"You really think that paint's gonna come out?" the woman asked her, lifting her thinly penciled eyebrows, which were stark against her fresh-looking face. Her hair was pulled back into a severe bun, but the woman couldn't be older than twenty-five. "They'll be filed with the other evidence."

"Evidence," Sadie repeated, pausing at the doorway of the little room where she'd been told she could change her clothes. She'd really liked those jeans; they didn't make her hips look nearly as wide as most styles did. The idea of her clothes being evidence—tagged and indexed in some computer somewhere—was kind of creepy. Would that show up on her police record?

The room was solid concrete, with no windows or mirrors, and Sadie was glad they didn't make her undress in front of someone else. That would be terribly embarrassing. The paint had dried against her skin, and she had to peel off the clothes in places. Patches of paint were left behind all over her left side. Hopefully it was a basic latex paint that would come off with a little soap. The scrubs fit like a cloth garbage sack, and she was glad there was no mirror for her to see how they looked. She folded her paint-covered clothes as best she could—the paint had dried quite stiff, making it tricky to get it right—and let herself out of the room where Officer Gall was waiting for her.

"Gray's never really been my color," Sadie said, trying to smile as she handed over the clothes. "So I guess it's good you took my picture already." Her fingers still had several spots of paint on them that she hadn't been able to wash off after the pictures.

Officer Gall smiled politely and took the clothes.

"This way, Mrs. Hoffmiller," another female officer said. Wait, no, this was a female *detective*. Sadie didn't have much experience with female detectives, but she followed her obediently until they came to the door of what Sadie knew to be an interrogation room. She stopped and looked up at the woman holding open the door. She was Latino or Greek or something, with her hair pulled back in a bun just like Officer Gall's and the same no-nonsense expression Sadie had seen on Pete's face when he was working a case.

"They said I was just coming here for some photos," Sadie said, tugging at the hem of her top.

The woman nodded and then smiled a smile that didn't reach her eyes. "And since you're here, we thought we'd ask a few questions—it's all about efficiency." Efficiency Sadie could understand, but she doubted that was the only motivation for this interrogation. She decided to play it out a little longer and entered the room, sitting down on one of the hard metal chairs as casually and comfortably as she could.

The detective—she hadn't given her name yet—took the opposite chair, holding Sadie's gaze for a few seconds. Sadie didn't let herself get stared down, but when the detective finally looked away, she wondered if maybe she should have allowed the other woman to win.

The detective put a file down on the table between them and pulled open the cover, scanning the page before looking up again. "I must say this is one of the most interesting records I've ever read," she began, watching Sadie carefully. "Not even a speeding ticket up until a year ago, then . . ." She let out a breath, closing the folder and leaning back in her chair. "Maybe you can summarize it for me," she said, smiling in a way that was not at all comforting. "Paint me a picture, so to speak."

Sadie hesitated for a minute but remembered she'd told Pete she had nothing to hide. Why should she play games? Not giving her own explanation wouldn't help anything, so she might as well keep her power and show them that she was on the same side of this as they were.

"Well," she said, tucking her hair behind her ears. "It all started when my neighbor was murdered last year. She'd been baking, or at least that's what it seemed like when . . ."

Sadie had just gotten to her adventure in Florida when there was a knock at the door. She stopped talking and blinked a couple of times to reorient herself to the right time and place. It was easy to become lost in her past adventures, especially when she had such an interested audience.

Detective Lucille—that was her last name, not her first name—was still leaning back in her chair, but her posture had become looser as Sadie had unloaded her recent history. Without a word, Detective Lucille rose, opened the door six inches, and whispered something that Sadie couldn't hear. After about thirty seconds, she shut the door and turned back to Sadie.

"That's rather fascinating," the detective said, sitting down and looking at her watch. Sadie could only guess that she was commenting on Sadie's recent history and not on the secret conversation she'd just had through the door. "So, what brought you to Boston?"

"Babysitting," Sadie said, wishing she could continue the story she'd been telling. She didn't like fast-forwarding through Florida, especially the end.

"And how did you meet Delores Wapple?"

Sadie didn't feel any hesitation in sharing exactly how she knew Delores Wapple. She didn't leave out anything.

"You believe in ghosts, then, Mrs. Hoffmiller?" Detective Lucille asked after Sadie explained about the voice she'd heard the night before and the lights that came on once the power returned.

"Not really," Sadie said, then frowned. She didn't believe in ghosts—never had. So why hadn't she just said no?

"But you said yourself that there was no explanation."

"I don't think ghosts are an explanation," Sadie said quickly. "Someone must be wanting it to seem supernatural, that's all."

"And who would do that?" the detective asked. There was a new undercurrent in her voice. Sadie suspected that talking about these inexplicable things was making her sound crazy, but how could she leave things out if she was determined to be completely honest with the police?

"I—I don't know," Sadie said with a surrendering shrug. "I've been assuming it was Mrs. Wapple." She paused, leaning forward slightly. "And, as horrible as this sounds, do you think she could have hurt herself on purpose?"

"Why would she do that?"

"Well, a vendetta of some kind."

"A vendetta against you?"

Sadie nodded. "I mean, look at all the weird things happening: her hat in our house, and then her calling me to come over only to find her suddenly unconscious. Maybe she wasn't really unconscious, but just pretending so that I'd get in trouble. After all, I was covered in paint, making it impossible for me to pretend I wasn't there, right?"

"She'd have to really hate you to go through all that trouble, don't you think?"

The idea of anyone hating her was hard to take, but she was the one who'd thrown out the hypothesis. "I guess," Sadie said, slumping in her chair. "All I did was take her some cookies."

That reminded her of Gabrielle. Should Sadie mention her? Was it important? She was hesitant to get into that part of the story because she wasn't sure what the police would make of her going to the banquet last night.

"Ri-ight," the detective said, leaning forward and putting her elbows on the table. She looked at Sadie hard, as though she could read her thoughts, and her intensity rendered Sadie absolutely silent. She wished the other woman *could* read minds, then she'd know Sadie was telling the truth.

Detective Lucille looked at Sadie in silence for nearly ten full seconds; Sadie waited her out, not sure what other option she had.

When Detective Lucille spoke, her voice sounded loud in the small room. "I'm going to check out a few of these details. I'll probably need you to come back tomorrow so we can finish up—is that a problem?"

"I'm happy to help," Sadie said, glad to hear they were done for the day. She was relieved no one had read a Miranda warning to her and that she hadn't said anything that would make them hold her at the police station. That meant she'd done a good job, right?

"We appreciate your cooperation," the detective said, standing up and taking a moment to straighten her slacks. They had bunched up at the top of her thigh, leaving unsightly wrinkles behind. No doubt the bunched-up fabric had been cutting into the detective's legs as well, making them as uncomfortable to sit in as they looked.

"You ought to look into wide-leg slacks," Sadie said helpfully as she stood. But her smile fell when she met Detective Lucille's eyes. "You've got wide hips like I do," Sadie said quickly, wanting to soften the other woman's expression by explaining why she'd brought up the subject and pointing out their similarities. "I find that a wider leg gives me the best compliment, evening out my curves and drawing attention away from my problem areas. Plus the fabric isn't so tight on my thighs that it climbs, ya know?"

The detective continued to stare at her for a moment, and Sadie swallowed as the scrutiny seemed to press upon her. Surely Detective Lucille could appreciate the tip, right? Sadie had been grateful for it when Joann Proctor from the Senior Center had passed on the advice to her a few years back.

"Did you just tell me I have big hips?" Detective Lucille finally said.

"Oh, well, I didn't mean to imply that was a bad thing, just that . . ." Sadie began. Detective Lucille stared at her with a flat expression. "Um, I just meant to point out that certain styles were more, uh, flattering than others when . . ." She looked at the ground and kicked at a crack in the concrete floor with the toe of her clog as her face and neck began to burn. "Never mind."

"Uh-huh," the woman said, turning toward the door. Sadie made a mental note not to comment on the body shape or size of any law enforcement officers in the future—well, maybe anyone who wasn't a really good friend would be insulted. It wasn't worth the risk. She followed the detective, her cheeks flaming at having made the unintended insult. They walked through a series of hallways toward the front of the police station.

"Your daughter's been waiting for half an hour," Detective Lucille said. "She said she'd take you home."

"My daughter?" Sadie took a few quick steps in an attempt to catch up with the other woman. Not only did Detective Lucille have wide hips, but she had long legs as well. Sadie must have misunderstood her comment that Breanna, Sadie's daughter, was here to give her a ride home. Breanna was in England eating crumpets and shepherd's pie in between cleaning out monkey cages.

They reached a door and Detective Lucille held it open, leaving just enough room for Sadie to go through, which she did.

"You just be sure not to leave Boston for another day or two, you understand?"

"Of course," Sadie said. "I don't have anywhere else to go."

"We'll be calling."

Sadie looked out into the lobby area of the station and watched as a tall woman with bright auburn hair stood up from a chair. Her hair was short and spiky on one side, but arched over to the other side where the spiky points softened into smooth and sleek layers that followed the curve of her face in a way that was almost flattering. Not Breanna. Jane Seeley.

Jane threw a magazine on the chair and stretched her red lips into a huge grin that did little to soften the sharp features of her face. Her fingernails were bright purple, and she wore a black-and-white striped shirt—vertical stripes, not horizontal like a convict—and light-blue skinny jeans. She wore red sneakers and red hoop earrings in graduating sizes in all six piercings in her ears.

"Mama," she said loudly, heading toward Sadie. "You finally ready to go? I've been waiting for, like, ever, and this place smells like socks."

CHAPTER 21

Sadie felt she had no choice but to play along with Jane until they left the station and hurried toward a little red compact car Sadie remembered well. Jane had driven all the way to the East Coast for her article? Wow.

The police had kept Sadie's clothes but given her back the coat they'd let her grab before they left the house, and for that she was grateful. It was nearly 8:30 and had been dark for hours. Once the sun went down, the day had turned from chilly to brittle. The snow had stopped and was mostly melted, except for where it clung to the concrete in patches. Once they were inside the car, Jane started the engine and cranked the heater.

"What are you doing here?" Sadie finally asked as Jane pulled into the traffic on Washington Street. "And why did you tell them you were Breanna?"

"I didn't tell them I was *Breanna*, just that I was your daughter. I worried they'd make a big deal about me seeing you if I didn't claim to be family."

"And how did you know I was there?"

"Pete called Shawn, Shawn called me, and I called Pete and,

voilà, I dropped everything to come to your rescue." She looked over at Sadie and smiled, very pleased with herself. Jane's new hairstyle was, as usual, too trendy for Sadie's tastes, and the new hair color too bold for Jane's skin tone, which was on the pale side. And her clothes had to belong to a very tall fourteen-year-old somewhere. That Jane would lie to the police about who she was wasn't all that surprising—she was Jane, after all—but Sadie hoped it wouldn't come back to hurt her later. Should Sadie call Detective Lucille when she got home and explain?

"Aren't you glad I came?" Jane asked.

"Yes, I am," Sadie said, not wanting to be ungracious. She decided that voicing her concerns about Jane's lie to the police wasn't necessarily a priority. "But you didn't have to drop everything. I'm sure the officers would have taken me home."

"Maybe," Jane said. "After they parboiled you, mashed you into a pie, and baked you at five hundred degrees."

Cooking analogies were not Jane's strong suit, though Sadie was impressed Jane knew what parboiled meant. "It wasn't like that," she said, unsure of why she felt the need to defend the police. They hadn't been overly nice to Sadie, but they hadn't been terrible either. They were just doing their job. She smoothed the fabric of her gray scrub pants and realized that no one had told her how and when to give the clothes back. She certainly had no reason to keep them, though they were rather comfortable in a shapeless and unattractive way.

Jane turned onto Green Street and became part of the slow-moving herd of vehicles on the narrow street. "Oh, honey," Jane said as though talking to a child. "It is *so* like that."

"No offense," Sadie said, trying to keep her tone easy, "but you've only been here for the ride home, so you don't know the whole story."

Jane smiled and picked up her iPhone from the middle console. With one hand on the steering wheel, she started toggling through her phone.

Sadie double-checked her seat belt to make sure it was secure. "Um, I don't think it's safe to be—"

She was cut off by the sound of a horn from the car behind them. Traffic had sped up but Jane had not. Sadie startled, but Jane caught up with the other cars without even acknowledging the problem.

"Here you go," she said, handing the phone over to Sadie. "Tell me what they left out." Her tone oozed vindication, and she made a quick jerk to the right, changing lanes fast enough to get honked at again.

Sadie took the phone somewhat reluctantly and pulled it closer to her face so she could read the tiny print. The first headline said "Colorado Woman Detained for Questioning in Jamaica Plain Assault."

"Goodness," Sadie said, scrolling down to the next one, which read "Jamaica Plain Woman Hospitalized; Is the Babysitter to Blame?" She could stomach only a few more titles before she put the phone back in the console and looked out the window, trying to get hold of her turbulent thoughts and emotions. *Not again* was the only thought that kept spinning through her mind.

The memory of another article that questioned her character was suddenly fresh in her mind. The writer of *that* article—the article that had changed everything for Sadie a few months ago—was sitting less than two feet away and driving like a true Bostonian.

"How could those stories be out so fast?" Sadie said. "It's only been a few hours."

"Do you have any idea how many reporters spend their day listening to police scanners in their cars so they can rush to the scene of a story?" She shook her head as though censuring this breed of ambulance chasers. "Once they grab hold of an angle, they don't let go."

"I'm tired of being an angle," Sadie said, folding her arms over her chest, her residual anger toward Jane resurfacing. She thought she'd gotten over the betrayal she'd felt when the article had come out last August, but perhaps not; her pain felt as sharp as ever at this moment.

Jane didn't answer, and they both remained silent for the rest of the drive. Sure enough, there were no less than six cars parked along the curb in front of Mrs. Wapple's house, where yellow tape stretched across the front door. As soon as Jane parked, a fresh-faced, twenty-something-year-old girl stepped out of a black Ford Escort and came toward them with a bright smile on her face as though applying to be their newest BFF. The doors of the other cars clicked open, and Sadie dropped her head, horrified by the new development. What would Heather and Jared think of their house being on the news?

"I've got this," Jane said, hurrying to get out of the car. By the time Sadie had opened her door, Jane was nose to nose with the girl, towering over her in both height and overall presence as she calmly but boldly told the woman in no uncertain terms that she was not welcome here. The other people kept a distance, but Jane looked them over to ensure they understood they were included in her instructions. Sadie wasn't sure whether to wait for Jane or not, but when she saw a man in a truck down the road snapping pictures, she hurried to the front door, certain that Jane could fend for herself. She just wanted to get away from it all and find her sanctuary.

Her foot was on the top step when the front door opened and Pete stepped out. He didn't hug her, but he smiled as he took her hand and pulled her inside. Once they were over the threshold with the door shut behind them, he gathered her in his arms, and Sadie heard and felt him let out a long, deep breath. Sadie closed her eyes and let herself completely melt into the embrace, wishing he would never let her go and that she could feel this safe, this secure, forever.

It didn't last long, however. A moment later there was a light tap and Sadie pulled out of the embrace to open the door. The reporters were chatting with each other on the street, but staying away from the house.

"Can I come in?" Jane asked when Sadie didn't invite her inside automatically. Sadie nodded quickly and stepped aside. As she closed the door, she noticed that Pete had installed the eyebolt while she'd been gone. She glanced at him, pointing toward it, and he shrugged as though he knew it was too little, too late. Sadie lifted the chain and slid it into the lock on the door, feeling better anyway.

Pete said a polite hello to Jane before turning to Sadie. "How'd it go?"

"Okay, I guess," Sadie said as Jane dropped onto the couch and immediately pulled her phone out of her pocket, texting or going online or something. Sadie took off her coat and hung it in the closet while she continued her explanation. "They said they might have more questions for me tomorrow and that I shouldn't go anywhere, but they didn't hold me, didn't even question me all that . . . energetically. Mostly they wanted me to explain my record."

"Good," Pete said with a sharp nod. "That's really good."

Sadie looked past him into the kitchen. "Is that pizza?" she asked, nodding toward the boxes as her stomach growled. Why hadn't they eaten the beans she'd made for dinner? Then she remembered the cinnamon twists she'd set out to rise just before going over to Mrs. Wapple's. They were surely ruined by now. What a waste.

"I'd already ordered it before I remembered you'd made those beans. Sorry. But the pizza helped take the boys' minds off everything else."

Sadie forgave Pete easily. Compared to everything else, wasted beans were barely worth noting.

"Pizza?" Jane said from the couch.

"Would you like some?"

Ten minutes later the three of them sat around the kitchen table. Jane was on her fourth slice of pizza, while Pete kept lifting and lowering his water glass, making rings on the Formica tabletop. Sadie had passed up reheated pizza in favor of dried-out beans. She was glad she'd tasted them that afternoon when they had been at their prime so she could fully appreciate how delicious they could be. She hadn't worked up the strength to check on the cinnamon twists still covered with a dish towel on the counter. There were only so many failures a girl could handle at one time.

"Thank you for bringing Sadie home," Pete said to Jane. "I hope it wasn't too much of an imposition."

"It was actually a nice break," Jane said. "I've been knee-deep in college kids for the last week and I'm ready for real conversations, if you know what I mean."

Shawn is a college kid, Sadie thought to herself, but she lacked the energy to worry about Shawn and Jane's possible relationship right now. "Will you be heading back tonight?" she asked.

"I already booked a room at the Longwood Inn over in Brookline. After I knew I was coming, I made some calls and lined up a couple interviews for tomorrow, adding a little Harvard into my Yale-heavy research."

"Oh, good," Sadie said, relieved that Jane hadn't come just for her. She was feeling more comfortable with her as the intensity of the police station experience wore off. "I'm glad you didn't waste your time, then."

Jane looked at her. "Helping you wasn't a waste of my time, if that's what you're implying."

That's exactly what Sadie had been implying, but she was embarrassed for having been caught. Jane continued. "I just like to multitask, that's all."

"Well, I really appreciate your help."

"No problem," Jane said with a quick shrug as she picked a piece of pepperoni off her pizza with her purple fingernails and popped it into her mouth. "I'll be around tomorrow too if you need help with anything else."

"Thanks," Sadie said. "That's very generous of you. The boys' mother will be back tomorrow evening, so I guess we'll be off the clock by then."

She looked up at Pete, noting the tightness around his eyes. He must still be feeling bad that this mess had happened on his watch. But Sadie was pretty confident that once Jared and Heather understood what had happened, they would calm down. She wondered why Pete didn't have the same confidence, however. Maybe because Jared was *his* son. Maybe because of the mysterious Michaels?

"So," Jane said, drawing out the word until both Sadie and Pete looked at her. "Shawn said some weird stuff's been going on around here."

Sadie and Pete shared a glance. "Did he?" Sadie asked, stalling for time.

Jane shrugged. "He was worried about you," she said. "And he needed to talk to someone—you know how he is."

Sadie did know how Shawn was; the boy had never been able to keep his thoughts and worries to himself. That detail of his personality made it strange that he was so good at the PI work he'd taken on these last few months. But that wasn't what held Sadie's attention. Instead she was trying to suppress the jealousy she felt at not being the one Shawn talked to. Jane was watching her intently so she simply nodded in response, hoping her face wasn't too easy to read.

"Well, after he told me about it," Jane continued, "I did a little research on Delores Wapple, just for the sake of curiosity, ya know, to see if she had any . . . connections to weird stuff."

"What kind of weird stuff?" Pete asked, leaning forward slightly. Sadie watched the detective mask descend over his face, a combination of careful intent and open-minded interest.

"Wicca, gypsies, poltergeists."

"You can research that kind of thing?" Sadie asked.

"Oh, yeah," Jane said with a nod. "If you know where to look."

Sadie didn't glance at Pete this time. They had both assured one another that they didn't believe in ghosts or witches, but Pete hadn't heard his name whispered in dark corners of two different homes. He hadn't had doors slammed in his face and wet gusts of wind come from empty hallways. Sadie didn't believe—*she didn't*—but she was curious and couldn't pretend otherwise.

"Did you find anything?" Pete asked when Sadie didn't.

"In fact, I did," Jane said, smiling triumphantly. "Her father fancied himself a kind of medium and wrote articles on things like séances and crossing over earthbound spirits."

Sadie and Pete both blinked at her, which apparently encouraged her to continue.

"He was one of the early experts in modern ghost hunting, and he was one of the first people to publicly introduce the idea that earthbound spirits were here by choice rather than some kind of damnation."

"Earthbound what?" Sadie asked. Surely she was not having this discussion.

Jane turned her dark brown eyes to Sadie. "Earthbound spirits are souls who have died but haven't gone into the light. Don't you ever watch *Ghost Whisperer* reruns?"

Sadie shook her head. "Not my kind of show." She looked up at Pete, who simply held her eyes before turning his attention back to Jane. Sadie was sure he wasn't buying any of this either, but he was used to letting people say whatever they wanted to while appearing to reserve judgment. Sadie wished she were better at that.

"Well, anyway," Jane said, "Daddy Wapple wrote about this stuff back in the late seventies. Most of what he wrote hasn't been archived digitally, but I found references to at least a dozen articles in old collections around the country. I found one or two of his articles online, though I had to dig forever to unearth them. They were very Melinda Gordon." She looked at Sadie. "That's Jennifer Love Hewitt's character in *Ghost Whisperer*—I can't believe you've never watched that show! Her husband is totally hot." She shook her head. "Anyway, if spirits don't go into the light when they die, they become earthbound spirits and can wreak havoc among the living. They are basically what we think of as ghosts."

"What kind of havoc?" Pete asked, still guiding the discussion.

"They thrive off energy, right? So, they get people all freaked out using air movement, temperature changes, and electrical surges. They can even move things sometimes, but they have to be totally ticked off to do stuff like that."

"Electrical surges?" Sadie repeated, thinking of the exploding lightbulbs and power issues they'd had.

"Big time into electrical," Jane said with a nod. "Energy is energy, so they mess with it." She shrugged like that was a small detail. "Anyway, isn't that kind of thing pretty similar to what you guys have been dealing with?"

Sadie and Pete remained silent, neither of them wanting to agree it was a possibility.

"So you believe that the experiences we have had are linked to ghosts?" Pete asked in a perfectly level voice.

Jane looked at him without apology. "Maybe." She said it simply, but Sadie's thoughts were going in a totally different direction while Jane continued speaking. "It's pretty rare for earthbounds to hurt people, but it's been known to happen. Daddy Wapple swore that they had a spirit in their home and that it liked to short out the toaster. That's how he first got involved in all that ghost busting stuff." She shrugged again.

"But why would spirits bug us?" Sadie said. "Heather said nothing like this has happened before. So why now?"

"Unfinished business is the number one reason earthbounds hang around," Jane said with an air of authority. "Maybe Daddy Wapple isn't done yet."

Sadie almost chuckled, it was that preposterous, but quickly moved forward in her own growing theory. "If the dad was into this stuff and believed in it, then that kind of interest likely trickled down to his children. Now, assuming that's what happened, and one of these children wanted to . . . bother someone, they would have a lot of information from which to draw to make things appear as though ghosts or spirits or something spectral was taking place, right?"

Sadie was thrilled to find a family history that supported the theory she'd already discussed with both Pete and Detective Lucille.

"Excellent point," Pete said, nodding. "But it still goes back to motive. Why do this?"

"If it's a spirit," Jane said, not letting go of that possibility, "they just like to stir the pot. You can get rid of them, though, and then things go back to normal. Easy breezy."

They all were quiet for a moment, until Pete pushed away from the table and stood, picking up his glass. "Well, regardless of who or . . . what is behind it, Mrs. Wapple isn't there anymore, the police are investigating now, not us, and I'm hopeful we'll get a full night's sleep tonight."

Sadie smiled, but she couldn't smile away the heaviness in her heart. As much as she wanted this to be done, it wasn't. The knowledge that Mrs. Wapple's father was involved in spirits and such was very uncomfortable to her and opened even more questions. "I wonder how Mrs. Wapple is doing," Sadie said as Pete took his glass to the sink.

Pete leaned against the counter. "I called the station for an update while you were gone. They didn't give me much, but they said that her skull had been fractured. Luckily, the knife wound in her side wasn't serious."

Sadie pushed her empty bowl of beans away, suddenly feeling sick to her stomach. "Has she regained consciousness? Is she going to be okay?" All along Sadie had assured herself that Mrs. Wapple would be fine. It made her feel very foolish to have assumed she hadn't been seriously injured.

"I don't know," Pete said, giving her a sympathetic look that helped her know he understood her concern for the Witch of Browden Street, weird or not. "They didn't tell me that."

Jane pulled out her phone again and started scrolling. "One of the articles talked about that." She kept scrolling, then stopped. "'The victim has regained consciousness and her condition has been upgraded to stable, though she will remain at the hospital for further evaluation,'" she read out loud.

"At least she's getting the care she needs," Sadie said, feeling a little better about the "further evaluation" part. "Hopefully social services will get involved and she'll end up in a better situation in the long run."

Sadie felt her desire to find answers drain out of her, replaced with fatigue and plain old sadness. She shook her head, more ready than ever to let this go. "Regardless of what might have been behind what's happened here, it's over now, right?"

"Let's hope so," Pete said, pushing away from the counter.

"In case it isn't, keep in mind that I came to help," Jane said. She put down a half-eaten piece of pizza and brushed her fingers off over the box, her bright purple nails flashing with the quick movement. "Any way I can." She stood up from the table and shrugged again. "It won't hurt my feelings if you want to leave it all at the feet of the police and let them figure it out, but I think we also need to face the facts." She looked straight at Sadie. "You have a history, this story is already in the press, and it's all just weird enough to get more and more attention from here on out. There's always the chance that it will just go away—let's hope it does—but if you decide to do a little homework on the sister, Mrs. Wapple, or even the possibility of ghosts, I'm happy to help." She paused a moment. "I mean, maybe figuring out some explanations would be a kind of closure to everything. Totally up to you, though."

CHAPTER 22

Sadie held Jane's eyes and decided to look at this from a different perspective. Jane wasn't trying to make her believe in phantoms—she wasn't even trying to make Sadie feel obligated to launch an investigation—she was just offering her help, and much less forcefully than she had in previous situations.

Sadie smiled and put her hand on the younger woman's arm as something much closer to gratitude and companionship pushed some of her doubt and hesitation out of the way. At Sadie's touch, Jane tensed a little bit and for a moment her assured expression dropped enough to show a whisper of vulnerability, reminding Sadie that it was usually a lot of hurt that created the toughest exteriors.

"Thank you, Jane," she said with sincerity. "For everything, really. I'll call you in the morning, okay?"

Jane nodded and took a step back, causing Sadie to drop her hand. "Okay," she said. "Do you need help with the dishes or anything?"

Jane was offering to do dishes? Sadie was seeing a whole new side of this girl tonight.

"Don't tell Sadie, but we used paper," Pete said, coming back to the table and sending a wink in Sadie's direction. "Thanks for the offer, though."

They walked Jane to the door and watched her climb into her car and drive away before Pete locked the front door and the new eye-bolt—checking it twice. There was still one car parked at the curb, but Sadie was encouraged that the other reporters had left. Hopefully that meant that something far more exciting had happened and they had tossed her story aside like a stale crust of bread.

The curtains had been drawn when the police were there earlier, and Pete hadn't bothered to open them up. For Sadie's part, there was nothing outside that window she had any interest in seeing.

"It was nice of Jane to come," Pete said, heading toward the back door, Sadie trailing behind him. "I was going nuts being here with the boys, knowing you were there alone. It was a huge relief when she called and said she was heading to the station." He locked the back door and slid the new chain into place. Sadie was so glad he'd remembered to install the extra security, even though she hoped there would be no need for it.

"It *was* really nice of her," Sadie agreed. She took a deep breath and let it out as Pete double-checked the window locks over the sink. She knew she should deal with the failed cinnamon twists and over-cooked beans tonight—she hated leaving the mess for morning—but she couldn't make herself do it. They weren't going anywhere, and she was completely overwhelmed by far more important things.

While Pete finished securing the house, Sadie waited for him to ask her some questions about the police station, or about exactly what had happened at Mrs. Wapple's house, but he seemed distracted somehow—not interested in talking things out. Strangely, that was okay with her. She was looking forward to the oblivion of sleep.

The two of them went through their nightly routines, and Sadie tried to ignore the intimacy of brushing their teeth next to one another in the bathroom. Pete finished first and gave Sadie a minty fresh kiss on the cheek before retiring to his room. Sadie closed the bathroom door and took a shower, scrubbing at the red paint still on her hands. When her skin was raw, but paint-free, she turned off the shower, dried off, and dressed in the pajamas she'd brought in earlier.

She opened the door a few inches to let the steam escape and began lathering on all the creams and serums that kept her looking a youthful fifty-two instead of her true age of fifty-seven. She was applying anti-crepe neck cream and thinking about how the paint can had been so perfectly rigged for her to kick over when the bathroom door suddenly opened. She jumped to the side and lifted both forearms in a block before seeing Pete standing there. She lowered her arms, both a little embarrassed by, and a little impressed with, her reflexive action.

"Sorry," he said with an apologetic smile. "Sneaking up on you probably isn't a good idea right about now."

"I'm a little keyed up, but it's good to know that taking the advanced self-defense course at the Y is paying off."

Pete nodded. "I just . . . Well, I was thinking about what you and Jane were discussing—about looking into Gabrielle or Mrs. Wapple tomorrow."

Sadie rubbed the excess cream into her hands; she didn't want to draw attention to her neck with Pete watching her in the mirror. She also hadn't made up her mind about if she would take Jane up on her offer. Part of her wanted to drop it completely, but the other part impelled her forward, encouraging her to learn everything she could. Her hair was still wet and she felt a drip of water slide down the back of her pajamas—the pink-and-white polka-dotted ones she only wore when she wanted to look nice in her jammies.

"Do you trust me?" Pete asked suddenly.

She leaned against the counter as she continued rubbing the lotion into her hands. "What kind of question is that?" she asked, trying to keep her tone light despite the fact that the name Michaels surfaced in her mind. "Of course I trust you." And she did, very much. Did he trust her?

Pete crossed his arms over his chest and looked at the floor. He was tense and unsure of himself, something that rarely happened. "Do you remember what I told you about not getting as involved as you could in this case?"

"After I decided to go to the hotel to talk to Gabrielle?" Sadie asked. He nodded. "Yes, I remember."

"Well, I'm not sure where the police are with this, and as much as I support law enforcement as a whole, I don't know these people and Boston's finest has a rough history that has me worried about how *your* history is going to play into this. It's hard to make sense of why you keep finding yourself in these situations, and I've no doubt the police are having a hard time with that too. Cops hate coincidences and patterns." He took a breath while Sadie tried to keep her expression neutral, even though she was aching to defend herself. Was he questioning her too? Is that what he was getting at? Was it only *her* history that he was worried about?

"Anyway," he continued, "I just wanted to tell you that while I can support you doing what you feel you need to do, and I acknowledge that in the past your determination to get to the heart of matter has made all the difference, I can't help you with this one, and I shouldn't really know the details anymore."

Sadie felt herself exhale the breath she hadn't realized she'd been holding, but her surprise was sincere. "You think I *should* look into Gabrielle?"

"I'm saying I can't be a part of it—at all."

"But I should try to figure her out?"

Pete didn't say anything, allowing Sadie to think over what he'd said exactly. If she continued, it was on her own. Or, rather, she and Jane on their own. The fact that he'd said what he'd said and hadn't told her to stay out of it—like he usually did—almost felt as though he were giving her his blessing . . . sort of. She had to keep dissecting his words in order to find the specific intent of what Pete was saying.

She grabbed hold of the only thing that stood out. "I can't talk things over with you anymore?"

He held her eyes for a few moments, obviously wrestling with what to say, what to tell her. It was tempting to just come out and ask him about what she'd overheard on the phone but she didn't want to take away his chance to confide in her because she *did* trust him and she wanted him to do this his way.

"I love you, Sadie."

That brought Sadie up short. It had been said before, in greeting or parting, or signed on a note he left on her windshield at the grocery store when he'd recognized her car in the lot. The words had become as comfortable on their lips as the kisses that sparked more than just chemistry these days. But he'd never said it with this kind of weight before, as though his loving her explained something more than his feelings and tapped into more than their future. He reached for both of her hands, and she stepped closer, their entwined hands between them.

"I love you too," Sadie said, her chest constricting with rising emotion as a horrible thought entered her mind. Did he fear that whatever he wasn't telling her would crumble what they had to-gether? He looked so heavy, so concerned and . . . scared.

"Are you okay?" Sadie asked.

Pete squeezed her hands. "Sure," he said, but he was looking at their hands, not her eyes. "And I know things will work out in the long run. I just need you to know that it's okay for you to follow your gut instincts on this. I trust them, and I don't want you to ignore them because of my inability to be involved."

"I wish you *could* be involved," Sadie said. "I think we make an amazing team."

Pete smiled. "Just be careful, and don't forget how much I love you and how proud I am of the woman you are."

Talk about cryptic! But Sadie didn't dare question him about it; the fear in his eyes was burrowing into her.

They stood there for a few more seconds, and finally Pete let go of her hands and kissed her quickly on the lips. "Good night," he said when he let go.

"Good night," Sadie answered as Pete turned and went back into his room. She went into her room a few minutes later and shut the door behind her while pondering the exchange. She stopped when she caught sight of her laptop plugged into the charge cord and rest-ing on the dresser. Everything she needed to know could be only a Google search away, but was it a betrayal of Pete for her to investi-gate *him*?

Did she want to know who Michaels was?

Would it change everything?

His words came back to her: "Do you trust me?" She abso-lutely did trust him but wondered if he really trusted her. If he did, wouldn't he have told her? Then again, he didn't know she'd over-heard his phone call. And yet there was something *preparatory* in what he'd told her—*be careful, remember that I love you.* Pete himself had told her to trust her gut instincts. *And* he'd pointed out that her investigations in the past had been important—they'd made a difference. Would he find it at all surprising that Sadie would dig into his past if she had reason to do so?

She thought of how troubled Pete was, how vulnerable he had looked, and her heart ached for him. He had so much pressure on him right now, but she also trusted that whatever he couldn't bring himself to tell her was something that would not destroy what they had between them.

She retrieved her computer and made herself comfortable on the bed. As she flipped open the screen and waited for it to wake from its electronic sleep, she looked at the bedroom door and simply hoped that her gut instinct wasn't leading her astray on this one and that whatever this secret might be, she and Pete really were strong enough to handle it.

CHAPTER 23

Once the new browser window had come up, Sadie typed in the URL of her favorite journalistic archive website. It had been a wonderful resource in the past, and she felt only a small twinge of guilt that Pete was the one who had showed her the site in the first place. She didn't have access to police records like he did, but Pete taught her how to make a pointed search of public information and of previously published articles dating all the way back to the sixties in some cases.

As she typed Pete's name into the search bar, Sadie did a quick review of what she already knew about his basic history. He had been born in New Mexico—Santa Fe—played baseball in high school, and served four years in the army via the ROTC program after graduating high school. He married Pat after finishing his time in the military and then completed his schooling and joined the police force when he was almost thirty and his girls were young. Jared was born a few years later, completing their family. The family moved to Fort Collins about thirteen years ago, then after Jared had graduated from high school and started his undergraduate work at Colorado State, Pete and Pat had moved to Garrison. Pete had said something on the phone about fifteen years ago. That would have been when he was in New Mexico. Was Michaels someone he arrested back then? Was this Michaels person the reason Pete had left his home state?

Although the website spared Sadie from the thousands of useless links she'd have encountered through a traditional Google search, there was still plenty of chaff to sift through. It took about fifteen minutes for Sadie to skim through the results until she found a link that matched the time period Pete had mentioned on the phone. She opened a scanned image of an article from the *Farmington Daily Times*, printed fourteen years earlier.

Sadie took a breath, then zoomed in on the image and started to read about whatever it was Pete didn't want her to know about his past.

Detective Under Investigation; Landscaper Acquitted

The investigation into who killed Lamar Nutson in his Flora Vista home last April took a shocking turn on Thursday, June 4, when Ricardo Fruge, Mr. Nutson's former landscaper, was released from the San Juan County jail where he's been held without bail for the last two months awaiting trial.

Mr. Fruge called 911 to report having found Mr. Nutson lying on his bedroom floor April 2 of this year, a victim of an apparently random attack involving multiple stab wounds and a blow to the head. Mr. Nutson was airlifted to University of New Mexico Hospital in Albuquerque, where he died two days later as a result of his injuries.

Mr. Fruge had worked for Mr. Nutson for several years but had been recently fired for having pawned several pieces of equipment belonging to Mr. Nutson. Mr. Fruge claimed to have returned to the house to repay Mr. Nutson for the equipment, but was arrested two weeks following the attack due to evidence which was not made known to the public. Today, Mr. Fruge is a free man but refused to make any comment as his lawyer drove him away from the jail.

Yesterday, Detective Peter Cunningham, four-year veteran of the Farmington police department, was put on administrative leave pending an investigation into his work on the case. According to an official police spokesman, Detective Cunningham is not a suspect in the death of Mr. Nutson, but is suspected of using unapproved methods of investigation when he accepted the help of Terry Michaels, a self-proclaimed psychic. The information from Ms. Michaels led police to Roberto Fruge. However, current information has proven the information was not viable and that the search of Fruge's father's home was done without a proper warrant. Evidence discovered during that unlawful search is now suspect. What action will be taken against Detective Cunningham is as yet unclear, but according to the spokesman, "It's unfortunate that proper protocol was not followed in this case. We are doing all we can to repair the situation and bring Mr. Nutson's killer to justice."

There have been no other arrests since Mr. Fruge's release, and Detective Cunningham has made no comment.

"Oh, Pete," Sadie said, shaking her head as she bookmarked the page and returned to her search results. Using the new names she'd discovered, she looked for any other articles on the topic. She felt a little queasy as she imagined the implications of the article. Certainly Pete hadn't acted on a psychic's tip without fully considering the situation, had he? She knew him to be skeptical and cautious, but had he once been impetuous and brazen, seeking justice at any cost? Sadie found another article dated three weeks after the first one and pulled it up. This one was digitally archived rather than scanned in.

Psychic Arrested in Nutson Murder

Psychic Terry Michaels was arrested at a border crossing in Arizona yesterday. Ms. Michaels has been sought for questioning since her role in the original investigation of Lamar Nutson's murder was made public earlier this month. Police were unable to locate her and neighbors reported seeing her leaving town several days before her participation in the case had been made known. Attempts to locate Ms. Michaels revealed additional warrants from Utah and Montana, where she was a person of interest in two cases of fraud, one of which resulted in a homicide. Both cases involved successful businessmen who had been clients of hers. The connection was soon made that Ms. Michaels had met with Lamar Nutson twice before his death, apparently offering him information in regards to his late mother's wishes for his future. A spokesperson from the San Juan sheriff's office said Tuesday, "We are eager to question Ms. Michaels in regard to her association with Mr. Nutson and will be working with the other state officials."

When asked about the investigation taking place in regard to Detective Peter Cunningham, the original investigator into Mr. Nutson's murder, the sheriff's office had this to say: "Detective Cunningham will remain on administrative leave indefinitely as we continue to explore the timeline of events that took place." Mr. Fruge, Mr. Nutson's landscaper, was arrested in part due to the information Detective Cunningham received from Ms. Michaels. The landscaper was later cleared of that crime but has filed a lawsuit against the department for negligence and wrongful arrest.

Ms. Michaels is currently being held in a Phoenix jail awaiting extradition to Billings, Montana, where she will face charges of aggravated murder.

When she finished reading, Sadie understood why Pete had been hesitant to call the Boston police when things had started getting strange. But surely the police wouldn't think this somehow placed suspicion on Pete. The crimes were very different and on opposite sides of the country. Even so, Pete himself had said police hated coincidences and patterns and they would have no choice but to take Pete's past into consideration as they investigated the attack on Mrs. Wapple. Apparently he *hadn't* just been referring to Sadie's recent past.

She closed the second article and did some more digging, filling in the gaps until she felt she had a pretty good view of the big picture. Pete had been set up all those years ago by Terry Michaels, who had misled him because she was the person guilty of murder. It was a poor decision for Pete to have trusted her, but Sadie could only believe he'd been desperate to find answers. Why else would he accept help from a psychic? Regardless, he hadn't done anything illegal or immoral—he'd simply made a bad choice.

A glance at the clock revealed it was after 11:00—no wonder her eyelids were so heavy. She closed the computer and put it back on the charger, grimacing as she stretched out the kinks in her back. She should have sat at the desk to use the computer and not stayed on the bed. Her fall earlier surely didn't help, and she got an ibuprofen out of her first-aid kit in her suitcase. She'd likely be even more sore tomorrow, though she was grateful her injuries were only some sore muscles and a few bruises. She hadn't always been so lucky.

Her hair had dried in frizzy waves; it would need some serious attention in the morning. She checked on the boys one last time. Their room was across the hall from hers, and she wanted to be able to hear them if they needed her, so she left both bedroom doors open. Confident that everything was safe, she slid between the chilly sheets and pulled the covers up to her chin before turning to face the window.

Soft light glowed around the edges of the slats of the mini-blinds and Sadie's thoughts turned to Mrs. Wapple. Would the doctors take the time to give her a full psychological assessment in addition to the physical one? Was she going to be all right? Would Sadie dig deeper into Mrs. Wapple's past tomorrow? Would she investigate Gabrielle? Would she take Jane up on her offer to keep looking for answers in search of closure? What would the police think of the similarities between the Michaels case and Mrs. Wapple?

She took a deep breath and let it out slowly, trying to ease her mind and rest her soul with thoughts of peace and calmness while praying for sleep to overtake her and for the night to be uneventful.

The calm, peaceful sleep lasted for exactly one hour, as though someone were timing her REM cycles.

CHAPTER 24

BAM!
 Sadie shot up in bed, blinking and looking around, trying to figure out where she was and what had woken her up.

BAM!

Boston.

The boys!

She scrambled out of bed and ran for the bedroom door. When she heard the first boy start crying, her heart jumped into her throat, and she reached for the knob, instantly realizing that one of those BAMs had been her door slamming shut. She'd left it open when she'd come to bed.

"It's okay," she yelled to the boys as she pulled open the door, not even thinking about what might be on the other side. It was cold in the hallway as she ran to the boys' room. The door, which she'd also left open when she went to bed, was closed—the second BAM?

Pete came flying out of his room moments behind Sadie, his gun in his hand. Sadie looked at him long enough to note he was only in his boxers as he ran to the front of the house.

"It's okay," she said, running toward Fig, who was crying. The other two boys converged on her, and she pulled them close, kissing and whispering and assuring them everything was fine. She didn't even think about Pete again until the boys had calmed down and he reappeared in the doorway still dressed only in his boxers but had donned a T-shirt. Sadie turned her face away and kissed the top of Chance's head.

"The front and back doors are open," Pete said breathlessly. "No one's here."

"Someone came in?" Kalan asked, his eyes wide, even in the dark.

"No," Pete said, running a hand through his hair. "I mean, yes, or . . . I . . ."

"It's okay," Sadie said again, smiling at Kalan. "We're going to a hotel." She stood up and crossed the room to flip on the light. Everyone squinted, but she hurried to the dresser and began pulling out folded clothing. Her heart was thumping. "Boys, get your shoes and coats. Pete, go find your pants."

They didn't question her and immediately did as she said. By the time Pete returned, properly dressed, Sadie had the boys' things nearly packed into the overnight bag she'd found in the living room closet.

"Are you going to call the police?" she asked Pete as she grabbed an extra pair of socks for each boy.

Pete didn't answer and an unexpected wave of anger rushed through her, which she quickly tried to suppress. This wasn't Pete's fault, but she couldn't help but wonder what his hesitation to involve the police may have cost them over the last few days. She met his eyes, wishing she could tell him everything she knew. Instead, she said, "Call them."

He nodded and disappeared. Within ten minutes, a single bag

was packed and everyone's shoes were on. Sadie had put her hair under the faucet after she'd passed the mirror and scared herself. She doused it with gel and anti-frizz spray, which was a vast improvement over the Don King impression she'd had a few minutes earlier. In the meantime, an officer had responded to Pete's call, and the two of them had checked out the locks, specifically the new eyebolts Pete had installed that afternoon, both of which seemed perfectly intact.

"Is there a crawl space?"

"No," Pete said, shaking his head and putting his hands on his hips. "I asked my son."

"Broken window locks?"

"I've checked them half a dozen times."

They kept discussing and rejecting options until Sadie noticed the dish soap lying on its side in the kitchen. Forty minutes later, their best guess was that the lock on the windows—circa 1950—could have been jimmied open with a butter knife. Or maybe the intruder had disabled the eyebolt with a bit of wire—the back door-jamb allowed more slack than the front. Pete wasn't satisfied with either answer but even he had to admit that sometimes the "how" didn't get explained.

Finally, the officer gave them permission to leave for the hotel. Chance and Fig had fallen asleep on the couch by the time they were ready to leave; Kalan was barely awake as he watched *Cars*. Sadie and Pete herded the kids out to the minivan. It was after 1:00 and freezing cold outside. A drizzly rain was still falling, which had melted the snow but left behind slushy conditions. It would likely freeze during the night and make for a dangerous commute in the morning.

While Pete backed out of the garage, Sadie turned around in her seat and tried to get the boys to calm down. Fig was crying again and Kalan and Chance were trying to be brave, but Sadie's heart was breaking at the look on their tired little faces.

Pete pulled out of the alley and drove past Browden Street in time for Sadie to see the taillights of the responding patrol car disappear around the opposite corner. Sadie watched Jared and Heather's house, looking so silent and innocent. As they passed the alley that ran behind Mrs. Wapple's house, Sadie saw a person—a man—stand up from behind a car in one of the driveways farther down the road. He wasn't looking at the minivan. Like her, he was looking toward where the cop car had disappeared. Had he been hiding? She craned her neck around as they drove further out of sight. The man hurried down the alley with something under his arm. She couldn't make it out—maybe a box or a really fat newspaper?

"Pete," she said, hitting him in the arm. "Go back. Someone's in the alley."

"What?" Pete said, his tone sharp.

"There was someone in the alley behind Mrs. Wapple's house. Go back."

Pete shook his head. "No way am I going back," he said without even slowing down. "Call the officer and tell him to check it out. We need to get these boys to the hotel."

Sadie felt bad about not considering the boys, but she called the officer—he'd given Pete his card—and gave all the description she had, which wasn't much. The officer assured her that he'd look into it.

"You said you found a room?" Pete asked as soon as she hung up, clarifying that his curiosity was not engaged in the lurker from the alley.

Sadie shifted her thoughts and told herself that it was probably nothing—some neighbor on a beer run. She picked up the GPS she'd brought with her from Garrison, the one she'd nicknamed Dora. "The Courtyard in Brookline where I stayed those first nights," she said. "Parking's ridiculous, but we can't be taking the T." She typed in the name of the hotel. "I'm just glad they had two connected rooms."

"Turn right in point eight miles," Dora said a moment later. Pete followed the directions.

"Turn right in point three miles."

They pulled up to the hotel ten minutes later and quickly herded the boys inside. Within ninety minutes of the banging doors, Chance and Kalan were tucked into one bed of the queen suite and Fig was asleep in the king bed he'd be sharing with Sadie in the connecting room.

Pete was leaning against the wall when Sadie came out of the bathroom; she nearly screamed. He waved her back into the bathroom and then shut the door behind them.

"What's wrong?" she asked.

He cleared his throat. "I need to talk to you about something."

"Okay," Sadie said, instantly picking up on his obvious anxiety. She wondered what it was that caused him to be this nervous and then, just as he opened his mouth, she knew what it was. Terry Michaels. She was all ears and leaned against the counter.

"Have you ever wondered why I'm a detective in a small town police department?"

"No," Sadie said, shaking her head. "I assumed you wanted to be a detective in Garrison."

"I do want to," Pete said. "But I haven't been able to accomplish all I hoped to accomplish when I started out in law enforcement. There are things that kept my career from advancing."

Sadie was tempted to let him off the hook and tell him she

already knew, but she forced herself not to. She was curious to know what he'd say about it. "What kind of things?"

"Several years ago, when I was working in Farmington, New Mexico, there was a murder." He took a breath, looking between Sadie, the towel rack, and the tile floor before continuing. "The victim was a wealthy horse breeder who lived on the outskirts of town. We rarely had homicides in that town—plenty of assaults and property crime, but very few murders—and my partner and I worked every angle we could of the case. Nothing really panned out. The victim didn't have family; he wasn't involved in scandal. He just raised horses and made a lot of money doing it. A week into the investigation, a woman contacted me at home. She said she was a psychic and that she'd had a vision about the case." He sought Sadie's eyes for . . . understanding? Support?

"You believed her," Sadie said, hoping it sounded more like a question than the statement of fact she knew it to be. She wanted to hear Pete's side of the story.

Pete nodded. "At first I didn't. I told my partner about it and put a note in the file. A week later she called me again. She knew about a piece of evidence that hadn't been made public—a red bandana that had been stuffed into the victim's mouth. When all our leads dried up, I went back to her—on my own since my partner thought she was a crackpot. I don't know why I was willing to go against procedure and endanger everything by following her lead, but . . . it was my first murder case in that department and I wanted to make a name for myself." He shoved his hands in his pockets. "Anyway, the short of it is that she'd made a living out of conning wealthy men through her supposed psychic powers, but things had escalated over the last few years and she'd turned from criminal to pathological. She'd attempted a con on our victim but when he didn't buy into everything she said and even threatened to expose her as a fraud, she killed him. Then she led me to the evidence she had planted that implicated someone else.

"She later admitted that she chose me as the person to find the planted evidence because I was the newest detective involved in the case—the hungriest. It nearly ended my career altogether. It was only due to a flawless reputation up until that point and a few key people vouching for me that I was even able to keep my badge, but the career goals I had were instantly out of reach. It's all part of my official police record."

"That's why you can't be a part of anything I do from here on out."

Pete nodded.

"That's why you didn't want to call the police."

He hesitated, but nodded again. "Remember how I said the police hate coincidences and patterns?"

Sadie nodded, remembering that she'd already considered Pete's personal connection to that statement.

"They'll be calling me in tomorrow, and I'll have to go through the whole thing all over again. They'll look for connections to that case—and they'll look hard."

"Connections?" Sadie asked. "Are there connections?"

"Me," Pete said. "The Farmington case involved a psychic, and this one has had ghosts mentioned."

"No one believes any of this is based on ghosts."

"I'm starting to," Pete admitted, holding her gaze. "I don't know how else to explain how someone got inside the house."

Sadie didn't know what to say. He was open to the possibility of something spectral?

"When I went to Montana to take Terry Michaels's statement,

she told me that she would haunt me for the rest of my life." He stopped and groaned, shaking his head and running his fingers through his hair. "Listen to me. I'm losing it."

Sadie stepped forward and placed her hands on his upper arms. When he met her eyes with a hesitant expression, she smiled. "Someone's playing a game with us. And I'm going to find out who it is, okay? I know you had nothing to do with Mrs. Wapple's injuries, and I know you're an excellent detective. I don't doubt that while your choices in Farmington may have been flawed, your motive wasn't. And that woman *is* in jail, so the process seemed to have worked out okay in the end as far as finding the killer goes. This is going to be okay, all right? And I'll back you up no matter where tomorrow takes us."

Pete held her eyes before pulling her into an embrace, melting against her for nearly a minute before he pulled back, looking a little embarrassed, but relieved all the same. He dug into his pocket and pulled out a single key. "To Heather and Jared's," he said. He placed the key in Sadie's hand and closed her fingers around it. "Well, we'd better get to bed. Tomorrow will come whether we're well rested or not, and it's sure to be a long day."

Sadie agreed. They shared a quick kiss, and Pete passed through the connecting door to his room, closing the door on his side. Sadie climbed into the second bed of the night, but sleep didn't come easily. The ramifications of what Pete was up against reverberated in her head, and yet there was also a glowing ember of hope and gratitude that he had told her. That was a big deal, and it buoyed her confidence in their relationship to know that he trusted her.

Sleeping was a bit of a joke, but Sadie managed a couple of hours between two and seven. As expected, her muscles were tight and sore when she got out of bed, so she took another ibuprofen and did her best to ignore the discomfort. Once they were all dressed and ready, she and Pete took the boys to breakfast at the hotel café, and then she left them at the hotel for a day of swimming and pay-per-view movies. They'd agreed to allow Kalan to miss school so that Pete could have the peace of mind of keeping all three of the boys in his line of sight all day. He didn't ask Sadie where she was going after kissing her good-bye in the hotel room, just wished her luck and told her to be careful.

Sadie asked the front desk to call her a cab that could take her to the closest rental car agency. By nine thirty she was driving off the lot in a nondescript gray Ford even though she planned to take the T as much as possible. As she'd anticipated, the roads were slick, but most of the morning traffic had cleared, and she had always been a good driver, so she wasn't too concerned.

She drove straight to Heather and Jared's house. It took her nearly fifteen minutes to walk around the yard and through the house, taking in all the details and assuring herself that no one was there and nothing was out of place. It was hard to believe all that had happened there last night. After inspecting the house, she stopped at the end of the hallway where the kitchen and living room joined it. The hallway was about fifteen feet long, with one door at the end—where Pete had stayed—and two on the right—the bathroom and the boys' room. The room she'd been staying in was directly across from the boys' room.

She walked slowly up and down the hallway, stopping when she was between her doorway and the doorway of the boys' room, both of which were partially ajar. She looked between the two doors, then reached for the door of her room and pulled it closed as fast as she could.

BAM! Definitely the same sound she'd heard last night.

She reached for the boys' door and pulled it shut too.

BAM!

But how could someone pull both doors closed and not be caught? Pete's room was six feet away. And Sadie had been even closer.

She opened both doors before closing them just until the latch-thingy rested on the doorjamb. She grabbed the doorknob of her bedroom door and pulled quick—BAM—then reached for the boys' door and pulled it closed too—BAM. The sound was the same whether the door was partially open or mostly closed.

She thought back to last night. What was the time line? She'd shot up in bed at the first banging door; the other bang had followed almost immediately. She closed the doors most of the way again and played it out again. Pull door shut—BAM—time to sit up in bed. Pull other door shut—BAM. She turned and hurried for the back door through which she'd make her escape. By the time she'd made it to the backyard, she was pretty certain both she and Pete would have been in the hall. Cutting it close.

She left the back door open, then headed into the living room and opened the front door as well, like they'd been when they were all awakened last night. After returning to the hallway, she reset the doors, crouched down, and stretched out her arms so that she was touching both doorknobs.

One, two, three.

BAM, BAM, run to the . . . front door—it was closer than the back door, and she didn't have to navigate around a table—down the steps, through the open gate, and to the sidewalk. She stopped and turned back to the house, taking a deep breath in order to recover from the impromptu workout. How long did that take? Five seconds? Six?

She pulled her phone out of her pocket and headed back inside. She set her phone to stopwatch mode and returned it to her pocket, keeping her thumb over the button that would start the count. She took a deep breath, let it out, crouched slightly and then . . . pushed the stopwatch button. BAM, BAM, run to the sidewalk. She pulled the phone out of her pocket. Seven seconds. With another seven seconds she could be halfway to the corner.

She reset the stopwatch and was heading back inside for another try so she could analyze the combined data when she sensed someone watching her. She looked over her shoulder and saw a man standing on the sidewalk across the street. She felt her cheeks flame as he quickly looked away and continued on his way with his hands shoved deep into his pockets.

She ducked her head and hurried up the sidewalk, trying to imagine what he thought she was doing. Just before crossing the threshold, she glanced over her shoulder to see if the man was still watching her. He wasn't; he was heading up the sidewalk to the house on the corner.

Something in his posture and movements made her embarrassment disappear. Was he the person she'd seen lurking in the alley last night? Was he connected to this? She almost laughed—of course he was connected! She'd done this too many times to be lulled with the assumption of coincidence. After entering the house and closing the front door behind her, she called Pete.

"Hey," Pete said when he answered the phone.

She headed to the kitchen so she could shut the back door. "Hi, sweetie. Could I talk to Kalan?"

He was silent, and she could feel him fighting his desire to ask why. However, they both knew that would break the agreement they'd made. "Sure," Pete said after a few seconds. A moment later, a timid voice said, "Hello?"

"Hey, Kalan," Sadie said as sweetly and brightly as she possibly could without sounding drunk. "It's Aunt Sadie. I have a question for you; do you think you could help me?"

"Okay," Kalan said. He sounded more comfortable now that he recognized her voice.

Sadie pulled open the front drapes, giving her a good view of the other houses. "Who lives in the brown house on the corner across the street?"

"Um . . . by my house?"

"Yes," Sadie said. "Mrs. Wapple lives right across the street, and then on one side there's a white house. Two houses down the street on that same side is a brown house on the corner. It has a chain-link fence around the front and . . ." She scanned for something that would make this house stand out to a six-year-old. "There's a blue mailbox stand out front, but no mailbox on it."

"That's Mr. Forsberk's house."

"The one whose dog got run over?"

"Yeah," Kalan said. "His dog's name was Bark."

"Bark the dog?" Sadie asked.

"Yeah, Mom thought it was funny."

"It is funny," Sadie said, smiling about it. "Maybe he'll get a cat and name it Meow."

"And a bird named Chirp."

Sadie laughed. In her mind she was considering why Mr. Forsberk would be outside at midnight. And then her thoughts went even further—could he be the person slamming doors and breaking in? But why? Sadie hadn't even met him.

Kalan's laugh was so cute that Sadie hated to change the subject, but there was work to do. "Kalan, when did Mr. Forsberk's dog die?"

"Um, it was the day Mom had to go to school."

Sadie frowned, and yet the fact that Kalan remembered it at all meant that it might not have been as long ago as she'd originally assumed. She turned and hurried into the kitchen, heading for the calendar Heather kept by the phone. She used her finger to scan backward along the dates, stopping when she read *PTC 3:20*. Having been a schoolteacher for more than twenty years, Sadie knew education acronyms almost as well as she knew the properties of baking soda.

"Parent-Teacher Conference?" Sadie asked, moving her finger so she could read the date and calculate how long ago it had been. "Two weeks ago yesterday."

"I guess," Kalan said. "She took us to McDonald's on the way home."

"Did she go to the school to talk about you with your teacher in a special meeting? Did you give her some papers you'd done, and maybe some pictures you colored?"

"Yes," Kalan said, sounding impressed that Sadie knew this. "And Mrs. Call talked to her about tests. I'm ahead of abrage."

"I have no doubt you're above *average*," Sadie said.

"And I got chocolate milk at McDonald's, too!"

"Maybe Grandpa will take you there for lunch today."

"Really?"

"You should ask him," Sadie said, feeling conspiratorial but needing to get off the phone now that she had the information she needed.

"Okay." She could tell from the way his voice was suddenly muted that he'd abandoned the phone entirely. She could hear him begging Pete for lunch at McDonald's and smiled as she heard the other boys join in the chorus.

Pete came on the line. "Thanks a lot," he said gruffly.

"Oh, come on, as long as you find one with a PlayPlace, it's good physical entertainment for the price of a hamburger."

He grunted and they both went quiet. There were so many things they couldn't ask and wouldn't answer.

"So," Pete finally said. "I got a text from Heather right after you left. She headed for the airport after I texted Jared about going to the hotel, and she caught a red-eye flight. She lands at 11:14. The boys and I are picking her up."

"Oh," Sadie said, but it was a loaded one-word answer. "She texted you instead of calling? Does that mean she's mad and didn't want to talk?"

"That's exactly what I thought."

"I'm so sorry I'm not there to help explain," Sadie said, wondering if maybe that was a better place for her to be than here.

"A detective also called me; they want me to come in. I explained about Heather, and they said I could wait until she was back."

"Did they say what they wanted to talk to you about?"

"They weren't specific," Pete said. After a moment, he said, "Please be careful today, Sadie. Okay?"

"You've told me to be careful several times," Sadie said, unable to smile for all the wishing he were here. "I haven't forgotten."

Pete let out a breath. "That's good."

"Call me when you finish with the police," Sadie said. "Assuming we don't run into one another at the police station." But she hadn't heard from the police about her follow-up interview yet. Apparently Pete was the priority today.

"I will," Pete said. "Good luck."

"Thanks. You too."

She returned to the living room window, staring at Mrs. Wapple's house as she tapped the phone against her chin.

Her eyes drifted to the corner house, and she allowed her thoughts to move away from Pete and settle on something different. Mr. Forsberk's dog had been run over two weeks ago; well, fifteen days to be exact, but Mrs. Wapple had been attacked on the two-week anniversary of the dog's accident.

Without wasting another minute, Sadie headed outside—locking the door behind her—and crossed the street, walked down the sidewalk, and went through the gate in front of Mr. Forsberk's house. She could see his TV through the missing slats of the mini-blinds that covered his front window as she marched up the front steps and knocked sharply on the door—ready for . . . something. Preferably not a fight, but if it came to that, she was ready.

She felt the vibrations of his footsteps on the wooden porch before she heard his approach, and moments later the door was pulled open. Mr. Forsberk was tall, but his shoulders curled inward, making him look reduced. He had a receding hairline that amplified his already prominent forehead, but the hair he had left was scruffy and unkempt, a dull brown-gray color. His glasses were rimless, and his lips were too full for his face and the fact that he had no chin. "Hello?"

"Mr. Forsberk," Sadie said. "My name is Sadie Hoffmiller. I've been staying with the Cunningham children across the street, and I'd like to talk to you for a minute if I could."

CHAPTER 25

Mr. Forsberk invited her inside, but it was obvious he wasn't entirely comfortable having her there. The house was sparse and dusty and without a lick of femininity anywhere. The air smelled like coffee and bacon. The TV she'd seen through the window was paused on a tire commercial. No family photos or smiling couple portraits stared at her from the shelves of his mammoth entertainment center. The only thing on his wall was a poster of the original *Star Wars* movie. What ever happened to the actor who played Luke Skywalker, anyway?

There were all kinds of wires and things on the kitchen table, and bundles of cords and miscellaneous gadgetry covered all but one of the kitchen chairs. All those details added together meant that Mr. Forsberk was single and lived alone.

He didn't invite her to sit on the gray-black velvet couch, a throwback to the early 1990s, so she simply stood in the middle of the cluttered living room. He looked nervous, which, if he had nothing to hide, would make no sense.

"I'm sorry about your dog," she said to get things started, shoving her hands into the pockets of her coat and rocking back on her heels.

His eyes widened behind his glasses and his big lips parted before he looked down at his beat-up sneakers. "Thank you."

"Did you have him, or her, for very long?"

"Him. Yes. Eight years."

Sadie frowned. "What a difficult loss."

He nodded and scuffed his shoe on the carpet as though rubbing something into the floor.

"You were outside late last night," Sadie said, fast-forwarding to the reason she was here. "What for?"

His head snapped up and he blinked at her. She could fairly hear the gears in his head spinning as he tried to make up a lie. She smiled again—a warm, soft, trust-me smile. "I'm not trying to get you in trouble, Mr. Forsberk, but after the police drove around the corner last night, I saw you come out of hiding behind the car. I just want to understand the context of you being out so late and ask if you saw anyone else while you were out, that's all."

"Um, it musta been someone else, I don't—"

Sadie cut through his halfhearted response. "It was late and raining and cold—so your reason must have been important."

He didn't say anything, and she took that as a good sign even as she held him tightly in her no-nonsense-stare-with-a-smile that had sent many a second-grader into sniveling confessions for a variety of petty elementary crimes. "I already told you that I'm not trying to get you in trouble, I'm really not, but some strange things have been happening at the Cunningham house these last few nights. Last night those events sent us to a hotel. If you were outside, maybe you saw something or someone that will help me get to the bottom of the situation we find ourselves in." She was careful not to accuse him of the strange events; she didn't need him to be any more defensive than he already was.

He simply blinked at her again, but he looked scared, which meant he was hiding something. Her stare was working its magic; she could feel his resolve to play dumb crumbling as the seconds ticked by.

"What kind of strange things have been happening?"

Sadie hadn't expected that question, and it took her a moment to come up with an answer and determine there was no reason not to share it. "Well, um, lights going on and off, doors slamming, kitchen utensils laid out on the kitchen floor—someone's been getting into the house."

"Um." Mr. Forsberk pulled back and looked at his clasped hands. He mumbled something Sadie couldn't hear.

"Excuse me? I didn't catch that." She glanced at the clock on his DVD player, noting that he had a nice TV, extra speakers, and several game consoles.

He cleared his throat and spoke more clearly. "She's a witch. She can make things like that happen."

"With all due respect, Mr. Forsberk, and despite my sincere regrets about your dog, I don't believe that. Mrs. Wapple may have problems, but a supernatural power isn't one of them."

"She wanders around in the middle of the night. She killed Bark."

"You think she cast a spell on your dog and caused it to be hit by a car?" Her tone pleaded with him to listen to how crazy that sounded.

He didn't take the opportunity for reflection. "We were across the street when Bark suddenly started whimpering and running circles, like he was hurt. I tried to calm him down but as soon as I let go of the leash to pick him up, he ran right into the street." He paused and looked at the wall behind Sadie's head, his eyes far away and full of pain. His non-chin trembled. "It was awful."

Sadie didn't doubt that. She reached out and touched his arm, which startled him. "But a spell, Mr. Forsberk?"

"Something made Bark run into the street like that," he said, and even though his timid voice wasn't strong, clearly his convictions were. "He was always calm and well-behaved. He didn't even bark when the postman came to the door. Something done happened."

"And he'd never behaved that way before?"

Mr. Forsberk shook his head, but then stopped and seemed to reconsider. "Well, actually, he'd whimpered when we passed her house the day before. I thought he was upset by the argument I'd had with her at that same spot. He was sensitive like that; he'd have remembered. Once we were a couple of houses away, he was fine. But that was different than what happened the day she killed him."

Sadie nodded, but something was tapping at the back of her mind—something she remembered from years gone by when her friend Gayle's son had raised hunting dogs. She gave Mr. Forsberk a sincere look of regret. "I'm so very sorry for your loss," she said.

Tears welled up in his eyes, and he looked away, trying to hide his emotion. He nodded quickly, embarrassed, and folded his arms across his chest. "Thank ya," he said. He sounded so much like a little boy that Sadie wanted to bake him something.

"Other than the situation with your dog, which is really horrible, have you had any other issues with Mrs. Wapple?"

"She stole my mail. She didn't usually come out in the daytime, but I saw her stuffing envelopes in her coat and I yelled at her. Blake, next to your place, said he caught her stealing his mail too."

"When did she take your mail?" Sadie asked, thinking of the piles of envelopes and magazines she'd knocked over yesterday afternoon. She hadn't thought to see who the mail belonged to.

"Right after she moved in. Two months back."

"But it only happened that one time?"

"That I saw," he clarified. "I've had a few more things that never seemed to come, so a few weeks ago I took down the mailbox and asked the postman to use the mail slot." He nodded toward the front door, and Sadie glanced back to see the mail slot about three feet up from the bottom of the door. "I ain't had any problems since then."

"That's good," Sadie said. "So, what were you doing out last night?" she asked, getting back to why she'd come.

He didn't meet her eyes and shrugged one shoulder.

"If you saw anything, I'd really like to know." Sadie smiled softly at him.

"I had to go out," he said. "That's all."

"In the cold rain?"

He shrugged. Sadie waited, but after a few seconds she realized he wasn't going to tell her. Not right now. She didn't have any baked goods; how could she think he would roll over so easily when she was so poorly prepared?

"I gotta go to work," Mr. Forsberk said.

He was dressed in jeans, an old Red Sox sweatshirt, and tennis shoes. Maybe he was one of those eccentric computer programmers who went to space cadet conventions on the weekends. "Where do you work?"

"I clean carpets," he said, but without pride, which Sadie felt was a shame. There was nothing about hard work to be embarrassed about. She waved toward the mass of cables and wires on the table. "Then what's all this?"

He looked around and shrugged one shoulder again. "Just a hobby. I . . . build things." There was always so much more to people than first met the eye.

"What kind of things?"

"I like to take apart electronic things and rebuild them a little different."

Sadie didn't get it. Why would you want something to be different? "Like making a toaster toast faster?" she asked.

"Kind of," he said, his cheeks red. "I used to work at Radio Shack." He said it as though that was all Sadie needed to know to understand his hobby. He looked at his watch, reminding her that he had to get to work.

"Can I write down my phone number for you?" Sadie asked quickly. "You could call me later if you think of anything about last night." In the meantime she'd find some excuse to come back after he'd had some time to think about things.

He went into the kitchen and retrieved a pen and an old envelope.

"One last question," Sadie asked after writing down her number. "Do you like chocolate?"

"Chocolate?" he repeated, his eyes squinching up behind his glasses.

"You're from Philadelphia, right?"

His eyes got big. "Sorta," he said. "Harrisburg, actually."

Sadie beamed for having guessed the basic area correctly. She'd been playing a game with Pete when they watched TV the last few months, trying to peg certain accents. "Maybe you're more of a vanilla kind of guy?"

"Um, I like chocolate."

Sadie smiled. "Of course you do," she said with a nod. "And what time do you get off today?"

"Um, my last house is at two o'clock. I should be home by four thirty," he answered. "Why?"

"Well, the other day I took cookies around to the neighbors but I didn't have enough to go around, and now that I've met you I feel just terrible for not having made more of an effort to bring you a plateful. I'll come back tonight with something special."

He blinked. "Oh. Okay."

Practically an invitation to return! "Wonderful." He'd have worked hard for six hours and would be hungry, not to mention tired from his excursion last night. It was a perfect setup for a full confession. By five o'clock this afternoon, she was certain she'd know exactly why he'd been out so late.

She said good-bye and hurried down the block toward Jared and Heather's house while pulling her phone out of her pocket and hitting speed dial number six.

"Gayle," Sadie said as she looked both ways and crossed the street. She didn't want to be hit by a car like Bark had been, but then if her theory was correct, there was little chance of that.

"Sadie, sweetie, how are you?" It was early in Garrison—7:00—but Gayle was a morning person.

"Um," Sadie wasn't sure how to answer that.

Gayle saved her. "You're in the paper, sweetheart. I think you'd better stop leaving town."

If only being *in* town wasn't just as uncomfortable. "I know," Sadie said for the sake of manners and time, though she had hoped the *Denver Post* wouldn't have anything about her yet. "And I don't mean to be rude, but I'm in a hurry and need some information."

"Okay," Gayle said, not sounding offended; she was such a good friend. "What can I help you with?"

"Remember when Darrin used to train those hunting dogs?"

"Darn flea bags," Gayle said, and Sadie could picture her shuddering at the reminder. It was a testament to a mother's love that she'd allowed one dog, let alone the eight Darrin had at one time.

"He used a whistle to train them, right?"

"Yeah," Gayle said. "It was downright creepy the way he'd blow into that silver straw and the dogs would stop in their tracks."

"Aren't there dog whistles that actually cause pain to the dogs?"

"Sure," Gayle said. "But Darrin never used those. They're illegal in some states, and you don't really need them except in extreme behavioral issues, which we never had. Why are you asking about dog whistles?"

"Long story," Sadie said. "But you've never seen anyone use that kind of whistle then—the mean ones?"

"No," Gayle said.

"I'm wondering if that kind of whistle could make a dog go kind of nuts—you know, act all weird and not obey commands, things like that."

"I'm sorry," Gayle said. "I don't know."

"Would Darrin know?" Last Sadie had heard, he was still raising hunting dogs down in Durango. His full-time job was as an investment banker; the dogs were more of a hobby.

"I'm sure he would," Gayle said. "Would you like his number?"

Sadie had reached the front porch of the house and paused to dig the key out of her pocket. "Actually, could you call him and ask, then call me back? I've got a whole list of other things I need to do."

"You betcha," Gayle said. She loved to be involved; heck, she'd probably come to Boston if Sadie asked.

Holding the phone with one hand, Sadie fumbled with the key only to realize the door was unlocked. Again. It wasn't pulled all the way closed either. Sadie stared at it as a familiar cold chill rushed down her spine.

"Sadie?" Gayle said on the phone.

"Thanks," Sadie said, distracted from the phone call as she stood on the porch, the memory of locking the door when she left distinct in her mind. "I appreciate it."

"Sure," Gayle said. "I'll call you after I talk to Darrin."

Sadie slid the phone back into her pocket before reaching out and pushing on the door. It swung open easily on its hinges, and she took in the details as she stepped inside. Everything looked fine until she reached the kitchen. She stopped in her tracks. Every cupboard was open and every drawer pulled out. The kitchen chairs, which had been around the table when she left, were pushed up against the counter, seats facing in. That stupid gauzy ghost she'd ripped off the front door and stuffed behind the couch was hanging from the curtain rod on the back door. Chills crept up her back as she took it all in.

"I don't believe in ghosts," she said out loud as she calculated how long she'd been gone. Ten minutes, maybe twelve. She remained very still and considered what this latest event told her. Mrs. Wapple hadn't done it— she was in the hospital. She hadn't done last night's door slamming either. Sadie crossed her off the list. Mr. Forsberk, who had only recently become a consideration, couldn't have done this either—she'd been standing in his living room talking to him about his dog. That left Gabrielle, but what would she be trying to scare Sadie away from now?

"Knock, knock," she heard from behind her. She turned in time to see Jane step over the threshold of the open front door. Her hair was spiked to perfection, her face was bright, her mood elevated, and her eyes eager. "Okay, Sadie, Sadie, detective lady, where do we start?"

CHAPTER 26

J ane," Sadie said. "Um, I didn't expect you."

"You need to get over your issues with asking for help," she said, stopping between the kitchen and living room, where she leaned against the wall. She couldn't see the cupboards and drawers from where she was, and Sadie debated whether to find a way to keep her in the living room or let her come all the way into the kitchen. Sadie felt like she was back to square one, at least in regard to the strange things happening at the house.

"And we need to bang this out, right?" Jane said.

"Bang what out?" Sadie asked.

"Solving the mystery. We need to find whoever's behind all this, clear your name, and stamp a big ol' *solved* on this case."

"That would be nice," Sadie said, accepting the fact that Jane was here and there was no way to shake her. But was that really such a bad thing? "How did you know where I was?"

"It's nine thirty in the morning—where else would you be? Where are Pete and the kids?"

That's right, Jane didn't know they'd left last night. "Distracted," Sadie answered. "I'm on my own with this."

"Well, not on your own, per se," Jane said, grinning broadly. "You've got me. I knew you'd pick up the scent, though, so it's a good thing I showed up, right?"

Sadie couldn't help but smile back, impressed despite herself with how determined Jane was to be a part of this and how certain she was that Sadie wouldn't be able to let it rest. Sadie thought back to how she'd tried to leave Jane out in Portland and what Shawn had said about Jane looking up to her. Sadie decided to stop being so hard on Jane. And, the fact was, Sadie didn't know where to go from here. Without Pete to bounce her ideas off of, she could really use a partner on this.

"I don't think I could let it go even if I wanted to. It's apparently what I do now."

Jane nodded in agreement. "So, where do we start?" she asked, clapping her hands and rubbing them together.

Sadie looked into the kitchen. "Well, you better have a look at this." She walked to the front of the table and Jane followed her into the kitchen, stopping in almost the same place Sadie had been.

"Whoa," she said with a laugh, looking around. "It's like something straight out of the *Sixth Sense*."

"The sixth what?"

"A movie, came out in the late 90s—one of Shyamalan's thrillers. You had to have seen it. Bruce Willis? 'I see dead people'?"

"I prefer musicals," Sadie said, looking at the cupboards again. "Not ghost stories."

"'Well, you best start believing in ghost stories, Miss Turner—you're in one.'"

Sadie recognized the line from *Pirates of the Caribbean*. She'd seen every movie Johnny Depp had ever made—even *Edward Scissorhands*. What could she say, she had a vice. "It can't be ghosts,"

Sadie said, but even she heard the plea in her tone. Was she starting to fall for this? She shook her head; it was ridiculous.

She stepped forward and started putting the chairs back around the table. Jane stepped in and helped close the drawers and cabinets.

"I'm not ready to go that direction," Sadie said. "And I need to clean up the kitchen so if you want to sit, I'll keep my hands busy and fill you in on the details."

"Oh, do tell," Jane said before collapsing in a kitchen chair and putting her feet up on the table, ankles crossed.

"No shoes on the table," Sadie said automatically. Jane did as she was told, and Sadie pushed up her sleeves and then told Jane what had happened while she chipped petrified beans out of the slow cooker and mourned the dried-out, over-risen cinnamon twists. Hopefully the whoopie pies she planned to make would work out a little better; she'd certainly be more vigilant this time.

By the time she'd told Jane the whole story, she had the kitchen straightened and the ingredients for the whoopie pies set out on the counter. She'd experimented with traditional recipes for whoopie pies after her last trip to Boston; the kids had loved the filled cakes that were as big as the palm of their hands. Once home, she'd been disappointed with her attempts to replicate the treats until she broke one of her cardinal baking rules and used a cake mix-based recipe. It turned out to be the winner, making perfectly moist yet dense cakes that supported the thick cream filling perfectly and simple enough that Sadie didn't need to reference her Little Black Recipe Book, currently at the hotel. Lucky for Sadie, Heather was well-stocked on cake mixes and had everything else she needed for the traditional Amish dessert Sadie felt would only improve her chances of getting information from Pennsylvanian-born Mr. Forsberk. Perhaps the sugar content combined with the invitation of nostalgic feelings of his youth would help him trust her with whatever he was holding back.

"Okay then," Jane said when Sadie finished explaining. She didn't ask about the baking paraphernalia arranged on the counter. "Where do we start?"

"Well," Sadie said as she ripped open the cake mix box and pulled out the plastic interior bag so that she could cut the corner rather than tear it, which was high risk for inferior pourability. "Shawn has found some landlord information from Mrs. Wapple's former residence. I told him I didn't need it, but now I think it would be a good idea to get a more full-bodied view of the family. The landlord might have some important details."

"Agreed," Jane said with a nod. "What else?"

Sadie poured the cake mix into a mixing bowl and added the pudding mix, water, eggs, and oil. "Mr. Forsberk, the guy with the dead dog, was poking around outside last night. I already talked to him, but he's not giving up his reasons easily—hence the whoopie pies. He used to work at Radio Shack, and yesterday was the two-week anniversary of his dog's death, which he believes was caused by a spell cast by Mrs. Wapple."

"The plot thickens," Jane said, her grin betraying how intrigued she was.

"Like roux in a soup," Sadie said. She turned on the hand mixer, so they didn't talk for the next two minutes as she whipped the ingredients into a thick batter. It was important to mix cake mixes according to the directions in order to ensure positive results, and since this one said to mix it for two minutes, that's exactly what Sadie did. While it mixed, Sadie realized that Heather would be home soon. She looked at the clock and frowned. It was 10:10. If Heather's flight landed at 11:14 and Pete had to be to the Jamaica

Plain police department by noon then Heather would be home in just over an hour. Sadie turned up the speed of the mixer. It wasn't that she didn't want to see Heather, but she felt horrible about what had happened and didn't know how to explain it. It would be nice to put off the potentially negative confrontation until she was more prepared.

"Anything else?" Jane asked as soon as Sadie shut off the mixer. "Anyone else we should dig into?"

Sadie immediately thought of Pete. Even though she'd been trying not to think about it, it was forefront in her mind. Telling Jane was out of the question, but the information weighed heavily on Sadie. There was a connection between Mr. Nutson's case and this one . . . somewhere. Could she find it without Jane's help?

"Sadie?"

Sadie looked at Jane, realizing she'd drifted away from their conversation. "Oh, sorry. I think that's about it—just Gabrielle and Mr. Forsberk."

"You're sure there isn't anyone else that should be a person of interest in this case? We may as well dig up all the answers."

Sadie looked away, not liking the intent look on Jane's face or the way it triggered Sadie's guilt at withholding information. "That's everyone," she said, pulling out a cookie sheet to bake the little round cakes on. She hoped Jane wouldn't keep pushing; her determination to keep what she knew to herself was fragile.

"I used to date a guy who worked at Radio Shack," Jane said from the table while Sadie's back was still toward her. "I bet I could sweet-talk him into digging up some info for me about Mr. Forsberk."

"That would be great," Sadie said, looking over her shoulder to smile at her partner, a smile that had a lot to do with the fact that

Jane had stopped tempting Sadie to confess what she knew about Pete. "Your connections are amazing."

Jane shrugged, but was obviously pleased at the compliment. "When you've dated for so long without finding Mr. Right, you tend to get a pretty good cross section of society."

Sadie turned back to her cake rounds, not wanting Jane to see her smile fall at the mention of her dating history. She still hadn't resolved what was going on between Jane and Shawn, and while it seemed like the least of her worries compared to everything else, her children were never that far down on her list of priorities.

Jane started making phone calls in the living room while Sadie finished making the cakes. While they baked, she made the filling and obsessed about her son's possible relationship with Jane.

The first batch of cakes were just out of the oven when Jane came back into the kitchen, a cocky look on her face. "Well, the bad news is that Brian no longer works for Radio Shack, but he's engaged, which means he won't think me calling is some kind of invitation, *and* he gave me the number of someone else. I got a full job history and exactly why they wouldn't rehire Mr. Forsberk if he tried to reapply."

"They told you all that?" Sadie asked. This woman was magic!

"I posed as a small electronics company in Concord and knew all the right questions to get around the typical boundaries human resources sets up to protect them from, well, people like me." She smiled, very pleased with herself while Sadie squirmed. She'd been known to bend a story here and there to get some information, but she avoided outright lying and manipulation. Being in league with someone who didn't see things the same way she did could get sticky.

"Anyway," Jane said when Sadie didn't comment out loud. "Forsberk worked there for seven years and seemed on track to become an assistant manager in the Quincy store, but then he was fired for voyeurism."

"Voyeurism?" Sadie said, putting in the second sheet of cake rounds. "Isn't that filming someone without their permission?"

"Without their permission *when* they have an expectation of privacy. You don't sign an agreement to be on tape at a department store, but if the camera were in the fitting room, where you expect privacy, it's over the line."

"Do I want to know what he did?"

"I did," Jane said as though there wasn't any question about getting the nitty-gritty details. "The gal on the phone wouldn't tell me, of course, though she told me too much anyway and I could totally get her fired if I wanted to." She smirked and Sadie squirmed again. This was why she hadn't automatically called and asked Jane for help this morning. The woman's methods made her uncomfortable. Obviously not uncomfortable enough, however, or Sadie wouldn't be working with her. "But I did a few perfectly detailed Google searches and found the newspaper articles. Apparently, Little Nel had a—"

"Little Nel?" Sadie asked, looking over her shoulder while she rinsed the last of the dishes.

"Oh, his first name is Nelson—Nelson Forsberk—but he's such a dweebie guy that Little Nel fits, don't you think?"

"I don't think we need to call him names," Sadie said. "Nelson or Mr. Forsberk is fine."

"O-kay," Jane said, willing to go along with it but obviously not seeing the point. "*Nelson* developed a crush on a new female employee and bothered her so much that she requested a transfer to another store. After the transfer, he started coming to her *new* store, after which time he was written up for harassment. A month later she found a customized micro-camera installed in her home bathroom. She called the police, and they tracked the serial number of the different components of the camera to Nelson's Radio Shack and directly to a credit card purchase he made shortly after being written up. Radio Shack quietly fired him and likely settled with the girl. It was only made public in regard to an article about the increase in technological means of sexual harassment in the workplace. I've got a call in to the reporter who wrote the story but, seriously, you'd think after the whole Boston Strangler thing and the Craigslist Killer situation this town has had to deal with, they would do a better job of warning their citizens about creepy guys filming pretty girls without their consent."

"It must have seemed like such a small thing compared to those other stories," Sadie said, drying her hands on a dish cloth. She leaned against the counter, considering what Jane had discovered. "Mr. Forsberk had all kinds of wires and gadgetry on his kitchen table and told me he likes to rebuild things. Could he have bugged Mrs. Wapple's house?"

Jane looked adequately horrified by the idea, which Sadie found gratifying since Jane's unemotional attitude often made Sadie uncomfortable. "Why? He had the hots for the woman he worked with, but Mrs. Wapple doesn't seem like his type. Did the police find anything?"

"No," Sadie said. "At least not that I'm aware of. I'm just brainstorming. I don't know why he'd bug her house. He wanted nothing to do with her. But his dog *did* die two weeks before she was attacked, so there could still be a connection."

"Well, if he thinks she's a witch, maybe he was trying to find proof?"

Sadie frowned. "Maybe," she said, but that seemed so . . . trite.

"Why would he need proof she's a witch? Who would he need to prove it to? There has to be another motive."

"Or he's just crazy. Crazy people don't need motives."

"But they have them," Sadie corrected her. "In their own minds there's a reason why they do the things they do, even if those reasons make no sense to us. Judging from Mr. Forsberk's overall attitude toward Mrs. Wapple, I can only come up with revenge as a reason why he would be involved with her at all, which—"

"Which plays right into the possibility that he's the one who attacked Mrs. Wapple," Jane finished the sentence for her.

Whoopie Pies

1 box devil's food cake mix*
1 (3.4-ounce) box instant chocolate pudding
½ cup vegetable oil
3 eggs
¾ cup water

Preheat oven to 350 degrees. Mix all ingredients together with an electric mixer until smooth and thick—at least 2 minutes. Drop six large spoonfuls of batter onto silicone mat-lined, parchment-lined, or well-greased cookie sheets. Use the back of a spoon if necessary to flatten slightly so that each pie is no more than three-fourths of an inch tall. Bake for 11 minutes, or until cake springs back when lightly touched. Cool on pan 2 minutes before transferring to a cooling rack. Let cool completely before assembling pies.

Store leftovers in refrigerator. Freeze individually wrapped cakes in wax paper.

Makes 8 to 10 pies.

*Can substitute any other type of cake mix, but if so, change pudding flavor to vanilla or another, more suitable, flavor.

Filling Choices*

Buttercream
1 cup butter
4 cups powdered sugar
2 egg whites
½ teaspoon vanilla
4 tablespoons flour
4 tablespoons milk

Cream butter and powdered sugar together. Add eggs and vanilla. Mix until fluffy. Add flour and milk and mix until well blended. Use additional flour or milk to get the correct consistency—a thick but airy frosting. Layer filling between two cakes, bottoms together.

Marshmallow (Shawn prefers this one)
¾ cup Crisco shortening (do not use butter Crisco)
¾ cup powdered sugar
2 teaspoons vanilla
1 (7- to 8-ounce) jar Marshmallow Fluff

Beat shortening and powdered sugar together until smooth. Add vanilla and Marshmallow Fluff. Mix until well blended.

*Can add ½ teaspoon of a flavored extract to filling: mint, lemon, strawberry, orange, etc.

CHAPTER 27

Sadie nodded. "Exactly. And he was outside last night, hiding from the police."

"They say perps like to return to the scene of the crime; it reminds them of how powerful they were."

"I've heard that too. *Law & Order* talked about that all the time."

"And maybe he's the one who's been trying to scare you guys away, and when you saw him, he was trying to make his way back to his house without being seen."

Sadie rolled that over in her mind before shaking her head. "I timed it, and it took me only seven seconds to slam both doors and make it to the sidewalk. He could have made it back home with plenty of time to spare before the police showed up. Besides, the whole open-every-cabinet-and-drawer-thing happened while I was talking to him."

"He could be in league with someone," Jane suggested.

"I don't buy that either," Sadie said. "One unhinged person trying to scare me away is one thing, but two? Besides, he strikes me as a loner."

Mr. Forsberk *was* hiding something, though, and someone *had* lured Sadie across the street and into the strange setup where she found Mrs. Wapple. As a stranger to the neighborhood, she would make a perfect scapegoat if he chose his attack to coincide with Sadie's trip. And he had the perfect vantage point. But she couldn't get around the fact that she'd been talking to him during the time someone had come into Heather and Jared's house that morning.

"You gotta share your stream of consciousness with me," Jane said. "I'm working on my powers of telepathy, but they aren't finely tuned enough for everyday use just yet."

"Sorry," Sadie said, giving her an apologetic smile. "I was just thinking that if I separate the two parts of this situation into strange stuff and Mrs. Wapple's attack, Mr. Forsberk fits in better with the attack. Think about it—if he was determined to get revenge, maybe he could have used me as a scapegoat, making me a relevant suspect in her attack to keep any attention off of himself. It seems rather . . . overdone, but plausible."

"Keep in mind the only motive we know about is the dead dog—there could be more to it."

Sadie nodded and told Jane about the mail theft while she finished moving the first batch of cakes from the pan to the cooling rack. They would need to cool for at least another half hour before she assembled them. Not that she was in any hurry since she didn't plan to go over to Mr. Forsberk's until five o'clock tonight, but then she didn't want to be here when Heather got home either. She sat down on the chair opposite Jane and rested her hands on the tabletop. The second pan of cakes had about six minutes left on the timer.

"And the other part?" Jane asked. "The strange stuff?"

Sadie frowned but only shrugged her shoulders. She had no explanation for that since it couldn't be Mr. Forsberk.

"I know you don't want to believe it was a ghost, but what if it was? You asked last night why a ghost would choose you and Pete. Well, why not you and Pete? You're worried about Mrs. Wapple, and Mr. Forsberk is up to something, right? So what if there *is* a spirit specifically focused on keeping you involved?"

Sadie could feel her brow furrow as she looked at the tabletop despite Jane staring at her. The idea wriggled around in her head, but could she really even consider that? She was fifty-seven years old and had never heard of earthbound spirits until last night. To just believe in something that went against everything Sadie had ever believed before now seemed irresponsible, and yet Jane was so intent. She hadn't come right out and said it, but it was obvious that *she* believed it was ghosts. Or, she was at least willing to consider it a viable possibility, whereas Sadie just couldn't take it seriously.

"Do you think the reporter who wrote about the voyeurism is going to call you back?" Sadie asked, determined to change the subject.

Jane nodded. "Oh, yeah," she said with her trademark arrogance. "When someone follows up on your stories, you're always hoping to get another tidbit that will resurrect the thing. It's good journalism to call me back and see what I know. And the guy's got a good reputation—I always check—so I'll be hearing from him. I guarantee it."

"Do you think we could track down the girl Mr. Forsberk was bothering?" Sadie asked. "Maybe she would have some details about him that would better prepare us for when we meet with him later."

Jane nodded. "Possible," she said. "I think it would just take a stop into the Quincy store. All this went down just a year ago, so I bet there's someone there who would know where she was transferred to. And one of those interviewees I wanted to talk to today for my article is down in Milton, so it wouldn't be hard for me to do both."

Sadie nodded, relieved that they had given up talking about phantoms and were making a concrete plan of action. "Great. Why don't you work on Mr. Forsberk, and I'll get the landlord info from Shawn so I can learn more about Mrs. Wapple's history." This was always the hard part for Sadie. Only one of these lines would likely pan out, which meant a lot of their efforts would be wasted, and yet without knowing which line had the big fish on the end of it, there was really no choice but to cast them all.

All? She questioned herself. Was she really going to explore them *all?* Or was she picking and choosing by leaving Pete out? Ugh! Pete didn't do anything—why couldn't she let it go?

Jane twisted her arm so she could look at her watch, which was hidden between the two dozen black plastic bracelets on her wrist. "It's almost eleven. What if we plan to meet up at one? A friend of mine told me about a great little place called Wonder Spice here in JP. It's Thai. Do you like Thai?"

"I like everything," Sadie said. "And that sounds like a good timeline."

"If I have time, I'll try to get to the hospital and take a little peek at our witch—see how she's doing and if the sister's been around. We don't want to lose sight of the sister amid our new information."

"Oh, right," Sadie said. "We can't rule her out just yet, but I don't know if it's safe for you to go to the hospital either. People saw you at the police station; they think you're my daughter."

"They didn't pay any attention to me," Jane said, chuckling slightly. "They didn't even ask for my ID to prove who I was. Plus, I've got my wig."

"Wig?"

"It's a perfectly boring, shoulder-length, mousy brown thing that makes me look like the proverbial soccer mom."

Sadie looked at Jane's bright purple fingernails and the shirt she was wearing, all black except for the yellow Ms. Pac-Man and red words that said "Man Eater."

"Not to mention my journalistic wiles, which are secondary only to my feminine ones." She batted her eyelashes. "Don't worry, I know how to do this kind of thing, and I wouldn't do it if I didn't think there was something to be learned that made it worthwhile."

Sadie nodded, albeit reluctantly. "Okay," she said. "We'll meet up at one o'clock and compare notes. I might end up with some leads after I talk to the landlord, so this will give me time to follow up on them."

"Good," Jane said, slapping the table. "I think you and me make a killer team, Sadie."

Sadie smiled even though she didn't like Jane's use of the word *killer*. "Let's hope so."

Sadie gathered the ingredients for the filling—buttercream since Heather didn't have any marshmallow creme—and pulled out the second pan of cakes from the oven while Jane used the restroom. She'd just started mixing the filling when Jane returned.

"I guess I'm off to Quincy," she said, picking up her bag from where she'd left it next to the chair.

"Good luck," Sadie said with a smile. Jane nodded and let herself out the front door. Sadie finished the filling and put it in the fridge, then scribbled a note for Heather in case she came to the house, explaining that she'd be back for the whoopie pies that afternoon—she needed only four or five for Mr. Forsberk; the boys could have the rest. She didn't really have anywhere to go, but she wasn't up to staying and answering questions when Heather arrived.

She remembered passing a library on Sedgwick, and Sadie headed in that direction since she couldn't think of any better place to go. After locking the doors to the house, though it was beginning to feel more and more silly to do so, she took a long look at the house that still held so many questions. Was it safe for Heather to come back here? She made a note to talk to Pete about it, which reminded her that although Pete had an appointment with the police, she still hadn't been called back in. Had he taken their attention so much that she—the woman covered in red paint who discovered Mrs. Wapple—was no longer a concern? Poor Pete. She hoped things would go okay for him.

The sun was out and the snow from yesterday was long gone, but it didn't put a spring in her step or raise her spirits much as Sadie made her way toward the library. She had work to do, and it was hard to pay attention to anything else.

Her phone rang, making her jump, and she pulled off to the side of the road when she saw it was Shawn. He was on his way to class, he said, but quickly gave her the landlord information and then said how awesome it was that she and Jane were working together. Sadie scribbled down the information, thanked her son, and promised him an update later before pulling back into traffic and finishing her trek to the library.

She parked near the back of the lot and immediately jotted down a list of questions, or rather topics, she hoped to be able to discuss with the landlord. Then she dialed the landlord's number. The list was in her lap with her pen poised and ready to take notes.

"'Ello," the man said on the other end of the line.

"Oh, uh, hi. Is this Martin Delecorte?"

"The very same. How cun I help ya?" His accent wasn't Boston, more of a rural Oklahoma.

"Well, I'm looking for some information on one of your previous tenants—Delores Wapple. She lived with her dad, Timothy, in a rental you own up in Lowell, Massachusetts."

"Good renters, good folk. How can I help ya?"

"Well," Sadie said, not quite knowing what to do since he was making it so easy. "I'm trying to get a sense of the family and their connections. Did you know them at all?"

"I lived across the street. It used to be my dad's house; now it supplements my blasted social security checks, which don't go up nearly as quick as the price of cable television."

CHAPTER 28

O h," Sadie said, sitting up straighter. "Well, that's wonderful."

"How's Delores doin'? Can't say I haven't worried about her since she left."

"Actually, she's in the hospital, that's why I'm calling. We don't have much of a history on her and are trying to find people who knew her. Everyone here knows her as Mrs. Wapple, but it seems that Wapple is her maiden name, so it's created some confusion."

"Well, she ain't no missus, just Delores up around these parts, so I don't know about that. She's down in Boston these days, right?"

"Yes, a suburb of Boston—Jamaica Plain."

"I worried about them takin' her so far away. She likes things to be just so. What's she in the hospital for?"

Sadie briefly explained and was gratified to hear Mr. Delecorte offer a quick prayer under his breath. "Well, that's a shame," he finished. "Granted, she was a mite strange, especially in the beginning, what with the singing and the cats and all that, but I hate hearing she's had such a bad time of it."

"Singing?" Sadie said.

"Oh, she had a horrible voice, she did, but she would go out back and sing and sing and sing. Maybe that's what brought the cats in."

Sadie couldn't help but smile; she liked thinking of Mrs. Wapple singing to kitties. "She didn't do either of these things here," she said. "She yelled at neighbors and had issues with dogs."

"Oh, yeah, she don't like dogs. One here in the neighborhood got to one of her cats a few years back. Come to think of it, I didn't hear her sing much after that. Her dad said she took the loss hard, real hard. When her mother died, she about fell apart and that was the beginning of things that led to her needing to live with her father. You wouldn't think a dead cat would be that upsettin', 'specially since she had half a dozen of 'em, but she didn't come out for, well, it was a few weeks. She and Tim kept a wonderful garden; in fact they filled all the front flower beds with vegetables that were downright beautiful the way they had them arranged."

"Did they, by chance, plant potatoes out front?"

Mr. Delecorte laughed. "In fact they did—real nice foliage, for a vegetable. I probably would have said something about squash or tomatoes, but they were mindful of the way things looked."

"It sounds like you were good to the family."

"Ah, they were a good sort. I had my Jimmy; he wasn't quite right either. Didn't live past his twenty-first birthday—hit by a car back in '59. Tim and I could relate to one another, that's all."

Sadie wrote furiously and glanced at her list of topics so as to keep the conversation moving. "Did you know the sister—Gabrielle?"

"Never met her 'til Tim was sick, then she came around a bit but was always rather pinched for time. When Tim ended up goin' quicker than any of us thought, she came in, swept out Delores, and had the furniture put into storage. Don't get me wrong, she was nice enough, but, well, it seemed as though she'd grown out of her family, if ya know what I mean, and didn't know quite what to do with 'em. Her dad was sure proud of her, though, talked about her 'complishments all the day long. Right pretty thing too, if you don't mind my sayin'."

"Quite lovely," Sadie said. "I agree. But she wasn't much involved with the family?"

"Nope, like I said, she wasn't like them—more highfalutin."

Sadie moved to another topic. "Did Delores ever have headaches that you noticed?"

"Oh, yes," Mr. Delecorte said. "She'd do fine for awhile and then get struck somethin' awful. Sometimes she'd go to bed for days at a time. When she felt good, she was always tending to the garden, so if my wife and I didn't see her for a few days, we'd check in with Tim to see if we could do anything to help out."

Sadie was running out of questions and frantically searched for some more. When did she ever get someone so happy to talk to her? "I understand she didn't like doctors much."

"Not particularly, no, but Tim had a friend who was a doctor and would come visit without her knowin' what he was about. She just thought they was visitin'. Tim gave Delores her medicine but called 'em vitamins. She was fine with vitamins but not medicine, ya know. Part of her funny ways is all."

Vitamins? Sadie's mind flashed back to the night she'd helped Mrs. Wapple dig for potatoes. Mrs. Wapple had said potatoes had vitamin C. Had she made a connection to having felt better when she'd been on her "vitamins" and tried to find whatever solution she could think of with her fractured mind?

"Do you know what her medicine was called? I mean, what she was being treated for?"

"That's schizo-phrenia," he said. "Done been affectin' her since she was a young lady tryin' to go to college. Ain't nothin' she'd get cured of, ya know, but so long as she had the medicine she did okay, slept more and stayed calm. I don't know the name of the doctor-fella who was comin', though, and I a'course don't know what the medicine was called or nothin' like that. Ya know, my other boy, Dave, he lived up in Cambridge for awhile, everyone said that livin' in the city was as safe as anywheres, but he had a break-in that first month. They took off with his TV and his Mac Apple computer. Was probably done by the same guys who told him it was so safe, if ya ask me. Cryin' shame that Delores suffered under the hands of them city thugs."

"It sure is," Sadie said. "I only hope the doctors will be able to get her some help. I don't think she's been taking her 'vitamins,' and her headaches are pretty intense."

"Cryin' shame," Mr. Delecorte said.

"I don't know how often you come into the city," Sadie said, "but if you do, maybe you could look in on Delores. She's at Massachusetts General right now, though I don't know how long she'll stay, and I don't know where she'll go when she leaves. I don't think she'll be coming back home, though; I'm not sure she can take care of herself anymore."

"I'm not one for cities, but maybe my wife and I will look into it. I sure hate to think of somethin' happenin' to that gal. She done never hurt anyone herself, that be for sure."

Sadie didn't mention Bark's untimely demise. She was beginning to get a dual view of Delores—who she was and who she'd been. And while she might never have been "normal," Mr. Delecorte didn't seem to think she was that weird either. And, Sadie noted,

Mr. Delecorte had said nothing about her being a witch . . . cats notwithstanding.

"Delores has had some trouble up here—stealing mail from the neighbors and such. Did that ever happen when she lived in your rental?"

"Well, yes, it did happen some. She liked to collect things, like the cats, and she liked letters. Tim said that when Delores was little her mama would write letters to both girls and send them through the post so they would get their own mail. When things started going poorly, she seemed to hold on to that memory. When she didn't find anything from her mother, she started going through other people's things. Tim worried about that a whole lot, seein' as how it's a felony and all to tamper with another person's mail. He'd keep a lookout and return the mail when he found it. A few of the neighbors had a real issue with it, but it didn't bother me too much. She just wasn't right, that's all. She weren't tryin' to hurt nobody."

"Did people file complaints?" Sadie said, tapping the line where she'd written "Three complaints in Lowell."

"Some did, for sure, but not me. Like I said, it weren't really her fault, and she never opened the mail or nothin'. Just took it home and left it on the counter for her daddy to find and return all apologetic-like."

Sadie scribbled some notes and moved on to her next question. "Timothy wrote some articles back in the late seventies. Did he ever talk about that?"

"Tim had been a bus driver for the MBTA. He never wrote nothin' that I ever knew about. What was they about?"

"Well, they were about ghosts."

Mr. Delecorte went silent and Sadie felt herself cringe. "You're sayin' Tim wrote ghost stories?"

"Articles," Sadie corrected. "I'd heard he was kind of . . . involved in that kind of thing."

"Not here he wasn't," Mr. Delecorte said strongly. "I don't take up with that kinda thing, and I'm sure glad Tim never mentioned it to me. I'm a man of faith, not fantasy."

"I understand completely," Sadie said, wanting to assure him that she wasn't trying to make him uncomfortable.

"What was you needing this information for again?" Mr. Delecorte asked. "Who are you calling with?"

"Oh, I'm not calling for anyone," Sadie said. "I'm just worried about Delores, is all, and wanted to be able to give the police and hospital a better history."

"Ain't her sister helpin' out? I thought she was going to be takin' care of Delores. That's what Tim was sayin' toward the end."

"Um, she's . . . involved, but seems to be a pretty busy woman."

Mr. Delecorte harrumphed and Sadie agreed with him. It wasn't a good enough reason in Sadie's book either. She thanked him profusely and ended the call with a sigh of relief. She couldn't type in the car, at least not comfortably, so she went inside the library and sat at one of the small study tables. The building was relatively plain, but it had character in its window frames and hardwood floor, making it easy to feel at home.

As soon as she was settled, Sadie typed up her notes from the phone call. She'd fleshed out some of Mrs. Wapple's history, and that was good, but she hadn't discovered anything earth-shattering. Perhaps the most important detail was that Delores had been on medication back in Lowell and wasn't anymore. If she were schizophrenic, and unmedicated, her mental illness could be out of control, exacerbating her dislikes—dogs, kids, people in general—and rendering her incapable of rational thought—digging for potatoes, talking to people who weren't there, muttering about angry birds.

Nothing Sadie had learned would explain who would attack Mrs. Wapple and why, but she seemed more sick than sinister now that Sadie had been able to talk to someone who had positive feelings toward her. It was a shame that Mr. Delecorte and his wife hadn't been able to take over Mrs. Wapple's care. Instead, Gabrielle had obviously taken on more than she was prepared to handle.

Nothing Mr. Delecorte had said pointed toward anything scandalous or horrible enough that Gabrielle would be trying to scare Sadie away from it, and Gabrielle hadn't been any kind of villain in his report. She'd grown out of her family was how he put it, and it was an apt description. She was educated and had social status beyond what she'd been raised to. She wasn't taking the right kind of care of her sister, but she'd moved her closer, and she did check in on her once a week. Very basic things, but . . . it was something.

Sadie's thoughts circled around to motive again. Gabrielle was one of the few people connected to the weird things that had been happening, but she had no reason to do any of it. Additionally, she had many reasons *not* to. Presumably she was fine with her sister's situation until Sadie started trying to tell her what she was doing wrong. All she had to do was wait out Sadie's visit, not stage some big dramatic series of events meant to scare her off. Unless, as Sadie and Pete had discussed, she was a psychopath. Then her motives didn't have to be reasonable.

Hmmm.

It was barely noon, which meant she had another hour left before she would be meeting Jane at the restaurant. Sadie tapped her pen against her notepad, contemplating her options. She was on track with Mr. Forsberk. By the time Jane finished her parts, she'd have a lot of information on which to base round two with him this afternoon. That left Sadie with Gabrielle to look into, but she felt as though she'd exhausted that resource.

She went back to the notes she'd taken about Gabrielle and spent twenty minutes going through them, trying to find more leads on information. She found Gabrielle on a couple of social network sites, but there wasn't much personal information available. It seemed she'd worked hard to have a very professional online presence in place. Sadie tracked her job history and figured out when she'd graduated from school and when she and Bruce Handell had started dating, but there wasn't any *dirt* for her to dig through.

Sadie had heard about companies you could hire to "clear your name" online, so to speak, so that those old college frat party pictures or the political protest you'd attended didn't show up when the potential boss did a background check. Sadie wondered if Gabrielle had done the same thing or if she really had just lived a very professional, clean, good life—the perfect front for a psychopath. She also noted that Gabrielle hadn't been publicly connected to her sister's attack yet. When Sadie searched the news databases with Gabrielle's name, the only hits she got were for articles about the gallery or Bruce Handell. Nothing came up about her mentally ill sister.

There was unfinished business with Gabrielle, Sadie could feel it, but she'd run out of places to look for information. Would Jane be able to find something more? Sadie bit her bottom lip and considered that. She already felt as though she'd given Jane a lot to do while Sadie had just made one silly phone call. Asking Jane to take on even more was presumptuous. Or did it just hurt Sadie's pride to admit she couldn't do this all by herself? She called Mrs. Wapple's current landlord, but it went to voice mail. Worried that the police had made the same contact, Sadie chose not to leave a message, deciding to call back later instead.

Sadie decided to look up articles on Mrs. Wapple's attack to see if there had been any updates and spent another fifteen minutes reading a couple dozen different versions. There was nothing that she didn't already know and still no mention of Gabrielle.

Sadie was glad the story hadn't been picked up by the Associated Press and was therefore relatively contained, although it had shown up in the *Denver Post*. She assumed the story would pick up steam when there was an arrest made, assuming there would be an arrest.

At 12:35 she got a text from Jane saying she needed another half an hour; her interview had gone long. Sadie replied that was fine, then rested her head on her hand and wondered what she was going to do for the next hour until she and Jane could compare notes. Sadie's notes were rather pathetic—was there a way she could boost her results and use her time more constructively? Was there any lead she hadn't squeezed every last drop from?

Her eyes rested on the Google search bar on the computer, and she contemplated it for several seconds before she went ahead and typed in the topic she'd been avoiding since the beginning.

Ghosts.

She took a breath and clicked the search button, trying not to feel as though she'd caved.

CHAPTER 29

I t was a tongue-in-cheek search, to be sure. The sites were immature or Halloween-themed, impossible to take seriously. But Sadie kept reading, if only to convince herself of how ridiculous it was. Other than really poor grammar on most of the silly sites, there was little to interest her other than the profound belief these people had that spirits did exist. The more she read, the more her anxiety began to build. She was uncomfortable with this line of investigation and kept telling herself, "People can put anything online." None of this could be for real.

Then she had a burst of inspiration. She was in Boston, twenty minutes from the site of the infamous Salem witch trials during which time nearly two dozen men and women were executed for practicing witchcraft that was proven by scientifically unsound means. It was a tragic and dark story, and yet the fact that she was so close to such a nucleus meant that she had resources other than silly websites full of stories she had no way to prove.

In-person research was always more effective than reading, and since she already had a prejudice against this information, it made even more sense to go to the source and get exactly what she needed. She went back to the Google search bar and typed in "meta-physical store Boston" and discovered there were dozens of stores in the Boston area. She waded through the links and repetitions until she found an address in Jamaica Plain. She let out a breath and tried to push her prejudice aside as she wrote down the address in her notebook. A good investigator didn't ignore any options, regardless of how ridiculous they seemed. After packing up her things, she checked the time: 12:50. She had forty solid minutes, and she assured herself this was a worthy use of her time.

By the time she found the store, she was questioning herself all over again. She had to park almost a block away, but at least she didn't have to pay for parking. The shop wasn't part of the main downtown district in Jamaica Plain, filled with colonial and cottage-style buildings that housed antique shops, bookstores, and various cafés and delis. This block held square brick buildings with narrow doorways, cracked sidewalks, and heavy power lines draped between the rooftops. She speed-walked past a pawn shop and a bar with peeling vinyl stickers on the door saying they were open from 4: 0 to 2:0 , and pushed open a door painted bright green with the words WICK'D WHICH painted on a sign that hung perpendicular to the patched brick. Oh, boy.

The tinkle of a bell was the same one she heard every time she entered Marie's Bakery back in Garrison. For an instant she missed her town—missed knowing her way around, knowing what to expect and who she would see when she ran her errands. It wasn't the same for her at home anymore, but she missed what it once was.

The store smelled nothing like Marie's Bakery, however, and the musty, incense-heavy scent in the air chased away any feelings of nostalgia the bell had signaled. Floor to ceiling was covered with either shelves or banners depicting all kinds of symbols and visions of the undead. Near the door was a set of shelves with a handwritten sign that said POCKET ALTARS TO GO! Two women stood off to the side discussing different types of tarot cards; Sadie didn't tune in. Quite frankly this kind of stuff gave her the creeps. There were some teenage kids in the back corner of the store, and Sadie wondered if their parents knew they were here. Right after she came in, another woman entered who seemed to know exactly where she was going. Sadie wondered if it was always this busy or if the Halloween season had something to do with the afternoon traffic.

There was a counter toward the back and she went directly to it. A woman about Jane's age with unnaturally blonde hair but surprisingly normal makeup and clothes was ringing up a college-aged man with gauged ears—the holes were easily an inch in diameter. Sadie closed one eye and shifted so her line of sight passed through one of the holes until she realized the clerk was watching her. She cleared her throat and took a step back. The clerk smiled but didn't call her on it.

After the customer collected his bag of tricks, Sadie moved forward. The clerk looked an awful lot like a librarian, especially with the line of books behind her head. However, the book titles were things like *Unveiling Your Spirit Guides* and *How to Use Charms and Tokens*. It was hard enough to believe people read those books, let alone wrote them.

"Welcome to Wick'd Which. Can I help you?" She had a deep, rich voice; she'd be great on the radio.

"Um, yes," Sadie said. "I need to do a, um, cleansing." She'd decided the best way to get information would be to pretend to already have a belief and go from there. She'd gleaned enough from her Internet searches to get started.

"Okay, for what type of entity?" She cocked her head to the side and looked at Sadie with bright brown eyes.

"A ghost."

The woman smiled a little more, and Sadie sensed that the clerk had pegged her as a novice. So much for Sadie's Google education. "What kind?"

"I guess I didn't know there were different kinds," Sadie admitted. "The scary kind."

The girl laughed. "What signs have you seen?"

"Power going out, doors being slammed. Voices."

The woman frowned. "Voices?"

Sadie nodded, but she didn't like that frown. "Is that bad?"

"Rare," the woman said. "And not an *Antiques Roadshow* kind of rare." She leaned her elbows on the counter. "Tell me about the voice."

If not for the incense in the air and the set of large spandex bat wings hanging from the ceiling above this woman's head, Sadie could imagine they were talking over coffee about something totally routine. She decided to pretend that's exactly what was happening. "Well," she began, and then she laid out everything that had happened in chronological order and with intricate detail. Halfway through, Sadie stepped aside so that the clerk could help a customer. When the woman was finished, she said, "Thanks, Grace."

Grace—such a solid Christian name for a girl working in such a strange store. As soon as the customer was gone, Grace waved Sadie back, and Sadie picked up where she'd left off. She kept waiting for Grace's expression to change or show some kind of surprise, but it remained totally neutral.

When Sadie finished, she paused for breath and said, "So, what do you think?"

"Honestly," Grace said, scrunching up her face, "what you've explained is kind of a mixed para-phenomenon."

"A what?"

"Well, the electrical is classic earthbound spirit stuff. The rushes of wind and things being moved . . . well, that's anger-driven but also earthbound spirit-related. Cold mist?" She shook her head. "Old wives' tale. I mean, sure, you might be freaked out and get the chills, but they don't use moisture like that. And voices? Unless you're a sensitive, hearing voices isn't typical either." She cocked her head to the side and looked at Sadie a bit more appraisingly. "Are you a sensitive?"

"Oh, um, I get allergies sometimes, mostly just in the spring. I think it's the cottonwood trees."

She smiled. "Not sensitivity. Are you a *sensitive*—someone who can sense spirits? Have you had other experiences like this in your life?"

"Oh, gosh, no," Sadie said, trying not to laugh. "Just this, uh, one. I'm not sensitive to anything like this. I'm just trying to figure out what's going on." She paused. "I have kind of wondered if someone is, you know, pretending."

"Excuse me," another customer asked Grace from behind Sadie. "Where are your Goddess Watchtowers?"

"North wall," Grace said, pointing to her right. "Next to the rack of Mojo bags."

The customer thanked her and moved away. Grace's attention snapped back to Sadie. "The whole unlocking doors thing doesn't fit either. Spirits don't need to mess with locks."

"I guess that makes sense," Sadie said, considering how that tidbit worked so well into her growing theory.

"The thing you need to understand is that most ghosts are either angry, sad, or scared. If they decide they want your attention, they have limited ways in which to get it."

Sadie nodded. "But unlocking doors and calling my name isn't in their MO?"

"Not that I've heard about," she said. "And believe me, I've heard just about everything."

The phone rang and Grace answered by introducing herself to the caller. Sadie wondered what a woman like her—normal and smart—was doing working in a store like this. She looked toward the ceiling where a ten-foot snakeskin hung; Sadie wondered if you bought it by the yard like ribbon. Did the shop sell eye of newt to go with the scales of a snake? She heard Grace finishing the call and looked back at her, catching sight of the books behind the counter again. There was a sign off to the side that read "Have you searched our para-database?" That gave Sadie a whole new idea.

"Do you have a catalogue of books and magazines about this type of thing?" Sadie asked, waving toward the sign. "Maybe that would help me get, uh, familiar with all this."

"Sure do," Grace said. "Would you like me to recommend some reading for you? It's really a fascinating topic, despite the obvious weird stuff." She reached over her head and tapped the bat wings, causing them to swing back and forth slightly. "It's not all *Twilight Zone*."

"I've actually heard of some articles written by a guy named Timothy Wapple." Maybe reading more about what he wrote would help her see any connections to Gabrielle now that Mrs. Wapple was hospitalized and therefore had a perfect alibi.

"Do you know a title of an article?"

"I don't, sorry." Sadie considered texting Jane but that would mean admitting she was in this shop in the first place. She wasn't ready to fess up to that just yet. "I know they're old, late seventies or early eighties. Hard copy magazine, I think."

"We'll do our best," Grace said with a nod. "My aunt actually owns the shop and she has a pretty extensive database, but eighties magazines . . ." She whistled. "It might require a little magic."

She smiled at Sadie but Sadie could feel her smile in return was a nervous one. This woman wasn't going to cast spells on the computer, was she? Sadie was suddenly in a hurry to leave. "Not a big deal," she said, waving away her question, wondering why she'd bothered asking. "I don't mean for you to go to all the trouble."

"I have no problem doing a search," she said, still tapping at the keyboard, then waiting for a page to load. "And if we don't have it, my aunt's friend works at the Salem library and I bet she's got it."

"It's really not important, but thank you."

Sadie's phone beeped, indicating a text message. She pulled it out of her purse—she hated waiting for things. The text was from Jane.

The girl isn't with Radio Shack anymore. Not much from the reporter either. How is your stuff going?

Sadie hurried to answer.

Good info from landlord, doing some research right now. Heather's probably home. Are we still on for 1:30 at Wonder Spice?

When she read Jane's agreement, she looked up as Grace gave her an apologetic frown. "Sorry, I'll have to do a deeper search."

"It's okay," Sadie said. "I really don't mean to be a bother, and you're so busy." She felt silly and turned away.

"Didn't you need to do a cleansing?"

"Oh, right." How could she forget? After all, *that* was why she'd come in, right?

"Let me take your number, too. I might not have a lot of down-time—'tis the season for shops like ours—but if I do, I'll keep looking for those articles."

Sadie hesitated but realized there was no good reason not to cover this base just like she was trying to cover everything else.

Grace wrote down Sadie's cell phone number on the back of her own card and slipped it under the cash register so that only a corner of it peeked out. Then Grace moved away from the computer and came around the desk.

"Even if someone's having a little Halloween fun with you, a cleansing isn't a bad idea. I recommend doing them quarterly, and pretty much everyone has a spirit or two that gets a little hopped up on the holiday this time of year."

She headed toward the far left of the store. Sadie followed her, albeit carefully, and smiled at the two women they passed who'd been here when she'd come in. They were taking turns holding different crystals while closing their eyes thoughtfully and either nodding or shaking their heads. Grace stopped at a rack full of what looked like bottles of spices. Nearby, clusters of dried herbs hung from a ladder suspended horizontally from the ceiling. Sadie looked for a jar labeled EYE OF NEWT but didn't see any. They must keep that in the back. Maybe it was FDA-regulated.

Grace reached up to a shelf below the ladder and grabbed what looked like a small, oblong bale of hay bound up with blue bailing twine. "One smudge stick," she said in triumph. With her other hand she selected one of the bottles of spices and headed back to the counter, where she wrapped the bundle in tissue paper and put it into a bright red bag with the jar of spice. She handed it across the counter and tapped on her cash register. "That'll be $13.31."

"You don't think it's a ghost, though, do you?"

"Believe you can do this," she said, giving Sadie an encouraging smile, but not answering the question directly. "And see it through to the end."

"I think that's very good advice—with or without a ghost." Sadie smiled back as she plucked a twenty-dollar bill out of her wallet.

"Light the smudge stick, but blow out any flame so it's only smoldering. Open the windows a crack and walk through the house, waving the stick around. Make sure you get the smoke into corners and closets. I'd recommend you hold it over a pan or something so you don't get ash everywhere. Sprinkle it with the cinnamon every now and again."

"Cinnamon?"

Grace shrugged and tapped the bag. "It makes it smell better, and it has properties of protection that can't hurt, right?"

"I've always been a fan of cinnamon," Sadie agreed. She thought of her poor cinnamon twists—the spice hadn't offered much protection yesterday.

"Here's my card," Grace said. "In case you need anything else. I'll be sure to call you if I find anything about Timothy Wapple."

Sadie took the tiny rectangle that read GRACE OWENS—MEDIUM, MYSTIC. She had to remind herself of the urgency of her meeting with Jane to keep from asking Grace what a medium actually did and how it was different from a sensitive. She was curious, but didn't want to invite more talk of the strange stuff people believed. And she didn't have time, anyway. She only had fifteen minutes to find the restaurant.

"Thank you so much," Sadie said. She headed for the front of the store and nearly jumped out of her skin as a man pulled the door open just as she reached for the doorknob. He was gray—not pale; gray—and his eyes bugged out of his head a little bit. He didn't smile, but Sadie imagined she'd see fangs if he had.

"Hey, Bright," Grace said from her counter. "I've got your order in the back. It said to keep it refrigerated."

Sadie gave Bright a shaky smile and slipped past him in the doorway, not wanting to know what this man needed that required refrigeration; her mind was already spinning with unsavory possibilities.

CHAPTER 30

Wonder Spice wasn't hard to find since, as opposed to Wick'd Which, it was located on a quirky corner of the Centre Street downtown district. The spicy lemongrass smell convinced Sadie as soon as she entered that Jane could be trusted on her recommendation. A tiny Asian woman showed Sadie to a table for two when she said she was meeting someone and then brought her a glass of water. Sadie was drooling over the Thai-Cambodian menu items when someone put their hands over her eyes, instigating a moment of absolute panic.

"Guess who?" Jane said from behind Sadie before dropping her hands.

Sadie tried to smile, but she did not like that game. "I didn't hear you come in."

"I'm like a cat," Jane said, lifting her eyebrows as she slid into the vacant chair. "I've heard the Bo-Bo soup is out of this world." She lifted her menu and scanned it without saying hello.

Sadie quickly found it on the menu; it did sound good.

"And the Pad Thai," Jane said. "Have you had that before?"

Sadie shook her head. "I haven't, but I'm willing to give it a try.

I admit I don't make a lot of ethnic dishes. They require so many special spices and pastes I usually don't have on hand."

The waitress came relatively quickly and they both ordered the Bo-Bo soup and Pad Thai, then updated each other on their respective tasks. Sadie didn't know how to confess to having gone to a metaphysical store so she left it out for now.

"So nothing groundbreaking from the landlord?"

Sadie shook her head. "No. He was a very nice guy, though."

Jane rolled her eyes. "Well, that's helpful."

Sadie chose not to take that as an insult. "It's too bad you couldn't talk to the girl from Radio Shack."

Jane shrugged. "Yeah, but those are the breaks, right? I put another call in to the reporter who wrote the article. I don't like being ignored."

"Hopefully he'll call soon," Sadie said. The soup was delicious, an amazing blend of texture and flavors that Sadie couldn't immediately identify. The Pad Thai came just as they were sipping the last of the soup and was also delicious—the noodles cooked to chewy perfection, and the tangy spices just right. Sadie might be able to come up with a recipe for this one. She wondered if Pete liked Thai and would be up for experimentation. A quick glance at her phone informed her that he'd been at the police station two hours now. She hoped he was okay.

They were both halfway through their meals before Jane asked, "So, what's in the bag?"

Sadie looked at the red plastic bag she'd tried to tuck into her purse. The length of the smudge stick made it impossible to hide completely, however. For some reason she hadn't expected Jane to notice, which she realized was kind of ridiculous. That Jane *had* noticed, however, meant Sadie had to come clean. "I, uh, went to a mystical store to ask about ghosts and things, and I ended up buying a smudge stick."

"Serious?" Jane said, leaning over and grabbing Sadie's purse without even asking. She pulled the bag out and quickly removed the smudge stick, grinning widely. She gave Sadie a knowing look. "I knew you wouldn't be able to leave that alone. So, you're seeing it, aren't you?"

"Seeing what?" Sadie asked, twirling another forkful of noodles on her plate.

"Everything you guys have experienced and tried to blow off, it's totally on point with what I was telling you last night, right?"

"Well, some of it," Sadie said, meeting Jane's eyes. "But not everything. The gal at the store said voices aren't common and neither is cold mist. And why would ghosts unlock doors?"

Jane's smile fell. "They could unlock the doors just to throw you off."

"Why bother throwing us off when we don't know what we're looking for?"

Jane blinked, then went back to her plate, cutting another bite while Sadie kept explaining. She talked about how Grace was going to look into the articles by Tim Wapple and get back to her. "She could see the possibility that someone was trying to make it look like ghosts but hadn't done their homework."

"Huh," Jane said, after chewing and swallowing another bite. "That's really surprising. When I researched ghost phenomena, all of those things were there—symptoms, if you will."

"Which might go back to the fact that anything can be put on-line." Sadie didn't want to be too discouraging since Jane seemed to take the conflicting information hard. "Anyway, it was educational, and Grace was very nice so it wasn't a wasted trip—quite the opposite. I think we can put the ghost possibility to bed completely now and move on to the next item on our list."

"Gabrielle," Jane said.

Sadie hadn't actually gotten far enough to decide what to do next, but Gabrielle was an area they hadn't fully explored. "It's probably time," she said. "I just don't know what to do or where to start with her. I've researched her to the hilt and there's nothing that stands out. Of course you have access to different information than I do, so maybe I missed something." That seemed to cheer up Jane, and some of her arrogance returned.

"Everyone is hiding something," Jane assured her.

"And I believe one of the things Gabrielle is hiding is her sister."

"Interesting," Jane said, nodding. "I bet hiding the sister is part of something bigger, though. Maybe she lied to her friends about where she came from, or maybe she reached her social status using scandalous means that, should they be discovered, would ruin what she's worked for. Maybe hurting her sister was a way to keep her quiet about something else."

Sadie hadn't thought of any of that. "It seems risky. She's certainly been contacted by the police, and her inattentiveness would be a huge red flag to them. She could lose everything. And while the paint spill was certainly interesting, it was rather elementary too, like it was more to freak me out than to get the police's attention."

Jane looked at her plate while she cut a bite. "Unless she thought you might discover Mrs. Wapple but not go to the police. The paint would make it hard for you to pretend you hadn't been there."

Sadie considered that and shook her head. "It still seems weak and not all that inventive."

"Or we just don't understand the real reason. I think Mrs. Wapple had information Gabrielle would stop at nothing to protect."

"Maybe," Sadie said, resting her fork on the side of her plate. "But I can think of a dozen ways to silence someone completely without leaving any evidence behind."

"A dozen ways?" Jane said, her eyebrow raised and a smile on her lips.

Sadie blushed. "Not that I would ever use them. I'm just saying that if she wanted to silence her sister, why not silence her?" She felt horrible talking this way; it felt so dark and twisted. "Anyway, things just don't line up."

"Which means we must be missing vital pieces of information that would make things come together. Didn't you say that Gabrielle has a party at her gallery tonight?"

Sadie nodded. "She's made a big deal about it on more than one occasion; she's really stressed about it." Which, again, made it even harder to imagine that she'd hurt her sister at such an intense time. But, like Jane had said, if Mrs. Wapple knew something detrimental enough about her sister, none of that might matter. And, if Gabrielle were psychopathic, making sense of everything was a waste of time. That thought, however, invited a truly sick one to grab hold of Sadie's insides. Had Sadie's continued questions and prodding somehow influenced the attack on Mrs. Wapple? She put her fork down as her appetite left her completely.

"What?" Jane asked, watching her reaction.

"Nothing," Sadie said, unable to vocalize the possibility she could be to blame for what had happened. "This is just . . . hard, ya know? I hate to see such sad things up close. I really hope Gabrielle didn't hurt her sister."

"But if she did, we can be part of the solution, right?"

Sadie had to acknowledge that possibility.

"Right," Jane confirmed. "So Gabrielle's crazy busy today. We should go to her house."

"She's not there," Sadie said. "I'm sure she'll be at the gallery or the hospital all day."

Jane pointed her fork at Sadie. "Precisely," she said with a cocky grin. "What better time to have a look around than while she's so wonderfully distracted?"

"You mean break in?" Sadie shook her head. "We can't do that."

"Sure we can. You and me got skills, girlfriend. We can get inside in ten seconds flat. You brought your pick set, right?"

Actually, Sadie had invested in a pick gun, an electronic device that did all the pressing and poking for you. It was ingenious and so fast and easy to use that it made an ideal item to keep in her purse. At home, however, she still preferred the hands-on lock picks when she was practicing with her growing collection of locks. "I didn't mean we can't physically accomplish it. We can't break in; it's illegal."

"So is stabbing your sister."

"Which we don't know she did."

"But could find out if we got into her apartment."

Sadie could see her point, but she couldn't get past the breaking and entering part. "No," she said, shaking her head. "I won't break the law."

Jane let out a breath and stuffed a too-big bite into her mouth; chewing it caused her whole face to move. When she finally swallowed, she'd apparently worked out her frustration. "Fine," she said. "We can at least poke around outside, right?"

"She lives on Hemenway Street, probably in a multi-residence brownstone. I don't know what we'll find since that area is so densely populated."

"We can poke around outside the gallery too," Jane said, looking up at Sadie for the first time in the last several seconds. "I mean, we've got to do *something*."

Sadie didn't like feeling so prudish so she nodded even though the chances of finding something outside either Gabrielle's house or her studio seemed like a long shot. But this angle did need to be maximized. "Can you also do a search on her? See if you can find what I couldn't."

"Of course," Jane said, smiling again. "I'm happy to work my magic for you."

CHAPTER 31

They decided to take the T into Boston and were waiting in the Forest Hills station when Sadie's phone rang. It was an unfamiliar number.

"Hello?"

"Mrs. Hoffmiller," a familiar voice said. "This is Detective Lucille. We spoke yesterday at the JP police department."

"Oh, yes," Sadie said as a tremor washed through her. "What can I do for you?" She stepped away from Jane and the dozen other people waiting for the train so that she could have both some privacy and noise control. She plugged her other ear to better hear the detective and hoped that the noises of the station weren't too loud.

"Well, I'm mostly calling with an update," the detective said. "I thought it would be a courtesy for me to tell you that we've all but ruled you out as a suspect."

"Really?" Sadie said. "Gosh, that's a relief."

"I'm sure it is. Based on Mrs. Wapple's injuries and certain other details from the scene, we've determined that the attacker was taller than you and, likely, stronger."

Sadie had never been more grateful to be short and wimpy,

though she silently reminded herself that she was stronger than she looked. "I'm very glad to hear that," she said. A mental picture of Mr. Forsberk popped into her mind. He was tall and while he didn't look particularly muscular, she couldn't say for sure. The next person she thought of, however, was Pete. Apparently she wasn't alone in thinking of him.

"We've been speaking with Peter Cunningham this afternoon," Detective Lucille continued. "And I'd like to ask you some questions about him."

"Oh," Sadie said rather flatly. "Um, of course. When would be a good time?"

"Late afternoon—perhaps around five thirty? I should be ready for you by then."

That would still give her time to meet up with Mr. Forsberk. "I can do that," she said, though her stomach was wriggling with instant anxiety. Was she going to tell them everything she'd discovered? She didn't feel ready, but she knew she wouldn't lie about things either.

"We'll expect you at the station at five thirty, then," Detective Lucille said.

"Sure," Sadie said. They ended the call, and Sadie hung up, the sick feeling in her stomach growing stronger even as she told herself that since she had nothing to hide, there was nothing for her to be afraid of.

"What was that all about?" Jane asked from right behind Sadie, causing Sadie to jump and turn at the same time.

"Oh, it was the detective," Sadie said. "Apparently, they've determined whoever attacked Mrs. Wapple was taller than I am. I guess I'm off the hook." She smiled, showing the relief she felt so strongly despite the concern of meeting with the detective.

"Awesome," Jane said. The train approached with a hiss, and Sadie put her phone back in her purse as they headed toward the platform.

"Yeah," Sadie agreed as she lined up behind Jane and the other passengers. "And they don't want to meet with me until five thirty so we don't have to adjust our schedule."

"They still want to talk to you?" Jane asked, looking over her shoulder as the train lumbered to a stop and the line of passengers tightened even more.

"Yeah," Sadie said, trying to sound casual; she didn't want to give away Pete's role in this. "Just to verify some details."

Her phone rang again, and she hurried to answer it.

"Sadie," Gayle said after Sadie said hello. "Sorry it took me so long to get back to you."

"No problem," Sadie said, bringing to mind why she'd called Gayle in the first place. Oh, yeah, the dog whistle. "This is actually perfect timing," she said as she followed Jane into the train car.

The call cut off twice while they were on the train, but Gayle called back both times and was able to confirm Sadie's suspicions: dog whistles could be set to such a high pitch that they were un-detectable by humans but painful to dogs. "Darrin said he was at a dog show where someone in the stands had one—they never found out who—but they had to cancel the show. All those dogs—highly trained dogs, mind you—were howling and running around. The next year they had metal detectors at the entrance. The whistles can be really dangerous."

"That's what I thought," Sadie said, picturing the dog magazine at Mrs. Wapple's house. Had she seen anything else? "Thank you so much for doing the research for me."

"No problem," Gayle said. "Everything okay?"

Sadie sighed. What a question. "I think it will be," she finally said, wishing she was more confident than she felt. "I'll call tomorrow with more details, okay?"

"Sure thing, sweetie. You hang in there, okay? And let me know if you need anything."

Sadie thanked her and hung up to find Jane staring at her. She quickly recounted the phone call. "I could have looked up the whistles for you," Jane said when Sadie finished. "You don't have to ask other people to help you, that's what I'm here for."

"I know," Sadie said with a smile, feeling bad that she still didn't trust Jane completely. "But you already had a list of things to do, and I didn't want to put too much on your plate. As for Gayle, I called her before you even showed up."

"But I'd already offered my help."

That was true. "Sorry," Sadie said. "I guess I'm just not used to having a partner."

"Huh," Jane said, but she still seemed a little miffed. Sadie was too tired to explain herself again and leaned back against the seat. A teenage boy with earbuds was head-bopping to a song, and a teenage girl further down the car was sneaking glances at him every few seconds while two old women twittered in Chinese a few seats past that. Things were funneling together, Sadie could feel it, but she didn't know how the pieces fit together just yet. It was both exciting and anxiety producing.

I'll figure it out, though, she told herself, boosting her confidence. *I will figure it out.*

She had to.

When they exited the Back Bay station, Sadie blinked a few times, but it didn't clear away the gauzy shroud in the air. "Fog," she said, surprised since it hadn't been foggy in Jamaica Plain.

"Advection," Jane answered, shoving her hands into her pockets as they started walking.

"Advection?" Sadie repeated. "What does that mean?"

"The cold temperatures from the water mix with warming temperatures on land and create a fog. I was here one summer when it happened in August. Totally weird phenomenon. They were talking about it on the news this morning—said it would come through in time for the afternoon commute. Nice."

"It's kind of pretty," Sadie said. It blocked out the long-range views of the city, but gave an almost romantic tinge to everything else.

They went to Gabrielle's house first and, as Sadie suspected, there was little to see. It wasn't garbage day, and the houses had porches instead of yards. Gabrielle was on the middle floor of a triple-decker brownstone squished between an entire street's worth of triple-decker brownstones. They were able to chat with the neighbor who lived on the street level of Gabrielle's building, but she had only ever exchanged pleasantries in the hallway with her.

Jane was undeterred by their lack of success, and they immediately headed for the gallery on Newbury Street. Despite the fog, it wasn't terribly cold like it had been the last few days. Sadie took in the cozy feel of the city, nodded to people who didn't nod back—this was the East Coast, she reminded herself—and took in the changing leaves, the autumn wreaths on many a door, and the overall feel of downtown Boston. Though Sadie had never been a big city dweller, she could imagine herself living in a place with so much personality and history. Maybe if her kids didn't come back to Garrison—a possibility that continued growing all the time—she'd look into relocating to a place like this. Then again, she'd never been to Boston in the wintertime. She should make sure to do that before she made any definite decisions.

"A penny for your thoughts?"

Sadie looked at Jane, who also seemed to be relaxing on their walk.

"Just admiring the city," she said.

Jane looked around. "It is a pretty cool place, isn't it?"

"It is. I love the whole feel of it. You said you've been here before?"

"Several times," Jane said. "I had an aunt who lived in Cambridge. We'd come and visit every summer when I was growing up, and I spent a year out here before I went to college—that's how I know my way around so well. She's dead now, though."

This was the first time Jane had ever said anything about her childhood. From Shawn's comments, Sadie knew that it hadn't been ideal, but she was glad there were some good memories too. "Did you grow up in the East?" she asked, assuming that Jane must not have lived too far away if the family made a yearly visit to Cambridge.

Jane shoved her hands into her pockets and looked uncomfortable. "Yeah, kinda," she said, but didn't elaborate, which led Sadie to wonder if she'd suddenly remembered the less pleasant parts. Sadie had no desire to dredge up hurtful memories so she started talking about the first time she'd been here with Breanna and Shawn. Jane listened politely, and Sadie could only hope she enjoyed the trek down memory lane as much as Sadie did.

Before she knew it, however, she'd run out of story, and Jane was pointing across the street at a green awning over a bricked colonial building that had only somewhat been restored so as to keep the Victorian feel. They looked both ways but still got honked at as they ran across the street, stopping at the simple wrought iron sign that said Bastian Gallery mounted beside the beveled glass front door. It was the kind of place someone had to know they were going to if they hoped to find it, as it could be easily lost amid the splashier facades and brighter signage of neighboring businesses.

"Let's find a way to the back," Jane suggested. Sadie nodded and headed left until they found a narrow walkway between the buildings. It was dark and the fog meant they couldn't see what was at the end of the alley.

"I'm glad it's daylight," she said as she followed Jane through the fog. The buildings were so tall and the walkway so narrow that despite never having felt claustrophobic in her life, Sadie nearly ran into Jane's back as her feet seemed to unconsciously speed up. She breathed a lot better when they emerged into the space behind the buildings. She looked down the staggered brick store backs, a mix-matched hodgepodge of different types of brick and stone, accessorized by overgrown weeds and electrical lines as well as a Dumpster every thirty yards or so. Curb appeal was certainly not a consideration for the back lot.

"Green awning," Jane said, pointing to their left. "Same as the front, that's got to be it."

"But we're not going in," Sadie said. The fog made the back lot feel isolated despite the sound of traffic all around them.

"I know," Jane agreed. "We still need to know the layout. Let's start there and do a perimeter search in extending grids from the back door."

"Okay," Sadie said, impressed with Jane's command of the situation while still wondering what they might find.

"I'll go left; you go right."

"Got it," Sadie agreed. They approached the door, the solid gray metal stenciled with letters indicating that it was, in fact, Bastian

Gallery. They both began searching the ground for . . . whatever they might find. Sadie mostly found crushed glass and oil spots, though there was half a pack of soggy cigarettes and a pop can—diet cherry Dr. Pepper—beside the telephone pole about twenty feet from the door. She picked up the trash and headed toward the Dumpster pushed up against the building.

"Found something?" Jane asked from her position further down the lot.

"Just throwing these away," Sadie said.

Jane nodded and then continued her search.

Sadie lifted the lid of the Dumpster in order to throw the items in. When she dropped the lid with a reverberating thump, she noticed a piece of white paper partially under the Dumpster. It was bigger than a business card but smaller than a regular sheet of copy paper. She might as well throw that away too. She bent down and picked it up, giving it a cursory scan as she lifted the Dumpster lid again. She froze when she turned the paper over and saw a very familiar shade of red staring back at her.

She blinked and, still holding up the lid, took in every detail of the card she now recognized as a paint sample card, the kind Sadie had picked up many a time from her local paint store when looking to redo a room in her home. This particular card was the exact shade of red Sadie had been drenched in at Mrs. Wapple's yesterday afternoon. A shivery tingle radiated out from her spine, making her fingers holding the card ache a little bit.

"You okay?"

Sadie looked up to see Jane approaching and finally recognized the ache in her shoulder from holding up the Dumpster lid. She dropped it, the sound making her jump. She handed the card to

Jane, who took it and then turned it over in case she was missing something.

"That's the same color of paint from Mrs. Wapple's house," Sadie said, realizing Jane hadn't seen it. "I'd put money on it."

"Really?" Jane said, her eyebrows going up. "You're sure?"

Sadie nodded and the sick feeling that had bothered her off and on for the last two days came back. She looked at the green awning of Gabrielle's gallery. Sadie couldn't wrap her head around the proof that Gabrielle was involved. "I know we came here looking for evidence but . . . I'm shocked to have found this," she finally said.

"No kidding," Jane agreed.

Sadie looked at the card in Jane's hand, and her brain kicked into investigative gear. "We should check out local paint stores to verify where she bought it. I bet they have all kinds of records."

"She'd be an idiot to buy it locally," Jane said.

"Should I call the police?" Sadie asked.

"I don't know," Jane said, looking at Sadie with an expression as close to sympathy as she had ever seen on her face. "Will they find it suspicious that *you* found the sample?"

Sadie hadn't thought of that and hated thinking of it now. "But they already said I'm too short to have attacked her."

"That's what they *said*," Jane reiterated. She shook the card. "But this doesn't prove your innocence, and it's not strong enough evidence all by itself to get around the automatic suspicion they'll have about it."

"Then why did we come here?" Sadie asked, feeling panic rise in her chest. "If this makes things worse for me"—she waved at the card in Jane's hand—"what did we hope we'd find?"

"Hey," Jane said, putting her hand on Sadie's arm. "Don't freak out, this is still a good find. Now we know Gabrielle's involved. That's powerful stuff."

Sadie took a breath and nodded; Jane was right.

"Have a little faith in the process, Sadie," Jane continued, slipping the paint card into her pocket. "We're adding things up and eventually we'll have enough to take to the police, but we need to go one step at a time, okay?"

"Okay," Sadie said, feeling sheepish for her knee-jerk reaction. "You're right."

The creak of a hinge caught both their attention, and they simultaneously looked up to see the back door to the Bastian Gallery opening toward them. In a split second, they both darted around the side of the Dumpster, pressing their backs against the chipped paint. They looked at one another as they heard the sound of high heels crunch across the gravel. Sadie's heart was in her throat as she willed whoever was there not to come around the Dumpster. She was more grateful than ever for the fog that made her feel even more hidden.

CHAPTER 32

"I know," they heard a woman say. "I just need to get it out of my car—calm down." Sadie was all but convinced it was Gabrielle's voice and could hardly breathe.

"We're so totally behind schedule," said a monotone voice that did not match the urgency his words seemed to reflect. Sadie pegged the voice as belonging to Hansel, the man Sadie had spoken to when she'd called the gallery on Tuesday.

A little beep of a keyless entry sounded before Gabrielle spoke. "It's not my fault," she said. "You know that." A car door, or maybe the trunk of a car, opened. "I'm doing the very best that I can."

"I know," Hansel continued. "But I hate falling behind."

"You and me both," Gabrielle said. Sadie could hear the fatigue in her voice. "See, it's right here. We're good."

"Thank goodness," Hansel said.

The door or trunk slammed, and Gabrielle's steps could be heard hurrying back toward the building. A minute later the door hinges creaked closed. Sadie and Jane both remained totally still and silent for at least thirty seconds.

"She didn't lock the car," Jane said, stepping around Sadie and into full view without even checking to see if someone was there. Sadie was more cautious, peering around the side of the Dumpster before daring to come out of hiding completely. By the time she emerged, Jane had almost reached the black Audi parked opposite the gallery's door. Sadie hurried to catch up, looking around to see if anyone was watching. The back lot wasn't particularly isolated, but they seemed to be alone at the moment.

"What did you say?" Sadie asked when she reached Jane, who was appraising the car.

"She used her keyless entry to unlock the car, but she didn't lock it back up. I didn't hear the beep, did you?"

Sadie thought back, but it was hard to remember since she had been paralyzed with fear. "I don't remember hearing it," she admitted.

"Well, the woman is an idiot to leave her car unlocked in the city. And what's she doing driving to work anyway when she lives four blocks away?"

"I don't think we should break into her car," Sadie said.

Jane looked at her, then grabbed the door handle and pulled. In an instant Sadie was reminded of another time she'd done the same thing and set off a car alarm. She closed her eyes and braced herself, but heard nothing. By the time she dared open her eyes, Jane was leaning halfway into the car, rifling through the middle console. Sadie swallowed and looked around, hoping they were still alone. She sidled over to Jane as though maybe she could block her from view if someone showed up.

"Her car is immaculate," Jane said, standing and going to the back doors. "But if I'd hauled paint and played some elaborate hoax on someone, I'd get my car detailed too."

There was nothing in the backseat, Sadie could see that, and

Jane didn't waste much time on it. Sadie felt like her head was about to explode from her growing anxiety. Jane shut the back door and popped the trunk before shutting the driver's door.

"What a jerk," Jane said.

Sadie joined Jane by the trunk and saw a black duffel bag sitting inside. Jane had unzipped the bag and was sifting through the contents, which seemed to be an eclectic collection of clothing. "How much do you want to bet this is a bag she's packed for her sister and not taken to the hospital yet."

Sadie shook her head. The clothes certainly weren't Gabrielle's.

"Hey," Jane suddenly said, her hand stopping in the bag. She withdrew a small round container, like something face powder would be held in. She lifted it up for Sadie to see, and as soon as Sadie recognized what it was, she straightened.

"Stage makeup?" she asked.

"I guess," Jane said, turning it in her fingers. "I wonder what it's for."

"I know exactly what it's for," Sadie said, glancing at the gallery door. "The face Pete and I saw in the window. It was white— ghostly."

"Ah," Jane said, tossing the container into the air and catching it with a satisfied grin on her face. "Strike two for Ms. Art Gallery director."

"What's it doing in Mrs. Wapple's bag, though?" Sadie asked. "Seems like a strange hiding place."

"Except who would think to search the bag she's taking to her sister in the hospital?"

"Why not just throw it away?" Sadie said. She'd never quite understood why people kept evidence around.

"Maybe she secretly wants to get caught."

A car drove into the lot, and Sadie and Jane both instinctively ducked their heads. The car moved a good hundred yards down the lot before stopping. The driver quickly got out and disappeared through the back door of one of the other shops without looking their way.

"We need to get out of here," Sadie said. She hurried away from the car, and Jane joined her, but a few steps later, when they had almost reached the Dumpster again, she realized she hadn't heard the trunk close. She looked back to see that it was still open, like a giant maw on a sleek black beast. "Shouldn't we close that?" she asked.

"What for?" Jane challenged, taking the lead, which Sadie followed. "Why not give *her* something to figure out for a change?" She smiled at Sadie as she reached the walkway that would take them back to the T.

Sadie didn't argue, but she didn't like the idea of playing games. Still, she wasn't about to go back and shut it herself. As they crossed Newbury Street and continued toward the Back Bay station, Sadie imagined Gabrielle's reaction when she came outside and found the trunk open.

"Did you keep the makeup?" Sadie asked, her breath coming in short bursts due to the Jane's quick pace. Jane reached into her pocket and pulled out the container just enough for Sadie to see.

"I only wish we could see the expression on her face when she realizes it's gone," Jane said with a grin. They reached the stairs leading to the T station, and Jane returned the makeup to her pocket. They kept up the pace until they were sitting on the train heading back to Forest Hills. Sadie looked at her watch. It was 3:30.

"Mr. Forsberk will be home in an hour," Sadie said, moving ahead. "I think he's still worth looking into, even if things are pointing to Gabrielle right now. We'll just have to keep it short so I don't miss my appointment at the police station."

"Sure," Jane said with a nod. "I'm cool with that."

"And," Sadie said, her stomach tightening again, "I need to talk to Pete's daughter-in-law, assuming she's at the house. She's had time to settle in, and it's only going to get harder if I avoid the inevitable."

CHAPTER 33

I t still amazed Sadie how fast the T moved. They were back at the Forest Hills station within twenty minutes. Both she and Jane had parked their cars there, and they were discussing whether to drive together and leave one car at the lot, or drive separately when Sadie's phone rang. She dug it out of her purse, wondering if it was Pete, or maybe Grace from Wick'd Which. Her heart nearly skipped a beat when she saw that it was Gabrielle.

"What?" Jane said, turning to face Sadie while people streamed past them.

"It's Gabrielle," Sadie said as the phone rang for a third time. She considered not answering, but only for a moment. Sadie swallowed and answered the phone before the call went to voice mail. "This is Sadie," she said carefully.

Jane folded her arms over her chest, her already sharp features even edgier with the stern expression on her face.

"It's Gabrielle. I need to talk to you."

Sadie's eyebrows shot up in surprise, and she looked at Jane. Did Gabrielle know they'd been in the car? Or was she calling about something else? "Okay," Sadie said. "When? Now?"

"Not now," Gabrielle said as though Sadie should know that. "I have a reception in three hours that I have spent months preparing for and am now scrambling to make work."

"I'm sorry," Sadie said, and she was. "Can I help?" It was an automatic offer for Sadie; she always helped.

"Not hardly," Gabrielle said. "There's a café on Belvidere, or just off it, called Germaine's. Meet me there at nine thirty."

"Nine thirty?" Sadie repeated, scrambling in her purse for paper and a pen as Gabrielle rattled off the directions to the café. She found a receipt and bent over to use her thigh as a writing surface as she scribbled down the time and the directions. "It's called Germaine's?"

"Yes," Gabrielle said, sounding exasperated. "I'll come as soon as the reception ends. I'll be alone, and I expect you to be alone as well. I don't want to make a big production about this."

"Can I ask what it's about?"

"You said you wanted to help us," Gabrielle said. She hung up before Sadie had a chance to prod for more details. Sadie returned the phone to her purse as she smoothed out the receipt and reviewed the details.

"You're not meeting with her," Jane said as though it were fact.

"It's a public place," Sadie said.

Jane looked completely exasperated. "Are you kidding?"

"I'll be okay," she said. "I can't miss the chance to get a face-to-face with her. You have to appreciate the opportunity to get that kind of interview." She hoped appealing to Jane's journalistic instincts would put them on the same page. Every other meeting with Gabrielle had been complicated, a one-on-one was Sadie's best chance to figure out this woman. That Gabrielle had said she wanted help with something could either be a clever ruse or a humble request. Sadie was willing to risk it.

Jane shook her head. "I'll sneak into one of the other tables then so I can keep an eye on you. Make sure nothing happens that shouldn't."

"No," Sadie said. "I'm not going to take any chances of losing another opportunity with her. I'll go alone." Besides, as wonderfully helpful as Jane was, her strong opinions on what to do and how to do it were a little frustrating.

Jane clenched her jaw, and Sadie braced herself for further argument but Jane just nodded. "I'm driving," she said, turning back to the parking lot.

"Me too," Sadie countered, causing Jane to look at her with an annoyed expression. If she was trying to bully Sadie, it wasn't going to work. "It makes sense for us to each have our own car now that we know we'll be going separate directions at some point."

Jane didn't seem to like that but after a moment she nodded and continued toward her car, while Sadie headed to her rental car, which blended in with all the other vehicles in the lot.

A few minutes later, Sadie pulled up in front of Heather and Jared's house. Jane pulled up behind her, parking alongside the curb. Sadie took a breath, noting the ghost decoration was back on the front door—she really hated that thing. She saw a red head bound past the living room window, proof that the family was indeed home. She was not looking forward to this meeting, but she grabbed her purse with the bag she'd gotten from the metaphysical store and hoped this would go well.

"Do you mind waiting here?" Sadie asked after stopping at Jane's window en route to the door.

"Ah, I don't get to listen to you get chewed out by the mama bear?" Jane asked, grinning widely, apparently recovered from their earlier tension. Sadie was glad Jane was over their disagreement, but she didn't smile because the comment wasn't funny. She was scared to death of facing Pete's daughter-in-law, but she had to get the whoopie pies and she needed to make peace.

Jane shifted into park and pulled out her map of Boston and her phone. "I'll do some checking on that café you're going to. Germaine's, right?"

"You don't need to check on it, but thank you for your support," Sadie said with sincerity, glad they were a team again.

Sadie stepped away from the car, let herself into the gated front yard, and pulled herself up straight as she climbed the steps. Not wanting to overstep her bounds, Sadie rang the doorbell and then held her breath. Heather pulled the door open and stared at her.

Sadie forced a smile. "I bought you a smudge stick," she said, holding out the bag. "I hope you like it."

Heather stood there for a few minutes, the seconds becoming more uncomfortable with each tick of the clock. Finally, when Sadie was ready to kneel at her feet and beg for forgiveness, Heather took the bag and looked inside. Then she looked up at Sadie. "You bought a smudge stick? I thought you didn't believe in ghosts."

"I don't," Sadie said, glancing at the stupid decoration swaying on the door. "Not really, but . . . well, I'm so sorry about everything that's happened. I thought this might help, you know, in case you were worried about . . . ghosts and things. The gal at the store recommended quarterly cleansings and said they are especially helpful this time of year."

They both stood there awkwardly, and Sadie could feel Jane smirking at her from the car. She hoped Heather would invite her inside before she gave Sadie a dressing down.

"Have you heard from Pete?" Heather asked after a few seconds, surprising Sadie.

"No," Sadie said, shaking her head. "Have you?"

Heather shook her head and finally stepped back from the door, inviting Sadie in with a nod of her head. Sadie entered the house gingerly, closing the door and following Heather into the kitchen.

"I called his phone, but maybe I can just ask you a question," Heather said. She went to the counter and opened a cupboard.

"Sure," Sadie agreed, eager to be helpful in any way she possibly could.

"It's about someone getting in and out of the house," Heather began as she rifled through the cupboards. "I went to check on the spare key." She looked at Sadie. "It's not there. I wanted to make sure you guys hadn't used it before I made too big a deal out of it."

Sadie blinked. A spare key? Could that be the mysterious means of getting in and out of the house? Sadie hadn't even thought of that. It was so simple. "I didn't even know you had a spare key."

Heather dug around in the cupboard again. "Well, I haven't ever used it, but when we first moved in, we put one under one of the flowerpots on the side of the garage, just in case. I need to check with Jared to make sure he hasn't moved it sometime in the last three years, but if he hasn't, that part might be solved. Aha, found it." She stood up and set an 8x8 pan on the counter. She put the smudge stick inside the pan and began looking for something else in the cupboard.

"You're still going to do the cleansing?"

Heather looked over her shoulder and smiled. "My mom used to do a cleansing every summer. I've never done one by myself, though."

"Oh," Sadie said. "You don't seem too worried about the key."

"No one got hurt," Heather said. "And we won't be staying here tonight anyway. Pete offered to put us up in the hotel, but I needed to repack and take care of some things here. I guess I'm just putting off the worry. Oh, I wrapped up your whoopie pies," she said, waving toward the counter where several of the cake sandwiches were individually wrapped and stacked on the plate. "The boys loved them—thanks. Why are you taking the rest to Mr. Forsberk?"

"Oh, um, condolences for his dog," Sadie said. "Do you know him very well?"

"No," Heather said. "Roberta—she lives next door—said he's a weird guy, and he's always watching people so I keep my distance from him too." She turned to Sadie. "I have a lot of strange neighbors, don't I?"

Sadie smiled. "They're certainly colorful."

"I guess that explains why I enjoy the other women from church and playgroup so much." Heather frowned. "I feel horrible about Mrs. Wapple, though."

Sadie nodded. "So do I. I feel sick every time I think about it."

"I'm assuming she's doing okay," Heather added as she pulled a fire wand, complete with a childproof switch, out of the drawer.

"Me too," Sadie said. "And I think she'll get a lot of her issues taken care of now that a doctor is involved. I talked to her old landlord and he said she was taking medication and getting home visits from a doctor before she came here. I don't think she's had any medical care since then, which might explain her strange behavior."

"Why did you talk to her old landlord?"

Sadie shrugged and traced the wallpaper seam with her finger. "I just wanted to get a good feel of who she is and who she was. I thought it might help the police and the doctors."

"Oh," Heather said, looking at Sadie in an appraising way for a few more seconds. "You're an interesting person, Sadie."

"Well, I certainly keep finding myself in interesting situations."

She paused and finally brought up the elephant in the room. "You're not mad?"

"I was," Heather admitted. "Until Pete explained things to me. Whatever's been going on isn't your fault—or his—I can see that. You should have told us earlier though." She pointed the fire wand at Sadie and closed one eye to make her point. "I'm a little ticked about that."

"We should have told you sooner," Sadie agreed. "I wish we had. I'm really sorry, Heather. There is nothing worse than worrying about your children when you're too far away to do anything about it. I'm really, really sorry."

"Like I said, I know it's not your fault." Heather lowered the wand and inspected the smudge stick more closely. She seemed honestly excited to do the cleansing. "And I'll feel better when I get this over with."

"Do you need help?"

"It's not hard. I'd like to make sure the kids stay outside, though. Could you keep an eye on them for a few minutes?"

"Sure," Sadie said, eager to remain in Heather's good graces. It was 4:15, so everything was on schedule so far. "I'll just be out back. The lady said to sprinkle it with the cinnamon every now and again—I guess it helps with the smell."

Heather nodded as she clicked the lighter and put the flame to the end of the smudge stick. "Got it, thanks."

Sadie still thought the whole idea was just plain weird, but she headed out to the backyard.

"Hey, boys," she said, pulling the back door closed behind her. The temperature had to be in the high fifties, maybe even low sixties. The humidity still gave the weather an edge it wouldn't have had in Colorado, but it was much more tolerable than it had been the last few days. With a little luck, Pete and Sadie would finish off their trip with a few days of a vibrant Indian summer.

"Hi, Aunt Sadie," Kalan said before disappearing down the slide behind Chance. Fig pushed a big truck up and down a patch of grass. Sadie spent a few minutes playing with them before she noted the smell of burning sage in the air. She looked toward the house and saw the windows along the back were cracked open, allowing the smoke to leave—maybe the spirits too. She rolled her eyes.

It took another ten minutes before Heather proclaimed the house cleansed, by which time Sadie was feeling anxious about her timeline. She had to be to the JP police station by five thirty and then to her meeting with Gabrielle by nine thirty. She still had a busy day ahead of her.

Sadie made her good-byes and then put five whoopie pies on a paper plate. Mr. Forsberk was a bachelor; he didn't need the whole plateful. She was in the living room, shrugging into her coat when she got a text from Shawn asking how things were. She texted back a note saying that she'd call him later, then headed outside to make peace with Jane, who had been waiting for probably longer than she'd have liked.

Jane was out of her car, leaning against the passenger side door. She pushed off when Sadie came outside and started walking toward Mr. Forsberk's house, forcing Sadie to hurry to catch up with her. Sadie could do without the dramatics.

"I'm sorry," Sadie said as she caught up with Jane on the sidewalk. "I went as fast as I could."

"Right," Jane said. "I see how high I am on your priority list."

Sadie turned to look at her, needing to read her expression. Jane grinned and slapped Sadie on the shoulder. "No biggie," she said in a breezy tone. "Let's get this over with."

But Sadie kept staring, and not just because of Jane's quick shift in mood. "Did you do something with your hair?" Yesterday and this morning Jane's hair had been spiked, arching over her head before smoothing down to curve around her other cheek—very Manga cartoonish. But the spikes had been brushed out, and instead of the punky-impaler look, Jane's hair was soft and quite flattering. The style softened the too-sharp lines of Jane's features. But her hair wasn't the only change. "Are you wearing glittered lip gloss?"

Jane's cheeks pinked. She was blushing! Sadie quickly checked the sky to make sure it was still blue. "And you're wearing a sweater!"

Sadie didn't realize she'd stopped until Jane grabbed her arm to get her moving again, leading her across the street. "It's not a big deal," Jane said. "I just wanted to make myself a little more presentable."

"That sweater has a collar," Sadie commented. Glitter lip gloss? Collared sweaters? What was going on here?

"I can clean up when I need to."

Which took Sadie to the next part of her question. "Why do you need to clean up?"

Jane rolled her eyes and let go of Sadie's arm, shooing her through Mr. Forsberk's open gate. Sadie obediently climbed the steps. She knocked on the door and listened carefully for the approaching footsteps, trying to get back to the task at hand. She'd worried that Mr. Forsberk might not be home at all, but was gratified when he pulled open the door and blinked at her from the other side of his glasses. Then he looked at Jane, who smiled quite sweetly, and his face and balding head went red before he looked away, completely flustered.

"Hi, Mr. Forsberk," Sadie said, trying to make sense of his

reaction. He hadn't turned red when she'd been there earlier. "I brought you some whoopie pies. This is my friend, Jane."

"Hi," Jane said in a voice that caused Sadie to do another double take. It wasn't harsh and masculine, but rather soft, girlish, and casual. She put her hand out to Mr. Forsberk, who shook it quickly before dropping it. Jane fairly glowed while her lips sparkled. "Nice to meet you," she added.

Mr. Forsberk simply nodded.

"May we come in?" Sadie asked after a moment.

He moved to the side and Sadie let Jane enter first. She added a swagger to her step and gave Mr. Forsberk a dazzling smile that left Sadie almost as stunned as it left him. What was this, femininity? The sweater Jane wore was light green, a color Sadie had never seen on her, but it somehow worked with Jane's coloring and white skinny jeans. Her choice of footwear—red Converse sneakers—stood out rather starkly against this softened version of Jane, but she looked . . . pretty. Not that she wasn't attractive in the first place, but she had never played it up. At least not until now.

Sadie shut the door behind her and held the plate out to Mr. Forsberk. "How was work?" she asked.

"Fine," Mr. Forsberk said. "Th-thank you for the . . . pies."

"You're welcome," Sadie said. Jane had stopped in the middle of the living room and looked around appraisingly, her thumbs hooked in her jean pockets.

"Wow, you've got your own place," Jane said appreciatively, turning to face him. "That's so cool."

Mr. Forsberk's mouth went slack as Jane's glittery lips pulled into a smile, and she cocked her head to the side. "How do you like living in JP?"

"I . . . I like it," Mr. Forsberk said. "I like it a whole lot."

"I bet you do," Jane said, looking around as though his home were expertly decorated. She shifted her weight, jutting out one hip, which made her look as though she actually had a figure. What was she doing? "How long have you lived here?"

"Two years," he said quickly, as though eager to impress her. "I, uh, haven't really had the chance to clean up today."

He began gathering dishes and empty root beer cans from the coffee table, scurrying into the kitchen with them.

"Oh, gosh," Jane said with a girlish laugh. "There's always better things to do than clean up." She waved a hand as though dismissing the idea of housework entirely, then she moved toward the table. "Oh, cool, you're into electronics?"

"Sure," Mr. Forsberk said. He began explaining to her the same thing he'd told Sadie that morning, although this morning he'd sounded embarrassed and now, talking to Jane, he sounded like an astrophysicist the way he took such pride in his hobby.

Sadie knew she been completely forgotten but recognized the potential of such invisibility. She moved toward the end table and surveyed the contents. There was a remote control that looked as though it required a college degree to use, a few pieces of mail, and a stack of magazines—*Electronic House* and *Photography 101*. The third magazine in the stack had a familiar cover—a yellow Labrador with its mouth open and its tongue rolled forward. Sadie had a very vivid memory of the same magazine being overtaken by a spreading pool of red paint at Mrs. Wapple's. She picked up the magazine and glanced over her shoulder.

Mr. Forsberk was showing Jane some electronic gadget, which initiated Jane's tinkling laughter and flirty "oohs" and "aahs." Neither of them was paying Sadie any attention. The magazine title was *Bark*, like the name of Mr. Forsberk's late pooch, and the articles listed down the left-hand side were all about grooming, travel, and the ten things your dog wants you to know.

Exactly why did Mrs. Wapple have a magazine about dogs, anyway? Mr. Delecorte had explained why Mrs. Wapple hated dogs so much, and Sadie didn't think Mrs. Wapple would have changed her opinion so quickly. Sadie flipped to the table of contents, thinking about Mrs. Wapple's habit of stealing mail. Had she stolen Mr. Forsberk's subscription, requiring him to buy another copy? Her eyes stopped on an article titled "Inhumane Training: Become the Solution, Not the Problem." Sadie flipped to page sixty-nine and immediately saw the green tube-like whistle featured in the sidebar. Sadie flipped back to check the date on the front cover: October.

"Mr. Forsberk," Sadie asked, holding up the magazine. "Did you buy this?"

He pulled his eyes away from Jane and nodded. "Yes."

"But don't you have a subscription?"

He looked nervous. "How did you know that?"

"Well, you're a dog lover, and the name of the magazine and the name of your dog were both Bark, which means you'd likely be drawn to a magazine like this." She almost left it there, but instead finished sharing her thoughts. "And I saw this exact magazine at Mrs. Wapple's yesterday, along with a lot of unopened mail. I didn't look to see who the mail or the magazine were intended for, but I can guess that she stole your subscribed copy."

"That woman was crazy," Mr. Forsberk said with as much of an edge as Sadie had ever heard from him, putting her on edge as well. "This was a good neighborhood before she came. She ruined everything."

"You're right," Sadie said with a nod. "Everything changed when she moved in. She screamed at people on the street, stole mail, and hated your dog. You were trying to drive her away, weren't you? You wanted to get back at her."

His neck and face went red, which meant Sadie was on to something. "Mr. Forsberk, whatever you've done will be discovered by the police. You'll be in a much better position if you take the information to them yourself."

"What's this?" Jane asked.

Sadie stepped to Jane's side. Mr. Forsberk turned too and then reached for the box Jane was holding, which she quickly moved away. Mr. Forsberk remained frozen as he watched her sift through the contents.

Jane pulled out a plastic-looking box. "A recorder?" she said, looking at it.

Jane turned the box in her hand and pressed something with her thumb. A horrible screeching noise assaulted Sadie's ears, even though it wasn't loud. Jane turned the box again and must have found the volume because the squawking noise increased. It lasted a couple seconds before it stopped and a series of clicks sounded. Another pause and the screeching repeated, making Sadie cringe and put her hands over her hears, hitting herself in the head with the magazine she still held. Suddenly the noise stopped. Sadie looked at Jane, who was looking at Mr. Forsberk, who held a small black remote control in his hand. He slowly lowered it to his side, but he looked scared to death.

"Angry birds," Sadie said accusingly. "You planted that in her house to drive her crazy, didn't you? That's what you were carrying when I saw you last night. You wanted to get it out of her house before the police could find it." Sadie was disgusted and knew that her feelings were showing in her tone of voice. She looked at the remote.

"And you could turn it on and off any time you wanted to, couldn't you? Just by taking a walk."

Mr. Forsberk swallowed.

"And when it didn't work fast enough, you attacked her," Jane added. She'd given up on her flirty persona all together, and Mr. Forsberk looked even more horrified. "You could have killed her, you know." She threw the recorder back into the box.

"I didn't want to do that," Mr. Forsberk said, shaking his head and looking as though he were about to cry. "I just wanted her to go away."

"Well, I hope you're satisfied, then," Sadie said, throwing the magazine on the couch and putting her hands on her hips. "She suffers from migraine headaches and since coming here, she hasn't had her medication. Add that to her mental issues and you may very well have driven her crazier than she ever was."

"But I didn't hurt her," he said.

"Yes, you did," Sadie responded.

"I didn't attack her. At her house. Yesterday." His eyes were wide and his prominent forehead glistened with sweat as he started to panic.

"Call the police, Sadie," Jane said, throwing the box back on the table. "Tell them we found the man responsible for Mrs. Wapple's attempted murder."

"M-m-murder!" Mr. Forsberk exclaimed. "They said she was okay."

"You better hope she is," Jane said, fire in her eyes as she stared at the man who was nearly her height. "Or you'll get the chair."

Mr. Forsberk's eyes bugged out of his head, and Sadie hurried to rein things in. It was time to help him see them as his allies. "You need to turn yourself in. We can help you do that." She was due at the police station in half an hour; how would it be to show up with Mr. Forsberk and his confession in tow? That would certainly take some of the spotlight off Pete, who had been there for nearly five hours now.

"I didn't hurt her," he said again, pleading with Sadie to believe him, which, of course, she simply couldn't do. "I didn't do it!"

Sadie stepped toward him and tried to put a comforting expression on her face. "I'll go with you to talk to the police," she said. "I'll help you explain."

"I can't go to the police," he said, his eyes darting back and forth in a way that alerted Sadie to the fact that he was going to run. "They won't let me go this time."

"Well, you're right about that," Jane said with disgust, watching him with narrowed eyes, her arms crossed over her chest. "They'll lock you up like the sicko you are."

"Jane," Sadie said, giving her a pointed look. "Cool it."

But it was too late. In the split second it took for Sadie to look at Jane, Mr. Forsberk grabbed the edge of the table between him and Jane and threw it toward her, causing the piles of electrical equipment to fall onto Jane as she stumbled backward into the wall, losing her balance and falling to the floor.

"Jane!" Sadie said, taking a step toward her friend before turning her attention back to Mr. Forsberk in time to see his back disappear down the hallway.

"Mr. Forsberk!" Sadie yelled before going after him, dodging a recliner and the toppled table. It wasn't until she entered the hallway that she realized there was a back door at the end of it. She called after him again as he darted through it. Sadie stayed in pursuit out the door, down the back steps, and through the chain-link fence, but he was much faster than she was, and by the time she reached the alley behind his house, he had disappeared around the corner.

She took a few futile steps in that direction before realizing there was no way she could catch him. "Oh, biscuits!" she said as she stared at the corner. Then she turned back to the house while gulping for air. When she reached the top of the back steps, she nearly collided with Jane, who was coming out. They both screamed and jumped back.

"He's gone?" Jane asked when they had both recovered.

Sadie nodded, still winded from her exertion.

"What a creep," Jane said, looking toward the alley.

"He's scared," Sadie said, pushing down the desire to reprimand Jane for being so hard on him. She headed inside. "We need to call the police."

"I already did," Jane said. "They're on their way."

"Great," Sadie said, but she could hear the flatness in her voice. She did not look forward to explaining any of this and yet, she had to admit her heart was a little bit lighter having solved one of the many mysteries threading through the situation. Sadie imagined Mrs. Wapple in her home, her head pounding with a migraine, while voices swirled in her mind, only to have a screeching, squawking noise burst out of some unknown place and make both of her conditions worse. That poor woman.

Less than five minutes later, a car pulled up in front of the house. When Detective Lucille came through the front door, she looked directly at Sadie while two uniformed officers entered behind her. She raised her eyebrows. "I think you've got some explaining to do."

CHAPTER 34

After fifteen minutes at Mr. Forsberk's house, Jane and Sadie were told to follow Detective Lucille back to the station to finish the questioning. They both agreed and hurried down Mr. Forsberk's steps. "Do you think they'll find him?" Jane asked.

"Eventually," Sadie said. "He doesn't strike me as the street-smart type who can keep himself underground for long."

They looked both ways and crossed the street. Some of the neighbors were out, surely wondering what had drawn the police to their street again, but neither Jane nor Sadie paid them much mind.

"Should we drive together?" Jane asked but before Sadie could answer, Jane stopped on the sidewalk. Sadie had moved a couple of steps before she realized Jane wasn't with her and turned to face her friend.

"What?" Sadie asked just as Jane started moving again, slowly this time. Her eyes were fixed on her car, and Sadie followed the line of sight. For a moment she didn't see whatever it was that Jane was looking at, but then she noticed the slight drop of the left side of Jane's car and realized the tire was flat; the rubber looked like a puddle beneath the rim. "Biscuits," Sadie said.

Jane's word wasn't nearly so kind. She reached the car and crouched down to inspect the flat tire and cursed again. After a few seconds, Jane stood, shaking her head. "Wonderful," she said dryly. "Now what?"

"Drive with me," Sadie said quickly, putting her hand on Jane's arm and pulling her back toward the sidewalk. Sadie's rental car was parked a few feet up the curb and she fished the keys out of her pocket. "We'll figure out the tire after the police station."

Jane was hesitant at first, but agreed to Sadie's terms. Sadie grabbed her purse from Heather's, and the flat tire was quickly forgotten once they reached the police station. Almost immediately, she and Jane were taken into different rooms for questioning. As had happened yesterday, Sadie expected more yelling and posturing than she got at the station. Detective Lucille mostly listened and asked clarifying questions as needed about Mr. Forsberk. After that, Sadie was left alone for over half an hour. When Detective Lucille came back, she told Sadie an APB had been issued for Mr. Forsberk. They were just getting started again when the detective was called out of the room. Sadie waited another twenty minutes, her nerves ready to explode. It had to be getting close to eight o'clock. She needed to be in Boston by nine thirty to meet with Gabrielle.

Finally, Detective Lucille returned, but she didn't sit. "We'll need to finish this tomorrow," she said. "Detective Cunningham says you're staying at the Courtyard."

"Um, yes, I guess so," Sadie said. She hadn't even thought about where she was staying tonight. Did that mean Pete had reserved her a room? She also realized that in all the questioning, the detective hadn't asked her anything at all about Pete, and yet when she mentioned him just now, it was almost casual, not the way Sadie expected his name to come up. She wondered how his questioning had gone and if he was still at the station. She'd love to tell him everything she'd discovered today and find out what had happened on his end.

The detective pulled open the door, waving Sadie out of the room. Once in the hallway, the detective gave an officer instructions of what to do with Sadie and then disappeared into another room. Sadie looked around for Pete, just in case fate could have them cross paths in the hallway, but she didn't see him. Just before Sadie was shown into the waiting area, an officer returned Sadie's purse, which they had kept while she'd been questioned.

Jane was waiting for her and when Sadie entered, she threw aside the magazine she'd been flipping through. "About time."

"Sorry," Sadie said, glancing at the wall clock while digging her keys out of her pocket. "I've got to hurry and catch the T. Can you drive me to the Forest Hills station?" She held out the keys to Jane, who regarded them for a moment before taking them out of Sadie's hand.

"Sure," Jane said and turned toward the door.

"Did they question you?" Sadie asked as they headed to the parking lot. It was a warm evening, but Sadie could feel the weight of rain yet unshed and hoped it would wait until she was snuggled in her bed at the hotel, which she hoped wasn't too far in the future.

"A little," Jane said. "But I didn't have much to say. I just told them I was tagging along with you. They asked where I was staying and said they'd call me." She shrugged as they approached the car, and she used the remote to unlock the doors. "I've been waiting forever."

"Sorry," Sadie said for the second time, moving around to the passenger side. Jane wasn't on her rental agreement, and she knew she shouldn't be letting her drive, but it would be much simpler for

Jane to drop her off than to switch drivers once they got to the station. "What about your car?" she asked as Jane pulled open her door. Sadie did the same, both of them sliding in and shutting the doors in tandem.

"I haven't called AAA yet. I'll take your car back to the house and get it figured out. At least that will give me something to do."

Sadie ignored the reminder that Jane wanted to come to the meeting with Gabrielle. She was tired of arguing the point. Jane started the car, looking over at Sadie. "Does it seem weird to you that my tire is flat?"

Should it? Sadie wondered, attempting to switch gears. "I guess I saw it as frustrating, but not suspicious. You think it's a concern?" She tried to figure out why anyone would flatten Jane's tire but not her own.

Jane shrugged. "Everything's a concern right now," she said. She shifted into reverse and looked over the seat while backing up. "I still don't think it's a good idea to talk to Gabrielle by yourself," she said as they pulled out of the police station parking lot. "It's not safe, and I can't help but wonder if my flat tire is an attempt to make sure you're alone."

"That's not reasonable," Sadie said. "You could just take my car, or the T, if you were coming with me—but I gave my word I'd be there alone." Sadie knew Jane was still unhappy about it. When Jane didn't speak, Sadie said, "I can handle myself."

"You've thought that before and not been able to handle yourself."

Portland. Sadie took a breath. Would she ever live that down? "I've been trying to have a conversation with this woman for two days, Jane. And I'll be in a public place."

"So why does she want to talk to you now?" Jane asked.

"Because she wants answers."

"Because she's going to slit your throat."

Ew. Sadie shook away the image. "I'll be fine," she said again. "I feel good about the meeting."

Jane was silent while they waited for a light to change. Sadie tried to think of something she could bring up to both fill the time and change the subject.

"So what's the deal with you and Shawn?" Sadie asked, determining that Jane, of all people, could appreciate the straightforward question.

Jane paused a few seconds and shifted in her seat. She didn't look at Sadie. "Well, what does he say?" she asked carefully.

"Nothing," Sadie said, shaking her head. "But I haven't asked."

"Then what makes you think there's something between us?"

"You're smiling," Sadie pointed out, not liking the subtle grin Jane was trying to hide. It creeped her out. "For starters. And Shawn keeps talking about how great you are."

Jane turned the wheel, still smiling, and shrugged one shoulder. "I am pretty great," she said. "You have to admit that much." Her attitude was instantly different, lighter. Whereas she'd been annoyed and frustrated before Sadie had mentioned Shawn, she was now perfectly at ease. Sadie didn't necessarily like the shift.

"I just want to know what's going on."

"What can I say—Shawn's a pretty awesome guy," Jane said almost nonchalantly. "Is it that strange that I might be drawn to that?"

"He's twenty-one years old," Sadie said. "I'm not trying to get in the way of things, that's not what I mean, but the age difference is a bit of a concern for me."

"And how much older were you than Eric?"

Sadie felt a tremor run through her at the mention of her ex . . .

something. He hadn't been a boyfriend, but she'd thought about it. Sadie still didn't know exactly how old Eric was—things hadn't gotten that far—but the age difference wasn't the reason their relationship had ended. Besides, Eric didn't have anything to do with this conversation. Jane was trying to distract her. "So you *are* interested in Shawn."

Jane made a right-hand turn into the Forest Hills station. "Here we are," she said, pulling up to the curb and shifting into park. She turned to look at Sadie, who reached for her purse from the floor of the car. "You'll call me when you're done?" Jane said. "Or anytime during the meeting that you need backup? I'll call AAA and get the tire taken care of in a jiffy."

Sadie nodded, realizing that the tire might be exactly what she needed to keep Jane out of this. She felt bad for finding a silver lining in Jane's frustrating situation, but it winked at her all the same. Jane wasn't one for following Sadie's directions, and Sadie did not want Jane to ruin this meeting. "Don't follow me, okay? Let me do this my way."

"You told me not to and I won't. Be safe though."

"I will," Sadie said, opening the door.

"I won't see Shawn if you don't want me to," Jane said, stopping Sadie's exit. Sadie turned to look at her, the door open a few inches. Jane's expression was sincere if not a little bit vulnerable. "I can tell you're uncomfortable with it."

Sadie felt like a jerk. Jane had been helpful on many cases, and she'd come to Sadie's aid here in Boston and was offering her help any way she could. "It's not that," she said, softening. "I guess maybe I feel . . . left out. He's my son. I like to know what's going on in his life."

"We've only talked on the phone and through e-mail," Jane said.

"I haven't seen him in person since March. But you've raised a remarkable boy."

"He is remarkable," Sadie said, glad to know there hadn't been more happening behind her back. She wanted to say something about how Shawn was also sweet and naïve and so different from Jane, but there was no way to say that without being rude so she just smiled. "I'm not against it," Sadie said. "But it will take some getting used to."

Jane shrugged one shoulder and smiled softly. "No worries. I'm in no hurry. We're just . . . getting to know one another right now, that's all."

"Okay," Sadie said, pushing the door open all the way and feeling better. It was still hard for her to accept a relationship between them, but knowing the truth of it gave her a sense of peace and inclusion. "Thanks for clarifying, and thanks for the ride and everything else. I don't know what I'd have done today without your help." Of course there were a few things she was unhappy about—like going through Gabrielle's car and running Mr. Forsberk off—but for the most part, Jane had been a huge asset.

"That's what I'm here for," Jane said. "Call me when you finish talking to Gabrielle."

"I will," Sadie said.

Jane was pulling away when Sadie realized the extra few minutes of discussion had put her in even more of a time crunch. She practically ran for the train, glad she was familiar with the process so she could pay her fare quickly and still make it through the doors before they closed. She collapsed in a seat and caught her breath as the train moved forward. Once she felt settled in, she opened her purse and pulled out her phone, relieved it was there since she hadn't taken the time to double-check everything after her purse was returned to her at the police station. She thought about calling Pete, but decided to text him so as not to interrupt anything.

Call me when you can! Big day. Are you okay?

A few minutes later, the train hissed to a stop at the Back Bay station, and Sadie took a deep breath when the doors opened. She stood up slowly, allowing her fellow passengers to lead the way, and squared her shoulders for whatever might be ahead.

Here goes nothing.

CHAPTER 35

Germaine's felt more like a pub than a café. The walls were exposed brick with huge abstract paintings on the tall walls and a varnished concrete floor. The tables and chairs were made of a thick, dark wood, and a bar spread across one end of the room.

Sadie chose a table for two with a good view of the door and looked over the menu before setting it aside. She was too unsettled to eat and kept going over her meeting with the detective. She was uncomfortable both with what she had said and what she hadn't said, and while she was proud for having not lied, she hadn't told Detective Lucille about this meeting. Granted, the detective hadn't asked, but Sadie was already imagining how she could explain having left it out. There could be no explanation other than the fact that Sadie had wanted to meet with Gabrielle and telling the police would have made that impossible.

She looked at her watch: 9:09. Being this early wasn't efficient, but she hadn't been able to risk being late by taking a later train, and since she wasn't big on the nightlife of the city, there wasn't anything else to do but come here and wait for the meeting with Gabrielle, which, she hoped, would resolve whatever issues were left to be resolved. She wondered how Mrs. Wapple was doing. She wondered if Jane was still mad about not coming. She wondered if Pete was avoiding her.

While she waited, she scribbled down a possible timeline of events, starting with Bark being hit by the car and ending with Mrs. Wapple being found in her bedroom. It wasn't until she finished that she realized there was no mention of the paranormal stuff on her list. The more details she learned that were based on fact, the more everything felt separate. Like two different things at play. After pondering that for a minute, she wrote out a list of questions she wanted to ask Gabrielle, ordered a Diet Coke to keep her awake, and started making a list of places she still needed to see on her trip, assuming that tomorrow she would wake up with a huge weight off her shoulders, ready to debrief with Pete, see her son, and be a tourist again. Shawn called but she let it go to voice mail before sending him a text that she'd call him later. He replied almost immediately.

I'm on my way to Boston. Should be there by 2 am.

Then she had to call him.

"What do you mean you're on your way?" Sadie asked when he picked up. "You have class tomorrow."

"I talked to Jane. She said she's really worried about you. She thinks you're in trouble."

"I'm not in trouble," Sadie said, annoyed that Jane would go to Shawn. "I'm just fine, and you need to go to class."

"I'm already in Auburn," Shawn said. "I made sure not to call before I was too far to go back."

And Jane didn't tell me? Sadie thought. That girl took far too many liberties.

"If it were me in this situation, you'd have been there two days ago."

"I already finished college!" Sadie retorted.

"I'll see you in a few hours, Mom. Text me the name of the hotel when you're done being mad at me." He hung up, and Sadie dropped the phone on the table before crossing her arms over her chest. Did everyone feel her so incapable that they had to circle around her? Was that Jane's motivation too?

She went back to her list in hopes of distracting herself. It worked a little too well, and the next time she checked her watch it was 9:41. She looked up at the heavy wood and glass door in case Gabrielle happened to be standing there waiting for Sadie to see her. She wasn't there, though. Instead a couple was leaving, him holding the door for her as she put on her hip-length jacket.

Sadie scanned the bar, which was fuller than it had been when she arrived, but Gabrielle wasn't among the crowd that, thankfully, wasn't loud and obnoxious. Sadie went back to her list of things left to do in Boston, adding Walden Pond and taking off Fenway Park, though that might take some explaining to Pete and Shawn. Her list didn't distract her as much as it had before, and she checked her watch every few minutes, scanning the bar again every time she looked up. With no sign of Gabrielle, Sadie texted her.

Are you coming?

When two minutes passed without a response, she called. It went to voice mail. Sadie left a message and then bit her lip when the clock above the bar hit ten o'clock straight up. She did not have the time or patience to be stood up right now!

Sadie called directory assistance and requested the number for the gallery. Someone picked up but then hung up before Sadie had a chance to say anything. Sadie pulled the phone away from her ear to verify that she had full service and her phone hadn't simply dropped the call. She had four full bars. She called back and this time the line was busy. Sadie started to worry, even though she tried not to. She tried the gallery again—still busy—and called Gabrielle's cell again—no answer. After thirty seconds of planning, Sadie left five dollars to cover the tip and the cost of her drink, which she hadn't even finished, and headed for the door. On the street, she sent Gabrielle a text.

Is everything okay? I'm coming over.

Then she put up the collar of her coat and pulled out her street map, quickly calculating the shortest walk to the gallery. Her muscles ached, and her head felt heavy on her shoulders. The fog was less than comforting, but Sadie would take fog over rain or snow. Sadie walked as fast as she could and hunkered down in her jacket to fend off the increasing cold. This had been one of the longest days of her life. She hoped it wouldn't stretch out too much longer, but she couldn't go home with this unfinished.

CHAPTER 36

Sadie reached the gallery in six or seven minutes—bless the laminated street map and a heightened sense of concern—and looked through the beveled glass of the gallery's front door. Other than a frosty light coming from the back of the building, she couldn't see anything. She pulled on the handle, fully expecting it to be locked, but the thumb latch depressed easily and she pulled the door open.

"Ms. Marrow?" she called out as she moved across the threshold and adjusted the strap of her purse on her shoulder. Sadie could smell the fruity vapor of the wine from the night's reception, but the stillness of the gallery made the building feel barren. Sadie shivered even though it was warmer inside than it had been outside. She wondered if she should call the police, but she didn't want them to know she was working on the case. Hopefully there was just a misunderstanding about the time of their meeting.

"Gabrielle," she called louder as she stepped forward on the polished hardwood of the gallery. The light was coming from a room up ahead and to the right, but she could hear nothing, which made her stay silent too. Gabrielle was here—so why couldn't Sadie hear her moving papers or talking on the phone?

She kept her glance darting ahead, cautious of the dark corners that seemed to be encroaching on her. The paintings on the walls looked like open holes in which anything could be hiding. The similarities to her discovery of Delores yesterday—dark building, one light drawing her in—made her shudder from déjà vu.

"Gabrielle," she called again. "Are you here? It's Sadie Hoffmiller." Finally, she reached the portion of wall just outside the lit room—an office. Sadie peeked around the doorjamb, giving herself a moment to assess the scene before she planned her next move.

The first thing that caught her eye was hair, cascades of it pouring over the desk as though sprouting from the veneer itself. An instant later, however, she realized it was Gabrielle Marrow, facedown at her desk with her long hair and array of extensions billowing out around her as though poetically arranged just so.

"Gabrielle," Sadie gasped as she dropped her purse by the doorway and moved forward. She saw an empty wineglass a few inches from where Gabrielle's hand lay outstretched from beneath her hair, fingers gracefully curved as though she had been reaching for one more drink when she passed out.

Sadie put her hand on Gabrielle's back, and Gabrielle's body shifted beneath her. The shift must have hit the mouse or a key on the keyboard because the computer screen in front of Gabrielle came to life, capturing Sadie's attention completely.

The background was white—a document—with tight lines of perfect letters. Sadie leaned in, anxious to read what Gabrielle had been typing.

I have done all I can to leave the past behind me, but it continues to claw its way into my life until I can no longer abide its toll. Let Delores heal and find whatever measure of existence is her due, but do not tell her I'm the one who nearly took that away from her. Let her believe I simply faded—as I have surely been doing all my life despite my vibrant attempts at normalcy—and simply disappeared. I love her, in my way, but with her in my life, there is no room left for me, and I would rather end my own life at the height of my success than renegotiate the terms.

Sincerely,

Gabrielle Marrow

By the time Sadie finished, her heart was in her throat. Suicide? She reached under Gabrielle's hair enough for her fingers to find where Gabrielle's pulse should be. Her eyes fell on the orange prescription bottle tucked beneath Gabrielle's arm. Sadie didn't realize she'd been holding her breath until she felt Gabrielle's weak heartbeat under her fingers.

"Wake up, Gabrielle," Sadie said, shaking the woman's shoulders. She didn't respond. "Oh, please, don't do this."

When Sadie still couldn't rouse her, she left Gabrielle and fumbled for her phone in her purse. While waiting for the call to connect, she heard something from the direction of the gallery and for the first time wondered if she and Gabrielle were the only two people here. Where was Hansel? Had the police found Mr. Forsberk? The furniture and filing cabinets were pressed up against the walls of the tiny room; there was no place to hide. But maybe she hadn't heard anything at all, maybe it was just her own blood rushing in her ears.

She moved toward the doorway, listening intently. A swish? Was it really?

"Nine-one-one. What's your emergency?"

"Yes, my name is Sadie Hoffmiller," she said, turning back to Gabrielle. Sadie reached out and touched her hair, willing her to be okay. "I'm at the Bastian Gallery on Newbury Street and—" Suddenly the room went dark except for the glow of the computer monitor. Sadie turned quickly toward the doorway and screamed as something white came directly toward her face. She could barely make out the edges of the object and raised her hands to block it. The white apparition drove into her, propelled by a force she couldn't see. The phone clattered to the floor. She smelled something chemical—sharp and metallic—before the whiteness mashed against her face.

Cloth. Soft. Wet.

She grabbed an arm holding the smelly cloth and tried to pull it away from her face. In the process, she fell against the filing cabinet and pain sparked through her hip as she slid to the floor, the cloth still held fast against her mouth and nose. Relentless. She was partially propped against the filing cabinet, her clogs sliding on the hardwood floor as she tried to get her footing. The edges of her thoughts began to get fuzzy, and she realized the intent of the cloth against her face wasn't simply to prevent her from seeing who was holding it. She tried to hold her breath, but it was too late. Something was slowing . . . her thoughts and . . . taking away . . . her ability . . . to . . .

CHAPTER 37

S adie awoke with a splitting headache to find herself in a box. There was a humming and bumping beneath her ear, which was pressed upon cheap carpet. It smelled like old motor oil and new carpet.

Despite the smell and her aching head, she took deep breaths, then coughed when her lungs protested against the dank air. It took a few more breaths for her to realize she was moving. It took several more seconds and the honk of a horn for her mind to clear and process the clues that told her she was in a car—or rather, the trunk of one. Despite her drugged state, panic began to radiate through her body, causing her heart to race and her head to pound even harder. She had to get out of here! She tried to lift her head only to have dizziness swirl around her like a vortex. Her head fell back to the carpet with a thump, and bile rose in her throat. Her head was still pounding, her heart racing as the panic threatened to consume her completely.

You have got to calm down, she told herself, and clenched her eyes shut while forcing herself to take a deep breath, fighting the urge to gag. She held the breath and then exhaled it slowly, consciously relaxing her feet and hands, then her arms and legs, her hips and shoulders. Her hands were tied together in front of her, which initiated another wave of panic before she forced herself to relax again. She knew she didn't have a chance if she couldn't focus her thoughts.

How had she gotten here?

She remembered finding Gabrielle. She remembered dialing 911 and . . . then it all came back to her. The note. The panic. The spectral whiteness coming toward her and then . . . nothing. Sadie felt her throat thicken as she realized she hadn't completed the call to 911. Panic seized her chest again, but she pushed it away with the absolute knowledge that she had to get out of here. She had to focus.

She kept her eyes closed and took deep breaths of the musty air, forcing herself to relax her breathing and her heart rate while focusing her thoughts on her own survival. Once she had herself under control and could think rationally, she began talking herself through the situation as any reasonable person would do.

Unfortunately, you are tied up and locked in the trunk of the car.

Fortunately, you are not unconscious anymore.

She felt better already, and moved on to the next affirmation.

Unfortunately, you are sick and feeling suffocated and dizzy.

Fortunately . . . She drew a blank. *Fortunately* . . . The word hung in her mind and she raced to find something hopeful—anything!

Fortunately . . . There had to be something!

Fortunately . . . *think, Sadie, think!*

Fortunately . . . *that's it!*

Sadie's thoughts ignited and hope surged through her. She liked to have the TV on when she baked, and she always baked a lot in the fall and Shawn had gotten her hooked on survival shows. She knew exactly what to do when trapped in the trunk of a car.

She blinked her eyes to clear her vision and looked around for the trunk release—a standard safety feature in most cars manufactured during the last decade. There! She could see the small plastic pull cord set against the top of the trunk above her, green and glowing up and to the right, but when she reached toward it, searing pain flared in her shoulder. She tried again, but the release seemed miles away. She couldn't reach it. What were her other options? She was on her back and tried to straighten out her legs which felt tangled around each other.

There was nothing else to do but kick out a taillight. The car seemed to be going slower than it had been, but not as though the driver planned on stopping. What would the taillight feel like from the inside? She remembered that a plastic bracket held the taillight in place. What could she break it with? There weren't many options.

She needed to turn her head toward the back of the trunk so that her foot would have the necessary trajectory, and she gasped as fire ripped through her shoulder the moment she moved. The pain was paralyzing and brought tears to her eyes. How was she supposed to escape with bound hands, a bad shoulder, and limited motor control? It wasn't a question she was going to waste time answering. She had to stay focused and believe there was a way out.

It took clenching her teeth and allowing herself to whimper to withstand the pain, not only in her shoulder that had been giving her problems for months, but also in her left hip that had banged against the filing cabinet in Gabrielle's office. She felt sweat breaking out on her forehead even though she was shivering from the cold. She took a deep breath and tried to push the pain away as she'd done before. After what felt like forever, she was positioned as well as she could be—the trunk wasn't roomy—her knees pulled up until they touched the top of the trunk once she was aligned with the left taillight.

With her shoes on it was difficult to feel the difference in texture that would tell her she had located the bracket, so she used the toe of her left shoe to push off her right one. The car was still moving; she didn't allow herself to think about whether or not the driver would be able to tell what she was doing. With only a sock on, she was better able to feel where the topography of the inside of the trunk changed. Because her sneakers had ended up drenched in paint, she'd worn her clogs tonight and was grateful for the thick wooden sole. Taking a deep breath, she pulled back her still-shoed left foot and kicked as hard as she could using a heel-first jab kick that she'd been told could break three boards, though she'd never bothered to try.

Needles of pain shot up her leg, and she pursed her lips together as hard as she could to keep from crying out. Despite the pain, however, she'd felt the bracket give beneath her heel. Just a little. Just enough. She pulled back, braced herself and kicked again and again and again, ignoring the white-hot pain in her leg at each impact and the stars bursting behind her eyelids. With each kick, she felt a slight movement until finally her foot seemed to push through the trunk itself.

Cold air blew in and the red of the taillight cast a faint glow into that corner of the trunk. It wasn't much, but it helped her to see a little bit. She used her foot to push the taillight out of its casing as the car slowed down, rounding a corner. She held her breath, waiting for the car to speed up, but it didn't, and she started moving faster, trying to decide what she was going to do if the driver of this car opened the trunk. The car began to slow down even more. Sadie's head nearly exploded when the car came to a stop. She scrunched up against the back end of the trunk so that she would be in a position to defend herself with a few solid kicks.

Someone outside the car screamed. Sadie froze. Another scream—it was a woman—and then yelling. Something hit the outside of the trunk not far from Sadie's head, and she ducked automatically. It hit again, once in the same place, then again on the other side of the trunk. Sadie's heart was in her throat. What was happening? It was obviously a fight. That meant someone out there had to be on her side, right?

Hope flared in her chest. Maybe someone had seen the dislodged taillight and put the pieces together!

"Sadie!" she heard someone yell. It startled her—someone she knew was out there!

"Help me!" she yelled back and began banging on the top of the trunk with her right foot. Her arms were against her chest, trying to minimize the pain-searing movements. "Help!"

Her screams were answered with another thud against the metal above her head, more rustling, and screams she couldn't decipher. Blood pulsed in her ears. Who was out there?

And then it went quiet. For nearly ten seconds, Sadie couldn't hear anything at all. Then there was a timid knock above her head.

"Sadie?" said a quiet voice. "Are you in there? Are you all right?"

Jane?

CHAPTER 38

Sadie didn't answer right away. She didn't know what to say. *Jane?* There wasn't time to consider much of anything before she heard a click. The trunk popped open a fraction of an inch. She braced herself as the lid slowly lifted, revealing Jane, backlit by a set of headlights cutting through the fog. Jane wore a gray hoodie over her shirt, but it was askew and a light rain was causing the shoulders to darken. They were on a dark road without streetlights, both sides lined by woods.

"We've got to get out of here," Jane said.

"What happened?" Sadie gasped, not moving, staring as Jane wiped at the blood on her face. She wiped it on the leg of her jeans before reaching her hand into the trunk. "Wait," Sadie said, trying to make sense of things as Jane grabbed her forearm. "What are you doing here? I—" The pain took her breath—and her words—away, and by the time Jane had pulled her into a sitting position, Sadie was gasping in an attempt to recover.

Sadie stared out of the open trunk as Jane pulled her forward by her bound hands, helping her get out. Jane's little red car was parked behind them with the headlights pointed slightly to the right so that

Sadie wasn't blinded. She looked from the car to Jane's face, where she could see a cut on her bottom lip. Her left eye was red and swelling quickly. "What are you doing here?"

Jane wiped at her chin again. She looked at the blood, and Sadie noted the lack of reaction she made to it. "We've got to get out of here," Jane said again, fiddling with the cords around Sadie's wrists. She pulled a knife from her pocket; Sadie flinched when Jane flipped out a three-inch blade and cut through the twine without a second thought. The knife disappeared back into Jane's pocket as quickly as it had appeared. "He might come back. I'll explain later."

He? Panic washed over Sadie, and she hurried to comply with Jane's attempts to get her out of the trunk even though the pain was overwhelming and she had to bite her lip to keep from screaming. When she was finally free of the trunk and on her own two feet, Sadie realized her sock-covered foot had sunk into the mud spreading along the shoulder of the road. She put all her weight on her leg so she could lift her socked foot up, and a searing pain ran down her other leg. She looked behind her at the car that had held her captive. It was black. When she saw the Audi symbol, her eyebrows rose.

"Gabrielle's car?"

"Yeah," Jane said, allowing Sadie to lean heavily on her shoulder to get her balance.

"Who was driving?" Sadie asked, still looking at the car as she pictured Gabrielle slumped over her desk. Had the 911 call been enough?

Jane shook her head. "I don't know who it was. He was wearing a black ski mask."

"He drove with a mask on?" Sadie asked, imagining that would draw a lot of attention. As a conscientious driver herself, she knew that she'd certainly notice if someone in a black ski mask were be-hind the wheel of another car. "How do you know it was a man?"

"He was built like a man," Jane said, sounding annoyed by the questions. "And maybe he pulled it on when he realized he was being followed, I don't know." She grabbed Sadie's right arm and pulled her toward the red car, forcing Sadie to stumble into a walk. "We need to get of here."

Sadie pulled against Jane's grip. "Wait," she said. "Let's check the car. If you took him by surprise, he may have left something behind." Even as she spoke, she looked at the thick woods beside the road. Chills ran down her spine as she imagined her kidnapper watching them from the trees.

"What?" Jane said. "No. There's no time."

"Exactly," Sadie said, nodding and pushing away visions of the Headless Horseman galloping out of the woods. "No time but right now to figure out who is behind this. There's two of us and only one of him. Cover me." She took two quick and painful steps toward the car before Jane's hand grabbed the back of her coat.

"Did you hear that?" Jane said, looking at the trees to their right.

"I didn't hear any—"

"Shhh," Jane said. She moved toward her car with careful steps, leading Sadie with her as she continued scanning the woods around them.

Sadie could hear the sound of other cars in the distance but couldn't tell how close they were. Where were they anyway? How long had Jane been following her?

"We've got to get out of here," Jane said, still tugging Sadie.

If they left the car, the man, whoever he was, would simply come back and drive away. The only male suspect they had was Mr. Forsberk; they had to verify if it was he who'd kidnapped Sadie.

"It will only take a minute to look through it," Sadie said. She tried to break free of Jane's grasp without being too abrupt, but Jane's other hand had her coat pulled too tight for Sadie to wriggle out of it. "Jane," she said sharply, her patience waning quickly. "Let go—I need to check the car. He could be connected to everything else—the missing piece we've been looking for. Why else would someone kidnap me? What if it's Mr. Forsberk?"

"You're not thinking logically," Jane said, still pulling Sadie toward the car. "The drugs are obviously clouding your judgment."

"I am thinking logically," Sadie said. "My head is perfectly clear and—" She froze.

Jane yanked hard on Sadie's coat, causing Sadie to stumble toward the car. Pain shot up her injured leg, and she reached out to catch herself on the hood of Jane's car with her good arm.

Drugs? How would Jane know about that?

Sadie's eyes darted to Jane's windshield, spotted with misty rain. The windshield wipers were off, as was the engine. If Jane had pulled over behind Gabrielle's car, why would she have taken the time to turn off the car? The hood was cold, which was equally confusing. The engine should still be warm.

Things started clicking in her mind, and she felt as though the ground were beginning to spin.

She thought of the forearms she'd grabbed at the gallery and grabbed Jane's arm as though needing it to steady herself. Sadie's hand nearly wrapped around Jane's forearm, and even through the fabric of the hoodie, she could feel the slender strength. "Sorry," she said quickly to cover what she'd done as she let go. "I can't seem to get my balance."

"It's fine," Jane said, still tugging Sadie toward the passenger side. "But we've got to get out of here." Sadie went along with her. What choice did she have? She was being bombarded by other thoughts that made her head pulsate.

Jane had made it to Boston in record time after Pete told her Sadie was being questioned by the police yesterday.

Jane had been the one to discover the paranormal connection of the Wapple family that no one else had confirmed.

Jane had known Gabrielle would be at the gallery tonight and the when and where of Sadie and Gabrielle's meeting.

Jane hadn't wanted Sadie to go to the meeting.

The question of "Why?" darted in and out of the facts presenting themselves in her mind, but Sadie had to ignore it. Understanding the reason would not protect her right now, and she had no doubt she needed protection.

All her thoughts came together in the time it took for Jane to help Sadie into the passenger seat of her car. When Sadie realized what was happening, she panicked and put her hand on the door to push it open while Jane hurried to the driver's side. But then what would she do? She was in the middle of nowhere, she was still woozy from whatever had rendered her unconscious, and she was banged up so much that trying to run away would be useless. The only sure way out of here was to go along with whatever Jane had planned.

Jane slid into the driver's seat, where she started the car, turned it around, and began speeding away.

Sadie's heart was thumping, and it was all she could do to keep breathing regularly. She couldn't do anything about the shaking that had taken over her arms and legs. How was she going to get out of this? She could only trust her gut from here on out, and play this game as carefully as possible.

CHAPTER 39

"Where are we going?" Sadie asked as Jane drove down the road at breakneck speed. Though the road was remote, there was a gas station within a mile. Sadie looked at it longingly as they passed. Jane's car had been cold, which meant it had already been there, which meant Jane must have been driving Gabrielle's Audi. Could she have brought her car to the location when Sadie was going into the city? Maybe Jane then caught a cab back to the city . . . but why? And how could she have fixed the tire and parked it in the woods and gotten back to the gallery by 10:00?

"We're going to the police, of course," Jane said, looking at Sadie quickly. The cut on Jane's lip was still seeping, and Sadie had to fight the temptation to look for a napkin in the glove box. Had Jane injured herself to fake the attack? And if she'd really done all this, why would she take Sadie to the police? "You've been kidnapped, and the police need to know what happened," Jane continued.

Sadie nodded. It was the right answer. But it made no sense. Possible motives came to Sadie's mind—greed, revenge, profit, envy, power—but none of them quite fit. Why would Jane do any of this?

"Don't you want to know what happened?" Jane asked as she

turned onto a busier road. Sadie watched as the headlights coming toward them from the traffic traveling in the other direction appeared through the fog. She wondered how many of those travelers would save her if they knew she needed help. How could she possibly signal them?

"Yes," Sadie said, barely able to get the words out but knowing she had to keep Jane talking. "I'm so confused."

"Well, I waited for you to call me, but you never did, so I tried calling you and you didn't answer. I called like three times—nothin'." She was talking as though relaying a story about a party or concert she'd attended. Her eyes danced in the flickering lights of the oncoming traffic as the growing drip of blood slowly snaked its way down her chin.

Sadie couldn't look at her and used her right arm to hold her left arm across her chest in an attempt to keep it immobilized. It throbbed, however, and she didn't seem to have full movement in her wrist and hand, though it hurt too much to know for sure. She stared out the front windshield and tried to appear calm while Jane told her story. Sadie mentally reviewed what had happened over the last few days. Had Jane found the spare key and used it to get in and out of the house? Was it Jane who had set up the paint and placed the phone call that lured Sadie to Mrs. Wapple's aid? Was it Jane's voice in her bedroom and in the hallway of Mrs. Wapple's house?

Sadie thought of the horrified look she'd seen on Jane's face when she'd speculated that Mr. Forsberk could have bugged Mrs. Wapple's house. If he had, he might have heard something Jane hadn't expected anyone to know. And yet Jane had carried that off perfectly too.

"So I drove to Germaine's," Jane said, "but you weren't there. The waitress remembered you, though, and said no one had joined you. I knew you must have gone to the gallery so I went there just as Gabrielle's car pulled out of the parking lot. But it wasn't Gabrielle behind the wheel. I tried to call you again, but it went to voice mail so I followed Gabrielle's car because I just knew something wasn't right." She turned to look at Sadie. "You know how sometimes you just know exactly what you're supposed to do."

Sadie nodded. She did know that feeling and sure wished she had it right now.

"Anyway, we kept getting further and further away from Boston, and I was really freaking out, and then he got off the interstate and I knew following him would be harder, but I kept the perfect distance and then he pulled over." Jane was smiling over her recital of what Sadie knew *hadn't* happened. It was hard not to point out the obvious holes in her story. Why not call the police? How could she have called Sadie three times before she even left to go up to Germaine's?

"As soon as he stopped, I jumped out of my car and ran over to him. I clocked him before he even got all the way out of the car, see?" She held out her hand where the knuckles were red and scratched. Sadie could imagine that punching the trunk of a car could do that kind of damage. "We had a pretty good little brawl, but you probably heard all that."

Sadie nodded again but felt sick to her stomach. Sick enough that she worried she would throw up. Tears welled up in her eyes. She could feel Jane looking at her but couldn't meet her eyes.

"Are you okay?" Jane asked.

Sadie was cold, and she couldn't stop shaking. The nausea was getting worse by the minute. How did Shawn factor into this? Had the paramedics reached Gabrielle in time?

Jane's hand on Sadie's shaking leg made Sadie jump in her seat and instinctively pull toward the door. "I'm fine," Sadie said, forcing herself to relax. Was Jane behind *everything*? The unlocked doors? The face in the window? Sadie thought about the trip to the gallery this afternoon. Jane must have planted the paint sample for Sadie to find. The stage makeup could have been in her own pocket when she opened the trunk. So many details, such flawless execution. It was so bizarre, so . . . unreal.

Jane stared at her too long, and Sadie swallowed. "I think I'm in shock."

Jane nodded and looked back to the road. More details came into focus in Sadie's mind. Was it Jane who had her kicked out of the hotel? The security guard had called her Mrs. Hoffmiller, while Gabrielle *had* always called her Mrs. Hoffman. She took a deep breath and prayed for a way out of this. *Stay calm. Keep your wits about you. Be wise.* Sadie took a breath and sat up a little straighter.

"Are *you* all right?" Sadie made herself ask. She had to try to act natural, the way she would act if she *wasn't* putting all this together in her mind. Jane changed lanes, cutting off another driver, but didn't react when the car swerved to the side and honked loudly. Sadie stared out the windshield and tried to hold back her rising fear. "He beat you up pretty good," she added when Jane didn't respond. She tried to keep her tone light even though it killed her to be kissing up. "I don't know what I would have done if you hadn't gotten there in time to follow Gabrielle's car."

"I don't know what you would have done either," Jane said with a cocky half grin. She leaned toward the door, driving with one hand. "It seems like I'm always there when you need me, doesn't it?"

"Yes," Sadie said, nodding, wondering if that was Jane's motive. Did Jane want to be the hero at any cost? Even if it meant creating the events that necessitated her coming to the rescue? The black thought clouded Sadie's mind as something Shawn had said came back to her:

"She really looks up to you, Mom." Was this somehow Sadie's fault? Had Jane used Mrs. Wapple as a means for being needed? Sadie closed her eyes against the tears. When she opened them a moment later, she had to blink rapidly to clear her vision.

"What's wrong?" Jane snapped, glancing at Sadie suspiciously. Pete had said psychopaths hated being questioned and felt justified in whatever they did so long as it worked toward their goal. Sadie thought of the way Jane smiled about lying to people, the overall arrogance she exuded that whatever she did was right.

"I'm . . . just"—Sadie took a breath—"I'm just so grateful, Jane." She sniffed and let her left arm rest in her lap. She needed a tissue, but of course she didn't have her purse with her, and she didn't want to ask for one. Finally, she wiped her nose on the sleeve of her jacket, dropping yet another rung on the ladder of humility and desperation. "You're a hero, Jane."

Jane beamed, though the arrogance took away from the brightness. "I guess I am," she said, happy to own the title. "You're lucky to have me around, aren't you?"

"I sure am," Sadie said. "How far are we from the police station, do you think?"

"I don't know," Jane said. "Why?" She was shifting so quickly between arrogance and paranoia that Sadie knew she needed to be careful.

"I bet Pete is worried sick," Sadie said. "Do you think I could use your phone and call him? I'd like to let him know that . . . you're taking care of me and that because of you I'm all right."

"It might do him good to worry about you a little," Jane said. "You know, there are things in Pete's past, Sadie, things you should know about."

Sadie nearly defended him, but her mouth stayed closed. "Really?

Then maybe I should call Detective Lucille. Someone should know we're coming so that they're ready for us, don't you think?"

Jane considered that and then reached into her coat. "I'd rather you call Pete," she said, toggling through her phone with one hand while driving with the other. Sadie really wished she had a chance to fasten her seat belt. "He might be a detective, but he's not the one who saved you, was he?"

"No," Sadie said, looking hungrily at the phone in Jane's hand as she tensed with anxiety. "He wasn't there when I needed him."

"No kidding," Jane said. "In fact, he's pretty much failed you in every way this trip. He couldn't protect you, could he?" She handed Sadie the phone. "Just hit the call button," she said, saving Sadie from having to respond to Jane's stated failures on Pete's part.

Sadie hit CALL and forced herself to breathe as she came up with a split-second plan. Pete had told her the police hated coincidences and patterns. She could only hope she could point them out enough for him to recognize the important details. Right after the second ring, Pete answered. "This is Detective Cunningha—"

"It went to voice mail, Jane," she said loudly, directing the comment toward Jane. "I'll just wait for the beep and leave a message." She put the phone back to her ear and prayed that Pete would play along. She cleared her throat, hopeful that this would work since Pete had fallen silent, and then started talking as though she'd heard the telltale beep. "Pete, it's me, Sadie. Jane's bringing me to the JP police station right now. You'll *never* believe what happened, and I can't tell you everything right now but, basically, Jane saved my life. She's a hero, Pete, and she's taking me to the station so that we can both give statements about the man who tried to kidnap me in Gabrielle's car. Jane got there just in time to follow him. It's been *really* scary, Pete, and if not for *Jane* being in the right place at the right time, I

Josi S. Kilpack

wouldn't be here right now. I just want you to know that I'm okay, and I'll be able to explain everything better when I see you."

She stayed on the line for another second even though she'd run out of things to say, mindful of Pete on the other end, trying to make sense of what she'd just told him. She wished she dared say something else or ask him to hurry to the station to meet her there. "Bye," she finally said, then hung up the phone. Jane immediately snatched it from her and put it back in her pocket.

While she'd been on the phone, Jane had exited the freeway. The silence was brittle, and Sadie could feel her heart hammering in her chest. *Hold on,* she told herself, the fingers of her right hand gripping the armrest. *Hold on.*

Sadie started recognizing the buildings and intersections of Jamaica Plain, but the fog had rolled in like it had in Boston and that, combined with the dark of night, made it harder to see exactly where they were. Jane began telling her story again, adding more details to increase the level of her heroism.

"How did you fix the tire, Jane?" Sadie asked. "Did you call AAA?"

"Turns out someone had just let the air out of it. I have a small pump in my emergency kit in the back." She pointed her thumb over her shoulder. "It was pretty slick."

How long would that take? Sadie wondered. If Jane dropped Sadie off at the T station in Forest Hills at 8:20 and then went back to get her own car, pumped up the flat tire, and drove to the remote road, left her car, ran to the gas station and called a cab, could she still have made it to the gallery by 10:00?

"I'm glad," Sadie said. "I'm sure whoever did it expected the repair would take longer." Had Jane done it herself to make sure they drove together? Had she hoped that would keep her with Sadie for

334

the meeting at the café? Or was she making it all up as she went along?

Salvation was less than a block away once they turned onto Washington Street.

Jane put on her blinker and began to slow down when the police station appeared. Sadie counted four police officers appearing out of the fog like sentries, but she didn't see Pete among them. It was a futile hope to expect he would still be at the police station, but as Jane pulled to the curb, Sadie saw Pete push through the front doors. Her chest became tight, and she grabbed the door handle, ready to run as soon as the car came to a stop. Pete held her eyes, and she couldn't blink for fear of losing the connection.

"What's wrong with them?" Jane said, the car still moving.

Sadie looked from Pete to Jane and then to the police, not sure what she meant, but then she noticed the expressions on their faces. Grim, austere, professional. That blasted detective face was worn by every one of them, Pete included. The officers had their hands on their hips or at their sides; one had his hand on his sidearm. Their dispositions were not subtle. "They've probably just had a long day," Sadie said. She forced a smile and hoped Pete would get the message to follow suit and play things cool.

"Something's wrong," Jane said.

"No, no, nothing's wrong," Sadie said quickly. "Everything's fine, just pull up."

Instead, Jane hit the gas and pulled back into traffic.

CHAPTER 40

"No!" Sadie screamed as Pete's face moved past her window. "No, Jane, stop!" She pulled on the door handle, but with the car moving the automatic locks were in place. She pulled again anyway. "Stop!" she shouted. She craned around in the seat, but Jane was really punching it, and the only thing Sadie saw were the police scattering in the wake of Jane's dramatic exit.

"You can't trust anyone," Jane said, taking a corner so fast the tires squealed. She drove into oncoming traffic to pass a truck, then pulled back into their lane and laid on the horn to get the car ahead of them to move out of the way.

"Jane, please," Sadie said, a catch in her voice. "Please, stop, go back. You don't want the police to think you have something to hide." She looked behind her again, hoping to see flashing lights, but she saw only regular headlights and endless fog.

"They can't be trusted, Sadie," Jane said, swerving around another car. "I should never have tried to take you back. They'll turn you against me. Everything's gotten too out of control."

"That's ridiculous," Sadie said, her fear giving way to anger.

"Take me back, Jane. Let me explain what happened. Running away will only make things worse."

Jane started to slow down at a red light, but at the last minute, she stomped on the gas again and shot through the intersection. Sadie didn't know where they were, only that there were cars lining both sides of the streets and tall buildings on either side. "Let me out of this car this instant, Jane!" Sadie yelled, pressing herself against the door so as not to be flung around.

"Don't yell at me, Sadie!" Jane screamed back. "And don't tell me what to do!"

The yelling spurred Sadie to go silent as she remembered who she was dealing with. She couldn't afford to let her emotions and fear overwhelm her ability to reason through this situation. "I'm sorry," Sadie said in calm tones. "Where are we going now, then?"

"Stop asking so many questions," Jane said sharply. Her hands were gripping the steering wheel tightly and her jaw was set.

Sadie pinched her lips shut and looked around, trying to figure out where they were. They passed a street sign: Green Street. But she couldn't tell which direction they were heading. "Um, did I tell you Shawn's coming into town?" she said, hoping she could calm Jane down. "He said he'd be here around two o'clock."

"I told him to come," Jane said, just as sharply as before. "*I* did, Sadie. Gosh, you just can't give me credit for anything, can you?"

"I-I'm sorry," Sadie said. "I, um . . ."

"You don't appreciate anything I do for you," Jane said, cutting her off. "I work your cases, I come to Boston even though you won't invite me for dinner, I bring your son to you—I've done so much and yet you see Pete at the police station, and it's like he's the one who saved your life, not me."

Sadie didn't know what to say for fear of making it worse but noted that Jane clearly saw Pete as a threat.

"It's not like I ask for much, Sadie," Jane continued. There was less traffic now and she'd slowed down a little. Sadie looked in the side mirror but still didn't see any red and blue lights. Where were the police? "All I want is a little appreciation and acknowledgment, but instead you keep things from me, you avoid me and try to do everything yourself. What does it take to convince you how much you need me?"

Sadie remained silent, but Jane reached over and slapped Sadie's leg. Her face was hard and angry. "You can't even answer a simple question?"

They passed a sign on the side of the road that said Jamaica Pond with an arrow pointing forward. Sadie knew where she was now. Jamaica Pond was a small lake surrounded by woods and a walking path. If Sadie could get out of the car and into those woods . . .

"I do need you, Jane. You've helped me so much, and I've been very ungrateful." Sadie could see the glowing orbs of an upcoming traffic light in the fog, which was thicker than ever, but that might work in her favor. She glanced at the passenger door, lining up the unlock button and the handle while she calculated how quickly she would need to move between them, wishing she'd thought of this option when she had been in front of the police station. A roll on the pavement would be better than staying here with Jane. Safer, too.

"Yes, you have been ungrateful," Jane said, but she seemed slightly appeased. "I know how people think, Sadie. I know how to get information no one else can get. I know how to ask the right questions and be exactly what people need me to be. You don't have any idea what I'm capable of, no idea what I can do when I put my mind to it."

Jane rolled to a stop behind an SUV turning left at the T inter-section. Once they completed the turn, they'd be following the road that wrapped around the pond. There were still no sirens or police lights behind them. Sadie couldn't believe the police weren't pursu-ing them. How could Jane get away from a whole police department so easily? Ahead, however, Sadie could see trees shrouded with thick fog; it must be worse due to Jamaica Pond being so close. There was no fence around the park, meaning she had a straight shot to the trees she could use as cover.

Jane kept talking, but Sadie's focus was elsewhere. The light turned green, and Sadie rested her right hand on her leg, waiting and trying not to think about the upcoming pain. The SUV acceler-ated slowly, and Jane had no choice but to follow. She pulled into the intersection and turned smoothly.

As soon as they were on Jamaicaway, Jane began accelerating. Sadie took a breath, said a prayer, and then pressed the unlock but-ton, pulled the handle, and threw herself out of the car and toward the curb, hoping she'd stay out of oncoming traffic.

She knew there were probably squealing tires and horns, but the ricocheting pain she felt in her hip, shoulder, and everywhere else overtook all her senses for a minute, causing her to scream despite her determination not to make a sound. Within moments of impact, however, she scrambled to her feet and ran—or rather, limped—into the fog-steeped trees, cradling her left arm with her right and trying to maintain her balance.

She kept going and cut left, heading for the thickest grove of trees she could see despite visibility being less than fifteen feet. She couldn't hear anything other than the sound of her own breathing and heart rate but she kept going, sure that Jane was right behind her, waiting for Sadie to look over her shoulder and see her there so she would have her moment of power. Sadie continued running and felt the adrenaline pumping, overtaking the pain, at least for now. Thank goodness!

A tree root took her off guard, but she was able to fall to her right side and better brace the impact. The dirt and leaves were a much softer surface than the pavement had been, but it seemed to take forever to get to her feet, her balance thrown off by her overall disorientation. She hobbled to an area dark with trees and shrubs and slid down the trunk of a large oak. She tried to reposition her left arm and catch her breath. She pulled her knees to her chest as best she could and focused on taking deep breaths to dispel the panic.

She hoped Jane would just leave her, knowing that trying to find her would increase her chances of getting caught. When a minute passed and then another without a sound, Sadie felt her hope increasing and her breathing and heart rate even out. She would wait as long as she had to—an hour if necessary—then she would find the walking path that looped the lake and walk to a different entrance. She'd find a phone, call the police, and tell them everything. They'd find Jane and all of this would be over. The fantasy was clarifying in her mind, and she could even visualize the look on Pete's face when she saw him again. It would all work out.

"Sadie."

She froze. It was the same throaty whisper from her bedroom the night the power had gone out, the same voice she'd heard in the hallway of Mrs. Wapple's house. Sadie was instantly washed with a cold sweat.

"Help me, Sadie," the voice said. "Help me!"

Sadie couldn't breathe, and then the voice laughed, this time sounding just like Jane.

"You think you can hide from me, Sadie? You think you can get away from *me?*"

Sadie pressed her back against the tree. The fog and dark shadows of the copse of trees she'd found refuge in made it impossible to see much of her surroundings. And yet, Jane couldn't be far away. How had she found her? Did she truly know where Sadie was?

"I can hear your heart racing, Sadie," Jane said, her voice coming from Sadie's left. Sadie shrunk against the tree even more. "I can smell the fear on your breath."

Sadie closed her mouth and stayed absolutely still, fear pricking at every part of her. It had seemed like such a good idea to get out of the car when she did. But had she put herself in an even more dangerous position by showing that she'd seen through Jane's game? Would a better opportunity have presented itself if she'd stayed in the car and kept playing along?

"Why have you made things so difficult, Sadie?" Jane said. She was closer, but on Sadie's other side. "Can't you see that I did all of this for you? Haven't you realized that even if you did get away from me, I'd find you again?"

"Sadie!"

Pete!

It was all Sadie could do not to call out for him. As it was, her whole body responded and tears came to her eyes. Jane was closer than he was, though. If Sadie called out to him, Jane would get to her first. She was sure of it.

"Sadie, we're here," Pete's voice called out. "It's going to be okay. Stay where you are."

Jane had fallen silent, but Sadie heard a shuffle of leaves to her left. Too close to be Pete. More movement could be heard in the distance, though. Pete had said "*We're* here," so he must have other officers with him. All Sadie could do was wait to be found. As quietly and carefully as she could, she bent down and removed the remaining clog from her foot. It wasn't much of a weapon, but it was all she had to defend herself.

More movement to her left, closer. Her heart was in her throat. She couldn't breathe. She could hear the murmur of men's voices, but they weren't loud enough for her to gauge their distance from her. She closed her eyes and tried to stay calm, but her whole body was beginning to shake and the pain she'd held at bay was coming back. She had to let her left arm rest in her lap in order to hold up the shoe.

"Sadie," Pete said again, but his voice was further away. She nearly called out again. "Hang in there, Sadie, we're coming."

Another shuffle of leaves to her left convinced her she couldn't stay. She might have to find Pete herself instead of hoping for rescue. The idea of moving was terrifying, but she had no choice. He was going the wrong way. If he got out of earshot, she'd be more lost than ever. She tried to move as slowly as possible, mindful of how easy it would be for her to make the slightest noise and draw Jane's attention.

She had only just gotten to her feet when a hand snaked around her and pressed over her mouth and nose before she could manage a scream. The hand pulled her backward and, though she kicked and tried to break free, within seconds she was on her back on the leaf-covered dirt. She swung the shoe wildly and made contact, but in the next instant, the shoe was ripped from her hand and Jane Seeley was pressing a knee into Sadie's chest. Sadie couldn't breathe, and she clawed at Jane's arm with her good hand until Jane repositioned her hand so that only Sadie's mouth was covered. Sadie inhaled as deeply as she could through her nose, fighting for air, fighting to keep her thoughts above the panic.

The blade of Jane's slender, silver knife was suddenly inches from Sadie's face. Not long ago, the knife had cut through the bindings around Sadie's hands. Now it held her captive. "I suppose sometimes ignorance really is bliss," Jane whispered, her voice deceptively sweet. She turned the blade, causing the muted light to dull and catch depending on the angle. "On the other hand, when someone knows too much . . ." She lowered the blade, and Sadie felt the cold metal press against her neck, just below her right ear. "Well, we run out of options rather quickly, don't we?"

Sadie wanted to close her eyes, but she didn't dare. She instead stayed very still, hoping to give Jane a false sense of victory. And yet, did Sadie have the strength to make a final attempt at escape? Between the pain in her body and the fear in her mind, she felt powerless and completely spent.

"All I wanted was to matter," Jane said. "All I wanted was to be important to you, but you couldn't do it, could you? You forced my hand, Sadie. You made me do things I hadn't wanted to do in order to get your attention, your allegiance. And yet you still withheld your gratitude, didn't you?"

Is that how it happened? When Sadie hadn't embraced Jane, had Jane raised the stakes bit by bit? But it had fallen apart tonight. Jane had planned Gabrielle's attack, the abduction, and Sadie's triumphant rescue, but Sadie had figured it out. What if Sadie hadn't? What if it had gone as smoothly as Jane had expected it to?

Sadie's body began to shake again. Jane's knee on her chest allowed only shallow breaths. She worried she would lose consciousness. Jane smiled. "But I'll settle for your fear," she said, a hiss in her voice. "I'll settle for the look of absolute horror in your eyes. I've played my hand flawlessly, Sadie. You, on the other hand, are going to lose the game entirely."

She lifted the knife, and Sadie had a clear view of what was about to happen. She threw herself to the side as quickly and as hard as she could, but she was unable to deflect the knife entirely and white-hot pain ripped through her right side. Jane lost her balance and had to take her hand off Sadie's mouth. Sadie screamed, but not a moment later, something knocked Jane to the ground.

"Get out of here, Sadie," Pete's voice said.

"Pete?" she cried out, her whole body hot with pain.

"Go!"

Sadie tried to move away, but her battered body wouldn't respond the way she told it to. She gasped for air.

She heard a grunt and a curse and turned her head enough to make out two bodies wrestling to the side of her. Sadie screamed "Help!" to get the attention of the other officers while she grabbed at the ground in an attempt to pull herself away. "Help us!"

The scuffle beside her continued, but she heard the sound of approaching footsteps through the trees. "Over here!" she called. Another grunt, a hit, and then the sound of quickly retreating footsteps. First one set, and then another.

"You'll never be free of me, Sadie," Jane's voice said, trailing away. "Never!"

Sadie screamed as a hand touched her arm, and she looked up into the face of an unfamiliar officer. "Stay where you are," he said, and took off, presumably in the direction of Jane and Pete. Another officer took his place almost immediately, his flashlight beam moving over her body to assess her injuries.

"Ah you Sadie Hoffmillah?"

Sadie nodded, but could feel consciousness begging her to let go. "I've been stabbed in the side," she gasped, glad she'd been able to turn enough that the blow wouldn't have hit anything vital. "Pete Cunningham is in pursuit."

"We know," he said. The faintest sound of sirens could be heard cutting through the fog, but Sadie couldn't allow herself to relax. Pete was still out there, and he didn't know what Jane was capable of.

A minute later, beams of flashlights bounced toward her through the fog as she felt her thoughts getting fuzzy. A minute after that she was loaded on a gurney by the paramedics and carried out of the woods. She kept looking for Pete, waiting for him to come back and assure her that everything was okay, but he didn't appear before the ambulance doors were closed. The EMTs started an IV, applied pressure to the gash in her side, and put an oxygen mask over her mouth. The ambulance was pulling away from the curb as Jane's words still echoed in her head: "You'll never be free of me, Sadie. Never!"

CHAPTER 41

It was late, but Sadie didn't know how late; everything had happened so fast. Detective Lucille had met Sadie at the hospital. There were questions asked and answers given. She was assured that Pete was okay, but had overheard two officers discussing the fact that Jane had gotten away. Now that Sadie was alone in her hospital room and the pain medication had started to take effect, she had trouble recalling what the police had asked her exactly and what she'd told them. Shawn had come, and the reunion had been good medicine before he was taken away to give a statement about his communications with Jane.

The light in her room was off, dousing the room in darkness, and she was trying not to feel anxious about it. She concentrated on taking full breaths and ignoring the panic that was poking at her from the dark shadows that stalked her mind. She heard the door handle turn and tensed as light expanded into the room. She didn't breathe until Pete came around the curtain.

"Hey," he said, pulling up a chair to sit next to the head of the bed.

Her relief at seeing him was so intense she started to cry. Pete lowered the side rail of the bed and leaned in as close as he could, one hand smoothing her hair, the other holding the hand of her good arm. He pressed his face close to hers, as close to an embrace as he could manage, and whispered that everything would be okay. She wanted to believe him, but it wasn't that easy.

Once she calmed down enough to talk, she asked, "Did they find her?"

"Not yet," Pete said, his voice still soft and comforting. "I'm sorry, Sadie." He pulled back a little, and that was when Sadie noticed the bandage on his arm. She let go of his hand to touch it, and he moved his hand to his lap, attempting to hide the injured arm from Sadie's view.

"She cut you." She looked into his face and noticed scratches on his neck and left cheek. It brought tears to her eyes all over again.

"A few stitches is all it took," Pete said. "The Boston PD have made it a priority to find her, and they've posted an officer at the door of your room to make sure you're protected. You're going to be okay, Sadie."

"Am I?" Sadie whispered.

Pete lowered his head so he was close again. "Yes," he said. "You are. You're the toughest woman I know. Pretending to leave a voice message was brilliant, and if you hadn't handled yourself as well as you did, who knows what would have happened. You should be proud of yourself. You used your head, and because of that, we know who's been behind all this. You cracked another case."

"This one's different, Pete," Sadie admitted. "This one was my fault." She looking at their clasped hands instead of his eyes or his injured arm. She didn't want to cry again. How bad were his injuries, really? He would downplay it no matter how serious it was.

"No, this one was Jane's fault," Pete stated.

"But she came to Boston because of me."

"She came to Boston because of who and what she is."

"If I had listened to Advice Number Three and kept my nose out of things, none of this would have happened."

"You're right," Pete said with a nod. "Mrs. Wapple would be as crazy as ever, Mr. Forsberk would still be tormenting her, and her sister would still not be stepping up to her responsibilities. Everything would be as *perfect* as it had been before you cared enough to try to help Mrs. Wapple."

"I still don't understand," Sadie said, unwilling to accept Pete's attempts at absolving her. "Why was Jane so angry with me? Why did she do any of this?"

"They found a file full of articles about you in her hotel room," Pete said. "I talked to Shawn and he said she was always asking about you. Over the last few days, she was calling him constantly, asking what you were doing, where you were."

"Shawn," Sadie said, her heart dropping. "She used him. Poor Shawn, I bet he feels horrible."

"He does," Pete said. "But would you say it's his fault since he was giving her the play-by-play that told her everything she needed to know to stay a step ahead of you?"

"Of course not!" Sadie said, offended by the suggestion.

Pete smiled. "So why are you to blame?"

Sadie looked down at their hands again. He didn't understand. Jane got close to Shawn because of Sadie. Everything Jane had done pointed back to her. It was a heavy weight to carry and she didn't know how to let it go. Pete's thumb softly stroked the back of her hand in slow, rhythmic circles.

He kept talking. "Timothy Wapple was never involved with ghost hunting. He never wrote those articles Jane told us about.

The security guard from the Copley Marriott identified Jane as the woman who asked to have you kicked out of the hotel. She had registered as a guest, which was why they took her side. Your phone was in her car along with a bottle of chloroform. Gabrielle's car, on the other hand, has thus far been Jane-free—no evidence at all that would point to Jane as a suspect. Had you not figured it out, there's a good chance we wouldn't have either. Jane would have recounted her story and everyone would have accepted it as the truth. She'd have been the hero she wanted to be, and you'd have been even more indebted to her."

Sadie shook her head. "There were so many details she had to get just right."

"She had a long dark wig in her hotel room. Along with the face makeup you said she had in her pocket, it explains the ghostly face we saw in the window. The police also found a handheld, whisper-quiet humidifier in Mrs. Wapple's house—that accounts for the cold mist you felt. They traced the call for help you received to one of those disposable cell phones. And the attendant at the gas station near the road where Gabrielle's car was found verified a woman being picked up by a cab around 9:00—they're looking for the cab driver now to verify the details. As for how she didn't get caught by us those times we were *right* there . . ." He shrugged. "She's fast, quiet, and—"

"She knows how people think," Sadie said, looking up at him and remembering what Jane had told her.

Pete nodded. "The police are working on a timeline that shows just how premeditated every part of this was. Jane might be psychopathic, and she may have had to rewrite her game plan when things didn't go her way, but she knew exactly what she was doing."

And she's still out there, Sadie thought to herself. Jane had said

Sadie would never be free of her and despite all the lies Jane had told, Sadie didn't think that threat was one of them.

"Sadie?"

She looked up into his face, absorbing all the tenderness she saw there.

"You've been through a lot, honey, but you're getting the very best medical care. The police will keep you safe, and I won't let anything else happen to you, okay?"

Sadie smiled, trying to engrave his words into her mind and take confidence in them. "Thank you," she said, giving his hand a squeeze. "For being there when I need you the very most."

"Ditto," Pete said, leaning forward to kiss her forehead. "I'll stay until you fall asleep, okay? And then I'll be back before you go into surgery in the morning."

Sadie had managed to forget that the shoulder surgery she'd been avoiding for months was now an absolute necessity. The cut in her side had required a total of twenty-seven stitches, internal and external, but the doctors expected it to heal well. The other bumps and bruises and strains and sprains would also heal on their own. Everyone remarked how lucky Sadie had been that she hadn't sustained more injury, given her age. Sadie didn't feel very lucky though, no matter how hard she tried to believe it.

Pete brought her hand to his lips, kissed it, and looked deeply into her eyes. "Everything's going to be okay," he said again.

Sadie nodded, tears in her eyes, and tried to hold on to his solid reassurance.

CHAPTER 42

"Mrs. Hoffman?"

Sadie looked up from the word search she was trying to do with one hand and was startled to see Gabrielle Marrow standing at the foot of her hospital bed. She attempted to sit up straighter, but between her shoulder, surgically repaired and supported by a fashionable foam-enhanced sling, and the stitched-up stab wound in her side, it was painful.

"G-Gabrielle," Sadie said, and then looked past her to another woman who resembled Mrs. Wapple. She was an inch or two shorter than Gabrielle, without Gabrielle's posture or poise, but her brown-gray hair was plaited into a single smooth braid that hung over one shoulder. She wore a lime-green sweat suit, and her skin and eyes were clearer than Sadie had ever seen them. "Mrs. Wapple," Sadie said in greeting, stunned to see both of them.

"Delores," Mrs. Wapple said, shaking her head before making brief eye contact. "I'm Delores."

"Okay," Sadie said with a nod, realizing that she'd never resolved why Delores went by Mrs. Wapple. It didn't seem to matter anymore, though, and Sadie assumed it must have just been the result of Delores's confusion. "Hi, Delores."

The officer who had been posted at her door since she'd been admitted stood just behind the two sisters, and Sadie nodded at him so that he could return to his post. Sadie looked to Gabrielle and lifted her eyebrows in question. She hadn't expected to see the two of them again and didn't know what to say.

"Social services found a facility for Dee, at least for a little while." Gabrielle looked over her shoulder at her sister, who was looking around the room and not paying them much attention. It was obvious that Delores wasn't . . . normal, but she looked so much better than Sadie had ever seen her. Even her fingernails were clean and shaped. "She's doing a lot better," Gabrielle said with a smile, and Sadie smiled back, relieved to have them here—it was a closure she hadn't expected. "We wanted to say good-bye," Gabrielle said. "Before you went home. I also feel like I owe you an apology."

Sadie shook her head. "No, you don't. I'm the one who caused this. If not for me, none of it would have happened." Despite four days in the hospital and the resolution of many things—Shawn was back at school, Pete had gotten the time off he needed to stay in Boston, and her injuries were healing well—she couldn't resolve the guilt she felt at having drawn Jane to Boston where she'd used Mrs. Wapple as a way to get to Sadie. A million times a day she went back over what she could have or should have done differently.

"*Something* would have happened eventually," Gabrielle said. She glanced at her sister again. "And regardless of how it happened, we both got some help. A social worker is coordinating things for Delores and me, and we're going to do better than we did. You were a part of that." She ducked her head slightly. "I just wanted you to know I appreciated it, and I'm sorry I was such a witch."

The word startled Sadie and she glanced at Delores, who was touching all the flowers in the arrangement Pete had brought her after the surgery on Saturday. Gabrielle didn't notice Sadie's reaction and continued. "It's just . . . well . . ."

"I know," Sadie said, realizing that Gabrielle didn't want to be critical in front of her sister. "I'm glad you both have the support you need."

Gabrielle took a few steps closer to the head of the bed in order to take Sadie's good hand. She squeezed it lightly and Sadie squeezed back. "Thanks," Gabrielle said quietly. Sadie just nodded due to the lump in her throat at the sincere gesture.

Gabrielle had joined Delores at the foot of the bed when Pete stepped into view, causing an immediate silly grin to break out on Sadie's face and the lump in her throat to disappear completely. He was dressed in pressed slacks, a blue button-down shirt, and a tweed sports coat. He must have gone shopping since he hadn't packed such dressy clothes originally. She wondered if he'd come from the police station, where he spent most of his time when he wasn't at the hospital.

"Pete," she said, as though she hadn't seen him for days, which wasn't the least bit true. He took another step, and Heather appeared behind him. "Heather!" She'd had a good long talk with Pete's daughter-in-law where they had resolved the lingering issues between them, and she couldn't be happier to see her here.

"Oh, this is Gabrielle Marrow, and you know Mrs. . . . You know Delores Wapple." She looked to Gabrielle. "This is Pete Cunningham, my boyfriend, and his daughter-in-law, Heather."

Pete greeted them both and shook Gabrielle's hand before Heather did the same. When he turned to Delores, she was looking at him with an adoring expression that made her eyes look wider and her cheeks fuller.

"You're very handsome," Delores said, causing Sadie to suppress a laugh and share a smile with Heather as Pete's cheeks pinked up. He dropped his hand when Delores didn't take it.

"Uh, well, thank you," Pete said.

"Isn't he handsome, Gabby?"

Gabrielle smiled and put an arm around Delores's shoulder. "Come on, Dee, we need to go. The van is waiting for us." She looked over her shoulder and winked at Sadie, which made Sadie smile even wider. Heather sat down on the edge of the bed, but Pete remained standing.

"Good?" he asked, nodding toward the door, which Sadie took as a question about her conversation with Gabrielle and Delores.

"Very good," she said, surprised at how much better she felt knowing they didn't hold anything against her.

Pete nodded. "So are you sure you're ready to leave?"

"Are you kidding?" Sadie said. "Four days of hospital food and the hourly monitoring of vital signs isn't as fun as it sounds."

Pete laughed.

"I came along in case you needed help getting dressed or anything," Heather said. "But it looks like you have that covered. You look great."

Sadie shrugged, downplaying the two hours she'd spent on her hair and makeup that morning—having one arm made it a challenge. Getting dressed had been tricky, but a nurse had come in to help her. Sadie wasn't exactly sure how she would do on her own tomorrow, but she didn't want to make a big deal about it for fear of having to stay in the hospital even longer. They'd already kept her longer than usual due to her being from out of town and in need of police protection.

"Well, I'll let the nurse know you're ready. They have some paperwork for you to sign, and then I'll bring the car around, will that work?" Pete looked between the two women.

"Sounds good," Sadie said. Pete leaned in for a quick kiss and made his exit, leaving Heather and Sadie alone.

"I think he likes you," Heather said, nodding toward the doorway Pete had disappeared through. "I mean really, *really* likes you."

Sadie blushed while smoothing the covers over her lap. "Thank goodness. I thought for a minute Delores Wapple was going to give me a run for my money."

Heather laughed. "The boys can't wait to see you," she said, lifting Sadie's plastic bag of personal effects onto the bed.

"I can't wait to see them," Sadie said, though she frowned at the sling that would limit her interaction.

Heather picked up Sadie's slippers and tucked them into the bag. "The boys told me about a swirly cake you made, and Pete figured out they were talking about a pumpkin roll. He helped me find your recipe book, and I made it to celebrate your release, though it's probably not as pretty as yours."

"It's dark where it's going anyway," Sadie said. "Pretty makes no difference to me, and it sounds wonderful." Anything would beat canned tapioca pudding.

Heather laughed and tucked her hair behind her ear. "Pete agreed it was a perfect celebration dessert, seeing as how you have had so many roles while here in Boston."

"Rolls?" Sadie repeated. Heather wasn't referring to Sadie's weight, was she?

"Well, you were a nanny for a little while, then a ghost hunter, and finally an investigator. You've been busy."

Sadie laughed. Oh, that kind of role. "I seem to be busy no matter where I am."

"I must have caught some kind of domestic bug from you because I put on my mom's famous pot roast this morning. I'll whip up some Yorkshire pudding once we get home. You're in for quite a feast."

"Bless you," Sadie breathed. She was starved for homemade food.

Heather continued to smile, but a new expression on her face shifted the mood in the room. "Has Pete been keeping you updated on everything? With the case, I mean."

"Mostly," Sadie said. "Why, did you hear something?"

Heather shrugged. "He was filling Jared in before we left and said Jane still hasn't returned to her hotel room. They've got the Denver PD watching her apartment. It's really scary, Sadie, to think she's still out there."

"Yeah, it is," Sadie said, knowing she should act brave. But she was very anxious about Jane hiding somewhere, waiting.

"They found her family, but she hasn't had contact with them for years. Apparently this isn't the first time she's become . . . obsessed with someone either, though it never got this far. Maybe I shouldn't tell you all this."

Sadie shook her head, reaching out her good hand to Heather who took it. "Ignorance is *not* bliss," she said. "I prefer knowing what's going on." But she could feel the all too familiar constriction in her chest. It was the same fear that made it hard to sleep at night and made her anxious when she was alone. She told herself—and everyone else who asked—that she was doing better, that every day helped her feel stronger and calmer. But it wasn't true.

"I should also warn you that Pete doesn't want you to go home. His sister, Jared's Aunt Brooke, lives in Las Cruces, New Mexico, and Pete's going to try to get you to agree to do your physical therapy there."

"Thanks for the heads-up," Sadie said, giving Heather's hand a squeeze before letting go. "I want to go home, and no offense, but there's no way I'm going to meet Pete's family on my own."

"That's what I thought you'd say," Heather said with a nod. She stood up and looked around the room. "Is there anything else we need to pack up?"

"Just the flowers," Sadie said. "Oh, and this." She handed Heather the word search she'd been working on.

Heather tucked the word search in Sadie's bag and raised the bed just as a nurse brought Sadie the paperwork she needed to sign. Within a couple of minutes, Heather was pushing Sadie down the hall in a wheelchair while Sadie held her bag and Pete's flowers in her lap. Normally Sadie would be embarrassed to appear so feeble, but everything still hurt, and she was happy to keep her movements to a minimum. They were the only people in the elevator when the doors closed, and Sadie found herself brave enough to bring up something to Heather she'd wanted to talk about.

"Did I ever tell you about the exploding lightbulb?"

"Sure," Heather said, moving to the side of the elevator so that they could make eye contact. "Or, well, Pete did."

"I can't explain it," Sadie said bluntly. "I've tried, but it had nothing to do with Jane."

Heather crossed her arms and lifted her eyebrows. "That's . . . interesting." She smiled and Sadie knew exactly what she was thinking. "Don't tell me you're starting to believe in ghosts."

"I don't know about that," Sadie said, chuckling self-consciously.

"But I've lost a lot of people I loved, and I've felt them, from time to time, lifting me up, pushing me forward, helping me make sense of something difficult. Maybe . . . maybe something like that played a part in this."

"It *is* the first thing that got your attention," Heather said. "Maybe someone got everything started, knowing you would take it from there."

Instead of feeling self-conscious about her role, a calmness inside whispered that things had happened the way they happened because they were supposed to. In addition to being the babysitter and the investigator, Sadie had played her role in helping Delores . . . and Gabrielle. Perhaps even Mr. Forsberk, assuming he learned a lesson from all of this and got the help he needed. The thought that her involvement could be a good thing, despite the people who were hurt along the way, embarrassed her, but the embarrassment passed quickly and of all people, Timothy Wapple's obituary photo came to mind. *Why would the grave end his love for his daughters when life never got in the way?*

The elevator came to a stop and Heather pushed her toward the main entrance where Sadie could see the minivan parked at the curb. She was eager to finish the conversation before they reached Pete, knowing he wasn't as open to this topic as Heather was. "I can't help but wonder if maybe Mr. Wapple wasn't ready to leave until both of his daughters were safe."

"I can't think of anything else that would keep me here," Heather said. "Knowing my children needed me? What bigger motivation would a parent need?"

Sadie nodded. "I agree," she said, pondering it even more.

The main doors whooshed open and Pete stepped out of the van, hurrying over to open the passenger side door.

"I think," Heather said as their opportunity to talk became shorter and shorter, "that there's a lot more going on than we think there is, and the bigger picture is just too big for any of us to see clearly."

For a moment Sadie reviewed the tragic loss of her husband, Neil, more than twenty years ago and the death of Pete's wife not so long ago. She and Pete certainly wouldn't be together if not for those dev-astating turn of events, and yet she couldn't imagine a life without him anymore. It felt so right. She thought about other trials of her life that had shaped her and wondered how many hard things like Terry Michaels had made Pete into the man he was—the man she loved.

"I think I can live with that explanation," Sadie said as Heather brought the wheelchair to a stop. "In fact, I kind of like it."

"What explanation?" Pete asked, coming to her side in order to help her stand.

Heather lifted her eyebrows at Sadie as if wondering how Sadie was going to get out of this one. "Just that maybe faith isn't any more complicated than simply believing there is a purpose behind hard things and allowing God the latitude to do it His way instead of ours." Did that mean Sadie's anxiety would go away? She didn't think so, at least not immediately. But did it mean that perhaps she could learn something from that too?

"Perhaps," Pete said as she gained her feet. Sadie took in a sharp breath at the pain that shot up from her ankle. He helped her to the car and had to lean across her in order to put on her seat belt. As he pulled away, Sadie reached out and touched his cheek with her good hand. He stopped, his face a few inches from hers.

"Thank you," she said softly while Heather got in the backseat and pretended not to notice.

"For what?" Pete asked.

"Everything."

He smiled and leaned in for a quick kiss. "Right back at ya, Mrs. Hoffmiller. I feel the exact same way."

Pot Roast and Yorkshire Pudding with Gravy

Pot Roast
2 tablespoons vegetable or olive oil
3- to 4-pound pot roast (chuck, top round, rump, bottom round, or brisket)
1 can beef consommé
1 quart of water
2 bay leaves
½ teaspoon pepper

In a 6-quart cooking pan, heat oil on high heat until it just begins to smoke.

Braise meat in oil, cooking each side a few minutes at a time until nearly burnt to seal in juices. The oil might splatter, so cover pan with a paper towel or grease screen, but don't cover with a lid as that makes it difficult to get the right "crust" on the meat. When braised on all sides, add consommé, water, bay leaves, and pepper. Reduce heat to low, cover, and simmer roast for at least 6 hours, adding water if it reduces to less than 3 inches.

Yorkshire Pudding
¼ cup drippings from pot roast
2 tablespoons butter
4 eggs
2 cups milk
2 cups all-purpose flour
¼ teaspoon salt

After the roast has cooked for six hours, use a large spoon to skim off some of the grease from the top of the liquid in the pan. Put one-fourth cup of the drippings into a 9x13 pan. Add butter to pan, and preheat oven to 450 degrees. Put all other ingredients into a blender and blend for 20 seconds. Stop and scrape down the sides of the blender. Blend another 10 seconds. Set aside. Put pan in oven to melt the butter and allow it to blend with the drippings. Cook until it's bubbling—about 5 minutes. Add batter to pan and return it to fully heated oven. Bake 20 minutes, or until edges are crispy.

Note: For individual puddings, heat drippings and butter and divide evenly between 12 muffin cups. Add equal portions of batter and bake 15 minutes at 450 degrees.

Gravy

3 cups pot roast stock
2 tablespoons cornstarch
⅓ cup water

While Yorkshire pudding is baking, move roast from pan to serving platter and cover with foil to let it rest. Taste stock and adjust the flavor by adding water, Worcestershire sauce, or salt and pepper accordingly. Remove all but 3 cups of stock (adjust thickening if you want more gravy). Increase heat under pan containing the stock to high heat, bringing stock to a boil. Mix cornstarch and water in a small bowl, making a slurry. Stir until smooth. Using a whisk, slowly add slurry to stock, whisking quickly to keep gravy smooth. Cook two minutes. (Add more slurry or more water to reach desired consistency of gravy.)

To serve, use a fork to pull roast apart into portion sizes. Cut Yorkshire pudding into 12 servings. Serve roast and pudding on a plate, covering both with gravy. Green beans or peas make a good vegetable side dish.

ACKNOWLEDGMENTS

I wrote this book during a difficult and busy time of my life and through the process have gained insights into the Lord's hand in my life and the blessing of so many people who have kept me sane and made this book possible.

Thank you, once again, to the fabulous staff at Shadow Mountain who make my story readable: Jana Erickson (product director), Lisa Mangum (editor, and author of *The Hourglass Door* series, Shadow Mountain, 2009–2011), Shauna Gibby (designer), and Rachael Ward (typographer). These women make an amazing pit crew or cheerleading squad, depending on the day—thank you.

I am once again indebted to my writing group: Becki Clayson, Jody Durfee, Ronda Hinrichson (*Trapped,* Walnut Springs, 2010), and Nancy Campbell Allen (*Isabelle Webb* series, Covenant, 2009–2012). These women are such troopers and make the rate at which this series is coming out possible. I also had several beta readers who gave me suggestions on how to get the book to blend just right: my dear friends Melanie Jacobson (*The List,* Covenant, 2011), Julie Wright (*The Hazardous Universe* series, Covenant, 2011 and beyond), my wonderful aunt, Sandy Drury, and my sister-friend-therapist,

Crystal White—each of whom made significant contributions to the finished product and saved me much sanity while sacrificing their own since none of them got to read an actual final draft.

As always, this book would not be complete without the crew of Sadie's Test Kitchen, who hone the recipes into the masterpieces they become: Don Carey (*Bumpy Landings*, Cedar Fort Inc., 2010), Danyelle Ferguson (*(dis)Abilities and the Gospel: How to Bring People with Special Needs Closer to Christ*, Cedar Fort Inc., 2011), Whit Larson (Whitty Baked Beans), Sandra Sorenson, Laree Ipson (Laree's Ginger Cookies), Annie Funk, Michelle Jefferies, Megan O'Neill, and our newest baker, Lisa Swinton. These people are amazing. Without them, there would be no culinary in this mystery series.

Thank you to my wonderful husband, Lee, for letting me do my marathon write nights and weekends even though he's been in a busy and difficult part of his life too. He is the keystone to *everything*. Thank you to my kids, who support and put up with me as well as the school lunch program that ensures they have one square meal a day five days a week for two-thirds of the year. Thank you to the fans who encourage, the friends and family who put up with my whining, and the other writers whose books I get to enjoy when I am in desperate need of a break.

How grateful I am for the gifts I have been given, both through struggles and successes. I know my Father in Heaven loves me and is growing me every day to be the person He knows I can be. I am grateful for the part in that process that my writing plays, and to all of those people who make it such a rewarding journey.

Enjoy this sneak peek of

Banana Split

Coming Spring 2012

CHAPTER 1

"Have you been snorkeling before?"

Sadie looked up from adjusting her life jacket. Konnie was the last woman, other than herself, still in the small boat that had taken them offshore where the snorkeling was *nani*—Sadie hoped *nani* meant wonderful and not deadly.

"Years ago," Sadie said. "In Waikiki, when my children were younger."

"I'm not sure that even counts," Konnie said with a tinkling laugh. Her wide smile fit perfectly in her round face. Her black hair was in one long braid down her back, only a few curly tendrils framing her face. "Everyone knows Oahu has the worst snorkeling in the islands. Here on K'auai, on the other hand, it's amazing."

"I can't wait," Sadie said, but her tone was flat. She felt guilty about lying. She was still trying to figure out why she had come. She didn't like boats or sand or swimsuits, but she'd accepted Konnie's invitation simply because she'd refused most of the others Konnie had extended on behalf of the Blue Muumuus, a group of local older woman similar to the Red Hat Club Sadie had seen in her hometown of Garrison, Colorado.

"The weather is perfect today," Konnie continued. "And the tide is just right. You won't believe the variety of coral you'll be able to see."

Sadie nodded, peering over the side of the boat with trepidation. Coming to K'auai was supposed to cure the anxiety that had overwhelmed her after what happened in Boston. Despite three months in this tropical paradise, however, Sadie was no better than she had been before. Only more isolated.

The water was clear enough that she could make out the shape of the coral beneath the shifting surf, but it was unnerving to think of the world hiding beneath the surface of the water. When Sadie had come to Hawaii before with her children, she hadn't been a big fan of being *in* the ocean, but her displeasure then was nothing like the terror she felt now. But she was determined not to let her anxiety get the best of her in front of this woman who was trying so hard to be Sadie's friend, so she swallowed her fear and forced a smile.

When Sadie had moved into the condominium complex almost three months ago with plans to stay awhile, Konnie had immediately befriended her. She didn't even care that Sadie was a *haole*— Caucasian—or that she was a newcomer to an island not always open to mainlanders. Konnie was big and loud and wonderful in every way, which was a little bit scary to Sadie right now. Well, everything was scary to Sadie right now.

"It'll be fun," Sadie said, but she could feel her sweat glands kicking in despite the breeze that whisked away any rising temperatures. They were only a quarter mile offshore, not far from a small village too far north to be frequented by the tourists who flocked to the southern part of the island, and too underdeveloped to be attractive to those who sought out the North Shore. It would have been a beautiful drive coming up here from the town of Puhi, where Sadie was staying, if Sadie had been able to focus.

"I'm going in," Konnie said, getting to her feet and causing the boat to rock back and forth. Sadie forgot to breathe until Konnie sat her voluptuous self on the side of the boat and the rocking evened out. "You can lower yourself in if you'd rather not jump."

A moment later, Konnie put on her mask and fell backward over the side just like an islander who had spent half her life in the ocean—which was exactly what she was. The ensuing wave caused by Konnie's entry made the boat rock more than ever, and Sadie clung to the side with both hands. Konnie surfaced moments later and yelled for Sadie to jump in. "One of the tour companies brings tourists out here around noon—time's a wastin'."

Sadie nodded, hoping she looked confident as she sat on the side of the boat and let her legs dangle over the water. She chose the side opposite her companions—Konnie and five other members of the Blue Muumuus—so that if she freaked out once she hit the water, the boat would hide it from their view. She could then join them once she was sufficiently recovered.

"You're okay," Sadie said to herself under her breath, eyeing the water and keeping her breathing even as she double-checked the clasps of her life jacket. She was the only woman who had chosen to wear one. "You'll be just fine. You're the youngest and spryest woman here. You can do this."

She looked over her shoulder, where six backs bobbed in the water, the tubes of their snorkels looking as though they were poking out of their heads. The stillness of their bodies bothered her, and she looked away, pulling on her mask and putting the mouthpiece of the snorkel in place. Another deep breath filled her with just enough courage to finally plunge into the water. She hadn't considered that the snorkel would fill with water, though, and so her first attempt at breathing was salty and wet. She headed for the surface and spit out the mouthpiece and the water, coughing and sputtering. Her heart was racing, and she felt a wave of nausea as she gripped her life jacket with both hands and went to work convincing herself she wasn't drowning. After taking another minute to get her bearings, and berating herself for being so dramatic, she put the salty mouth-piece of the snorkel back into her mouth. She practiced breathing through her mouth for another minute. Maybe four.

Konnie rounded the boat, her mask pushed up on her head. "Are you okay?"

Sadie gave her a thumbs-up, took a deep breath, and put her face in the water.

The coral reef was full of fascinating shapes, colors, and tex-tures. Grasslike anemones swayed as though blown by a breeze. The water was clear enough that she could see every detail of the scene below her. *It's beautiful,* she told herself as her heart rate increased. *Ethereal. Amazing.* And yet her lungs wouldn't allow her to draw a full breath. She watched a parrot fish lazily moving a few feet away as though she weren't there. But she was there. In their world, trying to appreciate the resplendence while battling a full-fledged panic attack due to the fact that their world was completely creepy! Some of these things were poisonous, and there were certainly creatures lurking at the bottom ready to pull her to the depths and never let her go. She'd seen *Finding Nemo.*

After only ten seconds she had to lift her face out of the water. She couldn't breathe, couldn't subdue the terror. But with her head lifted, she was aware of her feet now being even deeper in the water. She tried to pull her feet up, but would that really deter the horrible sea monsters lurking beneath her? She'd seen that movie about the surfer who lost her arm to a shark. What did she look like from the bottom of the sea? A Hostess cupcake like in the commercials? She spat out the mouthpiece and tried to inhale, but it was as though her throat was no longer connected to her lungs. She couldn't get the air in. Why not? What was wrong with her?

She turned toward the boat, knowing she had to get out of the water. Once she reached the side, however, she couldn't figure out how to get in. The rim was too high for her to grab onto. Her gasps for breath were ragged, noisy. She couldn't see any of her group. What if she passed out in the ocean? Would the fish eat her before anyone discovered she was gone?

You are being ridiculous, she told herself, ripping off her mask in hopes it would help her breathe. Over the last few months, she'd read several Internet articles about how to recover from anxiety attacks. None of the advice had talked about being in the ocean, but she clutched the sides of her life jacket even tighter and closed her eyes, trying to pretend she was simply resting on a punctured water bed. Her lungs opened up again. She took long, deep breaths and tried to clear her head. She felt oxygen returning to her brain and felt her body calming down.

Then something touched her foot, and her eyes flew open in renewed panic. She found herself thrashing toward the shore.

She had to get out of the water.

That the boat was right there and Konnie or the other women would certainly help her get in it didn't cross her mind until she was crawling onto the sand, coughing and sputtering, desperate to get away from the water. The sand turned from wet to dry and was littered with sticks, rocks, broken shells, and pieces of deformed plastic the tide had left behind. This wasn't one of the groomed beaches where machines cleaned up the shoreline before the tourists woke up. It was natural and messy, and her hands and legs were coated with sand as it stuck to her wet body. Something cut her knee, reminding her that she should stand up. But she didn't want to do anything that would slow down her escape.

Finally, she collapsed, the bulky life jacket keeping her face out of the sand as she once again focused on breathing like a normal human being. It felt like forever before she felt safe. Then her thoughts turned to how she would apologize to her new friends who must think she was absolutely bonkers. She wasn't so sure they weren't right.

The nightmares that had plagued Sadie in Garrison had led to insomnia and too many late-night infomercials that provided her with more kitchen gadgets and exercise equipment than she could ever use. When her friend Gayle, her son, Shawn, her daughter, Breanna, and her boyfriend, Pete, had sat her down for an intervention, they told her she needed to get away for a little while. Unwind. Relax. She'd been optimistic about the change of environment, and who wouldn't want to go to Hawaii? But although she was no longer ordering useless items off QVC, she stayed inside most of the time, and the only people she interacted with were the Blue Muumuus. She slept through the afternoons and was up most of the night, double-checking the locks every hour. The only time she left the condo was to clean the additional seven condos in the complex that were rented out by the week. The housekeeping job was her way of paying rent to her friend Tanya, who owned the complex but preferred her husband's ranch in Arizona this time of year.

"I need help," she admitted out loud to herself as water dripped off her hair, which was now past her shoulders, longer than it had been in decades. Before leaving Garrison, she'd had her stylist lighten it in hopes that she'd have more fun as a blonde. But she hadn't kept it up, and the color had faded to a brassy grayish-yellow. Two inches of gray roots had grown out since her arrival. The climate seemed to accelerate how fast her hair grew, and she lacked the courage to go to a salon. Most days she tied her hair back with a bandana and avoided mirrors.

Her senses began reorienting her to where she was, and she could hear the wind though the palm trees around her and the chirp and buzz of a million critters. The admission that whatever she was dealing with was more than she could handle on her own washed over her and filled her with both fear and relief. "I need help," she said again, wondering if it would be more powerful a second time. It held the same heavy certainty. She *did* need help, and she needed it soon. Things had happened to her, scary things that were obviously taking their toll on her mental health. She needed to get back to who she once was; she needed to feel whole again. While she regularly talked to her family and friends, she'd kept how bad things were to herself. She didn't want them to worry. What would they say if they knew the truth?

Finally she opened her eyes and flipped onto her back, staring up at the blue, blue sky and wondering how her life had gotten so out of control. Control had always been Sadie's foundation. It had gotten her through her husband's death more than twenty years ago. It had helped her raise her two children by herself. It had led to her being involved in several police investigations. But she'd lost her confidence in the wake of Boston, and her world had been spinning out of control ever since.

She got to her feet and looked out at the water that seemed so innocent now that she wasn't in it. The Blue Muumuus were back in the boat, coming toward her, and she felt overwhelmed by embarrassment and shame while grateful she wouldn't have to consider swimming back to them. They had always been so kind to her, and she had so little to give back. Now she'd ruined their adventure. Konnie waved her arms, and Sadie waved back to indicate she was all right. The salt water was beginning to dry the sand to her skin, making her feel gritty.

A small boat dock had been built into the rocks along the beach, and Sadie headed toward it so that the boat could pick her up. The floating dock moved gently beneath her feet when she stepped on it, and she froze for a moment, afraid she might fall in.

Konnie pointed the boat in Sadie's direction, and Sadie walked slowly down the weathered boards, dreading the explanation of her bolt to the shore. What could she tell them other than the truth? Hi, my name is Sadie, and I'm losing my mind. Congratulations on winning front-row tickets to the show.

When she reached the end of the dock, she waited for the boat like a penitent child, watching the water lap against the sides of the wood, black with barnacles and other sea life that gave Sadie the chills. Long strands of dark seaweed flowed alongside, like the hair of a mermaid from some long ago fairy tale. Sadie watched it move, looking so fluid and graceful, and tried to draw calmness from its easy motion. After a few seconds, however, she realized the seaweed was black, not green. Despite her misgivings, she bent down to get a closer look into the water and was soon on her knees, peering at the underside of the dock, where what she thought was seaweed was actually hair connected to a human head.

Scrambling to her feet as fresh panic descended like a hammer, Sadie screamed for help at the same moment that she lost her balance and plunged headlong into the sea that had already claimed one victim.

About the Author

Josi S. Kilpack grew up hating to read until she was thirteen and her mother handed her a copy of *The Witch of Blackbird Pond*. From that day forward, she read everything she could get her hands on and accredits her writing "education" to the many novels she has "studied" since then. She began her first novel in 1998 and hasn't stopped since. Her seventh novel, *Sheep's Clothing*, won the 2007 Whitney Award for Mystery/Suspense, and *Lemon Tart*, her ninth novel, was a 2009 Whitney Award finalist. *Pumpkin Roll* is Josi's fourteenth novel and the sixth book in the Sadie Hoffmiller Culinary Mystery Series.

Josi currently lives in Willard, Utah, with her wonderful husband, four amazing children, one fat dog, and varying number of very happy chickens.

For more information about Josi, you can visit her website at www.josiskilpack.com, read her blog at www.josikilpack.blogspot.com, or contact her via e-mail at Kilpack@gmail.com.

IT'D BE A CRIME
TO MISS THE REST OF THE SERIES . . .

ISBN 978-1-60641-050-9 $17.99

ISBN 978-1-60641-121-6 $17.99

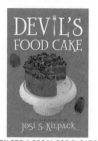

ISBN 978-1-60641-232-9 $17.99

ISBN 978-1-60641-813-0 $17.99

ISBN 978-1-60641-941-0 $17.99

BY JOSI S. KILPACK

And for an extra treat, enjoy *Pumpkin Roll* on audio

ISBN 978-1-60908-925-2 $39.99

Available online and at a bookstore near you.

www.shadowmountain.com • www.josiskilpack.com

SHADOW
MOUNTAIN

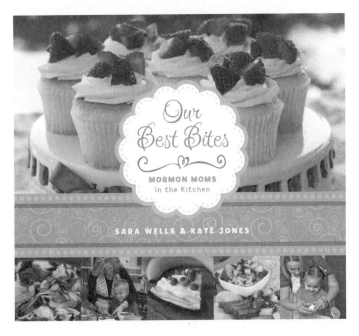